T0148509

the
Broken
Line

the Broken Line

LORI GALE

authorHOUSE®

AuthorHouse™
1663 Liberty Drive
Bloomington, IN 47403
www.authorhouse.com
Phone: 1-800-839-8640

Published by AuthorHouse 2/1/2013

ISBN: 978-1-4817-1260-6 (sc)
ISBN: 978-1-4817-1261-3 (hc)
ISBN: 978-1-4817-1262-0 (e)

Library of Congress Control Number: 2013902133

I would like to thank all of you that read The Broken Line and offered your heartfelt opinion. You have been a blessing and an inspiration.

To Paul McCall: You're brilliant! Thank you for the lovely illustrations.

— LG

CHAPTER ONE

San Francisco

Saturday was wash day. And it wasn't the laundry.

Clear water flowed over then beaded up on the white racing stripes of Elaine Bennett's classic 427 Shelby Cobra. A soft chamois absorbed the droplets and restored the sparkle to the vintage car. An appreciative owner stood back and admired the lines, just as many men had when she stepped out of the muscle car. She was never really sure if they were admiring her or her machine, but either way, both had a knack for turning heads.

Noticing a smudge on the chrome roll bar, she lovingly rubbed it out to reflect her patrician features. "Perfect," she purred, and walked around the car touching up any real and imagined flaws. The ringing of the phone broke her concentration for only a moment while she applied the necessary elbow grease to polish the chrome grill and bumper.

A throwback to days-gone-by, the answering machine beeped and announced the caller to be her twin brother, Lane. He droned on and she wished he would get to the point. Her attention was riveted on her car until he mentioned their parents.

"...Look, when you get this message, call me," he tersely instructed.

Scrambling to her feet, she tripped over the bucket, spilling some of the contents. "Shit!" she exclaimed, racing toward the phone. She picked up and breathed, "Hello."

"Screening our calls?" he harassed.

"What's up with Mom and Dad?" she asked, ignoring his remark.

"Their plane is missing," he answered with very little trace of feeling.

"What do you mean missing? Someone stole the relic?" she mused.

He didn't laugh. But then again, he didn't emote much at all. Elaine could have sworn that he was hatched, even though she knew that could not be possible. Still, a girl could dream.

"The plane went down shortly after takeoff. Somewhere near Juneau," he informed.

"They've crashed?" she clarified.

"Yes, they've crashed. I've coordinated the rescue efforts, and to this point, they haven't been able to locate them."

"What about the emergency beacon?"

"Somehow it's not working."

"How does that happen, Lane? Dad's old, not careless."

"I don't have all the answers, Elaine. You know as much as I do."

She doubted that, and took a collective breath. "What do I need to do?"

"Nothing. Just sit tight and pray they're okay. I'm working on it from here."

She took another breath to control the vile words rising in her throat, because she couldn't remember the last time he worked on anything but his career. His family wasn't any exception. She started scribbling notations on the pad next to the phone. "How long have they been missing?"

"Less than twenty-four hours," he answered. He waited for her response. Surprisingly she was quiet. "By the way," he started cautiously, changing the subject. "I ran into Jack the other day. He's organizing a company in the DC area. He mentioned to me that you haven't signed the papers. Is there a problem? Do I need to look them over again?"

"No on both counts, Lane. Twenty-four hours?" she asked, bombarding him with a series of questions to see just how on top of things he was. "What efforts are they putting into finding them? Was the plane on radar? How long after takeoff did they go down? Who can I contact at the airport in Juneau?"

"I told you I was taking care of it," he insisted.

"That's not good enough, Lane. They are my parents, too."

"Sam Winston is the contact at the airport. But I have a congressional representative from Alaska coordinating with the Coast Guard and the Alaska National Guard. Everything is under control, Elaine. Just let me handle it from here. You just sign your divorce papers. Get on with your life, and let Jack get on with his."

"I'll sign the papers when I'm damn good and ready to. Obviously you've forgotten whose copy of the divorce papers you looked over. It wasn't my copy, Lane. It was Jack's. Thanks for your help," she spat out with layered sarcasm.

Hot tears stung as she slammed the receiver into its cradle. Like the chrome of earlier, she rubbed out the annoying misery and concentrated on the notations she had made during her conversation. She called Information and got the number for the airport in Juneau and phoned Sam Winston. He wasn't available. She left her name, cell phone number and the reason for her call.

She sat for a moment and collected her thoughts. This was not her area of expertise, and she definitely knew it wasn't Lane's. Swallowing her pride, she placed a call to Jack Phillips, her ex-husband. That is, whenever she signed the papers.

He picked up almost immediately, his deep timbre reverberating through her, as it had several times before. She almost hung up at the sound of his voice.

"Hello?" he answered, thankful for caller ID.

She hesitated.

"Elaine? If you're going to call and you don't want to speak to me, you should star sixty-seven and blocked your number from appearing on my caller ID," he informed with mock seriousness.

"There's a problem," she said quietly.

"With the papers?"

"No," she emphatically answered. "My parents' plane crashed and they're missing. Efforts to find them…" she trailed off.

As much as he was tempted to hold their divorce over her head and force her hand, he liked his in-laws, and he still loved his wife. "What can I do?" he gently asked.

She heard the tenderness in his tone, but more importantly, the sincerity. "What kind of connections do you have within Congress and the Coast Guard? Lane says he's working with a representative from Alaska and the Coast Guard, but God only knows his motives."

"Between the two of us, I'm sure Lane has the better connections. He is, after all, going to be confirmed for a federal judgeship, so he has the inside track. What have you learned?"

"I've got a name, Sam Winston. I'm not sure of his position at the airport in Juneau. Lane gave me the name. I've placed a call to him and left a message."

"You didn't call me first?" he asked with mock hurt. But if the truth were known, he felt a twinge, because she had always relied on him. He had always been first in her life for everything and anything.

"Where are you?" she asked.

"DC."

"That's a long way from San Francisco."

"I can be there this evening," he offered.

4

"No. I need you to see if you can learn more about the congressman from Alaska and find out what he's doing first hand, please."

"You haven't given me his name."

"I don't know his name. Since you seem to be on better terms with my brother than I am, I imagined you could get information more quickly than me," she remarked.

"I'll call Lane as soon as I'm through with you." He grimaced at the silence on the other end. "I'm sorry. That was a poor choice of words. What were the folks doing in Alaska?"

"Of all things, they were going fishing."

"Mom went fishing?" he asked in jest. A throaty laugh danced in his ear. He missed Elaine's naturalness, not just her manner, but her beauty. She seldom acknowledged and definitely didn't take seriously her good looks. In fact, the exact opposite was true; she loathed the many occasions she was being considered for opportunities or getting her way simply because she was pretty. "How long have they been gone?"

"Almost a week. Dad said they were going for three weeks to mix a little fishing with a scavenger hunt. Of course, Mom referred to the scavenger hunt as antiquing. Simon, Margaret, Harold and Joyce were also going."

"Were they on the plane, too?"

"Probably not."

"Which plane?"

"The Waco. If that's the case, the friends weren't on the plane. Hopefully I'll learn more when Mr. Winston calls me back."

"What's Winston's number?"

There was a deliberate hesitation on her part. She could sense him doing the same thing as Lane, and she wasn't about to let him control her request.

He felt her apprehension, or rather, her animosity building, and he backed off. "It's okay. You handle him and I'll handle Lane." He waited for her response, and as quickly as she built up a wall, he tore it down. He knew she resented him for doing that, but that was part of their charm together, and when they were together, they were good. "I can be there this evening," he hinted again.

"I'm okay. Let's just promise to keep in touch on anything we find. Okay?"

"Okay. Where will you be?"

"Probably here at the house, but you can reach me on my cell phone."

"Which house?"

"Firehouse."

"You've finished renovating that?"

"Yeah, I had to, you sold our other house, remember?" she retorted with a little more bite than necessary.

"Yeah," he replied, happy her spunk was returning. "Take care. When I hear something, I'll call. You do the same?"

"Yeah," she whispered. "Jack?" She hesitated, wiping a wayward tear from her cheek. "Thanks," she added quietly, and hung up.

CHAPTER TWO

The drive over to her parents' home was a chilly one, considering she rode her other vintage piece of hardware—a turquoise and white 1951 Indian Chopper. Slowly she navigated the bike through the streets of Pacific Heights, or as the natives referred to it, Pissy Heights. She pulled into the nearly nonexistent driveway of Kash and Leslie's resplendent 1895 Victorian home, then into the garage on the lower level. Just in time. As quickly as the sun had shone, the clouds had moved in, and drizzle was covering the street.

Elaine shook out of her back pack and leathers and changed into her most comfortable pair of jeans and her favorite sweatshirt that read, *"Ball U"* from her alma mater, Ball State University, in Muncie, Indiana. Her mother often chastised her for wearing that vulgar piece of clothing, but her father always gave her an approving wink and thumbs up whenever he saw it. One motherly request she always honored was removing her shoes when entering the house. Boots aside, she padded quietly looking for Nook and Cranny, two precocious cats.

She easily found Cranny, the fatter of the two, surveying the world from her perch; the top of the refrigerator. Her intense blue eyes followed Elaine's every move while she brewed her favorite blend of Blue Mountain coffee in her father's latest coffee contraption. Thankfully, she was adept at mechanical objects. Lane, she mused, would have to go without. The only thing he was good at was opening and closing his mouth in judgment of others. *What a gift*, she thought.

As the coffee brewed and spread its mouth-watering aroma, Elaine walked around admiring her handiwork as a renovation specialist in architecture. Her company, *The Three R's*, represented the "reading, 'riting and 'rithmetic" of renovation. She had taken Great Grandmother Bennett's home and used the disciplines of restoration, reconstruction and rehabilitation in renovating the Queen Anne structure. Reflecting the personalities of the occupants, Elaine blended traditional with contemporary in the flow of the home. Many rooms reflected her mother's preciseness, while some of the rooms showed her father's sense of adventure from his days as an archeologist.

Coffee in hand, Elaine wandered, waiting for any call on her cell phone. None came. Meandering into her father's study, she opened and closed drawers of his desk until she found his address book. Recognizing several names, she found the phone numbers of those that were to take the trip. She dialed up Simon and Margaret Hughes and fully expected to get their voice mail, instead Margaret picked up.

"Hello?" Margaret answered.

"Mrs. Hughes?" Elaine clarified, remembering her manners.

"Oh, Elaine. How are you, dear?" she inquired in the genteel manner Elaine had become accustomed to with all of her parents' friends, especially her mother's.

"Fine," Elaine stammered. "I thought you and my parents were vacationing in Alaska this week."

"Alaska? Oh, my goodness, not this time of the year," Margaret brought to light.

"I thought maybe it was a little cold for fishing. How about Bud and Joyce Reed? Did they go with Mom and Dad?"

"No, I saw Joyce yesterday. Is there anything wrong, Elaine?"

Not wanting to alarm her mother's friend, she lied. "No. I've been gone and I'm just trying to catch up with my folks. You know how they are. Always one excursion or another at a moment's notice. That's all. I'm sorry for disturbing your morning. Take care, Mrs. Hughes."

Elaine didn't even bother phoning the Reed household, she knew she would find Joyce and Bud safe and sound at home. Why weren't her parents safe and sound? She placed a call to Jack and got his damnable voice mail. "Jack? It's Elaine. When you have a moment, call me on my cell. Thanks."

She tried Sam Winston again and was told he left with the Coast Guard to search near El Captain Passage, near New Tokeen ; where they thought the plane went down from the last radar tracking. At least they were on radar; that she could scratch off her list. However, things were looking bleaker by the minute, and Elaine was Elaine, not Nancy Drew. Sleuthing was not her forte. She was an architect, not a detective. She paused for a moment and decided to take the architectural approach used in renovation—start peeling back this mystery, layer by layer.

She started in her father's office. The Chippendale desk he inherited from his great grandfather was messy as usual. Finding any clues would be a challenge, but deep down inside, Elaine was a closet slob, so she took to it like a duck to water. The duckling paddled for a while and found nothing, so she moved next door to her mother's study, or parlor as it was referred to by Leslie. Even as a kid, if Elaine wanted to be nosy and go through her mother's stuff she was always caught, and not red-handed, but just by her mother knowing that everything had a place, an exact place. Her mother could tell in a heartbeat if something was the least bit awry in her space. Either that, or Lane tattled. Elaine always preferred the latter.

This time she didn't care if she disturbed things and didn't return them to their exact position. Like Christmas gifts, her parents were masters at hiding things. Leaving her mother's office in complete shambles, she moved to the lower level that consisted of the garage, utility and mechanical rooms. When she found nothing there, she advanced floor by floor, room by room, until she was in the attic. Even the close space of the attic was neat and devoid of clutter. After another pot of coffee and hours later, Elaine was still no closer as to why her parents lied about their trip or why they were missing.

Exhausted, she leaned against the paneled wainscot and sipped her coffee. Remembering the attic during renovation, she recalled the hidden storage behind the wainscot was to remain intact. She was joined by Nook as she crawled around looking for the entry panel. He playfully rubbed and purred as she tapped along the wall.

"Oh, now you want to be sociable," she cooed as he arched his back and rubbed her thigh. "Or are you just being nosy?" A little of both, she concluded. She found the panel and gently encouraged it to pivot. Though the lighting in the attic was sufficient, the small storage space needed help. Pulling free her flashlight, she illuminated the area. There she found boxes and an old steamer chest. Dragging the chest out, she broke the lock and opened it. She knew immediately the contents belonged to her mother, and there would be hell to pay for breaking the lock and invading her mother's space. *Tough shit*, she thought. The leather bound journals were dated, starting with September of 1947.

Sitting cross-legged on the floor with Nook purring furiously, Elaine opened the journal and started reading her mother's neatly chronicled entry. It started:

New York City, September 1947

Elaine read a small passage as her mother described the Metropolitan Building and her boss, Sampson. As a child, she remembered a boisterous man of the same name, and by reading on, she knew he was the one. Like Nook, curiosity took over and she pulled free the boxes from the storage area and found them to be her father's journals. Like everything he did, there was no rhyme or reason to his filing system, just clutter. Painstakingly she arranged them in chronological order, and then she decided to correspond the two writings and see if they matched events or if they were separate accounts of their lives. Funny, she wondered if each knew the other had recorded events from their past.

Then it dawned on her that she came by all of this very naturally. When she and Lane were growing up, each kept journals. On occasions, Elaine would sneak a peek at his to see what devious dealings he was up to. Unlike the stoic imagine he projected, his writings revealed his soft, spineless ways. He may have been able to cajole his parents, teachers and what few friends he had, but his truth was known through his twin.

Elaine often dismissed the theory of twins and how they mirrored their sibling's intrinsic thoughts and feelings. She had no such connection to Lane, and she was sure he felt the same. However, there were those moments; recollections really, of shared events where she had written her thoughts and then read his, and shuddered that they were almost verbatim to hers. Those were the happy times, and according to Lane, few and far between.

Mostly his writings reflected the darker and extremely personal struggles he manifested through his need for power and control. His covet to be the top sibling. In reading his journals, Elaine could literally read between the lines and piecing together the whole story by using her own entries.

She sadly shook her head and cleared the images of Lane; twin love long removed, she concentrated on reading Kash and Leslie's journals, and using her quirky little gift, she blended them into one story. Hopefully, one with a happy ending.

CHAPTER THREE

After brewing more coffee and fixing her favorite—grilled cheese with tomato sandwich, she sat down in her father's overstuffed recliner and started reading the journals. His came first from the date noted, September 22, 1947. Elaine let her imagination take hold and allowed the story to be told in third person, removing her father as the primary, first-person storyteller. She treated his journal like the class she taught at San Francisco University, *The Drama of Architecture*. There, she required her students to choreograph or stage the architectural piece before ever putting pen to paper. She settled in and read about her father's adventure in South America, 1947.

SOUTH AMERICA, 9/22/47

It was hot, and Kash Bennett, for what seemed to be the umpteenth time, wiped his forehead with the back of his hand and then adjusted his squat position for a better look. Perspiration trickled down his tanned face and ran along the leather line of the camera strap that dug annoyingly into his neck. The discomfort was momentarily relieved when he focused one of the cameras at the opening of a well-concealed tunnel where jungle growth had been left unattended for the purpose of camouflage.

Bennett's partner and investigative reporter, Mike Marrow, sat cross-legged next to him, looking fresh as a daisy. The heat and humidity didn't seem to bother him as he prepared the reel to reel tape recorder that was positioned awkwardly on his lap. Affectionately he patted Ole Betsy, and with a few quick rotations, the tape was secured. He took a deep breath and turned her on.

The whir caused Bennett to snap his head toward Marrow and Ole Betsy. "Goddammit, Marrow. What the hell is wrong with that bitch?" he roughly whispered, burning a hole through the noisy relic.

"Sshh, baby. He didn't mean it," Mike cooed to his clamorous but faithful machine. He tenderly stroked her well worn leather sides, encouraging her to warm up more quickly.

Finally the recorder fell into the rhythm of a soft hum. Gone was the loud whir, only to be replaced by the unnerving sound of rusty mining car wheels that moved at an agonizing pace on the track just inside the tunnel. Tropical birds scattered at the grating twang, and suddenly an alarming stillness came over the jungle.

The high noon sun provided a generous amount of lighting. Bennett was silently thankful for the natural lighting as he tried to get more comfortable. The birds returned and so did their previous chatter. Gently he fed his lens between limbs and leaves for a better, unobstructed view.

Two men appeared from the tunnel, their fingers poised on the triggers of their semi-automatic machine guns. Concentrating, Kash snapped a shot of the two, noticing the difference between them. One was tall and well built. His uniform and manner were orderly. His comrade was short and sloppy. The uniform he wore was generic. It bore no insignias, military or otherwise. His give-a-shit attitude prompted Kash to focus on him.

After a careful scan of the area, he raised a short arm and gave an abrupt wave forward and three more men appeared from the tunnel, struggling to move a mining car on tracks that had not been completely cleared of jungle growth. The shutter clicked, and Bennett briskly advanced the film while refocusing, hoping like hell the birds were used to the rusty mining wheels and continued their chatter.

The car was brought to a screeching halt, and the Spanish they spoke was hurried and full of excitement as they examined the contents of the car.

In one motion, Marrow switched on the microphone and began to put words to Bennett's pictures. He nudged Kash. "This is it. September 22nd. Five men have appeared from a well concealed tunnel pushing a mining car. The sentries in front are well armed with semi-automatics. The best money can buy. The heat is stifling, and the bandanas they wear afford little relief from the heat." Like any good reporter, he embellished. He nudged Kash again. "I can't make out the insignia on the bandana. Can you get a close up?"

A cut nod and change of cameras was Bennett's reply, and Marrow continued his recording.

"One soldier has drawn his pistol and is beating what appears to be a chunk of dirt," Mike chanced. He turned to Kash. "You getting this?" He winked, knowing full well his competent partner hadn't missed a thing. He turned back to the soldiers and gushed, "Jesus, God! Is that what I think it is?"

"No wonder they're smiling," Bennett offered solemnly. "Emeralds on the black market will bring plenty." He paused as he refocused. "What are they saying?"

"Something about the brothers will be happy, and that there's more of this in the deep walls." Mike interpreted the hurried Spanish. He strained to hear their lowered voices and repeated the conversation into Ole Betsy. He listened some more then turned to Kash. "I'll be damned, it's true," he declared in a hushed tone. "They are going to overthrow Raul. And you didn't think this was a hot lead," he chided Kash.

"It's hot all right," Kash stated, "and the lead turned out to be good for a change, too."

Marrow switched off the recorder and gave it a reassuring pat for a job well done. "Let's get the hell out of here," he suggested. "We have what we came for."

The click of hammers and the prickling coolness of metal on their hot skin made them aware of the unexpected company behind them. Suddenly, it was hotter.

"Friend's of yours?" Marrow teased his partner, looking back at the mining car, trying to count the soldiers. He saw five. He wondered where these guys come from.

The sun glimmered brightly off the metallic surface, but then disappeared quickly when the axe blade made its swift descent and neatly severed the tightly coiled piece of rope that held together one side of the makeshift raft Kash and Mike used to cross the water. Diagonally, on the other, a second blade separated another coil.

While ropes were losing their tension, another set was tightening, and Kash sneered at the pain in his wrists as the gritty rope dug in.

Mike, on the other hand, was more vocal as he watched "Ole Betsy" and Bennett's cameras being tossed into the muddy water. "Shit! Hey, pal, that's..." His protest was brought to an abrupt halt by the insistent point of a knife blade under his chin.

The soldier stood toe to toe with him and displayed a mouthful of jagged teeth that were pitted and yellow from lack of care. He saw Marrow's obvious disgust and let out a short, dirty laugh. His breath matched his laugh. The point of the knife left Mike's chin and he winced as the soldier trailed the dull side down his torso and around to his bound wrists. He clenched his fists as the keen edge sliced neatly into his skin. Bright red droplets dripped on to the raft.

A cold smirk played on the mouth of the soldier. "Croc-o-diles," he whispered into Marrow's ear, and then he gave the same dirty laugh.

Adding insult to injury, he gently nudged Mike, urging him to board the shaky raft and prompted Kash to follow. Bennett stepped cautiously onto the unstable craft and as he anticipated, it wavered under their weight. He looked down and saw the end disappear into the muddy water, but also noticed the droplets of blood on the separating logs. A splash drew his attention to the opposite bank. He squinted to see better. Croc-o-diles! Marrow didn't have to speak; the slack in his jaw said it all.

The soldiers pushed the raft off with poles and gave a mock salute to the drifting amigos, and with the rest of their comrades, vanished into the dense jungle.

Mike looked to Kash for any suggestions, silent or otherwise. He got silence. After a moment in thought, Kash moved to the center and nodded for his buddy to do the same.

Consecutive splashes alerted them more crocodiles were on their way for a noon time snack. Marrow watched their activity closely, while Kash squatted and worked his wrists past his thighs. Using his index and middle finger, he reached into his boot and pulled free a three inch boot knife. He began cutting away at the rope that bound his wrists.

A weak, but happy smile spread across Mike's baby face, but the relief was short lived. A crocodile zeroed in on his helpless prey. Marrow closed his eyes.

With a grunt, Kash hauled his snared buddy more to the middle and quickly cut his hands free. "You can open your eyes now. I need them to help me find a way to the bank," Bennett said plainly, without malice.

Marrow peered across the still water to the bank, some forty feet away. "To me, the easiest way over is to walk on the water," he reasoned sarcastically. "However, the bigger question is how do you suppose we do that without falling in?"

The raft caught on something beneath the surface and came to an abrupt halt. Luckily for Bennett, so did Mike. Kash couldn't bear to hear anymore of his partner's sarcasm, especially since it was his partner that volunteered them for this assignment. He knew the way back to the bank, and by rights, he should have made his move and left Marrow to fend for himself, but like countless times before, he just turned thoughtfully to his investigative reporter and returned the favor. "Easy. Ya just gotta know where the rocks are. Or in this case, the stumps," he answered in a sickening sweet tone. "Just follow my line."

Tree stumps lined the marshy water along the bank for as far as the eye could see, giving the illusion of being a protective grid against intrusion into the dark soul of the eerie jungle. Kash jumped to the first stump and managed to maintain his balance. He surveyed the line of stumps he had chosen for his "walk on water". In order to make it safely, the walk required continuous movement from stump to stump.

"Once I get going, follow my exact line. Got it?" he called over his shoulder to Mike.

"Got it," Mike called out with skepticism.

Kash drew a deep breath and with speed and agility possessed more of fear than dexterity, moved from stump to stump. Marrow needed only slight encouragement as he witnessed the front edge of the raft disappear and reappear with a hungry crocodile struggling to board, and his brothers were not far behind. With a burst, he stepped on its forehead and propelled himself to the first stump. His walk on water was less acrobatic, but none the less, it got the job done. Safely on the bank, Kash extended a hand to his clumsy partner and pulled him up to a less vulnerable area.

Slightly out of breath, Marrow leaned forward against a tree for support. "I've got a great idea; let's get the hell out of here."

Bennett stared deliberately past him. He took his boot knife and pinned a snake to the tree where Mike was relaxing. "Sounds great. Let's go," he agreed and nonchalantly slapped Mike's shoulder before heading for the Waco. Marrow stammered slightly as he looked back at the silent creature then headed after Bennett and the safety of the plane.

The Waco, an open air cockpit seaplane, roared above the ominous jungle along with Bennett's voice to Marrow, "Thank God, my next assignment is shooting ancient Chinese art in Ming Tombs. That ought to be a piece of cake."

Elaine reread the entry again and again. Not because his

handwriting was so bad, but her father wasn't a photojournalist, he was an archeologist. His degree reflected he graduated in 1945 and she had seen numerous articles bearing his name shortly after that time period where he discussed his findings in archeology. Not understanding, she read on, only this time it was her mother's journals. Unlike her father's, she could read these with great ease. Her mother's penmanship was second to none. After all, she hadn't won all those handwriting awards for nothing. Picking up where her father had left off, Elaine started with her mother's entry of September 23rd, 1947.

NEW YORK CITY, SEPTEMBER 23, 1947.

The doorman smiled and opened the heavy brass and beveled glass door and admitted a tall, neatly attired person. "Good morning, Les," he greeted.

Les Scott felt the rush of warm air upon entering the Metropolitan Building, and gave a short nod to the stout and kindly doorman.

The marbled walls and terrazzo floor echoed the activity inside the lobby. The most notable was that of a woman who walked briskly past Les. Her stiletto heels clicked loudly on the polished floor and the sound reverberated harshly off the marbled walls. As Les walked to the elevator, the irritating sound finally became absorbed as its source exited the building. All in all, the lobby was a welcomed change of pace from the hustle and bustle of the city that morning.

The doorman nodded to the lady as she left, then turned to Les. He shook his head more out of appreciation than objection at the retreating figure. He noticed the dark, pinstriped suit only accentuated the tall, well-tailored and graceful line of that cat called Les.

Everyday was the same with Les; the overcoat was neatly slung over the left forearm, and the fedora, whether black, brown or blue, was always pulled provocatively low over the right eye. From head to toe, nothing was ever out of place, right down to the spit shined loafers.

Reaching the elevator, Les pushed the up button, and then looked back to the obviously overwhelmed doorman. The usually stiff upper lip curved into a tiny smile, and the uncovered eye closed in a seductive wink, leaving the doorman smiling.

The elevator rang up and Les disappeared inside. In over ten years as a doorman for the Metropolitan, he had never seen anything quite like Les. He liked Les. She was something else.

The constant drone of the elevator was almost as aggravating as the woman in the lobby, and Les was grateful to exit on the fourth floor and head down the hall to "World Magazine". Long, unhurried strides carried the cat past the double doors and into the office of "World" and the thundering roar of Sampson, emperor of "World".

"Francine?" Sampson growled from his den. "Francine, have you seen Scott this morning?"

Francine Tucker, a kindly woman in her mid-fifties, looked to Les with sympathy, for she knew that impatient tone all too well.

Les forced a smile and hung up her neatly folded overcoat on the rack with the fedora. "Sorry I'm late," Les gave a breathy apology. "It's like a jungle out there today." A final adjustment to the charcoal suit, Les gave a hopeless sigh to Francine and headed down the hallway to Sampson's den.

"Fran..." Sampson's booming voice trailed off after he saw Les leaning against the door frame. He took a final drag from his cigarette and snubbed it out. He squinted at Les through the smoke he blew out. "Where the hell have you been, Leslie?" he asked sharply.

Leslie Anne Scott responded with a flat look and pursed lips for added measure.

"Have a date last night?" he joked.

Leslie said nothing and her expression didn't change.

"I didn't think so," he concluded in a disappointed tone.

"Then why did you ask?" she countered.

"Because I'm a dirty old man. I love living vicariously through you, seeing how we dress alike, and all. You don't pee standing up, do you?"

If she could have given him a sterner look she would have. She tapped her foot instead.

"Come in and have a seat," he offered. He pivoted away from his typewriter and leaned back in his chair. The springs squeaked and protested greatly under his considerable girth. He watched as Leslie carefully sat down, and then propelled himself forward, his round belly butting up against his always cluttered desk. He drummed his fingers anxiously while he put his thoughts into order.

Leslie recognized that look and steeled herself.

"I'm taking you off of the Chicago assignment and putting Murphy on that," he finally informed. "I have something else I want you to handle."

"I see," she managed softly, trying hard to mask the hurt, not quite succeeding.

"No, you don't see," Sampson corrected immediately.

"This isn't the first time you've pulled me from an out of town assignment. I suppose I'm going to hear the same narrow-minded excuse as before," Leslie shot back, and then mocked Sampson's gruff voice, "Travel's just too rigorous for you." Leslie waited a moment for him to defend his position. He didn't, so she continued, "I don't think traveling to Chicago is that rigorous. Then again, I'm not the one being narrow-minded."

Sampson strained his sizeable belly closer against the desk and pointed a stubby finger her way. "No, but you could be the one being fired."

"I just don't think it is fair, that's all," she protested.

He dropped his finger and relaxed back in his chair. "Going on archeological digs in the middle of Mexico and South America is no place for a woman," he reasoned.

"You're absolutely right," she said, throwing her hands up in the air in mock defeat. "Chicago is no place for a woman, either. That windy city. That toddling town."

"That's right, not this time anyway," he said, not giving an inch.

Leslie found the strength and pushed herself out of the chair. It may as well been the electric chair, for every time she sat in it, she was given a jolt that was enough to kill. Kill her spirit, anyway. Like so many times before she was being pulled from an assignment in favor of a less experienced, male journalist. Once again, she was a second class citizen, and she resigned herself to that unwritten law. No matter how skilled she was as a journalist, or how hard she worked, or even if she thought like a man in preparing a story, she was always going to be one step behind her male counterparts. It just wasn't fair. She smoothed her jacket and turned to leave the suddenly oppressive room.

Sampson waited until she was almost to the door before he spoke. "On the other hand," he sighed, baiting her, "Peiping is a place for an experienced art journalist such as you."

"Peiping? As in China?" Her words were barely audible, and she didn't turn to face his smug expression. She summoned the courage and put aside her pride and met his squinted gaze.

"Yeah. Unless of course you want to stand there and argue with me *about the rigors of travel. Which, by the way, will get you fired," he warned with a wink.*

"I'm sorry," she apologized. "It's just that...Peiping, huh?" She still couldn't believe it as she took up her familiar position against the door frame. Her professionalism took over. "What's the story?"

Sampson thumbed through a stack of folders and pulled one out marked "Tombs". He opened it and found his notes on the assignment. "Emperors' Tombs being opened and ancient art of the Dynasty's and Forbidden City are being displayed for the western world," he read, and Leslie curiously stepped forward to his desk. "Anyway, anything and everything you need to know it is in this folder." He handed it to her. "Travel arrangements have been made. You leave tomorrow for San Francisco. There, you will meet your photographer. Bennett's his name. Take a few days to roam around San Fran, particularly Chinatown. Acquaint yourself, if you will. After that, you head out for Peiping and ten days of work and not much play," he concluded with a devilish wink, insinuating one thing.

Leslie didn't bite. Instead she gave a smile of thanks and said, "You won't be disappointed."

He swiveled his squeaky chair around to his typewriter and picked up where he had left off before their meeting. "I know I won't. By the way, there's an allowance for you to buy some 'normal' looking clothes. Use it." He finished hunting and pecking through a sentence and looked up at her playful glare. "You know, stuff like Francine wears. Skirts and dresses. I could never understand why you didn't wear normal clothes, Leslie."

"Because I like wearing abnormal looking clothes like you," she answered flatly.

"You think I'm narrow-minded, wait until the Chinese see you!" He resumed his slow process of reporting. "Go get you some normal clothes, Leslie Anne."

She always knew when Sampson was serious; he would refer to her as "Leslie Anne". A privilege reserved only for her mother. "You know, Sampson, if you had hair, Francine and I would have to draw straws as to who would get the pleasure of being Delilah," she bantered.

Sampson gave a loud, obnoxious laugh and rubbed his bald, shiny head.

Satisfied, Leslie Anne walked away tapping her leg with the newfound hope she was just assigned.

CHAPTER FOUR

Elaine stretched, removed her reading glasses and checked her watch for the hour. It was early evening and still no word from Sam Winston at the airport in Juneau. She punched his number on her cell phone and waited until someone picked up.

"Yes? I'm wondering if Sam Winston is back." Elaine asked. Her brow furrowed, announcing her mood swing. "What do you mean; he came back and went home? I want his home number," she demanded. "No. This is Elaine Bennett, and my parents are missing, and supposedly, Mr. Winston has been involved in the rescue. I just want to know the latest information regarding my parent's missing plane." She waited some more. "Just give me his home number...All right, how about his cell phone? Is that less personal?"

She was getting nowhere with the person on the other end and was assured that Mr. Winston would call her shortly. She hung up and reluctantly phoned Lane and thankfully got his voice mail. She left a terse message, imploring him to call her with an update. She called Jack, if only to hear his voice and soothe her fractured psyche. He didn't pick up his cell phone and she didn't leave a message.

She roamed the house, trying to find a link to her parents and their past. Something that would confirm the writings she had been reading, something to affirm her childhood hadn't been a farce, but everywhere she looked, everything she touched, seemed to be so pat. So perfect.

Settling into her father's chair, she resumed her reading. She imagined her mother in her fastidious way, traveling and observing the likes of San Francisco. Elaine smiled at such an image, and with warmth, she read further of her mother's account.

SAN FRANCISCO, SEPTEMBER 25TH

It was chilly and damp. Leslie Anne Scott shrugged into her overcoat and pulled the collar up to keep the wind off of her neck. She reached up to the crown of her hat and pushed down firmly to secure it, then located the address on the building. The number on the structure read eighty, blank, nine. The tarnished shadow of a six showed between the zero and nine. She slid her hand into the pocket of her coat and pulled out a piece of paper. The address on the paper matched that on the building. Eighty-sixty-nine.

Leslie surveyed the four-story dwelling with distaste and disbelief. It reminded her of some of the condemned buildings on the lower east side back home. Peeling paint, broken window panes and crumbling steps. She shoved her hands deep into her pockets and gingerly went up the steps. Her first attempt to enter was unsuccessful. The door was swollen from the damp weather and needed a little encouragement. A swift kick at the bottom to loosened it, and then she used her shoulder to push her way in. Since her entry was anything but graceful, she shut the door with a resounding slam.

The entryway was as bad as the outside. Dark and dreary woodwork bordered plaster walls in need of repair and several coats of paint. The colorful pattern in the ceramic tile floor was dull from neglect, and several pieces were missing.

Apartment 3-D meant only one thing, Leslie had to climb three flights of stairs. She reached a hand out and tested the banister and found it to be loose. One of the spindles fell out and dropped down the stairs, landing at her feet. She looked to the wall for a second support. No such luck and she began her ascent with obvious caution.

The building was relatively quiet except for a few radios playing and the creak of the stairs under her feet. Finally she reached the third floor and room 3-D was at the end of the hall. Leslie made her way down the dimly lit corridor, tripping slightly on a loose wooden plank.

She presumably reached room 3-D and cocked her head to read the number that was barely hanging on the door. It was 3-D. She applied a courteous rap to the door, hoping the number wouldn't fall off. There was no answer. She tried again, and then turned her back to look out the grimy window. She patiently waited for Mr. Kash Bennett to answer the door.

Kash thought he heard a knock on the door and stuck his head out of the small bathroom. He was right, but the second knock was more firm, bordering on rude. He stumbled past his sleeper bed and pulled the toothbrush from his mouth when he opened the door. He stared blankly at the back of a beige overcoat and brown fedora.

Leslie Scott didn't acknowledge his presence, annoyed that it had taken him so long to open the door.

Puzzled, Kash stepped out and laid a heavy slap on the back of his visitor. "Hey, Les. C'mon on in." His words were a little fuzzy from the toothpaste in his mouth.

Kash stuffed the toothbrush back into his mouth and chewed on the bristles to get the lather going again. Slowly Leslie turned her head and looked over her shoulder at the man that stood in the doorway of 3-D.

Bennett bit down hard on the foamy object in his mouth. He, Les, was a she Les. A very tall one at that, and dressed in a man's suit, too. He gave a small smile of embarrassment as he became conscientious of his dress, or lack of it. He stood before her in nothing but his boxers, and she unnerved him further with her cool appraisal. Needless to say, he assumed Les Scott to be a man and not a woman. He removed the toothbrush and wiped the excess paste from his mouth with the back of his hand, leaving residue on his whiskered cheek.

Stepping aside, he gestured for her to enter. After what seemed like an eternity, she passed through the doorway into what could have been considered the bowels of hell. If Leslie had thoughts of the inside of this apartment looking better than the outside, she was sadly mistaken. The first room that should be condemned—3-D. He caught sight of her disgust in her brown eyes and scurried about picking up old newspapers, remnants of Chinese food, dirty socks and old beer bottles. It didn't matter, whatever was in his path, he collected and stuffed into a cabinet beneath the sink. A sink that contained at least two weeks worth of dirty dishes. Probably every dish he owned was stuck in that sink, Leslie thought to herself. Kash hurriedly threw the sheet and blanket into the sleeper bed and folded it back into the sofa. Gathering lumpy, frayed cushions, he placed them haphazardly on the sofa and then extended an open palm for her to have a seat.

"Please, have a seat. Make yourself comfortable," he invited breathlessly.

Leslie removed her overcoat and fedora revealing a suit that matched perfectly her dark brown hair. She wouldn't have sat down had Kash not

23

made another gesture toward the sofa. He silently volunteered to take her coat and hat, but she refused with a "not necessary" smile.

"I was expecting you to be a man. I mean, um, Les is a man's name and I thought," he fumbled and gave a clumsy smile. "Well, obviously you're not a man."

His smile quickly faded when he caught the sarcasm in her eyes. Slowly she eyed him up and down, making him uncomfortable about his appearance.

Finally she spoke in a deeply rich and sensuous voice. "I wouldn't make that mistake with you."

The words came out softly enough, but with sting, and instinctively his hands flew and crossed in front of his fly, protecting himself from this particular type of Venus.

"I'd rather figure you a man to wear Jockeys," she added.

"Jockeys?" he questioned, a little confused by her remark.

"You know," she stated while looking at his boxers. "Training pants."

Kash gave a little shy smile of defeat. He didn't want to get into a verbal clash, not with this woman. It was obvious she was well versed in verbal combat. His smile faded. "Nice suit," he jabbed and then he headed toward the bathroom and refuge from the man-eating tigress in his living room.

CHAPTER FIVE

Leslie peered into the window of a Chinese grocery store on Stockton Street and then she stepped back and looked at the many crates of bok choy and wintermelons. Kash quietly watched her fascination with a wintermelon. It was large and shaped like a pumpkin with the white-green exterior of a watermelon. She gave it a thump and it answered back with a thud of fullness. The click of a shutter switched her attention from the melon to Kash.

"New." He patted the camera. "Wanna go inside?"

Leslie nodded and he opened the door to the grocery. Bushel baskets that contained snow pea pods and bean sprouts lined the front counter, and standing behind the counter, an elderly man and his wife greeted them with a short bow. Near the back wall stood large barrels of pickled cabbage, guy choy, assorted salted fish and duck eggs. Chinese sausages were strung with uniformity above the barrels. Kash looked on with guarded amusement as Leslie lifted the lid to one of the tins. Her aristocratic nose wrinkled at the escaping odor. The smell wasn't offensive, just different.

"Ducks," Kash clarified.

Leslie put the lid back in place and walked past him on her way to the door. "I knew that," she defended.

The architecture of Chinatown was much like that of the western world. There were very few traditional buildings with pagodas, or curved topped roofs with glazed tiles to reflect the atmosphere of the old country. Many things were much like that of the modern civilization, but there were still some things that had remained the same and constant.

Leslie soaked up every detail that Kash volunteered as they wandered through a crowded street market. "A lot of things have changed since the

Chinese first arrived in the beautiful land or 'Mei Kwok' as they call it. No longer are they just laundrymen, restaurateurs, railroad workers or fishermen. They now own businesses. Some legitimate, some not. Just like their western counterparts.

One thing that has remained consistent and traditional is the teaching of primarily Confucianism and the family status. The Confucian philosophers classified the family status into five relationships. Number one; Ruler and Subject. Number two; Father and Son. Number three; Elder Brother and Younger Brother. Number four; Husband and Wife. And lastly, number five; Friend and Friend."

"Sampson was right. The women are far down the list," she noted.

He calmly studied her refined features after her remark and became acutely aware of her sexuality. He silently chastised himself and continued his explanation of Confucianism, hoping one would lend themselves to his present situation. "There are also five Confucian virtues of which to practice; Love, righteousness, propriety, wisdom and faithfulness. By following the standards set by the Confucian philosophers, the Chinese have been able to endure many of the prejudices they have encountered since coming to the beautiful land."

His information was thoughtful medicine for Leslie and they walked in silence for a quite a while until they came upon a small gift shop and Leslie stopped immediately.

"May we?" she asked.

Kash replied by opening the door for his east coast visitor.

The little shop was crowded, but not with people. Rather with pieces of traditional Chinese art and artifacts. A kaleidoscope of colors blended together and it was hard to tell where one object ended and another one began. Carved jade and ivory forms of candy dishes, horses and dragons were enclosed in glass cases for protection. There were paintings. Wall to wall paintings. Most of them were landscapes. Beautiful and detailed, every inch of the canvas delicately and tastefully used.

Leslie grinned with satisfaction; a souvenir for Sampson. A ceramic figure with a bald, shiny head and a fat belly sat cross-legged before her. So many things about him reminded her of the emperor of "World". Right down to the obscene grin on his face. She wondered, though, if Sampson had a candy red stone in his navel. She shook her head of the image and *patted the round belly. Feeling the presence of Kash behind her, she turned to face him.*

"Someone you know?" he asked.

"Yeah, my boss," she laughed.

"We should be careful," he seriously suggested.

Her smile faded and she looked curiously into his gray eyes. "Why?"

"You're starting to have fun," he answered honestly. "Hungry?" he asked before she had a chance to remark about his previous comment. Surprisingly she held her tongue and nodded her head "yes" in answering his question.

Warm, caramelized hazel eyes gazed across the table and ran straight into what could have been described as a steel wall. Leslie Anne Scott lifted her cup of tea in a mock salute of cheers to Kash Bennett. A perfectly arched brow raised and a hint of a smile tugged at the corner of her mouth and dimples started to betray her lighter mood. Kash absentmindedly imitated her gesture with his glass of scotch.

She squinted in anticipation of the tea being too hot to drink and tiny laugh lines appeared, softly feathering out from the corner of her eyes. Putting the cup down, she ran a slender hand across the pale pink tablecloth, more out of habit than for any particular reason. Kash took notice of the fastidious manner in which she did it and everything else, from the way she dressed to the way she folded her napkin.

He took a sip of his scotch and tilted his head to one side as he studied her crowning glory. In his silent opinion, the bun was too severe. If he could have been sure she wouldn't have decked him, he would have reached up behind her, pulled it free from its restraining pins and raked his fingers through its dark richness, allowing it to fall free about her shoulders and soften her already striking features. He flexed his hand to check the instinct of wanting to feel the silkiness of those thick tresses and the smoothness of that milky complexion.

His appraisal of her continued to her naturally high cheekbones that required only a touch of blush and her lips that needed only a hint of color. Then there were those dimples. The one on the left was deeper and it was revealed even when she was speaking of the most serious of subjects; like his choice of underwear. Her nose was classically straight and symmetrical. In short, she had the look of an aristocratic snob and she was definitely the type to admire from a distance. A very long distance.

The cup was poised on her lips and she gave a guarded look to her dinner companion. Once again, she met the penetrating glare of his gray eyes. Any thought of taking a sip was abandoned and she put the cup down. She didn't look away, even though his stare was more intimate than before and certainly more unnerving.

"Chocolate covered almonds," Kash blurted. It was out before he realized. In a certain light her eyes reminded him of milk chocolate covered almonds. Refreshing and delicious. Refreshing like her quiet resolve and delicious like her looks. "Uh, chocolate covered almonds," he repeated and he didn't know why. "One of my favorites, and I've got a hankering for them. What say we go get some?"

"Okay." She nodded slowly, trying to get a fix on the stranger she was about to share the next ten days with in a land that was as unpredictable as his moody gaze.

Left. Right. Left. Right. Leslie kept in perfect step with Kash as they made their way down a deserted street. The steady beat of their footsteps were only interrupted when Leslie came to an abrupt halt in front of a Chinese bakery. Kash was around the corner before he realized she was no longer at his side. He stopped and backed up to find her with her hands cupped near her face, pressing her nose against the window, looking inside the bakery.

Impatiently he shoved his hands into his pockets, praying she wouldn't ask any more questions. He didn't mind her inquisitive nature, but he wasn't in the mood for it. Rather, he was in the mood for chocolate covered almonds; real and imagined. Maybe, he mused to himself, if she dressed more like a woman, she wouldn't have to press her nose to the bakery window.

She glanced over at him and he was suddenly serious again, awaiting the inevitable. "What are those?" she asked, tapping the glass and pointing to the only things in the bakery's display case.

Kash peered into the bakery at the objects, then back to Leslie. "Moon cakes."

She anticipated an explanation, but instead he startled her by pushing her hat back on her head, revealing all of her face.

Suddenly his hankering for chocolate covered almonds was satisfied and he began to explain the Moon Festival. "Moon cakes," he began softly, and then he stopped, more interested in the apparition before him than the content of his interpretation of the Moon Festival. She raised her eyebrows for him to continue. "Moon cakes are made for the Moon Festival or Harvest

Festival. According to the lunar calendar, the full moon is always on the fifteenth day of the month. The Chinese celebrate the moon's birthday each year, roughly at the end of September. Since the moon is a 'Yin' symbol, or it represents the female, this festival is obviously held at night. It's a very private celebration." He stepped closer, penetrating her guarded space. He liked the muted glow of the street light and what it did to her absolute and defined features, turning them dark and sultry. "And very romantic," he concluded, his eyes smoldering.

"How do you know so much?" she asked, deliberately breaking their intimacy.

"I'm a native."

"No native I know wears boxers," she teased.

The drizzle became rain and fell a lot faster and harder. Kash gave a sigh of relief. "We'd better go before you melt," he sharply threw back and headed for the confectionary and chocolate covered almonds.

Leslie's dimples deepened at their exchange. Clenching her fist, she gently thumped her chest like Tarzan and then followed after him.

CHAPTER SIX

A tiny tinkle announced Kash's entry into the corner what-not-store. Whatever one needed or desired, including chocolate covered almonds, they could find in this unique little store. Even though there were many items, there weren't many of those items available, but that was not the case with Kash's hankering.

He saddled up to the counter lined with canisters of cookies, candies, teas and herbs and mulled over what else he might want. A boy barely tall enough to see over the counter approached him.

"Help you?" he asked.

Kash leaned over the counter for a better look. "Yeah. Where's Papa?"

The boy pointed toward the ceiling.

"Upstairs?"

The boy nodded and pulled a foot stool over for a boost. It helped.

Kash took the canister of chocolate covered almonds and handed it to the small boy. "I'd like half a pound," he instructed.

The boy obliged and scooped out a generous amount into a small bag. He weighed it and placed it in front of Kash.

"That be…" the boy started.

Kash placed a bill on the countertop and headed for the door, wondering why Leslie hadn't come into the store. The ringing of the cash register clashed with the tinkling bell as he left. He looked left and then right and checked the car across the street but didn't see any sign of his east coast visitor. He opened the bag and started to indulge as he retraced his steps and headed for the bakery, hoping to find his new partner.

Carefully Leslie tried to secure the banging metal door in the alley next to the what-not-store. It had been rattling around in the wind for as long as she stood waiting for Kash, and with her patience on edge, she couldn't help but put in back into place. The muted glow of a yellow light bulb above the metal door was the only light, and trying to keep the door still from the outside was going to be impossible; the handle and locking mechanism was inside.

As she pulled the door back to inspect the device, she noticed the steps leading down below the street level. She wondered where they led, and since she saw no sign of Kash, she carefully headed down the small passageway. On her way, she didn't give danger a second thought, her reporter's curiosity getting the better of her.

At the bottom she turned to the left and then made several more turns to the left and right until she came upon a large oak door. It was approximately two inches thick and studded with bolts and the same locking mechanism as the first door in the alley. For these doors to be unlocked there must be an access from the inside. But where? Along the way there were several doors on either side of the corridor, but they were all padlocked. This door was slightly ajar.

Carefully she pushed it open to a small room only to find another door just as massive. The room was lined with boxes and crates and there was a passage to the other door where at the bottom a light shone. Quietly Leslie made her way to the door and peeked inside.

The room was dark except for a single light that hung down from the ceiling in the middle of the room. A Chinese man in his mid-forties sat on a stool at the only wooden desk in the room. Atop the desk was his grip with various tools and under his elbows a piece of black velvet. Looking through a jeweler's loupe, he placed a tiny black dot in the opening of the eye. Using the end of the tweezers, he gently packed it into place and secured the edges. He sigh was easily heard. With his job complete, he motioned for his young assistant to pack the gear.

The Chinese youth stepped forward and methodically packed the grip, while a third party emerged from the shadows. He was a Caucasian. His hands were shoved deep into the pockets of his overcoat and the black fedora he wore was pulled low, revealing only the tip of his nose, thin lips and square jaw.

The jeweler turned to him and proudly presented him with an octagon shaped pendant. Cautiously the stranger removed his left hand from his coat and accepted the piece. After a quick inspection his thin lips curved into a cold but satisfied smile. Turning back to the assistant, the jeweler gave both a triumphant and relieved nod of his head.

Outside, Kash sat in his car, munching away on his chocolate covered almonds. More than once he contemplated walking up and down the streets again in an attempt to find his visitor, but he thought better than to interfere in her research. Besides, it was raining and he was hungry for almonds. He would wait another five minutes and then go looking, again. After all, what trouble could she get into at this late hour? She was probably window shopping, he mused. He dug deeper into the bag of almonds. Nonetheless, she disappeared on more than one occasion during the day, shopping for this and researching that. She wasn't afraid to stray from his side to explore.

He popped a few more goodies as a black Buick sedan cautiously approached with its lights off. Instinctively Kash sank down in his seat and watched as the back seat passengers emerged from the car.

A light drizzle greeted them. They ignored it as they scanned the street and area for any unwanted activity. Confident the area was secure; they started toward the alley that was between the laundry and what-not-store. The alley was fairly clean of debris, with only a few pallets stacked here and there, and according to the signs posted, it was mainly used for loading and unloading of goods. Their walk to the alley and the metal door was deliberate, like the task ahead of them.

To hear better, Leslie eased the door open a little more, only to be shocked back by a loud bang that reverberated off the walls of the scarcely furnished room. It was accompanied by a stream of blood and brains that spewed into the darkness. The jeweler's eyes were wide and glazed as he dropped to the floor, dead.

The assistant stood motionless; beads of perspiration formed immediately on his brow and upper lip. His heart beat madly in his chest, threatening to erupt, while his blood pounded loudly in his ears. His eyes darted wildly back and forth as he searched the shadows for the door. It was to his immediate left.

Leslie's head snapped to the first heavy door as she heard hushed voices approaching. Searching her surroundings, she found refuge behind several boxes and crates that still allowed her a view of the door and what was happening in the small room. She sat so still that she hardly seemed to breathe, and hoped like hell her pounding heart wouldn't give her away.

A callous smile formed on the thin lips of the Caucasian as he aimed his Colt at the stymied assistant, but the pull of the trigger was interrupted *when the door was unexpectedly kicked open the rest of the way. The 45 was realigned toward the sound, sparing the assistant, who took advantaged and dove under the wooden table.*

Out of the darkness came a throwing star, penetrating the trachea of the Caucasian. Instantly he dropped the pendant to the floor, directly in front of the assistant. Simultaneously he started to empty the magazine of his Colt in the direction of the door, while desperately trying to dislodge the star from his throat. Blood sprayed up into his face as he frantically gasped for air. The more he attempted to suck in the precious oxygen, the deeper the star went into his windpipe.

Kash wasn't mistaken in what he heard, and he grimaced at the sound. Still he remained low in his seat and watched the opening of the alley where the shots rang out from. He only hoped Leslie was somewhere far from the action, and wasn't one of those curious cats.

The slide of the 45 locked into place and there was a final click. The magazine was empty and the Caucasian lowered the gun and staggered to the table. Bracing himself, he looked at the door. He squinted to see the damage incurred by his means of self-preservation.

One of his victims was lying supine in front of the doorway. Half of his face was missing and his chest was soaking red from bullet holes. Even near death, the Caucasian was pleased he downed an enemy. His pleasure was short-lived. The second intruder emerged unscathed.

The Caucasian watched the victor move toward him and he drew his hand into an agonizing fist of defeat. A deep-throated cough exploded and he emitted a stream of blood in the direction of his adversary. His body quaked and dropped heavily face down onto the desk, where moments earlier he had watched his comfortable retirement being placed into the eye of the pendant.

The weight of his body started to drag him down, and slowly he slid off the table, leaving behind a feathery trail of red. The pointed end of the star dug into a fracture in the wood, momentarily halting his descent. Gravity took over and pulled him to the floor, the star cutting a jagged line up his neck and under his chin. He crumpled in a heap, landing in front of the assistant. His ice blue eyes fixed upon the very thing that had cost him his life; the pendant.

The assistant quickly forgot the jeweler and the Caucasian as he realized the pendant was a valuable commodity. He stretched a greedy hand out to retrieve it while watching the deliberate steps of the intruder. The man stopped, and quickly the assistant snatched up the pendant and held onto it for dear life.

Carefully he started to back out from under the table, his eyes never leaving the position of the other man. Slowly he pushed himself onto his knees, careful not to raise his head above the desk. He steadied himself, both physically and emotionally. His senses had become magnified. His eyesight was sharp, and he could see clearly the small room that led to the tunnels and steps to the alley. His hearing was acute and he became aware of every sound, from the mice squeaking in the corner to the soft shuffle of the soled shoes on the floor.

He got his bearings and ran his escape plan through his mind again. Outside of the intruder, there was only one body to jump over enroute to freedom. Drawing his knees to his chest, he balanced on the balls of his feet and with his right hand he felt over his head to find the edge of the table. In the same motion he stood and pushed the wooden structure over into the body of the oncoming figure.

Without hesitation, the assistant took five running steps, jumped over the body in front of the doorway and headed through the maze of tunnels until he emerged in the alley, still clutching the pendant in one hand, and trying desperately to free the pronged object stuck between his shoulders. He hadn't planned on the assailant being so agile as to cast the desk aside and strike with a star.

The bump in the night was caused by Leslie angling for a better view, and when the Chinese man pinpointed her position, he made a beeline for her. Thankfully she was still cloaked by several boxes and crates, of which came tumbling down on the man as he approached her position. As he grappled with the load, she quickly exited the room and ran the maze of tunnels before finding the stairs and freedom from her nightmarish excursion.

The metal door announced to the world its protest as Leslie emerged, and it wasn't lost on Kash that his east coast visitor was smack dab in the middle of trouble. "Oh, shit!" Kash exclaimed as he saw Leslie stop to help the fallen man. He revved the engine of his '47 Biscayne, threw it into gear *and made a tight U-turn, bringing him in front of the alley. Reaching over he opened the door and yelled, "Get in, goddamn it."*

As she reached the street, the rain was pouring down in buckets and dripping off the brim of her hat, distorting her vision and her hearing. A pleading hand begged her to help. She knelt next to the young man as he frantically spoke Chinese. She didn't understand. "English? Can you speak English?" she asked.

He placed a quivering fist to her chest and mumbled the same phrase in Chinese. After a moment, he opened his fist and let the pendant fall into her lap.

It was like nothing she had ever seen before. It was octagon in shape, with a silver background and black dashes around the edges and something circular in the middle. She gave a silent plea for him to give her more information as Bennett cursed and ordered her into the car.

"Eye..." the Chinese youth said.

"I, what?" she repeated.

Then he fell silent, and through the pouring rain Leslie could sense the Chinese man from below starting to find his way up from the underground.

"For God's sake, Leslie, get in the car!" Kash ordered, as he helped her up and shoved her into the passenger's seat. "Goddamn it! Why couldn't you have gone window shopping?" he swore under his breath as he got in and slammed down the accelerator. The rear wheels spun and finally caught on the wet pavement, propelling them forward to safety. Or so he thought. He paid little attention to her irritated glare as he sped through the streets of Chinatown.

He repeatedly checked his rearview mirror as he drove north toward Little Italy. They were well on their way when he asked, "What did he give you back there?"

She ignored his question and stared straight ahead, while in her pocket she fondled the object of his question and pondered what he meant about window shopping.

Irked by her deliberate and apathetic attitude, he brought the car to a screeching halt in the middle of the street. Leslie stopped herself short of the windshield, while still managing her silence.

Fed up, Kash grabbed her shoulder of her overcoat, and it was enough to get her attention. She stared at the white-knuckled grip he had on her coat, but still said nothing. What little traffic there was seemed to be behind them sounding off their displeasure.

"You're embarrassing us," he proclaimed to her stony profile.

"I'm not the one stopped in the middle of the street," she challenged.

Damn, that didn't work, he thought. "Yeah, well, you could have been the one that was killed. What did he give you back there?" he asked again.

"Nothing," she replied through clenched teeth. Her cool façade melted momentarily under molten silver glare. She clinched her jaw and blinked deliberately, giving herself time to garner her composure. "Not a goddamn thing," she said with finality.

Neither one backed down in their clash of wills. It was Kash that ended the battle as he turned his attention past Leslie to something outside the car window. He recognized immediately the object sticking out from *the passenger window at them; a 45 caliber, drum fed, automatic Tommy gun.*

Leslie's smug expression of victory was cut short when Kash abruptly jerked her down to his lap. He collapsed on top of her as a barrage of bullets cut through the window and windshield of his new Biscayne. When the shooting stopped, Kash eased his head above the dashboard for a better look. Through splintered glass he saw his assailants make a three-point turn around and head for another pass at his car.

He shoved the power glide into gear, slammed the accelerator to the floor and made a hard left turn. It wasn't the prettiest maneuver, but he managed to miss an oncoming motorist, street light and fire hydrant.

He sat more upright to gain better control. Leslie took that as a sign she could get up. Kash felt her move and shoved her back down for safe keeping. Fully aware of where her face was buried, she shook off her indignation and placed her cheek on his rock hard thigh.

The peaks and valleys made driving rough and difficult at high speeds, and Kash placed a restraining hand on her shoulder as he wildly steered his car through the streets. He was almost home free when he checked the rearview mirror and discovered they had caught up.

The Buick closed quickly, and Kash saw the man lean out and fire the gun again. He ducked instinctively and grimaced at the staccato rhythm of the gun.

The clinking of the metal told him two things: They were too close, and they had hit his new car, again. A low groan escaped his lips as he negotiated a hard right and sped through an intersection. Running a red light, he swerved to narrowly miss two vehicles. His unwanted company was not so fortunate; they skidded to a stop to avoid a collision and stalled.

Kash made a quick left then turned left again into a dark alley adjacent to the Carlyle-Essex Hotel. The very same hotel Leslie was staying. He shut off the engine and lights, and then let out a rush of air that he seemed to have been holding since the beginning of the chase. It was finally over. Or was it? The answer to that lay in his lap.

Leslie felt the firm shake of his hand on her shoulder that all was clear and she could get up. She wasn't sure she wanted to for fear of meeting his hard, angry stare. Slowly she pushed up and met exactly what she feared. Though it was nearly dark in the alley, the light at the far end provided enough reflection for Leslie to see, not only the fury in his eyes, but the reason for his infuriation.

The windshield was a splintered mess with at least six bullet holes and the passenger door glass was almost nonexistent. It wasn't so bad that it couldn't be repaired, she silently reasoned. Still, she didn't dare look at Kash, but rather, she cleared her throat and stared at the building outside her fractured window.

"Where are we?" she questioned in a voice that was barely above a whisper.

"I'm fine, thank you," Kash shot back sarcastically. Stepping out of the car, he shut the door with a resounding slam, startling Leslie, and sending the rest of the passenger door glass crumbling to the ground.

Being careful of the broken glass inside, Leslie searched the floor board for her hat. She found it, and gently she brushed it off and got out of the car. The glass crunched loudly under her feet as she walked to the rear of the car. Nervously she fiddled with the brim of her fedora while watching Kash inspect the bullet holes in the trunk lid.

"Are you okay?" Her question was meant for him, but she directed it at her shoe tops.

"I'm fine. How kind of you to ask," he bit out sharply. "I just wish I could say the same for my new car."

That inconsiderate tone of his was all she needed to rejuvenate her battered psyche. Her head snapped up and her eyes narrowed in a fiery glare. "I'm sorry about your car. I'll pay whatever it costs to have it fixed," she offered coolly, masking the hurt she felt. Then she pivoted and walked past him toward the opening of the alley in which they entered. "Just send the bill to my office," she called over her shoulder.

"Where the hell do you think you're going?" Bennett called after her.

She ignored him and pushed her hat onto her head.

"Your hotel's the other way," he informed her.

Leslie stopped, closed her eyes, and felt the embarrassment creep up her neck and flood her cheeks. Summoning courage, she turned around and headed straight for him, then past him; not once looking in his direction.

Leaning against the trunk of his car, Kash could only shake his head at her stubbornness. "Wait a minute, will ya?" His request fell on deaf ears, and she continued down the alley. He half-walked, half-ran to catch up *with her, and when he did, he tugged at her elbow, encouraging her to stop.*

She pulled up at the opening of the alley and examined the activity in attempt to keep a persistent Kash Bennett at bay. There was very little going on, except for two cabs letting off their fares in front of the hotel.

Full of her indignant attitude, Kash pulled her around and forced her to look at him. Pushing her hat back, he discovered the weariness and vulnerability caused by the evenings activities. The tiny crease between her brows was more from being tired and frightened than annoyed. It was a scary thing that after one evening of her company he could read her so easily.

"May I walk you to your room?" he asked in a gentlemanly fashion.

Without waiting for her acceptance or objection, he started to guide her around the corner, and then harshly yanked her back, pressing her against the building.

A sharp intake of air was stifled by his cupped hand over her mouth, and a finger to pursed lips, motioning for her to be quiet.

The same Buick that had chased them earlier was making its way down the street. It stopped in front of the alley. Kash pushed her deeper into the shadows, but their forms were still outlined. The car didn't move. Bennett removed his hand from her mouth and drew her to him, molding his length to her.

Her voice was hoarse when she whispered, "Now what do we do?"

CHAPTER SEVEN

A groan caught in her throat as he took her lips in a bruising and demanding kiss.

"Go along with it," he ground out against her lips.

She did. Drawing him closer, she willingly participated. Maybe too willingly? The car finally moved on, and so did Kash. He continued his exploration of a sweetness he thought didn't exist. Reluctantly he pulled away from her slightly parted lips, surprised that the frosty woman before him could be thawed and display a raw, fiery passion.

Her eyes remained closed; her breathing irregular and her mouth was suddenly very dry. She was sure everything would return to normal momentarily. Deep down she was trying to convince herself she had enjoyed the moment. A moment she knew she was sure to regret.

Kash glanced at the opening of the alley and then back to Leslie. "They sure have gone to a lot of trouble for nothing, don't you think?" His words were surly.

Leslie closed her mouth and opened her eyes to his cutting stare. She didn't justify his remark with a response. It was just as well, it probably would have come out all wrong and added more insult to already enough injury. Besides, she was tired and all she wanted was a hot bath and a warm bed, and more importantly she wanted to put this evening to rest. She gave him a wan smile, hoping he'd back off, and he did.

"Suppose we go up to your room…" He was cut off by a provocatively arched brow. It brought a tiny smile to the usually stern line of his mouth. "…And take a look at the nothing he gave," he finished.

"Oh," she mouthed to his innocent proposal, and then they disappeared around the corner.

Kash pushed the door open and stepped inside the darkened suite at the Carlyle-Essex Hotel. He fumbled for the light switch on the wall to his right, but he didn't find it.

Impatiently Leslie brushed past him and hit the switch on the left wall. The room brightened, and a low whistle of appreciation came from Kash as he stepped inside the room.

Leslie shut the door and leaned against it while Kash journeyed through the short hallway into the body of the living room. His heels clicked on the cherry wood parquet floor, but they fell silent when he stepped onto the powder-blue and maroon on beige ornate area rug. The furniture was finished in dark lacquer mahogany, with velvet cushions that matched the colors in the area rug.

"Nice." His statement was simple and to the point. He turned and faced the unusually quiet Leslie Anne Scott.

She nodded in agreement. She looked down to break his unnerving stare and saw the dark stain on the sleeve of her overcoat. If she had any doubt before that the Chinese man was bleeding, they were erased as she touched the sticky sleeve.

When she looked up, Kash had made his way to the framed opening that led into the bedroom. This time he found the light switch and gave it a flip. The room lit up. He stepped inside and stood next to the four-poster bed. The beige spread had been pulled down and a wrapped mint was resting on the pillow. He helped himself to the treat.

Leslie watched him stuff the mint into his mouth, wad up its wrapper and throw it casually onto the nightstand. She shook her head, and then shook out of her overcoat as she walked past him. "Make yourself at home," she sarcastically invited him.

He winced at her reaction and quickly picked up the discarded wrapper and shoved it into his pocket. His gaze narrowed as she disappeared into yet another room.

A white light sprung to life, illuminating the bathroom. Built in at the top of the mirrored cabinet, the light shone brightly on Leslie as she stared at the reflection she knew to be her own, but not recognizing the drawn and haggard features caused by the night's activities. Hard to believe it was the same woman, who earlier that morning had left looking fresh and crisp.

Leaning forward on the marbled vanity, Leslie tried to focus on the tired image of herself instead of the figure that loomed largely in the background, and had taken a position against the door frame. She broke the contact with

Kash and plugged the drain in the sink, filling it with cold water. Slowly she attended to the sleeve of her raincoat and occasionally she would catch a glimpse of Bennett watching her.

"How can you afford to stay here?" he asked, looking over his shoulder into the well appointed bedroom, then back to Leslie. "I mean, being a journalist..."

"...And a woman," she finished his thought. Her voice had an edge to it as she spoke. "I can't afford it." Turning around, she faced him and leaned against the vanity for extra support. "World's picking up the tab on this one." She let a moment go. "As they do with all of our out-of-town assignments."

Kash knew that tone all too well and he backed out of the bathroom. He headed for the living room and the decanter of scotch he spied on the table behind the sofa. "Want anything to drink?" he called over his shoulder.

"Sure." Her answer was automatic, concentrating more on her fedora. Through a hole in the brown felt she poked a finger. "Damn."

"Preference?"

"Whatever you're having is fine," she muttered.

"What?" he asked rather loudly.

"Whatever you are having," she enunciated, wondering what was wrong with his hearing.

Kash poured a lightly colored drink from a crystal decanter into two snub glasses. He lifted his head as Leslie appeared from the bedroom. Her hands were shoved deep into the pockets of her pants and the solid black suspenders that held them up were draped against the length of her thighs. Gone was the brown fedora and blue paisley tie and undone were the first three buttons of her white dress shirt. Most noticeably, the severe bun of earlier was released and her dark tresses fell in a heap about her shoulders.

Either by instinct or practice, Kash stopped pouring the scotch, replaced the decanter and extended the half filled glass to her. All the while his eyes were glued to the creaminess of her throat. A throat, if he had a chance thirty minutes earlier, he would have gladly wrung.

Aware of his scrutiny, a hint of red crept into view near her collar as she accepted the glass. In an effort to shake the uneasiness she felt, she moved past him and stood in front of the window that provided a spectacular view of the lighted city below.

A devilish grin stole across his face as he closed the distance between them.

Leslie could feel the warmth of his breath on her ear and neck. Their eyes met in the reflection of the glass, but she quickly ended the intimacy by looking back to the city. "You have a lovely city at night," she politely commented, hoping to draw his attention to something else other than herself. It didn't work.

Thoughtfully he pushed her hair aside in the back for a better view of the nape of her neck. "And you have a lovely neck."

The compliment was followed by a soft and delicate kiss on the tender skin. It evoked a reaction she had never experienced before; heat rising up one side, chills racing down the other. Startled, she moved her head away from his persistence and drew her shoulders up in a shudder, attempting to shake the unnerving effect the stern line of his lips had created. She whirled around and stared at Kash to find his mouth set a mocking pout. Slowly her eyes made their way to his hooded gaze and found there was a gleam that he was happy with himself and the reaction his playful nip produced.

Right, Romeo, she wanted to say, but she took the direct, ladylike approach. "Just what is it you want, Mr. Bennett?"

"Nothing," he replied lightly and sipped his scotch.

He left her to draw on her own conclusion and made his way to the sofa. Plopping down, he propped his feet up on the coffee table and leaned his head back on the tufted back.

Leslie understood clearly what 'nothing' was and pulled it from her pants pocket. Placing her drink on the table, she perched herself on the back of the sofa and like a carrot on a stick, she dangled the pendant in front of Kash.

"I'm sure this is the 'nothing' you were referring to?" she cooed softly.

He stared deliberately at the swaying pendant, wondering why its value was so deadly. "So, this is the 'nothing'?"

He reached up and claimed the piece for a better look. It was octagon in shape, with a continuous black border on all sides. On each side, there was a trigram, and in the center was a perfect circle. Inside the circle, two tadpoles were intertwined with each other. One was silver, the other black.

Entranced, Leslie swiveled her legs around and dropped down onto the sofa next to Kash for a better look. A small cry of astonishment came *from her when he turned over the pendant and stared at the other side of 'nothing'.*

"God, that's beautiful. What does it mean?" she asked. The pitch of her voice was raised a notch, as was her curiosity, much to Kash's chagrin.

"I don't know," he replied softly. Even he was a little awestruck by the detailed beauty the backside offered.

The back of the pendant was silver, with the same black border that was on the front. There were also two hand painted symbols or characters. The first was at the top of the pendant. The second was to the right, near the lower corner of the second side. Without a doubt the most striking feature on the back was the colorfully painted dragon emerging from a waterfall. The full pendant, front and back appeared to be protected by a clear lacquer finish. Kash flipped it over to the front side and felt the face, somehow it wasn't the same as the back.

Leslie didn't give him the time to ponder. Ever the journalist, she pressed and pointed to the intertwined tadpoles. "What does this circle mean?"

Kash took his feet down from the coffee table and squared himself to her. His tone was sharp with impatience as he spoke. "You know, for someone who's a highly trained art journalist, and I use that term lightly, you don't know squat about one of the oldest forms of art, do you?"

"Well, for a native," she playfully thumped her chest, "you certainly say, 'I don't know' enough."

"I only said that once," he defended.

"Well, once is enough. For your information," Leslie pointed out, "I do know something about one of the oldest forms of art. You've never asked me anything about Egyptian art." Pleased with her defense, she pointed back to the pendant, eager to learn more. "Now, what's that in the middle?"

Taking a page from earlier that morning, Kash avoided a verbal clash with the seasoned veteran next to him and explained the united figures. "You are aware of Yin-Yang?"

She nodded.

"It's the symbol for Yang-Yin. Taoism, an ancient Chinese belief, postulated the Yin-Yang symbol. This," he pointed to the silver tadpole, "is Yang, or the male. It represents the positive, the bright, the warm, sun, heaven and dominance. The black tadpole is Yin, or the female. It's the negative, the dark, the secretive and the deep." He found it hard to concentrate on the explanation while sitting next to the only female he had

ever met that represented the Yin symbol so perfectly. Still, he continued, "It also represents the moon and the earth. It is said to be derived from a continuous straight line denoting the male principle and the broken line denoting the female. Like the trigrams."

"Trigrams?"

"These are trigrams." He pointed to the dashes on the pendant. "Each trigram means something in nature."

Starting at the top and going clockwise around the pendant, he described each trigram. "Water. Thunder. Earth. Mountain. Fire. Wind. Heaven and Lake. It is believed that the offspring of the Yang were hosts of good spirits called Shen, and the offspring of the Yin were the evil spirits, or Kwei. The Kwei inhabited man and his nature. They would lie in wait in the bushes and the tress. At night the men would carry lighted torches, bang drums, gongs and kettles to frighten away the evil Kwei, and the Shen , which by the way, is more powerful than the Kwei, would protect the righteous on earth. Especially those who offered sacrifices and prayers."

"Interesting." She looked at him thoughtfully, impressed with his native knowledge. Although she wasn't sure about telling him and expanding his already considerable ego. "There can't just be an offspring of either Yang or Yin? It takes two to tango."

His brooding gaze took a long, lingering look over her body, and when he spoke his voice was husky with intimacy. "Do you tango?"

"You'll never know." She reached over and relieved him of the pendant, turning it over to study the delicately painted dragon. She gently stroked the colorful centerpiece. "What about this?"

"What about it?" he asked, more interested in her face and her technique in the tango than the pendant.

"Are you sure you don't know what it means?"

"Um-hum."

"Hum. What are we doing tomorrow?" Her voice and expression held a new found energy and vitality.

"I don't know. What do you want to do?" he asked cautiously, fully aware of her look and tone.

"Go to the library."

"Oh, that ought to be fun," he teased. "Why?"

"Maybe we can find a clue as to what it means and why someone would kill for it."

Bennett considered her proposal then dismissed it quickly as unwanted trouble. "I believe that's why we have the police." He reached for the pendant, but Leslie clutched it in her hand and headed for the bedroom. "Don't you?" he urged.

There wasn't a response to his pleas, not that he expected one. That would have been too easy and predictable. Leslie Anne Scott was anything but predictable. The rustling of some papers and the closing of an attaché case were the only sounds coming from the bedroom. "Don't you?" he tried again.

Leslie finally reappeared from the bedroom with definitely more than just a notepad and pencil. She had suddenly acquired a spring to her step and a gleam in her eye. Easily she folded herself into the cushions of the sofa. "Where's your sense of adventure?" she lightly probed.

"I've had enough adventure tonight to last me a lifetime. I don't want or need anymore," he explained in a definite tone. "Give me the pendant and let me take it to the police." Again he reached for the octagon shaped piece, only to have her hold it at bay.

"Why?" she asked simply.

"Because there's already been one death, and who knows how many more over this pendant," Kash sternly reasoned.

"That's right," she agreed, totally confusing him.

"Right," he seconded. "All the more reason to let the police handle it."

"Aren't you forgetting something?"

The look on his face told her he had.

"Number one," she began, "we didn't see the killer." Which wasn't exactly true; she saw him and she would never forget him. "So, we can't make a positive identification. Number two, I have a bloody overcoat sleeve, and you have a bullet riddled car. Who do you suppose the police will have as prime suspects?" Her conclusion was logical and accurate to a degree, and Kash knew it.

"Motive?"

"Since when do the police need a motive?"

"Terrific," was all he could manage.

"Let's just use the extra day we have before we leave to gather any kind of information that can possibly be useful, then we can turn it and the pendant over to the police," she proposed.

"Okay," he conceded. "Can I use your bathroom?"

He gave in much too easily and changed the subject much too quickly for Leslie's liking, but before she could inquire further, he had put his drink down and was heading for the bathroom. A perplexing smile played on her lips as she watched his retreating figure and the ease in which he moved, sure and confident.

She curled up and started to sketch the backside of the pendant, but her thoughts went back to the broad shouldered stranger in her bathroom. That's what he was, really. He was a stranger, but yet, something was familiar. A familiarity she hadn't experienced for quite some time. Or maybe, it was just her vulnerability having a relapse. For her own peace of mind, she shoved those feelings and her thoughts for Kash Bennett to the farthest recesses of her mind and concentrated on sketching the pendant.

She was penciling in the final detail of the waterfall, when curiously she lifted her head. Listening intently, her brows knitted in a confused frown. Water? She heard running water. Why was he running the water? She unfolded herself and reluctantly got up from the warmth and comfort of the sofa to investigate. Absentmindedly she shoved the pendant into her pants pocket and moved toward the bedroom. Before she reached the opening, Kash reappeared, startling her. She ran a weary hand through her thick mane. Kash wished it was his hand.

"I've drawn you a hot bath," he announced, much to her surprise.

"A hot bath?" she repeated, and Kash nodded. "But, I'm not ready for my bath," she mildly protested.

"Well, I think you are," he insisted.

A stronger protest formed on her delicate mouth, but it was silenced by his index finger. He walked around her and gave a daring pat of encouragement to her bottom, prompting her toward the bathroom and the relaxing bath. "Can I use your phone?" he asked while pouring himself another drink.

"Why not?" Her reply was laced with indifference. "After eating my mint, drinking my scotch and using my bathroom, what difference does it make that you use my phone," she muttered to herself and slammed the bathroom door on his shameless behavior.

Typical female reaction, Kash noted as he sank into the still warm cushions of the sofa. For a moment he enjoyed their warmth, imagining what it would be like to have the source of the heat wrapped around him. The velvety smoothness of her skin beneath him, instead of the crushed velvet material. He shook the image from his mind and picked up the phone to place his call.

"Marrow?" he boomed.

Mike's sleepy voice was barely audible. "Bennett, do you know what time it is?"

"Sorry," Kash apologized. "Listen, something very important happened tonight and I thought you might like first dibs on it."

"Really?" Mike replied. Suddenly he was very awake.

"Really. Meet me at Lucy's in forty-five minutes."

"Where?"

"Lou-Cee's," Kash enunciated clearly. "You know, around the corner from the Carlyle-Essex? We only meet there once a week."

"Yeah, right," Mike agreed, getting the hint.

"Hey, Mike, come in a taxi, will you? I have a favor to ask of you concerning my new car."

"Oh. See you in about forty-five. And this, pal, had better be worth it," Mike warned.

"Say hello to Betty for me," Kash knowingly concluded.

Marrow turned to his companion, Betty and smiled. "Kash says, hello" he mumbled through a kiss.

"Um," is all Betty managed to say.

"He wants me to meet him in forty-five minutes," Mike volunteered.

"Hey, guys, I'm still on the phone," Kash chided.

"Then you'd better go," Betty said, breaking off the embrace.

"Can't. Something's come up," Mike informed with a devilish grin. "He'll have to wait."

Kash laughed and hung up the phone without further comment. He was swirling his drink when he caught sight of the drawing Leslie had done of the pendant. Not bad, he thought. Then it dawned on him, the pendant. He checked the coffee table, between the cushions, and the floor. Nothing. He made his way to the bedroom and politely knocked on the bathroom door.

"Leslie?" he cautiously called out.

Couldn't she even take a bath in private? The very bath he insisted she take. Opening the door less than politely, she stared him down, annoyed at his brazenness.

Kash smiled, enjoying her appearance, but quickly he pretended to be serious and even a little embarrassed. His eyes twinkled with delight at the current situation. What goes around comes around, he reminded himself.

She stood before him in just her undershirt and blue bloomers. He took in every inch, slowly, from head to toe. Wide, smooth shoulders tapered to a flat stomach. Followed by womanly hips and long, lovely legs. She had great gams! Firm and shapely. He didn't hide the fact that he was scrutinizing her feminine attributes. He repeated the process, starting at her toes and moving up. His gaze lingered on her breasts. They were ample, but considering her height, they somehow didn't fit. It was the only criticism of an otherwise perfect specimen.

Leslie, aware of his stare, crossed her arms in front of her bosom, forcing him to bring his eyes to hers. She blinked deliberately and tilted her head, waiting for him to utter some male nonsense. You're pathetic, she thought.

"I came to see if you have the pendant. It isn't in the living room, so I thought you might have it," he speculated. She didn't say a word, pressing him to continue. "I, uh, thought I would take it with me and find a safe place for it."

"I have a safe place for it. One where nobody will disturb it," she assured.

Kash looked at her chest and retorted, "Well, it certainly can't be there. It'll fall right through to the floor."

"Touché," she smiled, slamming and bolting the door.

Kash grinned widely at her reaction and yelled through the door, "Say, listen, if you need your back scrubbed, don't hesitate to call me. I'll be in the living room."

CHAPTER EIGHT

Alluring? Hardly. Leslie grinned at her reflection in the bathroom mirror. Her flannel jammies were buttoned up as far as they would go. The hotel terry cloth robe was tied securely at the waist, with its collar pulled up against her neck to protect against any intrusion. Heavy woolen socks covered her feet and she gave her toes an animated wiggle. With a final pat to the towel wrapped around her hair, she spun on heel and headed for the living room and what she was sure to be a quick goodnight to Mr. Kash Bennett.

Kash turned away from the window and watched Leslie enter the room. His brow knitted in a perplexing frown at her attire, starting with the wooly socks. She noticed, wiggled her toes for measure, then strolled over to the sofa and plopped down.

Kash rounded the sofa and stood next to her, silently chastising her choice of sleepwear. *God, doesn't this woman own anything feminine, outside of blue bloomers?* "Are you cold?" he asked, a touch of concern in his voice. "If you are, I can turn up the heat."

I'm sure you could, she thought. "No, I'm fine, thank you," she assured, flipping to the middle of her notepad. "Did you place your phone call?"

"Yeah, I did."

"Good. What time shall I be ready in the morning?"

"For?" he asked, still dumbfounded over her outfit and paying little attention to the conversation at hand.

"The library. Tomorrow morning?" she reiterated their plans.

"How's nine?"

She lifted her freshly scrubbed face and smiled sweetly. "Nine's fine."

"Are you sure you have a safe place for that pendant?" Kash prompted with discretion.

Leslie put down the notepad and made her way to the door. "The lobby?"

He took the hint and followed her to the door. "Lobby?"

"Tomorrow morning at nine sharp," she reminded him and opened the door. "Goodnight."

Kash drained the remainder of his scotch and handed her the empty glass. "Goodnight."

She watched him leave and quietly closed the door. Automatically she locked up and put the security chain in place. Reaching up, she yanked the towel off her head and shook her hair free, then she lazily unbuttoned the top two buttons of her pajama top and laid the collar back. Her fingers trailed across the silver pendant that was nestled in the hollow of her throat. She couldn't have thought of a better place for it. Yes, it was safe.

Lucy's Rathskeller was a tiny hole-in-the-wall joint below the street level on the outskirts of North Beach. Its blue and pink neon sign showed up nicely against its white brick front. Concrete steps, bordered by black wrought iron railings, led to a large, black plank door.

Kash reached for the brass handle, but the door was pushed open from the inside, startling him. A young couple, laughing loudly, rambled past him. He successfully opened the door and walked into the dark night spot. As usual, the smoke was thick and hung in the air, burning his nostrils and eyes. The jazz band had concluded for the evening, and the piano bar had taken over for the rest of the club hours.

Kash made his way over to the oak trimmed bar and gave Roscoe, the bartender, the thumbs up sign. Roscoe acknowledged the signal with a wide grin and quick wink. Staring at his strained reflection in the mirror behind the bar, Bennett was thankful for the smoke, and the pink and blue lights obscuring his haggard features. The nights' encounters, at the moment, seemed to be worse than anything he had ever experienced in covering the War, or even the recent assignment with Marrow in South America.

His thoughts were interrupted by a heavy slap on his back. Standing next to him was Mike Marrow, grinning and looking as natty as ever. Like someone else he knew. It wouldn't have mattered if the city experienced the worst quake in its history, Mike Marrow would still have come out looking jake. It was just like Mike; sunny side up.

Kash starred at Marrow's leather jacket and gave a reminiscent smile.

Hard to believe they had gotten their jackets at the same time during the War in London. Mike's still looked brand new, while Bennett's could have easily been mistaken for a World War I relic, instead of World War II.

World War II seemed like a hundred years ago and it was the first time Kash Bennett met Mike Marrow. Mike was a cocky, snotty-nosed reporter on his first major assignment, and Kash, the wily veteran, was assigned to be his photographer. Total opposites who became fast friends. They endured the War and so did their friendship.

"So, what's so important, old man that you had to drag me out tonight away from lovely Betty?" Mike asked right off the get go, shaking Kash from his stroll down memory lane. Kash didn't volunteer right away, so Mike turned to Roscoe and placed his order. "Hey, Roscoe. The usual, please. How about three olives this time?"

The rotund bartender frowned and narrowed his gaze.

"Hey," Mike defended. "I gotta keep my strength up." He smiled knowingly and turned his charming manner to Kash.

Bennett looked at his watch, then to Mike. "You're late."

Marrow gave his best tomfoolery smirk as Roscoe approached and placed in front of them their "usuals". Scotch, straight up for Kash and a vodka martini, this time with three olives.

Kash got up quickly and attempted to pay, but Roscoe gave a mighty laugh and waved it off, indicating it was on the house. Kash nodded his appreciation and nudged Mike to the back of the bar.

They picked a booth on the far wall, a part of Lucy's that was actually tucked under the street. It gave Marrow the creeps to sit there, but it was a favorite of Bennett's, so Mike obliged.

Sliding into the leather booth, they placed their drinks on the oak table and Kash sat back and enjoyed the music from the piano bar, as Mike impatiently tapped his glass. Kash gave a sidelong glance and smiled at his youthful restlessness.

"Come on, what gives?" Mike probed.

"Something happened tonight while I was in Chinatown," Kash said in a low voice.

Mike looked around, wondering why Bennett felt he had to speak in such a hushed tone. He went along and remarked accordingly. "What were you doing in Chinatown? Not chocolate covered almonds?"

Kash ignored the last comment. "I was with Les," he said. "We were doing research for the Peiping trip."

Marrow nearly choked on his martini. "Research?" he asked, not believing what he just heard. "You did research with the guy you're taking to China?"

"The guy's a girl," Kash corrected in an animated tone. "And she's taller than you." Then he gave Mike the once over. "And, she dresses like you, too. And..."

"And sounds to me like you're interested," Mike interrupted with a teasing wink.

"Naw," he lied.

His small laugh didn't mask or hide anything from Mike, who stirred his drink and kept his mouth shut. Likewise, Kash rolled his scotch in the glass and tried to convince himself of the lie he had just told. What man wouldn't have been burning with curiosity over such a long-legged beauty? He just wasn't any man, nor was she just any woman.

"So?" Marrow brought Kash back around.

"Anyway, we were in Chinatown and got separated, so I waited for her in the car. While I was waiting, shots rang out from an alley, then some nasty types showed up and the next thing I know, Leslie is cradling some poor bastard that was in the wrong place at the wrong time. He handed her something, which she insisted was 'nothing'."

"Nothing?" Mike asked with open palms.

"Um-hum," he said as he sipped his drink. "That's not half of it. We were discussing 'nothing' when a Buick pulled alongside of us and ripped my new car to shreds."

"No casualties?" Mike inquired.

Kash shook his head and nursed the rest of his drink. "But, there would have been if I had just a moment to wring her smooth, creamy neck."

"Oh, you are interested." Marrow gave his patented smirk, and then he became serious. "Then what happened?"

"They chased us for a while and I finally lost them in the alley next to the Carlyle, but not before they put a few more holes in the trunk of my new car."

"Just what is 'nothing'?"

"A Yin-Yang pendant," Kash informed.

"That's it?" Mike was truly disappointed, but he continued. "Why

would anyone want to kill for it? Was there anything special about the piece?"

"I don't know." Kash suddenly seemed exasperated by all the events that had taken place concerning his new assignment. Being shot at by the bad guys wasn't nearly as harrowing as being shot down by Leslie Anne Scott, and having to relive the experience with his extremely perceptive friend was fast becoming a burden. "Leslie seems to think the back of the pendant contains something important. It has two characters, and in the middle, a painted dragon. She wants to go to the library and research it. I want to go to the police and let them research it."

"Is it something we should concern ourselves with?"

"I don't know. I can't imagine why anyone would kill for it. Who knows, maybe we'll find something at the library."

"You saw it?"

Kash nodded and waved at Roscoe for a refill. He looked at Mike's hardly touched martini and ordered him another, as well.

"You saw nothing unusual in it?"

"Nope."

"Where is it now?"

"Leslie has it in a safe place."

"Leslie? Is that wise?"

Kash looked Marrow over. "She's bigger than you. Hell, she's nearly bigger than me. Trust me, it's safe."

"So, I take it, you want me to do what every good reporter does, snoop?"

"Exactly."

"Where exactly did this take place?"

"The alley between Chow Lee's and the laundry," Kash recalled.

"Isn't there suppose to be a maze of junk under that laundry?"

Kash didn't answer, but he was aware of public speculation that tunnels with rooms attached were under the laundry. Since Leslie wasn't volunteering about her venture, he wasn't asking.

"I'll start with our friend Flanery, since Chinatown is his beat, he should be able to enlighten me about any bodies in the alley." Mike said. Feeling braver, he asked, "So, what's Les like?"

"She ain't Betty."

Nobody is, Mike thought with a grin and finished his first martini.

Kash rubbed his tired, and most certainly bloodshot eyes, while an annoyingly chipper Marrow spoke on the phone.

"You say he's at a scene," Mike yelled into the receiver, over the noise at Lucy's. "Where?" he pumped. "Next to the laundry. No. No message. I'll catch up with him later. Thanks." He hung up and rubbed his hands together. "Now, what's that favor regarding your car?"

Bennett waved goodbye, then winced as his new car sped up the street, hugged a corner and disappeared from sight. He only hoped Mike had better luck in finding someone discreet to fix it then he had in driving it. From the direction Marrow was heading, Kash knew fixing the car was far down on Mike's list, finding Flanery was at the top.

Like Leslie earlier, Kash pushed himself into his apartment building and started up the stairs. It had been a long night and all he wanted was t go to sleep in his messy, but familiar sofa bed.

The steps creaked under his weight while he fumbled through various keys until he found the one for his apartment. It wasn't necessary; the door was slightly ajar. With his index finger he pushed it open the rest of the way.

CHAPTER NINE

The glow in the dim hallway light was enough for him to see someone had intruded. Stepping cautiously inside he felt the wall for the light switch and flipped in on. Nothing. He tried again, still no luck. As if to be quieter, he held his breath and moved carefully, leaving the door open to light his way. He made it to the kitchen table and found the envelope containing his itinerary for Peiping had been opened.

Suddenly the door was slammed shut, and the light was gone. Automatically Kash blinked his eyes deliberately, trying to adjust to the dark. Before he could turn around, he heard a familiar sound, one he thought he had left in South America. He craned his neck forward when he felt the end of the cold barrel on his suddenly warm skin, and his uninvited guest encouraged him to put his hands on the table.

Kash obeyed with little protest as his eyes finally adjusted to the darkened room. Another click. A small pin light shined clearly on a drawing placed on the table in front of him. It was a rough sketch of the pendant. He stood motionless, staring at the drawing, and clearly sorry he had ever accepted the Peiping assignment with Leslie Anne Scott. Abruptly that thought came to an end as he was pushed down onto the table, and the end of the gun shoved deeper into the base of his skull.

"I don't know what you want," Kash lied in a hoarse voice.

The intruder realized and pushed harder.

"I don't have it. I don't know where it is." He nearly choked on the truth.

Not convinced, the intruder pistol whipped Bennett to prompt a more agreeable answer. Fury took the place of fear and Kash pushed himself off the table into the body of his unwanted guest, thrusting him backwards. A rapid presence of mind enabled the man to regain his balance and fend off a wildly thrown punch from Kash. With speed and accuracy, he delivered a blow to Bennett's abdomen, causing him to bend at the waist in agony. Simultaneously, he brought up his knee into Kash's face and the butt of his pistol down on the back of Bennett's head.

A groan fell from Kash's mouth along with a stream of blood, and without hesitation, the attacker was out the window and down the fire escape. Kash groped in the dark until he reached the window sill, and supporting himself, he watched the intruder speed away.

Startled, Leslie sat up in her bed and listened closely. Someone was banging loudly on her hotel door. She fumbled in the dark, found and turned on the light next to her bed. The banging continued as she stumbled out of bed and groped for her robe. Pulling it on, she walked through the living room to the hallway and flipped on the lights.

"Leslie!" Kash screamed at the top of his lungs. He ignored the angry stares of the guests who opened their doors to his commotion. "What?" he shot to them.

Before she released the safety chain and unlocked the door to Dante's fury, she buttoned her pajama top. Kash didn't wait for her to open the door to him. The minute he heard the door unlock and the safety chain removed, he charged in, pushing her back as he entered. He dropped his suitcase and tote, and then slammed the door shut to the curious onlookers.

Her gasp was barely audible when she finally got a good look at his face. A purple mark was forming on the right side of his lower lip, and his shirt had splotches of blood from a cut on the inside of his mouth. She reached up to touch his face, but he seized her hand in a hard, vice-like grip, and pinned her to the wall before she could speak. The light switch dug into her back and she arched to ease the discomfort. That was the least of her worries. The man that held her had a murderous rage in his eyes, and she didn't know why, but she was going to find out before the rage became a reality.

"What happened?" she managed softly.

His reply was anything but soft. It was rough like his glare and the hold he had on her. "Where the hell is that pendant?"

Leslie remained calm and lucid, despite the fury she faced. She narrowed her eyes and tried to penetrate the steel curtain before her, saying nothing. Hoping the momentary silence would ease his rage. She was wrong.

"The pendant?" he snapped. "I'm taking it to the police. Now!"

"Not looking like that, you're not," she said, changing the subject.

Reaching up, she gave him a persuasive nudge toward the living room. "Come on," she urged.

Reluctantly he let go of her wrist and followed her to the sofa. He stood and watched her take the decanter of scotch and disappear into the bedroom. The few minutes she was gone seemed like an eternity and he was notably relieved when she returned. He had hoped to see her carrying and handing over to him the pendant, not a dripping washcloth. His jaw tightened as she approached.

"Give me the pendant, Leslie." His tone was insistent, and stern, treating her like a disobedient child.

"Sit down," she returned the favor. Her tone equaling or bettering his.

Giving him a push with her fingertips, he landed heavily onto the cushions. A tiny groan came from his lips as he lifted his face to hers. For the first time, she realized he was vulnerable, and she examined his chiseled features, starting with his lower lip. She pulled it down and exposed a jagged cut. With all the tenderness she could muster, she applied the saturated cloth to the raw cut. Kash winced and coiled back from the pain.

"Damn!" He gingerly licked the wound. "Scotch is for drinking, not doctoring."

"Um. Something you obviously know a lot about, and have been practicing tonight," she threw back. "Besides, it's the only thing I have."

"No, it isn't," he corrected immediately. "You have the pendant."

She placed a quieting finger on his lips and wiped traces of blood from his chin and jaw.

"Aren't you the least bit curious as to what happened?" he asked solemnly, his anger subsiding, being replaced by self pity.

"It's obvious. You got the shit kicked out of you," she replied, paying little attention to his new mood, but happy his chilling wrath had succumbed to a lesser of two evils.

Leslie fussed some more with Kash's lip, preventing a retort to her statement. Annoyed at her persistence to add more insult to injury, he grabbed her wrist and pulled it away from his mouth.

He bent and shook his head at her nonchalant attitude toward his condition and what might have possibly happened. After all, he wouldn't have been in this shape had it not been for her. A lock of hair fell onto his forehead and he pushed it back into place.

That caught Nurse Leslie's attention and her brow furrowed as she inspected the back of his head, and the clump of red in his fine hair. Using the pad of her finger, she prudently touched the fresh break in his scalp. He jerked his head up and glared at her, not wanting any more of her nursing, or lack of it.

"I'm sorry," she offered.

"You should be. Why couldn't you have just left it alone when I told you to?"

"I think that bump on your head did more than just break the skin," she countered.

Kash gave a questioning look and she took a different, more sympathetic approach.

"Tell me, what happened after you left here?" She poked and pulled matted hair from around his wound. He winced and tried to move away, but she placed a restraining hand on his shoulder.

"Leslie, please?" he pleaded.

"It's all right," she reassured. "I'll be gentle. You left here and..."

He took up where she left off. "And, I went back to my place. The door was open, and whoever was there had gone through my things." He paused and remembered the condition of his apartment. "Made a mess of things."

Bewilderment flooded Leslie's features at his remark. How could it be any worse, she thought, recalling his messy flat.

"Um," he continued, "then he closed the door, and put a gun to my head. He turned on a pin light and showed a rough sketch of the pendant. He never spoke. We had a fight, and yes, I got the shit kicked out of me." He reached up and took her hand away. "That's fine, thanks."

"You need a cold compress," she suggested. "Sit still and I'll get you one."

Relaxation started to spread through Bennett's tension-filled muscles. At least when she came back, they could discuss rationally her turning over the pendant. He leaned back against the soft velvet cushions of the sofa and watched her leave for a second time. He didn't see her return.

Humming softly to herself, Leslie returned carrying a wet hand towel, with a bath towel slung over her shoulder. She started to speak, but stopped short when she saw Kash slumped over on the sofa. An understanding smile spread across her mouth and she retreated and came back with a pillow and blanket.

A soft plop and the bundle came to rest on the floor. Gently she cradled his head and checked his pulse in his neck. His breathing was deep and even, his pulse steady, reassuring her he was sound asleep.

It was a struggle, but she managed to remove his leather jacket without disturbing him, and she flung it across the room, not caring where it landed. Bracing him against her side, she slid off the sofa and let his body sink into its natural slump. She squared his shoulders and slowly unbuttoned his shirt. Her eyes lingered on his smooth, bronze skin and boldly let her fingers make a feathery trail across the hollow of his neck, down to the scoop of his undershirt. She smiled at his unknowing response; goose bumps. Now wasn't the time to be admiring his manhood, she reminded herself, but rather, making him comfortable for a night's rest, good or otherwise.

Somehow she couldn't get past the childlike serenity in his features as she brushed a strand of his reddish-blonde hair back off his forehead. A high, intelligent forehead and the usually deep crease between his arched brows was but barely a line in the tranquil state of sleep. Tiny creases fanned out away from the corners of his eyes, and the thick, brown lashes that framed his brooding glare remained still. His straight, symmetrical nose took in deep and even breaths, while his mouth, relaxed in sleep, was vulnerable. Gone was the tension it possessed earlier in the evening, but the mark under his lower lip had taken on an angry hue, and no doubt it would be touchy when he awakened in the morning, and more than likely, so would his mood. Of all the men Leslie had known, Kash Bennett could convey more by saying nothing, and just narrowing his eyes and tightening his square jaw.

Continuing, she moved to the end of the sofa and pulled his legs up onto the cushions. Grabbing the waistband of his pants, she squared his hips to match his shoulders, unbuckled his belt and unbuttoned his trousers to allow for some comfort. She removed his shoes and noticed his socks didn't match. She smiled. Staring at him, she tried to understand the feelings she was having for this man. They were such opposites; her striving for perfection in everything, and him; he couldn't have cared less about anything. She stopped and fiercely reminded herself, drawing a page from her past, that mixing business and pleasure caused only pain and heartache. Rapidly she buried that thought.

It nagged at her, though, while she placed the pillow under his head and covered him with the blanket, that she actually liked him. Why? She couldn't answer that question. They had absolutely nothing in common.

Well, that wasn't exactly true, she remembered. They did have exactly that: 'nothing'. It seemed that 'nothing' was the only common denominator between the two of them, and she planned on keeping it that way.

Weariness had finally made its way to her senses and she picked up the towels, disregarding the idea of applying them to his wound. Quietly she turned off the corner light, but left the other on, just in case he needed a night light. Stopping inside the bedroom, she looked over her shoulder at his peaceful form and whispered, "Sweet dreams, Mr. Bennett."

CHAPTER TEN

Book after book after book; a neatly manicured finger followed and tapped the numbers in sequence until finding the right one. The finger stroked the printed number and slid up the spine and pulled the book from the shelf.

Leslie turned it over and read the back, making sure that it was the book she wanted. It was, and she moved to the nearest table.

The library was quiet, except for a handful of people scattered about. Careful not to make any noise, Leslie opened her case, pulled free her notepad and flipped to the drawing of the pendant. She studied the characters, and then opened the book on Chinese characters to see if she could find any connection.

A low moan echoed in Kash Bennett's head, and a sour taste erupted in his mouth. The crease between his brows that was but barely a line during sleep was suddenly deep and threatening. Reluctantly he opened his eyes, faced the morning light and blinked several time, adjusting to his surroundings.

Surroundings that weren't familiar to him, but with a deliberate rub of his eyes he remembered the previous night and Leslie Anne Scott. Leslie? Without thinking, he quickly sat up and paid for it. "Oh," he groaned, messaging his forehead. He dragged his fingers through his hair, the stinging reminding him of the night's activities. "Damn it!"

He threw back the covers and swung his legs down to the floor. His voice was hoarse when he called out, "Leslie?" There wasn't an answer. "Leslie?" he called again.

The scratching of his eyes and forehead was interrupted by a polite knock on the door. There was a pause, then another rap. Slowly Kash rose, steadied himself and walked to the door. He pulled it open to find a room service attendant holding a silver tray.

"Good morning, Mr. Bennett," the attendant greeted. "Miss Scott asked that your breakfast be delivered at ten sharp this morning. May I?" He gestured with the tray.

"Sure," was all Kash could offer.

The attendant placed the tray on the coffee table, while Kash searched his pockets for money to tip him.

"No need, sir. Miss Scott has taken care of everything."

"Did Miss Scott also happen to mention where she was going this morning?"

"No, sir. Enjoy your breakfast."

The attendant left, closing the door behind him, while Kash meandered over to the sofa, eased down and stared at the silver tray. Finally he picked up the domed cover and revealed a perfectly poached egg atop hash; probably prepared by Leslie herself, he thought. On a separate dish, two slices of toast, with butter and jam on the side. A nauseous groan dropped from his parted lips and he put the lid back into place. Instead, he grabbed the silver decanter and poured himself a hearty cup of black coffee. He let the aroma and steam penetrate his foggy senses.

He pulled the phone up next to him as he sipped his coffee and requested the operator to place a call. As the phone rang on, Kash settled into the cushions, being careful not to spill his coffee. "Yeah?" Mike Marrow, please?" There was a deliberate pause. "Hello? What's wrong?" he asked in a concerned tone. The news hit him like an oncoming freight train. He jerked forward and dropped his coffee on the silver tray. "What?" he said in disbelief. "What do you mean Mike's dead? I just saw him last…" He stopped as questions flooded his mind, crowding the memories. "How?" he managed. "Murdered? Where?" His voice cracked with emotion as he repeated the answer, "In his car."

Unknowingly he slipped the phone into its cradle while staring at his perfectly prepared breakfast. His square jaw tightened, his gray eyes grew dark and he angrily heaved the tray off the table. He didn't feel the twinge in his toe when he kicked the table out of the way, nor did he hear the tray crash to the floor and slide into the wall, and most certainly, he didn't feel the searing pain from his wound as he raked his fingers repeatedly through his hair as he heard in his mind again and again, "In his car."

Hot tears stung his eyes and when he blinked, they fell down his roughened cheeks. He shut them and desperately tried to make them stop.

With a deep, shaky breath, he got control over his emotions. He had to. Mike wouldn't have approved of this unmanly show of feelings, he chided himself.

Several deep breaths later, Kash dialed his other close friend, Detective Francis X. Flanery. He was tough-nosed and determined to serve justice. He was a firm believer that a suspect was guilty, and thus must prove their innocence. He figured that attitude was erected from his Irish and English heritage.

For once, Kash didn't have to wait forever to be connected—Flanery came on immediately. His usual gruff self was slightly muted. "Where are you?" he asked Bennett.

"Why?" Kash cautiously asked.

"I know you're calling because you heard about Mike. So, cut the shit and tell me where you are."

"It was my car," Kash began. "I asked him to do me a favor regarding a little body work on my new girl."

"Yeah, well your new girl is destroyed."

"Nothing a little putty and buffing won't cure."

"It's going to take a little more than putty and buffing. It was torched beyond recognition, as was the occupant. The only thing I found recognizable was the pinky ring Mike wore. The one that matches yours. It was seared into what was left of his right hand. When I arrived, and I saw that, I was worried it was you, but when they pulled the body out, I knew it was Mike. He was such a …" His voice caught as recalled Marrow and his cocky way. "He was such a short shit. Cocky beyond belief. He would have given his eye teeth for you."

Kash felt the stinging tears returning and he steadied himself. "Who would have done this to him?" he asked Flanery.

"I was hoping you could tell me that. After all, he was in your car, and it's, or rather, it was a brand new car. Why was Mike being so nosy about the murders in the alley by the laundry and Chow Lee's store? Where did he get the information? Especially about the pendant?"

"What about the pendant?" Kash asked, sitting on the edge of the sofa.

"What about that pendant, Kash?" Flanery shot back.

"As far as I could tell, it was just a trinket that Leslie picked up," he explained, skirting the whole truth.

"Well, it's a mighty popular and expensive trinket." He hesitated before divulging more, but it was Kash he was talking to, so he continued. "One of the bodies belonged to someone in government service, if you understand my drift. He, too, was interested in that pendant."

"FBI, CIA?" Kash inquired as he found a piece of paper handy to take notes.

"He was a special officer, and his boss, Special Officer in Charge Charles Briggs informed me at the scene that Mr. Randall was a special courier, as a common courier was too risky for this particular drop. Something of importance is being transported via the pendant. Why the Tongs want it, I don't know. I wasn't aware their fingers were involved in our national security pie. But if so, that presents a whole new mess. What else can you tell me about the pendant and Leslie?"

"Nothing. The pendant didn't appear to have been altered, if that's what you want to know. Leslie, well, she's just a typical reporter. Like Mike."

"One difference, my friend; she's still alive. Or we better hope so."

Kash ignored the last comment, his mind couldn't handle the image of her being like Mike. He couldn't face that. "What about Randall? What do we know about him?"

"According to Briggs, impeccably loyal."

"To whom?"

"Good question."

"I've got to find Leslie."

"What, she's not next to you, Romeo?" Flanery gave a short laugh.

Kash ignored the comment and pondered the alley. "How many bodies did you find in the alley?"

"Four. Two were killed by the Tongs, and the others we speculate by Randall. The only one that didn't appear to belong was a jeweler. He was probably killed in the cross fire."

"All of the bodies were found in the alley?"

"Yeah, but you and I know that if we went tunneling, we wouldn't find shit. So, we accept where we found them. Yes?"

"Yes. I've got to find Leslie."

"You said that already. There's one more thing I need to ask you about."

"What?"

"I visited your apartment this morning, obviously because it was your car and…"

"What about my place?" Kash asked with an edge to his tone.

"You left in a hurry. That, of course, was difficult to pinpoint because your place is such a pig's sty. We found a nice drawing, too," he said, getting to the point. "Mr., excuse me, Special Officer in charge Briggs finds your trip to Peiping a little disconcerting. Especially with so much governmental unrest in that country. You understand?"

"Tough shit, I'm on assignment."

"Yeah, that's what I said, too. Not exactly that way, of course, but none-the-less, know that you are going to have company on your journey to China," Flanery warned.

"Let me worry about that. Just find out who killed Mike."

Flanery didn't sign off with his usual saying, instead he just hung up the phone. Kash looked at the receiver with contempt and slammed it down onto its cradle. He momentarily stared at his pinky ring and stroked it fondly, remembering when he and Mike had bought them. He smiled, closed his eyes and reflected on his friendship with Marrow.

When he finally opened his eyes, he stared down at the mess on the Oriental rug and snatched up a folded piece of paper marked "Kash". Partially saturated by the spilled coffee, it read, "Kash, I didn't have the heart to wake you, so I've gone to the library and Chinatown by myself. I'll see you later, Les."

His knuckles were white with fury as he wadded up the note into a tight ball and threw it to the floor. Better the note, than her, he thought. He got up and headed for the bathroom and got ready to go and find the good- for-nothing that was responsible for his miserable state.

CHAPTER ELEVEN

Leslie drew in a sharp breath of excitement and leaned forward and placed the book on the table. She compared the second character on the pendant to that of the illustration in the book. They matched. The character resembled that of a pitchfork with the handle. The book described it as the symbol for "mountain", and on the notepad, Leslie scribbled the notation next to the second character. "One down, one to go," she sighed. She took a quick glance at her watch, and then continued her search to find the meaning of the first character.

Kash paid the taxi driver and turned to face the bakery he and Leslie had stood in front of the evening before. He didn't make a move toward the alley because of the police activity. Instead he headed directly north to the small souvenir store they had visited.

He didn't get past the front door. A drawing that closely resembled Leslie was tacked to the entry wall. It was a three-quarter angle, and it didn't completely define her features, but it was certainly enough for him to identify it was her. Right down to the way she wore that damn fedora. Violently he ripped it down and stuffed it into his jacket pocket. There wasn't any sense in going in, he would have been recognized. He had to find her and leave as soon as possible, and he hoped Flanery was wrong about company.

Leslie compared the character in another book to that on the pendant. Finally, they appeared to match. The first character translated to "red". She made a note of it and examined the characters and their translations. She pondered what "red" and "mountain" meant to each other, and why they bordered a beautifully painted dragon?

"Symbolism in Chinese Art" was the third and final book Leslie had

pulled and she began the tedious task of reading and studying, hoping to unravel the riddle the pendant held most sacred and secret.

Kash had run out of time and patience. He had combed every inch of their visit from the day before, and in the process pulled down three posters of Leslie, all strategically placed. He crammed the last one into his pocket and flagged down a taxi. "San Francisco Library," he directed the driver.

Nothing. Leslie shook her head, disappointed she didn't find any new information about the pendant. The book confirmed the symbolism Kash had explained concerning the Yin-Yang sign, but it offered no new findings. As for the dragon, and its association, she learned it was tied directly to the Yang. Most commonly known as the "Demon Speller", the dragon had the horns of a devil, head of a camel, a demon's eyes, the neck of a snake, a tortoise viscera, a hawk's claws, the palms of a tiger, and the ears of a cow. Ears, which didn't hear—that was done by the horns. It was a queer looking creature, but the impact it had on symbolism and heritage in Chinese art and beliefs was overwhelming.

Leslie gathered the books and her attaché case, moved to the bookshelves and placed each book back where she had found them, then she quietly walked down the line of shelves and out of the library.

On the other side, Kash made his way down the narrow aisle of shelves in the opposite direction of Leslie. He quickly searched the library and found nothing.

Ironically, Leslie got out of the taxi at the same spot Kash had earlier; in front of the bakery. She glanced down toward the alley and saw enough police activity to warrant a change of direction. Before she headed north, she stepped inside the bakery and purchased one of the moon cakes for later on that evening.

The delicate aroma of jasmine sweetly assaulted her senses as she entered the tiny souvenir shop, and she was greeted by two men behind the counter. She browsed momentarily and then made her way to the counter. The younger of the two disappeared between the fold of the drapes, leaving the elder to Leslie. The elder acknowledged her presence with a mannerly bow and polite smile.

"I was wondering if you could help me," she inquired. "I have a friend who has a charming octagon shaped pendant with a Yin-Yang symbol on the front and a beautifully painted dragon on the back with two characters bordering it. Do you have anything like that?"

The elder pondered several moments, while the younger man slinked through the slightly parted sheets to rejoin them. "How about this?" the elder offered her a dragon necklace craved from jade.

"I take it you don't have anything like the pendant I've described?" she asked, a hint of dejection in her silky voice.

"I'm sorry, no," he apologized.

"Do you know of anyone who might have something similar?"

"No."

"It's really unusual, the dragon and the characters. Does that have any significant meaning?" she pumped, the journalist in her coming out.

"I have never seen or heard of such a thing as you have described," he regretfully told her.

Leslie nodded, not believing for one moment the old man behind the counter was telling the truth. She collected her package, left the store and hailed a cab to take her back to her hotel.

The inner brass doors of the elevator slid back to reveal the frosted outer doors bordered in brass. Leslie took an impatient step forward to vacate the elevator, but stopped short when the outer doors didn't open promptly. She looked back to the operator with resign, and he nonchalantly pressed a button and the doors finally opened. Leslie gave a curt nod of thanks, stepped into the hallway and headed toward her room. Her pace was slower than before, almost sluggish.

There were blue, pink and yellow bloomers. Kash snatched them all up in one fell swoop, along with a stack of neatly folded undershirts, and crammed them into a suitcase.

Leslie placed her attaché case and moon cake down on one of the chairs facing the sofa and peeled off her jacket. She looked down and noticed the stained rug. She tossed her jacket onto the sofa and walked into the bedroom just in time to see Bennett stuffing her personal belongings into her suitcase. Anxiously she stepped toward him and grabbed his arm in protest before he rammed home a charcoal pinstriped suit. "What are you doing?" she questioned in a sharp tone.

Kash shook loose of her hold, and struggled to finish packing the suit. "Packing!" he growled through clenched teeth. He turned back to the dresser and gathered her pajamas, while she tried to smooth out the suit.

"Why are we packing? We can do this tomorrow morning before we leave," she insisted.

Her suggestion fell on deaf ears, as he pushed her aside and threw the pajamas into the case. He looked at her, his brows knitted and his eyes squinted in a contemptuous glare. "We're leaving tonight."

"But," she protested.

"Tonight," he snapped and shoved her robe into her stomach. "Finish this."

He strode out of the bedroom and into the living room with Leslie right on his heels. He picked up his tote and suitcase from the sofa and placed them in the hallway by the door.

"Why are we leaving tonight?" she persisted.

"We just are."

Not pleased, Leslie blocked his way. "That's supposed to satisfy me?"

He gave her the once over and said, "I don't care what satisfies you."

For some unknown reason, those words hurt. "Frankly, you'll never know. What the hell is it with you?" She was frustrated and confused by his unprovoked anger.

"You." Bennett growled. His timbre was low and unsettling. Leslie tried to back away, but he was too quick, and he grabbed her by the arms and held her inches from his chiseled features. His grip was tight and rough. It hurt and so did his biting stare. "You. You couldn't leave it alone, could you? You had to put your pretty, aristocratic nose where it had no business being. Having disregard for not only your safety, but that of others, as well. You're not even qualified. You're just a goddamn art journalist. What the hell were you thinking?"

When he finished, she was still confused, but also livid at his brutal, malicious attack. "What are you babbling about?"

He didn't reply.

"I don't have to take this shit." She tried to wrestle out of his hold. "Let me go."

She struggled to free herself, but Bennett didn't relinquish the hold he had on her. If anything, he tightened it. "Oh, no. Not until you give me that pendant."

"Didn't we have this conversation last night? Didn't we agree that we'd use today to follow up any leads?" she recalled in an attempt to refresh his convenient memory.

"That was before I was pounded in my apartment. Before..." His voice caught slightly with emotion. "Before my best friend was found murdered in my car, and before I found your face plastered on half of the walls in Chinatown."

"What?" she asked with a nervous laugh.

Kash squelched the laugh as he sunk his fingers into the soft flesh of her arm and held her steady while he reached into his jacket and pulled free a piece of paper. A quick shake and the paper unfolded. Leslie swallowed dryly as its likeness to herself.

Aware she was at a loss for words; Kash gave his own explanation, as only he could. "It means lady that someone wants to put a shoe factory up your sweet little ass. It's all because of that goddamn pendant. Now, where is it?"

She refused to listen anymore and tried to once again break free. "Let me go, dammit!"

"This," he continued, "is a Chun Hung. It's a reward for you and your precious pendant. Where is it?" he demanded again. He planted her against the wall. He eyes scorched and burned past her cool façade. "Where is it?" he shouted at the top of his lungs.

"I don't have it," she answered shakily. "I sent it to the police, like we agreed if we gathered any information. Remember?" The rubberiness in her legs subsided when his grip eased and his brutal glare slightly relaxed.

She challenged him with an arrogant tilt of her head and a narrowing of her black stare. "Take your hands off of me."

He obliged and released her roughly, but she continued to stare him down.

"If you ever touch me again, I'll rip off your privates and feed them to you," she promised vehemently and with any dignity she could muster.

"What?" he asked, not quite sure he heard her correctly.

Stoked and feeling braver, she straightened her shoulders and clarified her statement. "You know, your balls."

"Is that what happened to yours? Someone fed them to you, Les," he taunted.

Seeing her jaw tighten, prompted Kash to yield a cynical appraisal of her, and as sharp as his words, he opened the door and walked out, slamming it behind him.

After locking the door, Leslie took in a shaky breath, loosened her tie and unbuttoned her shirt, revealing the cause for their angry display; the pendant.

CHAPTER TWELVE

Elaine had become so absorbed in the journals that she lost total track of time. Checking her watch, it showed she was well into the wee hours of the morning, and still no returned calls. While reading Kash and Leslie's journals, she had kept copious notes of her own for reference. If she had thought the annals would add clarity to her otherwise cloudy childhood, she was sorely mistaken. They only added more distance between herself and her parents. They obviously weren't what they seemed or portrayed to their children, family and friends. What of their friends? Were they the same? Shoving that thought to the back of her head, she glanced ahead in her mother's account and found their trip to China.

Looking at her watch again, she thought it best to take a break. Like the old saying, "One's mind can only absorb as much as one's fanny would let it." She was tired of sitting and she needed a moment to take in all that she had read; all that she had come to learn of her parents and their lives before their children.

Not the least bit sleepy, no doubt from all of the coffee she consumed during the readings, she pushed herself out of the chair and gathered the journals. After buttoning up the house, she headed downstairs to the garage.

Knowing the weather hadn't changed, Elaine decided to borrow her father's prized '47 Chevy convertible. Pulling off the tarp, she found the car in immaculate condition. One of the few things Kash Bennett took great pains in pampering. And pamper he did. He would spend countless hours in the detailing and maintenance of his "girl" as he referred to the convertible. Patiently, Elaine would wait for him to finish so they could go play pitch and catch or try out their latest fishing rods, while her twin brother preferred to accompany their mother to the latest ballet, opera or new museum exhibit.

Elaine and Lane were polar opposites, starting with the day they were born. They never shared the proverbial closeness many twins were known for. Instead, it was their dissimilarities that set them apart, both personally and professionally. They had nothing in common, and Elaine was more than happy to keep it that way. When needed, she would pull rank as the older sibling and egg her baby brother into submission. Even if she was only eight minutes older, when they were younger, it had been enough leverage to silence his petulance on more than one occasion. Adulthood was different. Unfortunately, Lane had a long memory, and ever since his first appointment as a judge, he had become increasingly harder to reason with. Thankfully there was a nation between them, but every once in a while, she could feel the intrusive long arm of the law, his law, into her life. This was one of those moments.

Mindful of the hour, and the precious piece of hardware she was driving, Elaine quietly shut the door of the '47 Chevy and made her way up the well lit step-street to her office; a cottage, courtesy of Nana Bennett. Of course, Nana had left it to both she and Lane. Even though Lane didn't want any part of the cottage, he did want his share of its worth, and Elaine was more than happy to accommodate his greed and paid him off. She was sure it wasn't his first, and most definitely wouldn't be his last, pay off.

Upon arriving, she fumbled with the keys as the rain drummed and fell off the awning. Unlike visitors, she knew which of the two angled doors she wanted to enter. Now to find the right key. She did and promptly dropped the chain. "Shit!" She griped as she looked at the door. She could only imagine the haughty stare of the stained glass peacock. Its head was provocatively tilted as it stared down its back to a trail of elegant feathers. In essence, he was looking down his beak at anyone who dared enter his domain at this hour, or any hour for that matter.

"Yeah, yeah, yeah," she answered its imaginary sarcasm. It wasn't the first time she felt that way about the twin cocks as she referred to the two full length stained glass peacocks that adorned the doors in the inverted "v" entry. Being a traditionalist in the strictest sense of renovation, she never replaced the doors. Instead, she renovated the house around them. The colors of the plume; peacock blue, spring green, deep purple, tangerine and buttered brown complimented and enhanced the centerpiece of the cottage. A place that had not only become Elaine's office, but sometimes her retreat, with its only access, a quiet step-street. Quiet it was, the slightest noise echoed down the small strip, and she winched as the keys clanked against each other as she found the lock and finally entered the office.

Blinking lights to her right alerted her to turn off the alarm. She did, and then reset it. A flip of a switch and the foyer chandelier sprang to life, illuminating not only the hall but the office and conference room, too.

She shrugged out of her jacket and dropped it over the half glass block wall that separated the two angled doors. Because of the hour, she subconsciously tiptoed into her office, but still the Venetian walnut flooring protested her late night calling. She flipped another switch and track lighting brought to life her drafting table, gently placing her backpack on top.

Above it, she examined a collage of several framed prints of the layout of the city. The centerpiece was an early rendition of the "City Beautiful" by Daniel Burnham, with other prints positioned around it; like the redesigned Civic Center. One in particular caught her eye and she used a magnifying glass to examine it further. The layout was from the late thirties and she recognized the area mentioned in Kash and Leslie's journals. She knew the vicinity and was well aware of the folklore that accompanied "Old Chinatown". She had heard and read, but never personally witnessed, the dens of Chinatown, and since reading her mother's account, her curiosity was piqued. Even more so, now that her hands were tied until someone called her with information regarding the whereabouts of her parents.

Not being good with idle time on her hands, Elaine examined the print further, grabbed a scrap piece of paper and made a makeshift map of the area. She corresponded it to an updated version, made the necessary street name changes. Opening her backpack, she dug through it looking for her own notebook and the copious notations she made while reading the journals. The pack yielded nothing, leaving one conclusion; her notes were somewhere in her parents' house.

Frustrated, but cautious, she retraced her tracks back to Kash and Leslie's. The process was made slower by the heavy fog rolling in with the ocean waves. Much like a newborn in sleep, nature's blanket nestled over the city and lulled it into what was surely only a momentarily peaceful slumber.

Elaine loved these moments in her city, but only when she was tucked away in the comfort of her home. Though she knew the city well, fog had the damnedest way of playing tricks on the mind. Its dreamy softness created shadows within shadows, alluring even the most alert to partake in its seductive dance. This on more than one occasion led to tragic consequences.

She slowed at what she thought was her parents street, only to find it was one more beyond the current selection. Pulling into the short driveway, she placed the vehicle into park and thanked the driving gods she had arrived safely.

Inside, Nook and Cranny greeted her with little enthusiasm as she found her journal between the cushion and frame of her father's chair. Pulling it free, she held onto it for dear life while she checked the phone for any messages regarding Kash and Leslie's whereabouts. If she thought she was frustrated earlier, this new feeling of exasperation was overwhelming. "Assholes. That includes you, Lane." She muttered the accusation, knowing she was correct in the assumption he was usurping her attempts in finding information regarding their parents, and she hated him for it. "Little prick," she continued as she made her way to the kitchen, convincing herself that Lane's attitude towards women was based solely on what she was sure was his little penis, or possibly CDS; *Crooked Dick Syndrome.* Either way, he had managed to irritate her from his far-reaching post across the country.

She popped water into the microwave and readied a cup of tea, and while she waited, she took in her handiwork. The renovation had been easy, as long as she kept her mother's proverbial and provincial fingers out of the pie. She successfully managed that for the better part of the house with the exception of the room she was presently in—the kitchen. There, Leslie was emphatic that she have state-of-the-art appliances and fixtures. Elaine conceded, but managed to keep intact the original hickory planked flooring, woodwork, cabinetry and plastered ceiling. Though each needed delicate repair, all were spared and made the final cut. For added convenience, an island was placed in the middle of the kitchen for extra prep space.

Elaine did get one consolation, her mother gave her permission to restore the lower-level kitchen; the original real-working kitchen of the house. The one the lady of the house would never enter. Elaine's mother included. She left the Sears & Roebuck cook stove in place and hung herbs from Leslie's garden from the exposed piping above. Next to the wooden washtubs and wringers, Elaine installed the best washer and dryer money could buy. She smiled at remembering the first time her mother used it. A tear slid down her cheek and interrupted the memory, as did the beeping of the microwave.

She steeped the tea and casually wandered through the house of her childhood. During the renovation she promised herself to not only restore the stateliness of the home, but the memories, as well.

She walked through the cozy breakfast nook into Leslie's study. A blend of Oriental, Inca and Egyptian greeted those that entered Leslie's private space. Though tastefully done, the room as a whole was a contradiction to her mother's particular personality—eclectic and mismatched. But each piece alone was so exactly Leslie. Just as they were arranged, meticulous and precise, showed it to be her little corner of the world. Like everything she did, her study flowed with an ease and grace Elaine only wished to possess.

As a surprise to her mother, Elaine had the office redone in a soothing gray and trimmed in a dusty rose, and in the farthest corner, where Leslie sat at her desk, she had a mural painted of her mother's favorite tree; a flowering pink dogwood. It matched perfectly the trim, and with the right lighting, sparkling white ceiling and threads of copper stripping accenting the trunk and branches, it easily became the focal point of the office. It was complimented by a *Lladro's "Springtime in Japan"* delicately perched upon the corner of Leslie's desk.

Meandering into Kash's domain, she spied Nook grooming himself in the overstuffed recliner. He stopped and momentarily watched her finger Kash's stuff. His stuff fit perfectly into the former smoking room of the house. It was strictly meant for men only, with its heavily paneled walls in natural cherry and beamed ceiling. In the middle, the beams collected at an octagonal center piece with a Bahamian fan that Elaine left in place to disperse the smoke from one of Kash's passions: cigars.

Like Leslie, Kash had an assortment of toys. Guy toys. Models he fashioned himself of his favorite real-life playthings: The Waco Seaplane, his '47 Chevy Convertible and Elaine's '51 Indian Chopper. As a child she waited patiently for him to allow her to help in gluing or painting the pieces. It was their special time together. She touched the turquoise and white Indian Chopper, and remembered the day she brought home the real deal for his approval and her mother's consternation. That very night he started putting together the plans for an exact model of her new toy, and when he finished, he presented it to her, only to have her place it on the shelf next to the others when she completed the renovation. That was the only time she saw his eyes glisten with emotion.

She mirrored him in only one way; his eyes. She wiped away a tear as she crossed the den into the living room. Before she left, she glanced back to the corner and saw "King George" as he was referred to; a fully armored figure replete with a King George sword. A Kash favorite.

More tears slid down her cheeks as she entered the formal living room. It was hardly formal. Comfortably formal as Leslie referred to it, but classically decorated, reflecting once again Leslie's quiet elegance. The cool sage color automatically adjusted one's mood and brought about relaxation and comfort, and at that moment, that was something Elaine was in desperate need of.

To help, she took her place at the wet bar that was nestled in the curve of the staircase that lead to the second floor, and grabbed a bottle of something. She didn't know and she didn't care as she added it to her tea. Taking a sip, she poured more until she was happy with the resulting taste and effect. She swirled the tepid liquid and fingered the mosaic pattern of the bar. Looking up she saw the same pattern in the twin skylights on the ceiling of the second floor. "Cool," she simply stated. She smiled and drained the rest of the tea, placing the cup on the bar; she headed up the curved staircase for the second level.

Her fingers trailed lightly on the rounded banister, stopping to double check the locks on the first story windows. Not that they were ever used, but for nothing more than something to do. The three double hung panes were jeweled hand-painted stained glass and somehow they had survived the years of natural disasters and everyday living, as did their second story sisters. They, of course, were stationary and for decoration only. The niches on the curved wall were filled with ceramic pieces by Leslie's favorite bay artist, Elaine.

Still to this day, she could never understand why her mother insisted on displaying her first attempts at sculpture in the prominent niches. When Elaine finished the renovation, she thought she'd surprise her mother with pieces of Lladro, but upon her next visit, she found her bulky work back on display and the expensive pieces tucked away in other parts of the house.

She glided up the rest of the way to the second floor sitting room, with its casual furniture, and straight through the angled double French doors into her parents' bedroom. She flipped on the lights and persimmon rust walls sprang to life. As she stood in the middle of the room, it suddenly dawned on her that she had no earthly reason as to why she was in the house at that hour. She should have been at home formulating a plan to locate her parents, not wandering through their most private of places, reminiscing about them as if they were passed.

Inwardly she slapped herself back to reality and walked into the master bath where she applied a much needed cold fix to her face. The cool water eased her anxiety and elevated her depleted energy. She caught a glimpse of her sluggish features in the mirror as she patted them dry, knowing full well she was in need of a good pressing.

Finished, she started to close the pocket doors of the closet; instead she entered the cedar lined walk-in. A deep cleansing breath brought renewed interest in the space. Of what she saw, mostly belonged to Leslie. As for her father, what Kash did have, could have fit in the linen closet. A clothes horse he wasn't. If it weren't for Leslie, he would have had an extensive collection of blue jeans, and blue jeans only. Even his blue jeans were hung with care and immaculately ironed and ready for wear—courtesy of Leslie.

Looking up at the shelving above, Elaine spotted several hat boxes. Remembering from her earlier search that they contained fedoras, she pulled one down and opened it up. Dusting off any imaginary lint, she put it on, cocking it over one eye. She turned and caught her reflection in mothers built in vanity mirror. She smiled at the sight, and if it weren't for her blonde hair and azure blue eyes, she could have sworn it was Leslie looking back at her—dimples and all.

She took it one step further and pulled free what she was sure to be the matching suit to the hat; a charcoal gray pinstripe suit, complete with shirt and tie. As she donned the outfit she started formulating a plan for retracing Leslie's steps that night in 1947 San Francisco. She knew damn good and well there weren't any such dens as described in her mother's journal, but she couldn't sit still and do nothing. After all, someone already had that job—Lane.

She reexamined her image in the mirror. "Not bad, old girl," she commented to herself. Smoothing the lines of the suit she felt something in the inner breast pocket. She pulled free a handkerchief with a most alarming surprise; the pendant described in Leslie's journal. Turning it over, she found the devastating beauty her mother wrote about. It was everything and more. She slipped the pendant on and secured it beneath the shirt and tie. The coolness on her skin sent a shock wave of chills spilling down her spine. It was exhilarating and exciting at the same time, and for possibly the first time in her life, she understood a small part of her mother.

CHAPTER THIRTEEN

Elaine took careful steps as she made her way from Columbus down Pacific to Stockton Street. She flexed her tingling fingers to encourage much needed circulation after the harrowing drive from her parents' home to the outskirts of Chinatown. The fog and rain had only intensified, each competing with the other for dominance in this particular upheaval. The rain dribbled off the fedora's brim and muted her vision even more, and for measurable irritation, it would occasionally run down her neck, chilling her already crisp self. She pulled up the collar on the suit jacket and shoved her hands into her pockets, seeking any warmth.

Before leaving the car, she memorized her notes and she slowed as she approached the block she was sure her mother had written about. It was an unusual block, in that; at least two-thirds of it had recently been purchased and renovated. She only knew that because she was asked to bid on the project, but due to other commitments, she declined. It was never clear who purchased the property, but during the projects bidding and renovation, the clients' portion was overseen by a local law firm. That was nearly a year ago, and for the most part, the only buildings to be completed were two large edifices divided by an alley and an unusual T-shaped piece on the street to the east. The stem of the "T" had two alleys separating it from the corner structures, which were in the pre-planning stage of construction. Had Elaine not been committed to other projects, she would have loved being involved in the renovation of the "T", as she called it. It not only was different in shape, but it had a courtyard in the back, and it was connected to another building using a prominent glass corridor on each side.

Making her way past the first enormous store front, a three-story shop stocked wall to wall with the latest and greatest in home furnishings, she stopped and looked down the alley at the building that was oddly connected to the "T". Leaning against roughened brick, she surveyed it and her surroundings. The alley was devoid of litter or paraphernalia of any kind. Any such nonsense would deter the tony crowd from frequenting the latest trendy restaurant that occupied the first floor. *God forbid*, Elaine thought, as the rain increased and her patience waned.

She glanced around and then headed down the alley toward the restaurant. At this hour, San Francisco as a whole reminded Elaine of New York; several sections appeared to never rest. They slowed, but they never stopped, and tonight this seemed to be one of those areas. Not that anyone was coming from that particular restaurant; they weren't. It had closed hours ago, but Elaine could hear and sense the traffic from other diners and nightclubs on the street outside of the alley.

As she made her way, she hugged the wall for protection against the rain and detection from the prying and curious. With every step, puddles announced her early morning intrusion, and as she neared the end of the alley, she heard a muffled banging to her left. The alley opened into another alley; one that was L-shaped and ran north, then east.

Checking her back, and comfortable that she was alone, Elaine carefully walked toward the sound. For a moment she hesitated. She didn't know why she was doing this, and why she felt compelled to continue, but she did. Her walk north took her past the back of the home furnishings store, and when she turned east toward the sound of the banging metal, the alley became the frightening reality of her worst bête noire.

Immediately she smelled the stench of human waste, the rain intensifying, not masking the pungent odors. If she hadn't known better, she would have sworn she had been transported to *On New Hong*, or "urinating alley", but she knew that tale to be off of Ross Alley, and she was nowhere near there. As much as she was afraid to breathe, she was equally petrified to move, but the rhythmic banging of the door urged her on. The lighting was worse than bad and she stubbed her toes several times, her outstretched hand groping for anything to catch her if she fell.

The glass corridor connecting the "T" to the restaurant gave her pause and offered a little relief from the darkness. The muted glow from the *Exit* signs provided some lighting. She stopped and let her eyes adjust to the newly found light. As she passed by the glass and brick corridors, she admired the architectural design in using beveled and stained glass with the original salvaged frosted glass pieces, and coupled with the roughened, uneven brick, the structure was now going to create more lore for future generations of architectural students.

She would have gotten closer for a better look, but a hissing warning shot her head around to the opposite side of the alley. It was followed by a chorus of the tiniest of cries she could remember hearing. "Ssshh," she soothed as she approached the mother cat. It was no surprise that she looked to be well fed, with the restaurant nearby, but Elaine was more concerned about her litter. As she neared the stacked pallets and boxes, the hissing and growling were replaced with a low, almost friendly purr. The feline accepted the gentle rubbing around her ears, but when Elaine made a move for her kittens, she arched her back and laid down her ears as a warning to cease further intrusion.

Her warning wasn't the only reason Elaine pulled back. Through the banging door, she swore she heard a plaintive wail. Abandoning her interest in the litter, she carefully moved toward the sound, and like that cat, if she weren't careful, her curiosity would get her killed. On her way, her stealth movement was interrupted with a stumble or two. "Goddammit," she hissed like the cat as she kicked at whatever caused her misstep.

She was a few feet from the door and she heard the scream again. She caught the swinging piece before it banged against the frame. She fought against the vacuum of wind to hold it in place as she walked through. Fighting the wind, she managed to secure the door, which then left her in total darkness. She flicked her lighter and took in the tiny space. It was no bigger than three feet by three feet, with two steps leading up to a landing.

She followed, pivoted and continued onto two more stairs and another landing that faced yet another door. She checked the knob, it was unlocked. A drafting of air blew the flame of her lighter over her thumb, scorching it. "Shit!" She dropped the lighter and shook her stinging hand. Her light suddenly gone, she willed herself to adjust and steady her jumpy nerves. The deep breath she took did nothing to ease her angst. She eased the door open, and a tiny security light was triggered with her intrusion. Quickly she retrieved her lighter and passed through the door. She shut it quickly, hoping that would kill the warning. It did.

Shielding the flame of her lighter, she looked left and saw a short corridor. Taking cautionary steps, she found it led to yet another door. Placing a hand on it, she found it to be cool, more than likely an outside entry. She retraced her steps and took the stairs down. She didn't know if her shivering was from the drastic drop in temperature or her nerves, but she continued anyway. Having a good sense of direction, she knew that after all of her twists and turns, she was heading west.

She came upon another landing, then more stairs downward. She looked back from where she came; she calculated she was down at least one story. The remainder of the stairs would take her down another story. Finally it flattened, and she walked a narrow corridor, her flame occasionally wavering in her haste to somewhere, anywhere. This was another set of steps, these leading up. She climbed the steep, tight passage. At the moment, she was a lot of things, but claustrophobic wasn't one of them. Thankfully.

Another landing, another door. Now she was heading south, but more importantly, there was a light. Dim, at best, but a light. It allowed her to extinguish her lighter. Good thing, it was almost out of fluid. Hugging the wall, she made her way, finding doors on only one side of the corridor. She suspected she was now under the basement of the restaurant, only because she could smell the remnants of dinner. Sweet, tangy spices filled her senses and suddenly she was hungry.

She ignored her urges, and the first door she came upon screamed "Stay away!" with its padlocked handle. It dawned on her the reason for coming this far; the cries of something human. They had stopped. Suddenly, the quiet was deafening, and she could hear her blood pulsating through her ears. Bravely and stupidly she continued.

More door and more locks. Until she came upon a small L-shaped hallway that led her back east. Only this corridor had doors on both sides and they weren't padlocked. She reached for one just as a frantic Chinese was coming from down the hall. Ducking into the room, she quietly closed the door and intently listened for their voices, but the chatter of sewing machines behind her gave her pause.

Stunned, there were women and children that paid little or no attention to her intrusion. They just sewed. On what, she didn't know or care. Until one little girl looked her way and smiled shyly. Elaine returned the kindness. She had heard the rumors, but never thought she would see it. She wondered if any agency of authority was aware. She gave it only a moment's thought as the knob she had been lingering on moved. She let go and looked for a place to duck and cover.

An elderly Asian woman shook the enormous piece of material she had been sewing, and Elaine took the hint and dove under its many layers as the door opened. She curled up, praying the floor would swallow and hide her. It only became worse when all of the machines were suddenly still. Whoever entered, gave what could only be construed as a stern lecture, only in Chinese, and Elaine understood nothing of what was being said. Why couldn't he have been speaking in French or Italian, she thought. Her knees prayed he would finish soon.

Instead, he moved closer; the tips of his shoes intruding her space. If she thought the blood was pounding earlier, its rush now was close to imploding, and her earlier pangs of hunger, were now waves of nausea. She closed her eyes and let his voice drone in her ears. She only realized he was gone when the elderly woman was tapping her shoulder, encouraging her to come out.

With great trepidation she managed to pull herself up and out of her hiding place. They exchanged smiles of thanks. Elaine was sure the woman thought she was there to help free her from this worst of human condition and bondage, and she looked around the room, she knew they were all depending upon her. She gave the old lady a reassuring pat, and as soon as she made her way to safety, she would contact someone, anyone, to help.

She listened at the door, and then with agonizing care, she eased it open. The sewing machines masked any noise she was creating. Slipping through, she resumed her search. For what, she wasn't sure, but she knew she needed more than just a room full of women and children sewing to have any swift action taken. The children were cause enough, but as quickly as she stumbled upon them, they could disappear. She needed more.

She zigzagged across the hallway, peaking into any door that didn't offer resistance. She knew she had found a gold mine of contraband, whether it was replications of priceless works of art, popular software or movies, stacks of green glassed serving trays, and as she made her way east, the rooms had increased in difficulty of skill and level of sensitivity, and so did her newfound courage. She was so incensed by what she had seen that her personal safety was secondary to those being held against their will. In the last room before the corner, the workers all wore jewelers loupes, and that was enough to convince Elaine she had seen enough and it was time to go, but the cries of earlier caught her attention again, and this time, they were accompanied by enraged voices. She recognized one of the voices from the sewing room, and from the size of his voice, he must have been huge.

As she rounded the corner a scantily clad young girl nearly ran her over, and not too far behind, the voices followed. However, one seemed to be having a great deal of effort moving. Elaine could only imagine why, and she wasn't about to stand around and find out.

Grabbing and righting the young woman, Elaine reversed her course and started to retrace her steps, running as quickly as she could, dragging the girl in her wake. Whistles blared off the walls, alerting more angry voices, she just knew it. Over the whistle; a pop. The bullet splintered and sent fragments of concrete into the air as well as their path. Elaine didn't know if it was a warning, or if they were terrible shots; she just kept running.

Rounding the corner, Elaine ran directly into the very thing she had recently been running from: Jack Phillips. "Oh, shit!" She collected herself and barely had a moment to stare with exasperation at her soon to be ex-husband and his sudden presence.

"Jack?" The Asian girl spoke perfect English. "Where have you been?"

He didn't answer, instead he led them down the corridor under the restaurant, and holding the door open to the tiny passage of stairs, he shoved the women through, and before he joined them, he waited for their pursuers. As they turned the corner, he fired his 9mm Glock, if only temporarily halting their pursuit. He slammed the door shut and shoved the latch into the locked position. He jammed a tire iron through the locking mechanism, hoping it would buy them some time. "Go!" He ordered, flicking his lighter in an attempt to illuminate the close passage. It did nothing but cast grotesque shadows, making their escape more harrowing then it already was.

"Yes, Jack, where have you been?" Elaine called over her shoulder with as much syrupy sarcasm as she could muster. He didn't answer, and just as well. If he had, it would have brought a halt to their flight. *There was plenty of time to rip him a new asshole later*, she thought. *And what the hell was he doing with a tire iron*, she wondered to herself.

Where she left off, the Asian girl took up. "Since when do we have a new partner?" she asked as they reached the flattened corridor. Her question wasn't answered as they heard teams from both ends trying to break through Jack's handiwork.

"Did you bring two tire irons?" Elaine asked, and as she turned back to Jack a rope was slapping her in the face. She swatted it as he pulled it taut and silently ordered her to begin her ascent. Instead she motioned for the Asian girl to go first.

"I don't give a shit which of you goes first. Just go," he barked, and the slender girl shimmied up the rope. His usually soft brown eyes were hard and brittle as he firmly encouraged Elaine up the rope.

"I haven't climbed in years," she admitted. "What are you doing here?" She couldn't resist asking.

Ignoring her question, he dryly replied to her climbing skills, "Like riding a bike." He gave her fanny an essential nudge upward.

She jerked her head downward at his feeble attempt in helping her climb the rope and she could have sworn she saw the corners of his mouth twitch with a smile, and then she remembered how to ride a bike and scampered up the rope—to where, she wasn't sure.

Above, the Asian girl lent a hand in pulling her up the rest of the way, and then they waited on Jack. Unfortunately, he was delayed as he fired shots into both stairwells before ascending. Deftly he managed the climb and as he was surfacing, more shots were fired from below. He kicked the access panel down just in time, as bullets struck the underneath side. Muffled voices could be heard scrambling beneath them.

It didn't take Elaine long to know where they were—one of the glass and brick corridors. The architect in her admired its beauty; the trapped woman in her searched for a way out. As they headed east toward the door she had seen when she entered, they were stopped in their tracks by more ominous looking men. These carried bigger guns. The women looked at Jack, who turned and fired at the stained and frosted glass of the corridor, providing an opening for them to escape.

He literally threw the women through the splintered mess, catching a look from Elaine that was more lethal than any bullet. "You want to live?" he shot back as he unceremoniously flung her into the alley.

Oddly, the men in pursuit didn't fire, nor did they rush their movements as they headed for the trio. That worried Jack. "Head for the pipe," he ordered in a hushed tone, fearing an ambush in the alley.

Despite her earlier interruptions, Elaine had made mental notations about the alley, and was bound and determined not to pussyfoot around. Ignoring his order and the pipe, she broke into a sprint and headed straight down the middle of the alley for the bend and hopefully freedom. She knew damn good and well Jack was beside himself over her choice, which was naturally, contrary to his.

Jack sent the Asian girl up the drain pipe and covered her action with sweeping gunfire. He did likewise for his fleeing wife, giving her cover as she neared the elbow of the alley.

Elaine was almost there, when she was broadsided and tackled to the wet ground. The wind left her lungs in a rush as she was righted and pinned to the disgustingly foul pavement. Gasping for air, she struggled against the leathered form above her. She stopped as he sunk his knees into the soft flesh of her shoulder and chest, demanding in Chinese as to know what she was doing in such a place at such an hour. Too petrified to answer, he told her she had some explaining to do.

There was a momentary silence as clips were changed and then the gunfire resumed, masking her effort to get relief. Bored with her attempts, and knowing she was a handful, the Chinese man drew a fist and threatened to still her aggression. In grabbing her shirt, his fingers encircled more than they bargained for. Curiosity relaxed his features as he ripped open the neatly starched garment and found a pendant nestled in the hollow of Elaine's throat. Yanking it free, he saw the back and recognized the dragon. Knowing the folklore that accompanied it, he leaned closer to her face, and said in perfect English, "Mr. Lin will be interested in hearing about this." He dangled the pendant in front of her stricken features.

He hoisted her up by the lapels of her jacket and applied a choke hold to encourage her cooperation. The pendant dangled and swayed back and forth from his fingers as he walked her back toward the shattered glass corridor. His booming voice spoke hurried Chinese and the gunfire stopped. Then he spoke his perfect English, "Oh, Jack? It's time to end this nonsense. There's nowhere to run. I promise, Jack, it will be painless." He nuzzled Elaine's neck. "For the both of you," he added.

Elaine didn't have a clue as to how Jack knew this animal, but later, like her, Jack had some explaining to do.

From the darkness, Jack called out evenly, "Let her go. She has nothing to do with us and our business." He waited a moment, then offered, "A simple trade: me for her."

"That's not like you, Jack. You've never had regard for hostages before. Why now? What is she to you?" The Chinese man asked, pulling Elaine closer. "A lover?" Looking beneath the bill of her hat, he appraised her sharp features and let a finger trail down her prominent cheekbone. "Yes. I can see that. No deal, Jack."

He steadily walked her to the fractured glass corridor where Jack emerged from the shadows and reluctantly he surrendered his weapons. If Elaine was disappointed, it didn't show. She had, through the years of being married to Jack, perfected the most serene of poker faces—and he knew it. Her face showed no fear, but her eyes shone with fury, and not for the man holding her captive.

Relieved of his weapons, Jack was pushed forward to join Elaine in what was sure to be a long walk to Mr. Lin's office. Sharp Chinese sent two of the four up the drain pipe to find Jack's accomplice. An encouraging shove urged the pair into the corridor. A lone gunman walked in tandem with Elaine's captor.

As they headed east in the corridor of glass, Elaine looked at the profile of her husband and said, "I take it you're not in reconstructive management?"

He narrowed his black eyes, warning her to cease. She obliged and stopped, bringing their procession to a halt.

"Are you telling me to shut up with that look, Jack? Well, tough shit, I'm not going to."

"Elaine," he warned with gentle measure.

"Don't Elaine me," she hissed back. "You and me; we're going to hash some things out before we meet with Mr. Whoever."

"Whomever," he corrected.

"Once again, who gives a shit?" she throttled back.

Jack looked back at his adversary, a defeated smile on his lips. "Women."

The man with the booming voice was at best Elaine's height, five-seven or so, and average in build. He smiled and motioned for them to continue up the stairs, the pendant showing the way. "You can talk on the way."

"You mean being lectured, don't you, Slim? That's why we've gone our separate ways. She likes to be on top, so to speak. You know, control things." Elaine was a lot of things; stupid wasn't one of them, and Jack recognized her ploy and egged her on. "Isn't that right, darling?"

"I need a little more than a minute before I lose control, Jack," she shot back sweetly.

That was all the time Jack needed to shove the lone escort into Slim, knocking them over like discarded chess pieces. He tried grabbing Elaine, but in a split second she stepped on the back escort, grounding his face into the roughened concrete, and reclaimed her pendant before Slim had a chance to recover it.

"Mine!" she exclaimed, placing a well polished loafer to his groan, stymieing any retaliation he felt rising.

Jack rudely shoved Elaine through the series of doors she entered in what seemed like forever ago. They had nearly cleared the alley when they heard Slim and more of his merry men approaching from the southern end of the L-shaped passageway. Shots rang out from above as they narrowly made it to the outside street.

Like their marriage, each wanted to go a different direction; so they did. Elaine to the south and west, and Jack to the north. Neither hesitated as they disappeared into the fog and light rain. The mist sealed quickly behind their fleeing forms, leaving no trace of their intrusion.

Elaine could hear the booming voice of Slim, and though he was speaking Chinese, she was sure he was ordering his men to divide and conquer. So as not to draw any attention to her actions, she slowed her pace. Feeling she was far enough away from the alleys, she reversed her direction and headed north, and when she felt comfortable that she was alone, she would head back east and to the safety of her father's car.

Jack's whereabouts crossed her mind only after she was suddenly yanked into an alleyway, her mouth clamped shut and his familiar voice low and steady in her ear.

"Ssh," he instructed as he eased his hold on her and then he planted her against the wall of the building.

A shaky breath tumbled from her parted lips as she searched his impassive face. "I thought you'd be long gone by now. After all, that is your trademark," she said, regretting the comment the instant it was out of her mouth. A moment of contrition flushed her features and she whispered, "I'm sorry, that was uncalled for."

He paid little attention to her as he placed a silencing finger to her lips, and searched through the mist and listened intently for any sign of Slim. Sensing none, he guided her out of the alley into a small crowd that was letting out from a late night movie theater. The crowd thinned as they made their way north.

Thinking they were in the clear, each relaxed their gait, though Elaine couldn't help but notice that with each step, the guiding hand on her waist became tenser. With good reason; in the distance a familiar voice pricked the hairs on their necks. Their quickened pace only increased the closing in of the voice.

Running out of options, Jack literally dragged Elaine into the only open-all-night store in the strip—Randi Andi's Playhouse Emporium. More like, let's play house, Elaine thought as she quickly glanced around and took in the numerous toys for all types of fun and loving couples.

Considering the hour, there were several couples perusing the latest and greatest in erotic gadgets.

Leather hoods with zippered eyes and mouths gawked back at Elaine as Jack pulled her to a corner of the store that represented S & M 101 with every conceivable item used in domination. She was sure this would be Slim's favorite section with its studded collars, heavy linked chains, clamps for nipples, and testicles, as well as various whips, whether plain leather, leather and velvet, or every horse lovers dream: riding crops.

The tinkling bell above the door drew her attention away from the grotesque hoods to see an even more horrifying site entering the cramped shop; Slim and his henchmen.

Jack ruefully yanked off her hat and shoved it as well as one of her favorite accessories, a leather hood, into her bosom for safekeeping all while keeping an eye on the new customers as they were greeted by the overzealous night clerk.

They had no more pushed him aside when the building wavered, causing displays to sway to and fro from a tremor that was more than incidental. Everyone breathed a collective sigh when suddenly another followed, sending several items crashing to the floor, and more importantly to Jack and Elaine, extinguishing the lighting.

With the lights out, there was only slight confusion - more amusement than anything. Tremors were commonplace in San Francisco and unless the ceiling caved in, these little blips were manageable. Playful naughtiness filled the dark shop while the night clerk searched for something to illuminate the space.

Jack took the opportunity to guide Elaine to the back of the store. He did this as if he had intimate knowledge of the place, and she wondered how that was possible. He definitely wasn't involved in reconstruction management, she reiterated to herself.

The blinding glare of a flashlight interrupted their progress. Elaine shielded her eyes, hoping their silhouettes didn't give them away.

"Sorry," the man apologized as the lights began to flicker up front and came back to life. He extinguished his manmade torch and called out, "Okay, Jay, lights are up."

"Wish I was," boomed a voice from one of the rooms.

Mixed laughter followed the comment, and as the rustling got closer, Jack tried several doors and found them to be locked. Then he discovered an empty room near the back. It could have been a closet for all they were concerned, but the sticky floor and stench of human excretions told them it wasn't used for storage.

The protest rising in Elaine's throat was cut short as Jack struck a match and found a nearly nonexistent candle to light. The murky glow provided enough lighting for him to examine their options. There weren't many. He removed his jacket and shirt and threw them under the small wooden bench behind his partner. He secured his hood and grabbed the riding crop, shaking it at a nonplussed Elaine.

Familiar voices approached as they opened and shut doors, interrupting acts of intimacy to put it at best, looking for Elaine and her soon to be ex. She took a shaky breath as she shrugged out of her jacket, struggling to undo her tie and shirt as the voices got closer. Damn, why weren't her fingers cooperating?

Jack helped; he tore the shirt from her, throwing it along with her fedora and jacket under the bench. As buttons bounced off the walls and stuck to the floor, he stuffed Elaine's head into the leather hood and zippered the eyes shut and more importantly, closed the mouth opening. A muffled response was stifled further as he dropped her to her knees with the crop and took his place on the bench.

If the claustrophobia of the room wasn't enough, the hood magnified it ten times. Nausea crept up her throat and became worse when her hands hit the floor, slid and stuck. "Shit!" she muttered between clinched teeth as she felt her head being jerked around and placed between what she knew to be Jack's rock hard thighs. She half expected something else to be rock hard, but to her disappointment, it wasn't. Just as well, she thought. As their door was yanked open, she held her breath when Jack shoved her deeper into his crotch, slapping her with the crop to ensure cooperation.

He paid little attention to the interruption of Slim's men, concentrating more on making his partner understand his domination, and that her submission was key to their survival. Surprisingly, she complied with his lead as well as his wishes.

She held her position until the door slammed shut; then in a rush, she was up, unzipping, tearing at the hood, trying to release its oppressive hold. Calming hands freed her from the restriction and eased the mask off, revealing her shattered confidence. A callused finger soothed the anxiety in her furrowed brow, and then as gentle as he had been, he roughly handed over her jacket, shirt and hat from under the bench.

He dressed before she slipped one arm into her mother's once neatly starched shirt. She finished as if she were in a dream, her movements sluggish and off center. As she pulled on the jacket, she tried to shake the feelings creeping into her reserve, and they weren't the ones of peril or danger, but rather of wonton intimacy.

Familiar with every inch of her soul, he recognized the want in her eyes as he blew out the candle and with that gesture, he snuffed out any hope of fulfilling any and all needs she had at that moment. He flexed his jaw in the dark at the thought of what was coursing between them, and then he eased open the flimsy door and peered out into the shop.

He didn't see or sense any sign of Slim and his men. The bell above the door confirmed their departure, but unwilling to take chances, Jack lead a slightly resistive Elaine through yet another doorway, constrictive corridor, down some more steps, until they were finally out in an alley behind the shop.

An alley she didn't know existed, and she wasn't about to ask any questions as to how he knew. Instead she let him drag her through more narrow passageways until they emerged onto a real street. Suddenly he stopped, causing her to run into his shoulder. "Would you mind telling me when you're going to do that?" she growled into his ear.

A firm squeeze on her captured wrist was his only reply.

"Shithead!" was her only retort.

Quietly they walked toward the area where she was parked; all the while she was wondering how he knew her location.

They were across the street from her father's car, when Jack demanded, "The keys?"

"I can get home from here," she replied, tugging on her snared wrist.

He tightened his grip.

"They're in my left pants pockets," she informed him.

Releasing her wrist, she fished out the keys and located the ignition key, and then she started her march across the street. Within seconds, he grabbed her hand and wrestled the keys from her.

"I don't need you to take me home!" she bit out.

Within seconds of his remark, he was shoving her into the front seat of the car and bringing to life its eight cylinders. When he engaged the power glide, they lurched forward until he got the feel for the eight-headed monster, and then he comfortably eased it through the city streets. Now, if only he could manage that kind of control over the blonde-headed beast sitting next to him, life would be grand.

"Slow down," she ordered. "You're going to tear the front end off this thing. Then, how would Daddy feel about you?"

He ignored her comments and asked, "Where did you get that pendant?"

"I'm sure you know the answer to that, and if not, ask Dad." She ran a sticky hand through her hair and shoved the hat back in place.

"I did meet your father on an archaeological dig," he quietly offered, trying his best to explain away the evening's events, and the very fact that he wasn't who he appeared to be their entire marriage. "I really was going to be an archaeologist. Travel the world, discover..."

"Save it for someone who cares, Jack," she interrupted.

"That was uncalled for," he solemnly shot back, fully intending for her to feel shitty about her remark, and just as he was ready to add more, a bullet pierced the body of the Biscayne's trunk, spreading shock and dismay through Elaine's already tense features.

Another bullet splintered the back glass and continued through the fedora she was wearing. Again, Jack dragged her down to his lap for safe keeping as he navigated the hilly streets, tearing the hell out of the front end. With every scrape, he could feel Elaine's face tighten.

Recalling her father kept a loaded 357 in the glove compartment, Elaine snaked away from Jack's lap to open it up and retrieve the hardware. Against her better judgment, she rose up and took aim at the motorcycle chasing them. She fired three shots, causing the bike to swerve and slow considerably. Re-aiming, she took a deep breath, and when Jack leveled the car, she fired the remaining bullets. The last one struck metal, causing the bike to veer sharply and catch on the wet pavement, spilling its occupants. She watched impassively as they were dragged down the street under the bike. Only when Jack rounded the corner did she turn away from the gore.

She threw the gun into the glove compartment and slammed it shut with her foot. She hugged the passenger door, getting as far away from Jack as possible.

"Where did you learn to shoot like that?" he asked.

"Ask Dad," she automatically replied.

There was stony silence as they reached Kash and Leslie's house. The only noise was that of the garage door opener allowing them access into the lower level.

Before the car was stopped, Elaine was stepping out and heading for the safety of the house, stripping sullied clothes as she went. Jack let her go as he secured the car and the garage. He would join her later, as soon as he assessed the damage to the car and his operation. Finding her parents was one thing, keeping her from interfering was another. He hadn't counted on her finding out so soon his involvement with her parents and their true profession. Elaine wasn't stupid, nor was she lazy or conniving; those were Lane's gifts. Thankfully, she was the exact opposite of Lane—hardworking and honest, trusting and decent, but above all, resourceful. Her profession had taught her that. Always peeling back layers to find the answers to the past. Elaine was an expert in stripping away layers. How Jack had managed to avoid her natural gift was a mystery to him. Or maybe she knew all along, and at some point she would trump him with it. She did have a tiny bit of deceit in her, after all, she was a woman, and that, as Kash often told him, was part of their charm—Leslie and Elaine.

He made his phone calls in the garage and then checked the security of the home. All was in place as he made his way up the stairs, past discarded clothing to the sound of the shower in the master suite. Following her lead, Jack stripped himself of his soiled clothes and entered the misty bathroom.

Elaine's form could be detected through the thick steam in the shower. Her hands were propped up against the wall, allowing the water to cascade down her back and run lazily down the length of her long, shapely legs.

Jack was mesmerized by her quiet, unassuming beauty. He barely disturbed the steam as he stepped into the shower behind her. She didn't acknowledge his presence. Typical Elaine, he thought, as he lathered up his hands and spread them across her lean back. The only admission of his company was a deep intake of air and a relaxing under his familiar touch.

"What took you so long?" she asked in a husky voice and then turned into his arms and mouth.

Her kiss was so deep, it rooted him to the tile floor, and he drank in the sweetness of her lips and tongue as the water fell over them, looking for a way to come between them. There wasn't the smallest space to be found.

He tasted the tangy scent of the evening on her neck and nipped at it gently to ease his hunger. She stirred and moved closer, and he could feel her melting into his flesh, and if it were possible for her to become one with him, at that moment, he would have welcomed it.

Lathering up her back, he seductively ran his hands down the curve of her spine to the roundness of her buttocks and back up again. Slowly he kneaded away the tension and she relaxed, granting him the access he had so patiently been waiting for.

Gently, he planted her against the cool tile wall and lifted her legs around him. He watched her face as he slowly found his way home. Her jaw flexed and a sharp intake of air let him know he was where he should be. Easily they rocked to a familiar rhythm, each helping the other reach that sweet point of no return.

Silently they sank to the floor. The only sound: the gently spraying water. Jack took a moment to open his eyes and study the woman in his arms. Her breathing was finally slowed and even and the furrow between her brows of earlier was now a tiny line. Jack loved the symmetry of her face; quiet and graceful, and when she lifted her lashes to him, she revealed a more pliable Elaine. He relaxed his tense features and waited for the spunky Elaine to catch her second wind. A deep breath steeled his resolve as she pushed her way up to meet his gaze. The water beat a gentle pattern on her back, and the droplets formed puddles around her soft curves.

With that deep breath, her shakiness was steeled and her tenacity returned. "Tell me about the company you work for, Jack." Her tone was firm and left him no wiggle room.

"I am in reconstructive management. Just not in construction." His answer was vague and he could see her putting together the pieces of any number of agencies that were covert and not accounted for in the Department of Budget's annual numbers to the Congress.

"Your primary business clients do start with a 'c', correct?"

"I help reconstruct misguided countries. Small, inconsequential countries."

"In today's world, there's no such thing, Jack. What were you doing in Chinatown, and who was the inconsequential woman you were with?"

"The less you know, the safer you are."

She pushed up and out of their embrace and turned off the shower. The shower head dripped dry, but Elaine's tone was pouring with sarcasm. "You sound like Lane. What's his involvement in your business?"

Jack stood and put up pleading hands for Elaine to silently understand his position. He didn't want her to be involved anymore than she accidentally was. "Look, for all I know, Lane is a judge, and a shitty one at that," he said, trying to appease her growing glare. To deflect telling the truth, he turned the tables on her and asked, "What were you doing in Chinatown, and what were you doing with the pendant?"

Unlike Jack, Elaine had nothing to hide. "I found my parent's journals. You know, the ones that describe their clandestine careers. Their bogus lives. Their..." she stopped short as hot tears stung her eyes. "How long have you known?"

He tried to gather her into his arms, but she backed out of the shower and found a towel to put between them. "How long has Lane known, and why didn't anyone think I should have known?"

"Lane's in the business of knowing. You're not. Your parents wanted it that way. They wanted you to be free to be you and do whatever you wanted in life. Knowing would have put you at risk, and now that you do know, you're unfortunately at risk."

"Was marrying me keeping me safe and giving me what I wanted in life?" she shot back.

"I married you much to the consternation of your parents."

"I thought you had married me because you loved me. You had met my parents long before I ever introduced you to them, hadn't you?"

He looked everywhere but at her. "I did love you." He regretted it the moment it came out. "I do..."

She cut him short with a look that could have instantly frozen hell. "You haven't told me why you were in Chinatown with that woman. China is a little bigger than small and inconsequential. What gives?"

"New, synthetic opium." It was all the more he was going to say, and at that, he had said too much.

His answers were too quick and too pat to be truthful, but she left it alone and proceeded to change into fresh clothing. Jack scooped up her towel and dried off, then went to Kash's closet and found a silk robe to put on. When he emerged from the closet, Elaine was nowhere to be found. He found her in her father's office, scanning some documents. He closed the distance between them and gently rubbed the newly tense muscles of her neck and shoulders. "It's nearly time for the sun to come up. Let's go back upstairs and get some rest. Then we can look at this with fresh eyes, put together a plan and try to find your folks." He caught a glimpse of her instant coffee and knew rest wasn't on her agenda. "I'll get dressed and we'll figure this out together."

She watched him pad up the stairs and knew they weren't going to figure this out together, and that it wasn't going to be figured out in any short time. "Wait for me," she called out after him and followed him upstairs to bed.

CHAPTER FOURTEEN

Elaine had carefully pushed the chopper out of the garage and lowered the door before she started the throaty beast. The Indian Chopper sputtered to life and with a quick flick of the wrist, it coughed out any resistance it was prone to have when newly started. She let it have a brief warm up and then put it into first gear and pulled out into the smoky morning air.

She drank in the moist air as she moved through the quiet streets of Pacific Heights on her way to her firehouse home. She had left a sleeping Jack in her parents' bed; a bed she shared in guilty pleasure, and she wasn't ashamed about it either. He was, after all, her husband, and she still wanted and needed him in a way only a woman could. It wasn't just a want that drove her to bed him, but a necessity. She needed him to be tired and sleep so she could copy the journals, transfer them to her PDA and formulate some sort of plan to track down her parents.

Her ride to the firehouse was without incident and she pulled into her garage and cut the motorcycle's engine and coasted to a stop. The Shelby Cobra reverberated the throaty sound of the chopper; his turn would be coming in less than an hour.

As much as Elaine wanted to scamper through the house and gather her belongings, her legs were suddenly sluggish, and her thoughts were just as unorganized. She was trying her best to shove some of the evening's sorted activities out of her mind and concentrate on the important tasks at hand, but everything about Jack Phillips kept creeping into that walled off part of her psyche. The part she promised that he and any other male wouldn't have access to ever again. It wasn't working, though. Instinctively she let a hand trail down her stomach, feeling, aching really, for his touch of earlier.

She flexed her hand and jaw and forced her attention on getting things together for her impromptu trip. She packed very little in the way of clothes, making sure to take only those items necessary for a trip to Alaska. She had been on enough fishing trips to know what to take and how well it would protect her from the elements.

Those trips to Alaska she enjoyed the most with her parents. It was their time together, as a family even though Lane, in his later years, wouldn't join them for all the tea in China. *Pussy*, Elaine thought. His lame excuses didn't fall on deaf ears, but they didn't diminish the torch his parents carried for him, either. On more than one occasion Elaine had a hard time biting her tongue and swallowing her bitter feelings regarding her brother's cavalier dismissal of Kash and Leslie as their parents. For some unknown reason, he thought he was the father. Of his own children maybe, but not of Kash and Leslie, and certainly not of Elaine.

"Fucking idiot," she bit out. That was all she was going to allow herself to feel and say about Lane.

After the evening's activities she wasn't taking any chances, and she shoved her father's 357 into the bag with extra shells and a quick loader. She looked at her watch and grabbed her pilot's attaché and headed for the Cobra. She packed her gear and gave a once over, knowing full well she had forgotten something, but there wasn't time to think about what it was.

Elaine settled into the leather racing seat of the Shelby Cobra and strapped in. She gave the key a quick turn and the power from the engine surged through her, exhilarating her from head to toe. If she could have married her car instead of Jack, she would have. From the time her father had given it to her, which was around the time she'd met Jack, the Cobra had been Mr. Reliable, never sputtering or hedging like Jack. It was a present from her father for a job well done on the renovation of Kash and Leslie's home. Like her Waco and Indian Chopper, the '64 Cobra was an original. Kash seemed to have scoured the face of the earth in search of this prized possession, much to the horror of Leslie, who would have preferred a nice, safe Volvo for their daughter's primary mode of transportation. But like father, like daughter - Elaine loved speed, and the Cobra was legendary for its muscle on and off the race course.

The garage door was barely open when the Shelby Cobra shot

out onto the street. Elaine let the car have its way and opened up the engine, zipping through her sleepy neighborhood. The mist was burning off with the rising sun and the open cockpit of the Cobra let the cool morning air flow over her drawn features. She was hoping the crisp air would clear the cobwebs and she could settle her jumpy nerves.

As she approached the Golden Gate Bridge, her mind was finally clear and her thoughts were as organized as they had been in hours. She had mentally plotted her course from California to Victoria, a city on Vancouver Island, then to her final destination; Alaska, and the fishing village her mother and father were headed to.

Once onto Highway 1, Elaine let the Shelby flex its muscle and tear up the coast toward her own private getaway; Bodega Bay a small town where she hid her passion for flying, among other things.

CHAPTER FIFTEEN

Jack groaned as he turned over and caught sight of the clock and the time of day. He looked to the other side of the bed and didn't find his companion of the early morning hours beside him. Eight-thirty was too late by half and he needed to find Elaine and make sure she hadn't made any goofy plan to find her parents. That was his job.

Rolling out of bed, he stretched to ease the kinks from a hard sleep. He walked through the master suite, gathered his clothes and put them on as he made his way downstairs, calling out for Elaine, "Elaine? Where are you?"

He reached the kitchen and found that the coffee maker had its timer set for nine o'clock. What he didn't find was Elaine. He checked the garage and found that the Indian Chopper was gone. "Damn," he ground out. Out of curiosity he checked the glove compartment of the Chevy Biscayne and found the 357 Magnum Elaine had handled with such skill the previous evening was indeed gone.

Back inside the kitchen, he hurried up the coffeemaker, found his cell phone and placed a call. "She's gone, and she's armed." He waited patiently while the party on the other side expressed their displeasure. "Look, she's not a professional and she will leave a trail. Just let me handle it. You stay out of the way. She catches any wind that you have a hand in keeping her from finding Kash and Leslie, and there will be hell to pay for both of us. My main concern now is keeping her alive and out of the way of Slim. He's seen that pendant, and old scores are always settled. Let me handle it." The call was terminated from the other end and Jack closed his cell phone to a new nightmare. "Shit," he said as he poured a cup of coffee.

A few sips later and he was heading out the door to find Elaine, Kash and Leslie, hoping like hell he could keep Slim and his men at bay. But he knew that to be wishful thinking.

CHAPTER SIXTEEN

The drive up Highway 1 produced a new urgency for Elaine. Usually this drive was filled with leisure and a familiar anticipation, but this morning, the usual excitement had turned into an uneasy intensity that had caused muscles to tighten and ache. She finally allowed that forbidden thought to cross her mind—what if her parents are dead? She winced at the notion. A blast of sea air forced her to shake that image from her mind.

To settle her jumbled nerves, she recalled more of the journals she had scanned earlier. She was thankful to have a photographic memory. It served her well in school, and now in recalling her parents' excursion to China, she could blend the two accounts and make one story. She picked up where she had left off; Kash and Leslie on their way to China. Recalling these entries, Elaine prickled with memory of her mother's account of London, 1946. Who was Mark Bauer Scott, and why didn't she ever tell her children he was her first husband? What was she hiding?

Bumpy. Uncomfortable. Noisy and chilly. Leslie pulled up the collar on her overcoat and stared out the grimy window of the plane at the twilight sky. The colors were beautiful and tranquil, but the tranquility was interrupted by an occasional sputter and the constant drone of the engines. The only thing worse than the annoying sound outside was the dead silence she shared inside with Kash Bennett.

She took a chance and gave him a sidelong glance, only to prompt the same scolding glare he had been yielding since they left the hotel. Quickly she turned back to the window and leaned her head against the cool glass. Certainly staring into the near darkness was better than facing the stormy gray of his eyes, she concluded. She focused her attention on the blinking red light on the plane's wing.

The plane rocked and dipped, causing her to bump her head, thankfully ending her hypnotic stare at the blinking light. She straightened up and drummed her fingers lightly on the tattered armrest and studied her surroundings. Like the armrest, the seats were well worn and badly in need of repair or even replacement. The cloth was frayed, scratchy and the cushions were lumpy, causing immense discomfort. Gray paint was peeling on both of the walls and ceiling and the battleship linoleum flooring was soiled, particularly in the aisle. Outside, the plane was still the same gray, but with streaks of brown on the wings, and it didn't have a logo. Leslie wondered if it was worthy of being flown, and if they would arrive in one piece.

With darkness already upon them, she decided there was no need in looking out the window anymore. There were two alternatives: sleep or converse with Kash. At that point, the latter was an impossibility, so she fidgeted, trying to find the latch to recline her seat. No latch. She squirmed some more, and in trying to become comfortable, she disturbed Mr. Bennett.

He slowly opened his eyes and turned his head to face her profile. Lightning bolts could have struck her dead and it would have been less painful than having to receive another scornful glare from Kash.

Yanking on her overcoat, she settled back into her lumpy station and looked out the window to find his reflection staring back at her. His hooded gaze was black as the night outside and his square jaw made harsher from the distorted cabin lighting inside. With a sigh, Leslie closed her eyes to the nightmare.

LONDON, OCTOBER 1946

The covers rippled from the playfulness of the couple beneath them. A woman's giggle is silenced and a low moan of pleasure takes it place. Suddenly, the covers become very still. For a moment they paused their affection, their lips barely touching and their profiles were sharp and silhouetted.

Suddenly he captured her mouth with such brutal savagery that she could taste the saltiness of her own blood. He too, could taste it, and he gently pulled down her lip to examine the tiny fracture. Like a snake striking its prey, he swiftly ran his tongue over the mark, soothing the tiny ache, causing a much larger one to take its place. Lovingly he took each lip and clung to them before he completely devoured her mouth, soothing the need creeping into her being.

Reluctantly he drew back and whispered, "I have to go."

Her mouth puckered in a childlike pout and she mouthed, "No."

Leslie Anne Walker Scott watched Mark Bauer Scott ease out of bed and slip into the olive green slacks of his uniform. She stretched lazily while admiring the man whom she had chosen to spend the rest of her life with in blissful matrimony. He was five hundred miles from handsome, but his zest for living was contagious and so very attractive, that she overlooked his too close eyes and crooked nose.

She pulled his robe up from the floor, slipped it on and quietly padded over to him. She playfully wrapped her arms around his waist and promptly unbuckled the belt he had just strapped into place. Her laugh was low and devilish, and he responded by pulling her around and pinning her against the dresser.

"Now, I told you, duty calls," he repeated.

Leslie nodded, and mocking him, she moved closer and ran her tongue the length of his jaw to his ear, causing him to shudder with excitement. "You've been reassigned," she informed. "To me. For life."

"Yes," Mark agreed. "As soon as I've finished this assignment. No rest for British Intelligence. Especially when it concerns one of our own."

Paying little attention to what he said, Leslie pulled his face to hers and kissed him softly.

"You can bet I'll enjoy being the dutiful husband," he muttered against her love swollen lips.

"Promise?"

"Until death do us part," he promised again. He released her, put his cover on and walked to the door. She followed, a brooding look on her face. He noticed and reassured, "I'm almost finished with this assignment, then I can start my new one."

"What is this assignment?" she asked, straightening his tie and brushing his jacket.

"Just like a reporter."

"More like a concerned wife."

He understood and quickly explained the assignment. "We have an informant amongst our ranks. Someone who's selling our intelligence to the highest bidder. Namely the Soviet Union."

"Do you know who it is?"

Mark nodded. "I'm to meet with him in an hour. That is if my new bride will let me."

"Does he know you know?" Leslie asked in a concerned tone.

He pulled her closer and playfully looked down the robe. "Probably," he answered absentmindedly. He was concentrating more on the creaminess of her skin and the anticipation of mastering her soft curves.

"Well, isn't it dangerous you going to meet him? Especially if he knows?"

"Probably." He felt a tightening in the pit of stomach and held her away. She felt it and smiled knowingly. "I'll see you in about two hours." He looked her up and down. "Don't bother getting dressed." He grinned and his limpid blue eyes danced mischievously.

Her laugh was low and husky and it was almost enough to make him stay, but he resisted the temptation and left briskly. Duty called.

Leslie bolted the door after him and then ran to the window to watch him drive away. She was already keeping track of the time until he returned.

The rain was coming down in sheets and Mark pulled the collar to his jacket up as he ran to the car. He paused briefly to see his new bride blow him a kiss, then he jumped into his car. "Lucky man," he sighed to himself.

Just as quickly as it took him to turn the key, the car exploded into an orange and red ball of flame with debris flying and striking the window where Leslie stood helplessly screaming. "No! Noooo!"

She ran blindly out into the wet street and tried to get near the burning mass of metal, but she was seized before she could get any closer. Slipping into uncontrollable hysteria, she screamed and struggled fiercely to free herself from the grasp of Gerald Bryant. Wrestling her to the ground, he pinned her with his weight and finally got her under control. His voice was stern and harsh. "He's gone. There's nothing you can do. He's gone, Leslie."

The orange glow from the fire illuminated her pain. The rain mixed with the tears and made it impossible to distinguish one from the other, but her raking sobs made clear her state of mind. Bryant gently lifted her and carried her away from the burning nightmare. She didn't hear the blare of the sirens or the crash of thunder.

Kash watched a restless Leslie wince and draw her brows into a deep frown while she slept and then he caught the lightening racing against the black night. One, two, three consecutive streaks and then there was a pause followed by a crash of thunder that rolled through the cabin of the plane.

Leslie bolted upright, an agonizing cry was kept in check. Her fingers dug into the armrest, struggling to keep the painful memory buried.

Kash intently stared at her and the beads of perspiration on her brow and upper lip. He noticed the tear that had slipped past her thick lashes and ran down her pale cheek. Abruptly she got up and stepped past him to go to the lavatory. He regarded her hasty departure with caution and wondered to himself what could have caused such unrest in the usually composed Leslie Anne Scott.

Leslie tried the handle to the washroom, it was occupied. She waited and used the back of her overcoat sleeve to wipe away the effects of her nightmare. Finally the door opened and a youthful Chinese man emerged. He stopped short when he saw Leslie and he scrutinized her features, causing her to blush with embarrassment. Their eyes locked for only a moment before she slid past him and entered the tiny compartment.

An unsteady breath tumbled from her parted lips as she looked at her reflection in the mirror. It was no wonder the man stared, she thought. Her complexion was paste white and her usually red lips were pale pink and dry. She turned on the tap and splashed her face with cool water and within seconds she could feel the heat in the back of her neck subside and the color return to her face.

She had calmed down when suddenly the plane took a dive, throwing her forward into the edge of the mirror. Regaining her balance, she braced herself as the plane leveled off. Looking up she was a trickle of blood running down her forehead. She wiped it away to spot a tiny gash near her hairline. Wetting her handkerchief, she applied it with some pressure to stop the bleeding. This assignment was not starting off well, she told herself, and if things continued as they were, she should be dead by the end.

The rocky walk from the lavatory to her seat was made even less steady by Kash's unnerving stare. He immediately noticed the tiny cut starting to welt up and take on a bluish tint. Unfortunately he noticed everything about her, but that didn't make his remark any less cutting. "I take it you didn't rest well."

Recognizing that tone, she turned to him, her eyes black with anger. "And I take it, that's none of your business," she snapped.

Ignoring her retort, he shot back, "You'd better buckle up, we'll be landing soon, and you don't want to bump your head. Again."

CHAPTER SEVENTEEN

A cloud of dust puffed and swelled around Leslie's feet when Kash dropped her luggage next to her on the dirt runway. Taking his in tow, he walked away, leaving her to fend for herself. She shook her head at his manners, or lack of them, and managed to carry her suitcases to their next plane.

She stepped inside the belly of yet another gray monstrosity and stopped. If she thought this plane was going to take on any improvement over the last, she was sadly mistaken. She felt an encouraging nudge from behind and reluctantly she continued inside.

There were very few people on the plane, and she noticed that none of them were sitting in seats. Instead they were perched on wooden benches that were fastened to the floor, and their luggage was either under the bench or out in front of them.

Kash threw his tote under the bench and slid his suitcase in vertically, establishing an imaginary wall between himself and his traveling companion. That suited Leslie just fine and she doubled his efforts by sliding her suitcase next to his, then placing her tote and briefcase directly under where she was to sit.

She waited for Bennett to sit, but he didn't. Tired of dawdling, she ran a hand over the rough wooden plank that was to be her seat. Kash gave a satisfied smile to her disgusted sneer and settled onto the bench.

Daintily she removed her silk handkerchief and began to dust off her area, including the wall. Irritation masked Bennett's face as he yanked the cloth from her hand and pulled her down onto the wooden bench beside him.

Splinter! Her buttocks tightened and her mouth puckered at the annoying discomfort of the sliver of wood that was puncturing her gluteus maximus. She leaned closer to him and eased the pressure and whispered coolly, "Thanks. Now I have a splinter in my ass."

Amusement twinkled in his gray eyes as he shoved her hat back. "Now you know what it's like to have a pain in the ass."

She gave a small smile of defeat, settled back and cautiously relaxed her fanny. She noticed the lighting was dull and sparse, but she didn't need much light to know that every eye was upon her. She felt a particular pair boring through her, and she turned to meet his stare. A stare she recognized from earlier on the other plane.

Uneasiness crept into her cool features. Realizing it, she pulled her hat down over her eyes, stretched out her legs and ignored the pain in her ass and heart.

The plane ride became bumpy, so Leslie grabbed onto the front edge of the wooden plank for support. There wasn't much there and the plane hit an air pocket, sending her into Kash's lap. She gave an apologetic smile as he righted her and took her hand, guiding it to a strap fastened to the wall, just above her head. "Like the bus," he informed.

She pretended she didn't hear him and asked in a whisper, "Is this plane taking us to Peiping?"

"Close enough."

Kash stepped off the plane and squinted his eyes against the bright sunshine. He looked across the runway and spotted their next mode of transportation and headed toward it.

Leslie's breathing was labored and her arm ached from carrying her cumbersome luggage as she finally caught up with Kash. He was placing his suitcase and tote onto the flat board of a wagon when she finally arrived. Promptly she dropped her case at his feet, and surprisingly he dutifully placed it next to his on the wagon.

"What is this?" she pointed to the wagon.

Kash brushed past her and jumped up into the wagon then motioned for her tote. Automatically she handed it to him. "This," he waved eloquently, "is your carriage, madam, and our transportation to the nearest railway station where we will take a train into Peiping." He beckoned for her to board, but she stood her ground, eyeing distastefully the rickety wagon. Bennett stared her down and spoke sternly. "Stop putting that nose of yours up in the air and get your fanny up here or we'll miss the train. It's at least two hours to the station. So, come on."

Leslie gave an indignant shake of her head and walked to the rear end of the wagon, remembering all the while the seemingly better accommodations arranged by World Magazine, and wondering what went wrong. Easy, Kash Bennett, she reminded herself as she angrily flung her briefcase at him and climbed aboard. A quick inspection showed old, wet hay, a pitchfork, and from the smell, manure.

Casually Kash dropped the case next to the others and then slid down on a pile of fresh hay. He then watched as Leslie picked her seat, literally. The splinter that had earlier caused such discomfort was easily extracted and discarded.

Now, if only she could do the same with Kash Bennett, she thought to herself. She looked around, trying to decide where to sit, and she figured where she was standing was as good as anywhere. It looked soft and safe. The hay wasn't exactly fresh, but it wasn't wet either, and it provided a safe margin of distance between her and Kash. In trying to become more comfortable she placed her hand into something mushy, and her face contorted into squeamish agony. "Oh, shit!" she groaned.

That's what it was. Once more, she removed her handkerchief and wiped her hand, carefully cleaning under the nails. She heard Kash's reaction, a boisterous laugh, and unexpectedly she threw the soiled material at him, hitting him square in the face. She squealed with delight at catching him off guard, and then held on as the wagon lurched forward and headed for the railway station.

Their wagon was the fourth and final to pull away. Leslie leaned forward and surveyed the countryside, recognizing many of the crops growing—wheat, corn and cotton.

The beginning of the fall harvest was taking place and the farmers were working diligently with their oxen and donkeys to bring in the crops. Along the road were several overloaded wagons drawn by donkeys and guided by frail looking farmers.

Leslie looked past the fields to the distant mountain ranges, their majestic peaks varied in size and shape, but all capped with the white of snow. She took in a deep breath and wished she hadn't. The squeal and smell told her they were fast approaching a pig farm, but the snort she heard wasn't from any pig, but rather, from a sleeping Kash Bennett. Like any child, he was able to sleep anywhere, anytime, she mused and leaned back to rest her own eyes.

The whistle blew and the train pulled to a stop at the platform. There were very few passengers on the train, allowing Kash and Leslie to disembark *quickly. By the time they had stepped off the train, their luggage had been unloaded and placed on a two wheeled jinrikisha.*

An older, slightly stooped porter approached Kash and gave a friendly nod. The smile he wore seemed permanent, but it was genuine. "Hotel?" he asked.

"Imperial," chimed Leslie.

The porter turned to her, caught off guard by her answering a question directed at Kash, but still his smile was pleasant when he acknowledged her response. A quick wave to the Pullman and Leslie watched in quiet panic as their bags disappeared quickly out of the station.

"He will meet you at the Imperial," the porter said, noting her concerned expression. Then he motioned for them to board the second jinrikisha.

Kash, who had earlier ignored his partner to the fullest, was suddenly very attentive—helping her board and then taking his place next to her. A deep throated giggle erupted from Leslie at their hasty start and she struggled to gain control of her windswept hat. Kash broke the stern line of his lips and allowed a small smile at her reaction and he firmly pushed the hat down onto her head. Their smiles faded as they became entranced with their new surroundings.

CHAPTER EIGHTEEN

Kash didn't have to fumble with the wall trying to locate the light switch, instead he left that to the English bellhop. No sooner was the door open, the light sprang to life, revealing a suite similar to Leslie's in San Francisco.

The bellhop pushed the luggage cart into the small hallway and unloaded the cases. Leslie brushed past Kash and the bellhop and inspected the living room. Tastefully decorated in rich cherry wood furniture and a complimentary vase full of freshly cut flowers added a welcomed sweet fragrance to her new home away from home for the next ten days.

She retraced her steps and watched Kash gather his belongings and walk briskly past her. He disappeared into a room and noisily dropped the cases. Curious, Leslie made her way to the doorway and leaned against the jamb and examined his quarters. Nothing special, she noted.

Kash picked up and tossed his bags onto the bed, and as before, he marched past her without uttering a single syllable. She hung her head in disbelief. One minute he was mad, then glad, then mad again. No wonder she was exhausted, she reasoned, Kash Bennett was like a faucet. Hot, then cold.

Faucet? Hot? Cold? A low sigh escaped her lips and she set out to find the bathroom, and a leisurely hot bath. She entered her bedroom, only to find it was a replica of Bennett's. A flick of the wrist sent her fedora sailing onto the dark blue spread of her bed. She tried the door handle nearest her and swung it open to find Kash, well...

"Do you mind?" he growled over his shoulder, irritated by her intrusion.

Color flushed her cheeks and she turned away quickly and shut the door, but she still could hear his grumbling as she walked away, leaving him in peace to finish his business. "Serves him right," she mused.

Loud, off key whistling assaulted Leslie's senses and rudely interrupted what was a peaceful slumber. Rolling over she pulled the covers up over her head and tried to block out the offensive sound.

Kash Bennett lightly stroked the beginnings of a new mustache. As he studied the new growth, the whistling stopped. He was pleased with the progress; the whiskers were short and sticky, but by the end of the trip, the mustache would be in full bloom. Using his tongue, he pushed out the purplish mark under his lower lip and rubbed it gently, hoping it would fade soon. "No after shave today," he told himself. After a quick inspection, he turned on heel, ripped open the door connecting to Leslie's room and let it slam against the wall.

Her eyes flew open and after a brief moment she finally let out a held breath. Bennett's voice was intentionally loud and harsh as he kicked the bed. "Rise and shine. We have a meeting in forty-five minutes, and I know how women are about getting ready in the morning. Of course, that might not apply to you."

Leslie yanked the covers down and stared at him through sleep laden eyes. He wanted to smile, but resisted the temptation. He knew he would love the sight of her in the morning. Her dark hair tousled, lips puckered and eyes dreamy from sleep. That alone caused his loins to tighten and he sucked in his gut hoping to control the urge that was building.

Leslie provided the rest of the control for him. With all the speed and enthusiasm of a snail, she crawled out of bed and headed for the bathroom. Her childish pout was laced with a look of despise and she slammed the door on him and his male urge.

CHAPTER NINETEEN

Exactly seventy minutes after leaving her San Francisco home, Elaine pulled into the driveway of a colleague in Bodega Bay. Charlie Warner was an architect, specializing in renovation of and development of the three E's; exclusive, expensive and eclectic hotels, spas and lodges in northern California.

His home base was Bodega Bay, and it was there that Elaine tethered her Waco Sea Plane, and on occasions, since her impending divorce, she was squired about by Mr. Warner sampling some of the finest resorts and lodges northern California had to offer.

She brought the powerfully built engine of the Cobra to a halt. She closed her eyes and took in a deep cleansing breath of sea air before Charlie Warner graciously opened her door, surprising the hell out of her. "Aaahh," she shouted at his gentlemanly gesture.

"Sorry," he said, jumping back at her reaction.

"My fault," she offered. "I've been up all night with worry and I guess I'm a little jumpy, that's all." She took his extended hand and unfolded her length from the Cobra. A quick stretch did wonders for her cramped muscles and joints.

None-the-less, Charlie admired her early morning grace. It was just too bad she had never taken him up on his many invitations to stay at his place. He knew she knew that he was the consummate playboy, and that was probably reason enough for her to politely decline his advances. Where Jack was ruggedly handsome, Charlie was just downright pretty. He rivaled Elaine for who had the more patrician features. Somehow it looked better on Elaine.

Elaine tossed the keys to her precious car to Charlie and then gathered her stuff. Charlie gave a wry smile as he eyed the keys and then the car. "I trust you," Elaine said as she made her way past him.

"Really?"

"With my car? Yes."

"I've got coffee," he said walking after her.

"To go?"

"If you wish. I was hoping we could visit, but under the circumstances, I'm sure you want to be under way. Any idea on when you'll return?" Charlie asked as he lovingly thumbed the keys to the Cobra.

"No idea. Did you get everything ready?" She asked over her shoulder as she made her way to her plane.

"Yes. The plane's ready and so is your so-called flight plan."

She gave him a warning not to start with her and her "plan" in finding her folks. He was there for moral support and that was all. "We've already had this conversation. How about that coffee?"

"Coming right up. You need help loading?" He asked as he made his way up the dock to his home.

"Since you're getting coffee, no," she called after him, a smile creasing her dimples.

She stowed her gear and in the 1931 Waco QCF-2. Like her Cobra, the Waco F-2 was a beauty and only recently had she been able to enjoy it fully. After acquiring it at an estate auction, Elaine knew by the looks of it that the plane needed a lot tender loving care and restoration before it would be safe to fly. She worked alongside her father and Charlie's father, Buzz Warner, as the Waco F-2 underwent a comprehensive rebuild. From remanufacturing the airframe to restoring the original instruments, the F-2 was completely overhauled to bring it back to its original luster and prestige. Of course Kash insisted on newer features like a 5 point harness for the front and rear seats, a Modern GPS/COM Transponder, all new electrical, brakes, pontoons and a computerized fuel monitor. All of this to keep his little girl safe, Elaine recalled, and oddly enough it was some of the same equipment he put on his own Waco Sea Plane.

She bit back the urge to cry all over again. She chastised herself, for she couldn't remember the last time she shed so many tears. Well, yes she could, and she had left him sleeping in Kash and Leslie's bed. She lovingly remembered his sleeping form earlier that morning. His mouth slightly open and the small snore that he emitted during his deepest of sleep. Strange how that little annoyance never bothered her. It was during his waking hours that Jack Phillips drove her totally insane. His need to control and her need to be in control was always going to be a stumbling block in their relationship. She was surprised their marriage had lasted as long as it had, and that was probably because they had miraculously kept busy with their own careers. Elaine, now knowing what she was married to, thought it was any small wonder she wasn't a widow. *Hum,* she thought to herself, *he must be good at it.* Or lucky. Her mind was treading in dangerous waters when a life preserver was tossed her direction, interrupting her thoughts.

"Your coffee, my dear," drawled a pleasant voice behind her.

She turned to face the hazel eyes of Charlie Warner. He was devastatingly handsome with the sun shining in his blonde hair and the morning light creating a prism of color in his fun loving expression. "Thank you," she said in a breathy tone she didn't recognize. She took a quick sip of the brew to stifle any potential embarrassing moments. "Um, good. Thank you, again Charlie for all you've done in prepping the plane. As soon as I find out anything useful, I'll call you."

She handed him the travel mug while she climbed aboard and strapped into the 5 point harness that her father insisted she install. Safely in place, she took the travel cup and placed it between her thighs. Its warmth was oddly comforting. Within a few minutes the chilly morning air was going to be piercing her very core. She gave a wave to Charlie below and then let the turquoise and indigo Waco turn towards its destination—Vancouver Island and the city of Victoria.

The Indian Chopper rumbled through the peaceful stretch that Highway 1 provided its travelers on its way to wherever Elaine was holed up. Jack wasn't happy about having to use this mode of transportation, but Elaine left him no choice. A shot up Biscayne was too noticeable and this wasn't any less conspicuous, but it was all he had in a hurry when he verified she wasn't anywhere to be found.

He pulled out his PDA and checked the status of her GPS; she was still in the same place; Bodega Bay. The exact coordinates would be available in about five minutes. He gave the motorcycle an extra tweak of gas and it responded by settling him deeper into the riders seat. He let the beast carry him towards what he was sure was a disaster in the making.

Charlie Warner ran a soothing hand over the Shelby Cobra and only imagined the kinds of comments and looks he was going to be receiving when he took it into town later that morning. His thoughts were interrupted by a motorcycle gearing down and coming to a smooth halt next to him. He examined the rider and knew immediately who he was.

"Mr. Phillips, I've been expecting you," he greeted and extended a hand to Jack.

Jack turned off the cycle and threw the kick stand down into place. He easily extricated himself from the chopper and handed the keys to Charlie. "Now, exactly when did she leave?"

"She's going to kill me for telling you," Charlie said, thumbing the keys, just as he had earlier with the Shelby's set.

"Look at it this way," Jack said, glancing at Elaine's muscle, "You'll get more opportunities than you could have ever imagined. Now, when and where did she go, Charlie?"

"Ten minutes ago, to Victoria," he replied without hesitation. "I suppose you want a ride to the air field for a quick trip to Victoria?"

"I take it you've arranged that?"

"Yes. Shall we take Shelby?"

"It's what Elaine would want," Jack replied with tongue in cheek. He got his gear from the saddlebag on the chopper and jumped into the passenger's seat.

A burst of power and the car slid sideways leaving Charlie's driveway. There wasn't any conversation as Charlie concentrated on maneuvering the Cobra through the twists and turns of the back road that lead from his home to the air field where a plane was waiting to take Jack to Victoria. He barely had time to breathe in the freshness of the Douglas Firs that lined the road before the high pitched whine of a motorcycle interrupted his lovely drive.

Jack snapped his head from his PDA to the sound and knew immediately the closing cycle was not taking a leisurely ride through the back roads of Bodega Bay. He watched as the cycle quickly closed the distance and it was on the left back quarter panel of the Cobra as he grabbed the wheel and turned the Shelby hard left into the path of the cycle.

A shocked Charlie instinctively let go of the wheel, let off the gas and geared the beast down as the car swerved and Jack struggled to keep it under control.

"Gas!" Jack screamed at Charlie. "Give it gas!"

Charlie snapped to and punched the Cobra's 427 engine. The spinning tires caught and crushed the unsuspecting wildflowers that lined the road. The wheels finally grabbed and lurched the car forward. While Charlie took control of the wheel and ran through the gears, Jack pulled from his duffel bag his Sig Sauer P229. As if he did this in his sleep, he checked the clip, snapped it back in place, chambered a round and flipped off the safety. A quick look over his shoulder revealed the motorcycle was righted and gaining.

Jack also knew there wasn't going to be just that one cycle. "Steady, Charlie. Keep me steady," Jack ordered and took a firm aim at the front tire of the motorcycle. One shot, one destroyed wheel. The cycle tripped and went down with its rider. Jack didn't bother observing the chaos, he caught sight of the trouble ahead; two Kawasaki Ninja ZX-14's were oncoming, in his lane. How appropriate the cycles matched their riders. They blended perfectly with their sleek machines; clad in black leather and full faced helmets with black face masks.

"Stay the course, Charlie. Don't flinch," Jack barked as he readied himself to take out the bikes and their riders.

As the riders got closer they rose off their tanks and pulled out two different types of weapons—one Glock and one throwing star. The cycles started to split, and the one on Charlie's left threw the star, and at the same time the rider on the right didn't get a chance to fire his Glock; Jack fired two rounds from his Sig, both through the face mask, jettisoning the rider from his bike and sending the cycle careening into and over the Shelby Cobra.

Charlie strained to keep the car on track, his right shoulder leeching blood over the handmade leather driver's seat. Jack didn't have a chance to check on his condition as he turned to see the second ZX-14 screech and turn around to pursue the Cobra. The throwing star had momentarily given him time to reverse his course and start his pursuit again as Charlie was desperately tried to staunch the blood and keep the car from plowing off the road into the thick woods.

It didn't take the cyclist long to catch up, and like his riding companion, he pulled a Glock and started firing rounds at the Cobra. The trunk reflected the skill of the pursuer, and with the same precision as before, Jack took aim and fired until his clip was empty and the rider was down along with his ride.

Charlie waited for Jack to give him the all clear before he brought the Cobra to a screeching halt, sending an unsuspecting Jack into the dash. An irritated look was replaced with one of concern as Jack took over and checked out Charlie's injury. He yanked a t-shirt from his duffel and then pulled out the throwing star from Charlie's shoulder. Applying pressure with the shirt, Jack threw the star into his duffel for future use, because he knew Slim would be sending more men.

Revenge was a strong motivator, and at the moment that was all Slim had since Jack had effectively compromised Slim's elaborate money laundering operation in New York. The only one to escape was Slim. Finding him in San Francisco was dumb luck, and then that was interrupted by the presence of Elaine.

No doubt Slim would seek shelter in the old country, but unfortunately with today's communication devices, he was surely to stay on top of his splintered empire. Money laundering for terrorists was just one of Slim's many diabolical operations, and probably the most dangerous and threatening to the country as a whole, but his latest foray into designer drugs from opium caused Jack great concern. Jack hadn't been able to pinpoint a supply, but his gut and certain intelligence told him Slim and his organization were placing twice the amount of exotic drugs and pocketing four times the money. He was hoping last night's venture in San Francisco would have yielded a least a sample of the new cocktail, but instead he and his Chinese counterpart, Shan Lin, found Elaine and that damn pendant.

A turn of the key extinguished the Cobra's engine and Jack got out and walked to the driver's side. He opened the door and assisted Charlie to the passenger's seat. As quickly as he killed the engine, he brought it back to life and peeled off to the airfield and his scheduled flight to Victoria and a rendezvous with Elaine and the new problem she has brought into his life.

CHAPTER TWENTY

Elaine silently cursed her choice to fly her open-air cockpit Waco plane to Victoria. The ride was going to be a slow and exhausting process. The slight head wind had turned into a crosswind and keeping the plane on course with the stick was proving to be bigger challenge than she wanted to face. However, the biggest hurdle was her lack of sleep. Her adrenaline had ebbed and flowed so much in the last few days that her body was now seeking its natural course, pushing for her to relinquish to sleep, but every time she felt herself giving in, she took a sip of Charlie's coffee. The Blue Mountain blend had enough kick to help her maintain her focus, and after each sip, she would suck in a deep, cleansing breath of cool salt air for extra measure.

Surely if she concentrated on the journals written by her parents, she would be able to stay awake and learn more about their clandestine lives, and somehow find a clue as to where they might be. She kept the stick level between her legs and pulled free her Palm Pilot. Earlier, she had scanned the journals and loaded them for easy access. Steadying the plane, she did the same for her feelings and read about Kash and Leslie's arrival in the Forbidden City.

CHINA, 1947

The receptionist's crowning glory reminded Kash of fudge swirl ice cream. A commotion of brown and white was twisted so tightly into a knot on top of her head, that Kash just knew she wouldn't have that first wrinkle. Only after he purposely cleared his throat, did the receptionist lift her head, causing him to ease back on his heels from his earlier intrusive stance. Slowly she raised her head and acknowledged their presence with a polished and genuinely fake smile. Kash returned the favor, and smiled inwardly at her flawless complexion.

When she finally spoke, her tone was stern and her English precise. All that was missing was the pointer clutched in her hand and poised to strike the knuckles of those that dared to be unruly. "May I help you?" she managed, not at all changing her pristine expression.

"We have an appointment with Mr. Bryant at ten o'clock," Kash replied with sugary sweetness.

Enough so, Leslie was sure she could feel a cavity developing. She and Kash waited patiently while the receptionist located their appointment in the daily log.

"Wait here and I will announce your arrival to Mr. Bryant," she instructed coolly.

She headed down the corridor, much in the same fashion as Leslie had earlier in the morning. Kash turned and found his highly trained and refined art journalist mocking the surly woman and he playfully scorned her effort, shaking a shameful finger in her direction.

"What? I was only doing what you were thinking," she defended.

"I was not," he countered.

"Oh, yes, you were," she teased.

"She's a crusty old Brit with very little personality and a weird hairdo."

"Hum. She probably learned to be that way from some crusty old photojournalist. Anyway, not all Brits are like her; the majority are sweet and sensitive, with a marvelous sense of humor."

She paused and watched him close the distance between them, and annoyingly he pushed her hat back. His hooded gaze licked over her outwardly composed features, while inwardly her stomach tumbled and pressed hard against her backbone, trying its best to shrink away from his intimate stare.

"You must be of German descent," she guessed, breaking the tension he had created.

Before he could respond, the lady he was sure was a former drill instructor, returned. "Mr. Bryant will see you now. Please follow me."

Gerald Bryant turned away from the window in his office as the door opened, and he watched as the receptionist extended a hand for Kash and Leslie to enter. After they crossed the threshold, she nodded to Bryant and promptly left the room.

Leslie took in a shaky breath as Gerald Bryant walked around his desk to greet Kash. They exchanged hearty handshakes and pleasantries, and then Kash turned to Leslie and motioned for her to join him.

Gerald showed only a trace of surprise when Leslie stepped forward and before Kash could introduce her, she and Gerald were embracing. Bryant took a step back and looked her over. Not much had changed in the two years in which he had last seen her, except for her attire. Still the porcelain features of a China doll, but the overwhelming stature of a jungle Amazon. A combination that both frightened and exhilarated him at the same time.

Leslie in turn took a brief moment to view the man Mark had regarded as his best mate—Gerald Allen Bryant. His boyish good looks were still intact, and his light brown hair that was streaked with blonde still invited fingers to rake through it, and Leslie couldn't resist stroking back into place a lock that had fallen across his forehead.

Unconcerned about the thoughts of anyone else in the room, she let her fingers trail lightly down his unblemished cheek, and prompted him to break into a wide smile, displaying his straight, white teeth and dimples that matched her own. And those eyes--sapphire blue, deep and lusty. They twinkled with delight at her display of affection. His deep, rich voice brought her back to earth.

"Leslie," he cooed, as he looked over her suit. "New look?"

All she could manage was a small smile.

"It suits you. No pun intended. You're still as lovely as ever."

She finally found her voice. "Thank you. The years certainly haven't dimmed your good looks, or your charm."

The line between Kash Bennett's brows deepened as he watched their affectionate display. "Apparently you two know each other."

"Know?" Leslie repeated. "I guess you could say that."

"Forgive me for my lack of manners," Gerald smiled, and looked past Kash to the darkened corner of the office, and beckoned for someone to come out of the shadows.

Kash and Leslie immediately took notice of an attractive blonde that stepped forward and stood at Gerald's side, where he formally introduced her. "Kash Bennett, Leslie Scott, may I introduce my assistant, Alicia Cameron."

She gave Leslie's hand a firm, no-nonsense shake, but delicately offered her hand to Kash, letting her gaze linger. "How do you do?" she purred in a husky voice.

"Nicely, thank you," he replied with velvety softness.

After what seemed to be a lifetime to Leslie, Kash finally released Alicia's hand, but still held her captive with his brooding gray gaze. Unlike Leslie, Alicia was small boned, but nonetheless, she still possessed a very ample and shapely figure. Her features weren't striking, but rather sweet, almost innocent. Warm brown eyes that held a hint of mischief, a turned up nose and a delicate mouth that was more than capable of seduction. Her shoulder length hair was carefully styled to accent her sweet heart-shaped face.

It was Leslie who broke the deafening silence. "So, Gerald, how long have you been the British Attaché in China?" she asked, shifting her attention from Alicia to the business at hand. She only hoped Kash would get the hint and do the same.

"I'm afraid not long enough," he answered, directing them to the chairs in front of his desk. "Please, be seated."

Kash and Leslie settled into round-back chairs, while Gerald perched himself on the edge of his desk and Alicia took her position behind Kash.

"Before we start, would you care for some coffee or tea?" Gerald offered.

"Black coffee would be nice," Kash accepted. "Thank you."

"Do you still take your tea the same way, Leslie?" Gerald inquired.

"Yes, thank you."

"One black coffee for Mr. Bennett and one tea with a little honey and a smidgen of cream for Mrs. Scott," Gerald instructed Alicia.

A sharp glare came from Kash upon hearing "Mrs." Scott. Leslie sensed his stare and ignored it, knowing full well he would ask later.

Standing at the door, Alicia looked to Gerald and asked, "Anything for you, Mr. Bryant?" Gerald shook his head and she excused herself.

Unbuttoning his jacket, Gerald relaxed and soaked up the sight of Leslie. "Your first trip to China, Leslie?" he asked, and she gave an affirmative nod. "Well, it's absolutely enchanting, and in its own way, very romantic." Not wanting to exclude Kash, Gerald turned his attention to the sullen figure seated next to Leslie. "And how about you, Bennett? You seem like a chap that's been about."

"A bit," Kash admitted, and looked at Leslie's sharp profile. "Apparently so has someone else." He left it at that, and looked back at Bryant. "What exactly is our purpose for being here?" he inquired strongly and to the point.

Alicia returned, thankfully, giving Gerald a moment to think out his answer to Bennett's direct question. Placing the tray on the coffee table, Alicia handed Leslie her tea and Kash his coffee.

"Actually, it's more diplomatic than anything," Gerald began. "With

the sudden influx of Russia and its imposing Communistic views, our government, and yours, think it is best to keep good diplomatic ties with the Chinese. It seems inevitable that Russia will have her way and Communism will find a place in China. So, naturally, we want to keep open the lines of communication with a country that has potential to become a powerful force, both culturally and economically."

Kash graciously listened to Gerald's politically motivated explanation and then asked, "So, when do we start our little end of the crunch?"

"That's a rather cynical way of looking at the situation, isn't it, Mr. Bennett?" Alicia noted a lilt of concern in her voice.

"Call me Kash, please," he quickly insisted. "Cynical, but honest. The ultimate chess game; the British on one side, with its white king and queen, the U.S. flanking the other side with its white knight, and Russia looming largely with her black rook. Dare the pawn, or China in this case, make the wrong move, since we know of all the pieces mentioned, the least valued and most expendable is the pawn." He finished his piece, but he knew that through only politeness he was allowed to express what he felt, and most certainly his comments would be forgotten by day's end, and they would still proceed with their end of the crunch.

"Do you play chess, Kash?" Alicia asked, emphasizing his first name.

"Of a different sort," he replied.

"Not like you to be so quiet, Leslie," Gerald observed, changing the subject.

She shrugged her shoulders. "I've only been here one day. That hardly qualifies me as an expert on the subject."

"Well, we'll have to do something about that, won't we?" Gerald's eyes twinkled madly at the insinuation of having fun, and especially with Leslie. "Alicia and I have a staff meeting that will last through the luncheon hour, then the afternoon is free. Why don't we meet you in the lobby of the Imperial at one-thirty and acquaint you with Peiping?"

Leslie darted a glance at Kash and he gave a curt nod of agreement. "Okay, you're on," she accepted.

Kash and Leslie followed Gerald and Alicia to the door and bade good bye.

CHAPTER TWENTY-ONE

The streets of Peiping were crowded with different types of people, much like New York and San Francisco, but the traffic was certainly in contrast to that back in the States, Leslie noted. Bicycles and jinrikisha took the place of cars and taxis. There were numerous buses and a handful of cars, mostly belonging to the government officials and foreign dignitaries, such as the British. Still many of the citizens transported themselves by walking.

Kash stayed about a step or two behind Leslie since leaving the British consulate and had enjoyed watching her reaction to the different types of street people of Peiping. What difference did they know, he argued. They thought because she was dressed in a man's suit that she was fair game, and it was obvious to him that she had no idea that she was a marked woman, so to speak. It would dawn on her sooner or later, but for the moment, he was going to enjoy watching the marked woman.

The line between his brows deepened when he thought of the marked woman as actually a married woman. Suddenly there wasn't as much enjoyment watching her, knowing she belonged to someone else, but something about her compelled him to continue his harmless observation. Maybe it was revenge, he thought, for her not telling him she was married.

Leslie frowned at the curious young women who had approached her on several occasions, then once again. They were chattering wildly in Chinese and feeling about her arms and shoulders intimately. Then it dawned on her, and with a definite shake of her head and stern glare, she sent them away.

She quickly dismissed the incidents and Kash Bennett's wide, astute smile, and studied the interesting combination of people surviving on the streets. On just about every street corner and alley opening, prostitutes and beggars could be found, and the opium dealing could easily be spotted, even to the amateur eye. Unlike New York, where the dealing was done behind closed doors, this was blatant and up front, cloaked for no one in particular, just those who wanted it.

Tired of the back view, Kash extended his stride and easily caught up and pulled level with Leslie. She gave a quick sidelong glance, and then concentrated straight ahead on nothing in particular.

"So, Mrs. Scott," he said, emphasizing the Mrs. "Would you care to do a little unofficial sightseeing or shopping before the official tour starts at one-thirty?"

They reached their hotel and Leslie paused outside of the entrance. Her look held no contempt and certainly no surprise at his emphasis on Mrs. She had fully expected that his curiosity would get the better of him and she didn't blame him for his round-about approach. "Thanks, but no. I think I'll go up to the room and start reading up on one of the oldest forms of art," she explained, hoping he'd understand and leave it at that.

"What, Egyptian?" Kash teased.

That brought a heart-warming smile to her face and relief to his. They waved goodbye and he watched her retreating back and shook his head at the twisting knot in his stomach. It was easy as hell to like her as it was to dislike her, but above all, easier to desire her, married or not.

He continued in the direction they were headed before Leslie abandoned ship at the Imperial. Around him he noticed the popular colors for dress were gray, black and white, all in tunic style topes and baggy pants. There weren't too many business suits in the streets of Peiping and he knew that the two men following him had made the mistake of wearing western wear, and that sooner rather than later he would know the reason for them trailing him and Leslie.

CHAPTER TWENTY-TWO

"Mrs. Scott, indeed," Elaine blurted out to the chilly wind; like it cared. Any evidence of being sleepy was erased as she read her mother and father's account of their meeting with Gerald Bryant in Peiping.

Elaine closed the Palm Pilot and let the news of her mother's first marriage sink in further than it did in the earlier reading of her Leslie's account of how her husband had perished in a car blast. Where did Elaine start in trying to understand and comprehend what she had recently read? Was her mind misfiring on connecting the dots where her mother's first marriage was concerned, or was it her heart not wanting to believe there was another Leslie had shared a part of her soul with before Kash?

She knew the answer to that question. "Poor, Daddy," she whispered to herself. "I can only imagine how you felt upon hearing that news." She took a moment and remembered her own husband and his tiny betrayal, and the funny thing is it wasn't another woman; it was his job. How he hid in plain sight for the entire length of their marriage, she didn't know, but then again, he had good teachers—Kash and Leslie.

She stopped feeling sorry for her father and considered her mother— Leslie, the reserved and precise matron of their family. When things went slightly south in Elaine's life, she clung to the quiet strength of her mother. It was a constant, and now when she needed that resolve, she had to look to herself and see if she had inherited that part of her mother she admired the most. It was one thing to look like your parents, another to reflect their character, their morals and their values. If Leslie had done her job, which Elaine knew she had, those traits and all others Leslie loved and admonished about her daughter would come to the surface and help her find her parents.

She also knew that if Kash and Leslie were in danger, they knew from their former training, they could find a way to help themselves and aid indirectly their daughter and everyone else searching for them. Even though they were in good shape, they weren't spring chickens anymore and that worried Elaine. As physically fit as she was, she could understand the stress taking its toll. But, then again, they were spies, and she was sure their resilience was tenfold. Still, she felt anxious for them.

Elaine thought back to how old her mother was during her first marriage; she was merely eighteen or nineteen. "You would have had my head if I had married that young," Elaine told her mother's memory. She smiled and allowed her mother to have her youthful love, because Leslie may have been critical of others at times, but she never judged their actions, especially those of her daughter's.

"I'll find you, I promise," Elaine choked out. "And then, you've got some explaining to do. Both of you." As quickly as the tears dropped, the cool air dried them and she made her final approach to Victoria, British Columbia.

James Bay in Victoria was home away from home for Kash and Leslie. They loved spending as much time in the capital city of British Columbia as they did in San Francisco, so their Victorian home in James Bay was always open and ready for occupancy and company.

Elaine easily spotted her second home on approach and guided her Waco sea plane past the 2500 foot breakwater that jutted out from the seawall and gently touched down in Victoria Harbour. She idled into a slip off of Wharf Street and was tied off for safety before she unbuckled and gingerly crawled out of the cockpit. She called over her shoulder to the attendant, "Top it off, please, and put it on my account." A curt nod of acknowledgment came her way.

It had been a long, arduous flight and the sight of their Victorian home and the smell of the activities only Wharf Street could offer brought relaxation to Elaine's weary self. She pulled free her small duffel bag and headed for her favorite haunt and a plate of their specialty—hot fish and chips. It was a tradition for Elaine that when she flew into Victoria and before she went home, she would stop for fish and chips and a crisp beer to wash them down.

It didn't take but a moment for Elaine to know she was nearly home when she opened the heavy formed glass paneled door to The Artesian Pub. The sounds and the smells enveloped her and welcomed her like the long-lost friend she was. A weary smile played on her lips as she made her way to the distressed maple bar with its fire engine red fused glass top. Droplets of water littered the surface and Elaine wiped a spot clean at the end of the bar.

The thud of her duffel bag hitting the plank flooring announced her presence to the bar maid and owner of the joint, Bailey Williams. A buxom woman, Bailey turned to Elaine and let out a snort reserved for only her finest of clientele. "About time you showed your sorry ass," she greeted and then went back to putting away freshly scrubbed glasses. "What do you want?" she asked, turning around and wiping her hands on the end of her apron.

"Want or need?" Elaine wearily answered.

"The need you've already had," Bailey said with a wink.

It brought a curious tilt of the head from Elaine and before she could say what she wanted, it slid across the bar and stopped smoothly in front of her. The Triple Bach sloshed only slightly in its frosted container and without hesitation; Elaine seized it and let the cold brew slid down her throat. Every time she drank Bailey's draft, it took her back to her teenage years, and sitting around in a circle with Nana Bennett, her good friends Minnie and Coatney, and their homemade bucket of beer. The community jar was always cold and the brew smooth and delicious. Not at all pungent, but sweet and full, like her Nana Bennett.

Her Nana was the best thing about those awkward years. Her San Francisco home was like her heart, always open and full of love. Nana Bennett was very much like her mother, only a little more relaxed and not quite as critical, but as Elaine knew from her father, his mother had been the original mold from which Leslie was cut. Opposites attract and that's probably why she and Nana always clicked. Much like Elaine and her mother had in recent years.

Elaine swallowed some more of her beer and with it, bitter memories of letting time slip by without engaging more quality moments with her mother. It was always so easy to be with her father. But her mother; she could never understand the need for the precision, the sometimes self-righteous manner that her mother lived her life, but when Elaine needed a point in the right direction, Leslie was more than happy to oblige. For a moment she lingered on that thought; whose compass would she use to find her parents now?

Any more thoughts of finding her missing parents were put on hold as Bailey laid before her a basket filled with freshly made fish and chips. The smell wafted up and reminded Elaine just how hungry she was and why this place was always her first stop in her second home town.

"Hmm, these are so good," she managed with a full mouth. "Oh, these hushpuppies. I love how you use caramelized shallots," she complimented as she licked her fingers and then dove into the fish, savoring their freshness. "Nothing so good."

"Except sex," Bailey countered with a wink, prompting another peculiar look from Elaine. "So, what brings you back home?" Bailey asked, changing the subject. Her sapphire blue eyes were burning with a curious desire to know why Elaine was back in Victoria so soon after her last visit.

Elaine swallowed and then wiped her mouth to give her enough time to think of an excuse as to why she was back in Victoria. "Mom and Dad forgot to clean up some loose ends, so I'm here to tidy up," she explained and then stuffed some more of the lightly battered fish into her mouth, enjoying the delicious concoction.

A new patron thankfully took Bailey to another part of the bar and Elaine slowed the consumption of her fish and chips. Taking a slow swig of her beer, she looked around the bar and noted nothing had changed since opening day.

As a favor to her good friend, Bailey, Elaine consulted with the local architect in transforming The Artesian Bar. The Artesian went from an abandoned waterfront cannery, with broken trundle windows, a leaky tin roof and a crumbling facade to what stood today; a traditionally sound brick building with a bright red corrugated metal roof and an interior that offered some of Victoria's finest artistic efforts.

The artistry started outside; before patrons set one foot inside, they were treated to the splendor of Victoria captured in stained glass in the three massive roof peaks. The middle peak was fall in all her glory. Rich crimsons, golden yellows and ponderosa pines lined the ripple-free blue lake, and like nature, the inverted triangle above the double doors reflected perfectly the image of the trees and lake. The right peak showed the flowering Dogwoods, their white and pink blossoms announcing spring and ushering in summer. The left peak captured the snowy crest of Whistler Mountain. Above the four stationary restaurant windows were rectangular transoms that showed off Canada's national symbol, a variety of colorful maple leaves.

The outside was rivaled only by the inside; the double doors opened into a cornucopia of glass, polished stainless steel and distressed maple. Two clear and formed fountains, shaped like a peak from Whistler Mountain, were on either side of the entrance. Their royal blue water continuously traversed valleys from the top of the mountain to the bottom where chunks of clear glass protruded and made the smooth water ripple and toss as nature had intended it to. Coins littered the bottom, twinkling from the eyeball lights beneath the clear fountain pond.

A curved wall of clear glass, anchored between two columns of red maple housed the hostess station. The panel reflected the pattern of the front doors, a torrential thunderstorm of raindrops splattering the glass and leaving behind their distinct impressions. Bearing to either the right or the left, the patrons had a choice family style seating booths on the outside walls, or tables and chairs in the main dining area.

The reason for The Artesian's name was directly behind the curved wall of the hostess station, a natural artesian well that was used when the cannery was open. It wasn't a well to pull groundwater from; it was a natural water source from the nearby harbor. The cannery built a holding tank around the well for the daily catch. When they were ready to process the fish, they would pull them from the holding tank. The owners always insisted they had the freshest stock because of that tank. Fresh or not, the cannery eventually went out of business, and for the longest time, the building stood empty, decaying and ruining the overall beauty of Victoria.

Then Bailey bought it and brought her brand of eclectic style and charm to the dilapidated structure. First thing she did was preserve the artesian well and then she put a tubular glass column in the middle of the tank that almost reached the exposed ceiling joists. At the top, four primary color spot lights shone on the column and illuminated the spider web design of the glass. The same fountain effect from the mountain scenes in the front lobby were extended to the artesian tank.

Elaine loved walking up the spiral staircase that surrounded the holding tank and watching how the different colored lights made the webs look real. The blue water trickling over the webbed glass reminded her of a dewy summer morning; that time just before a spider's web was dismantled for the day.

She laughed to herself as she recalled Bailey's decision to have a good old fashioned Halloween party for kicks, and she had over one hundred spiders of different shapes and sizes all over the tube. The guests were a little freaked, but the party was a hit. Now it's an annual gig and Elaine never misses it.

Elaine glanced upwards toward the second level where a party was starting to pick up steam. The sights and sounds of the party were muffled by the frosted glass partitions that reflected the Inner Harbor and the grandiose of the Fairmont Empress hotel. She gave a forced smile as Bailey broke the ice, literally; and served up a glass of Bailey's on the rocks as a night cap for Elaine.

The liquid traced a smoldering trail down her throat and sank into her full belly; a sweet warm glow spread through her being. She swirled the glass, played with the ice, then looked to Bailey. "What's on your mind, Bailey? You want to ask me something, so ask."

"I was just curious about Jack. I thought it was over between you two and then he shows up for carry out and tells me what a nice time he had with you in San Francisco."

The glass stuck on Elaine's lip, as did the words on her tongue. "Jack was here? When?" She drained the rest of her drink and hastily fished out enough money to cover her visit.

Bailey waved it off and was boxing up the rest of Elaine's fish and chips for later. "He came in an hour or so ago. You literally just missed him. Is he headed to your house?"

"Yeah, probably," Elaine absentmindedly replied as she gathered her things and headed for door. "Thanks," she called over her shoulder as she left the restaurant.

She didn't know if it was the crisp night air or the fact that Jack was at Bailey's less than an hour ago that chilled her to the bone. She headed up the street to find a taxi to take her to Kash and Leslie's summer home in James Bay, and to what she was sure was a mess.

CHAPTER TWENTY-THREE

The mess started the moment Elaine stepped onto the covered front porch of Kash and Leslie's James Bay home. Her heart thudded loudly in her ears as she stared at the slightly open front door. She glanced over her shoulder and saw the street was eerily quiet, and the cab that dropped her off; it was long gone. "Shit!" she whispered loud enough for her own benefit.

With all the bravado she could muster, she kicked open the door and stood staring at the pitch black of the foyer. If she could have listened more intently she would have, but it was also delaying the inevitable—entering into the home. She threw her duffel in first to cause a distraction; nothing, and then she carefully stepped inside.

Bam! The door slammed shut and so did Elaine; right to the floor. The air left her lungs as the weight upon her shoulders and back pressed down and clasped her hands behind her back. She took the hint and stopped struggling. Her attacker understood it as a sign of submission and whispered in her ear, "Good girl. Now keep still and I'll let go."

Elaine nodded in compliance and he relaxed his hold. A moment later he was sorry as she threw her head back and butted him square in the face. She heard something crack and took full advantage of him being more concerned about his busted nose than for her.

Rolling off of her, Jack grabbed his face and shrieked over the pain in his nose and mouth. "Dod dammit, Delaine. I dink you broke my dose."

"What in the hell are you doing here? And how did you know I was going to be here?" she asked in a harsh whisper that hurt her throat.

He sent a bloody stream of spit to the floor and wiped his mouth with his sleeve. "Charlie," he answered. "I dnow Charlie," he sputtered.

"Did you just spit on the antique Persian rug? And how do you know Charlie?" she said in the same severe low voice.

"Des, and he's bun of us."

"One of you?" she asked, amazing she was interpreting his screwed up enunciation. "No he's not. He's an architect." She thought a moment. "And my father an archeologist and my mother an art journalist." She went to flip the light switch and Jack pulled her away and planted her against the wall.

"Doe! We've got to be careful."

"We need to fix your nose so I can understand you on your first attempt."

"Latder," he said.

"What exactly has happened here?" She asked listening to her intuition.

Jack pinched his nose and spoke more plainly. "I had a friend stop by to make sure things were okay, but someone was waiting and they mistook him," he stopped and chose his words carefully. "The kitchen is a little messy. We can't stay here much longer."

Elaine slumped, relying on Jack for support. "Is this because of what you do or what I found?"

"A little of both, I'm afraid. Look, Slim's grandfather is someone Kash and Leslie had several legendary run-ins with and I'm sure Slim's heard about these bigger than life stories from his grandfather, Tu An Lin."

"Legendary in your world, maybe, but not the one I live in." Finding her legs, she started to push away from his hold but he stood fast.

He ignored her bitter tone. "Yes and my world has put you in harm's way."

She waited for the apology she knew wasn't coming and he worked on rearranging his nose while still holding her firmly against the wall. "What exactly is in the kitchen, Jack, outside of a mess? Hopefully not Charlie."

"No, Charlie's back home nursing a stab wound."

"Stab wound?" she asked anxiously. "How did that happen?"

"He was driving me to the airfield and we encountered a little trouble," he glossed over the details of Charlie's injury and her car's subsequent damage.

"What was Charlie driving?"

"He's fine. He'll be okay. It was just a flesh wound," Jack explained with a silkiness reserved for only his finest of screw-ups.

"You fucked up my car didn't you, Jack?"

"You kiss your mother with that mouth?" He asked as he cautiously looked out the side light of the front door for anything out of the ordinary.

"You weren't complaining earlier when my mouth was on yours and other parts of your body, so don't make this about me. Why are you here?"

"To keep you out trouble."

"If only you'd look at me when you say that. I know better, Jack. It has something to do with what I found, and it's not just that pendant."

He finally gave her his hooded gaze and the mocking twitch at the corner of his mouth betrayed his guilt. That damn pouty mouth. She licked her lips instinctively and immediately regretted it when he smiled knowingly. "We need to head straight out the back door. Like right now," he instructed, putting out of his mind their earlier shared pleasure.

"That won't be hard, Jack, it's a shotgun house. Just turn around and head straight and you will find the back door." She turned him around and pointed to the back of the house.

"Stay close and don't look toward the kitchen area. I promise it'll be cleaned and back to normal," he whispered and padded quietly to the back.

Elaine watched for just a second, then opened the front door and slipped out. Like Stan, she was making a new plan and it didn't include Jack. She was over the fence and hidden in the deep ground cover and bushes of Mr. and Mrs. Jackson's lavishly landscaped yard.

She knew it took only moment for Jack to realize she wasn't dutifully following him, and it seemed like forever until he made his way past her hiding spot. Thankfully he was headed in the opposite direction of her intended course. If it was one thing Elaine had learned in the last few hours; Jack was skilled at tracking. Especially, women.

It was a chilly walk to the wharf and her tied up Waco Sea Plane. The pier lights cast long eerie shadows; the creepy kind that sent waves of goose bumps up and down one's warm flesh. Elaine took a deep breath to steady her frayed nerves as she sought out her plane. The pier was quiet except for the rustling of her jacket and constant lapping of water against her plane's pontoons.

As like countless times before, she stored her duffle bag; checked and rechecked her plane before gently untying and climbing into the cockpit. She was primed, then she fired up. Like Nook and Cranny, the engine purred and waited patiently for her to put on her headset, finish her preflight routine and then begin her taxi to take off. She throttled up and was pulling away from the wharf when a shrill cry of, "Go! Go! Go!" cut through the night air.

She looked over her right shoulder to find Jack running at full speed toward her plane. He was motioning for her to get going. It took only a moment for her to see why; someone was closing the distance, and the gun he had was enough encouragement for her to understand Jack's point. But, unlike a car, you couldn't slam the accelerator down on the ancient Waco. She carefully throttled up while keeping a watchful on Jack. Just as she moved away from the pier; he lunged for the plane and landed awkwardly on the right pontoon; causing the plane to lurch slightly, and as it gained speed, Jack bobbed up and down off the pontoon and sea surf.

He held on for dear life as Elaine adjusted for his weight and coaxed her "baby" to pick it up. As her mind was racing to get the plane and Jack up safely, she heard the fire cracking sound of gun fire; but more importantly, she heard the twang of metal being struck by metal. It was only one ding, but that was enough for her. She quickly pulled back and climbed while Jack dangled and then found the strength to pull himself onto the pontoon and get a better hold, if that was possible. For Elaine was swerving to and fro to keep anymore gunfire from finding her baby.

She was up and over the seawall and well on her way out to sea when she looked over her shoulder to the pier and Jack's unhappy pursuers. She leveled off and roughly yelled to Jack, "Get in."

She didn't have to tell him twice, as he deftly pulled himself into the front cockpit of her Waco. She gave him ample time to strap in before she climbed and barrel rolled them. To say he wasn't expecting that was an understatement. His fish and chips of earlier reappeared and narrowly missed his pilot. Of that, he was thankful. He knew the moment they landed, she was going to be loaded for bear; and he couldn't blame her.

However, she didn't wait until they landed, "Some fucking super hero you are!"

It was all she said; and had to say. He understood perfectly. He lowered himself into the seat, as if that would help, and tried to find a way to get out of the cold wind and her scorching glare.

CHAPTER TWENTY-FOUR

It was at least an hour to an hour and half before Elaine finally had a sense of feeling safe and out of harm's way. She didn't bother asking Jack who the insolent son-of-a-bitch was that dinged her "baby", but she was sure he was a close friend of Slim's. By the sound of the twang of the metal, the bullet passed through the rear of the pontoon and out the topside; missing any vital. Lucky her, she thought. It was about the only thought she was able to produce in the chilly headwind. She checked her flight log strapped to her leg, then to the Garmin GPSMAP 496. She did a quick calculation for the sake of keeping her wits about her and knew she was close to a family friend's private lake. The Shasta family had accommodated the Bennett clan on more than one occasion, and she was sure they wouldn't mind her dropping by at such an ungodly hour for a quick stop to refuel both her plane and psyche.

Using her instruments and double checking with the GPS, she glided her Waco to Shasta Lake, a tiny speck in the beautiful countryside of British Columbia. It was nestled between the Rainbow and Fawnie Ranges. It was a stone's throw from Tweedsmuir Provincial Park; a favorite when her life was less complicated and her cares were limited to only what trail she would hike or were her and her father would go fishing. Those days were forever ago, and before she could reminisce further she was fast approaching her destination, and because she was more concerned about her wounded pontoon, than her passenger, she gently glided her Waco down onto the crystal clear lake and throttled down to a small idle, just enough to make it to the dock, and then she cut the engine.

She rubbed her eyes and unbuckled her harness; methodically unstrapped her log and shut down the Waco for the evening. She gingerly stepped onto the pontoon and then onto the dock.

With the Waco secured she stepped onto the pontoon and assessed the damage. It was as she suspected; nothing to worry about and most certainly nothing that would impede her progress. Then she looked to the passenger cockpit; there sat her biggest imposition. He gave a pale smile of resignation and slowly unbuckled and gingerly got out of his cockpit; joining Elaine on the pontoon. He said nothing as he stepped onto the dock.

"Well," she started, "the damage is minimal and it shouldn't prevent safe travel. I'm not sure where the bullet careened to, but it didn't hit anything vital in the plane." She gathered her duffel bag and jumped onto the dock.

Jack opened his field coat to find where the bullet careened to. He touched the left side of his sweater and when his hand reappeared, Elaine could tell by the light of the silvery moon that he had been bleeding. "Found it," he said in a strained voice. "I'm sure it's nothing vital," he guessed. He hoped.

As she reached him, the lights from the house came on and immediately the dock was lit up like a Christmas tree. They both blinked and adjusted to the brightness. John Shasta was making his way down to the dock; his Benelli Legacy shot gun draped in his arms, and he cautiously approached his late night guests.

"Evening, folks," he called out.

"John?" Elaine asked as she turned Jack around to face John Shasta.

"Elaine?" He asked happily, then recognizing her and the Waco. He also became aware of her passenger. "Jack?" His lighter tone of earlier gone when he saw Jack Phillips, the ne'er do well husband of his godchild.

Jack sheepishly smiled and replied, "Mr. Shasta. It's been a while." He extended his bloodied hand to find only empty air and a curious stare from John.

John looked to Elaine. "What happened, Honey?" he asked in a fatherly tone. One Jack understood to be more protective in nature than prying. He shoved his bloodied hand into his jacket pocket and looked to Elaine to explain.

"Jack slipped and hurt himself on the pontoon. You remember, he was always such a klutz." She slapped Jack on the back and walked over to John, giving him a hearty hug and kiss on the cheek. "I've missed you."

"I can tell," John said with a satisfied grin. "Mollie's gonna be so happy to see you."

"Oh, I haven't seen Mollie in forever," Jack piped up. "Still make those really great homemade biscuits and gravy?"

The looks he got from John and Elaine was enough to end his query. He quietly walked behind them; trying to keep his obvious discomfort to himself. He listened in on their private conversation.

"So, what brings you up here this late, young lady?" John asked with concern.

"Going to meet Mom and Dad in Angoon," she lied. "Got a late start, then I ran into Jack in Victoria, and the rest is history."

"Oh, that's right. Annual fishing trip, isn't it?" John remembered. Elaine nodded.

"Well, it's a little late to be heading out. So you'll stay the night, aye?"

"I'd love to. It'll be good seeing Mollie." Of that, she wasn't lying. She loved Mollie and her easy hospitality.

The log cabin was about seventy five yards from the dock, and like the pier, it was brightly lit. Elaine linked her hand inside of John's arm as they strode up the flagstone steps towards the cabin. She briefly took a stroll back in time when her family, along with John and Mollie Shasta rebuilt this home. During her internship in Seattle, Washington, the Shasta's cabin was destroyed in a fire. All that remained was the massive stone fireplace, and from that, Elaine created her first rebuild and restoration.

There were many firsts that summer; the least of which; her first glimpse of Jack Phillips. He was passing through on an invitation from Kash, and though his stay was brief, it was memorable. They never actually spoke to each other, just nodded, and then he was gone. That initial encounter should have been a precursor as to how their marriage was going to be; fleeting.

She gave a quick glance over her shoulder to find Jack lagging behind. He lifted his head and caught her concern; she immediately turned around to find Mollie Shasta opening a sliding glass door to greet one of her favorite guests.

As always, Mollie's hug was strong and she smelled of flour and cinnamon, and Elaine immediately knew that she had been slaving away in the kitchen. "What's in the oven?"

"Oh, a little something, something," Mollie replied with a wink. "Had I known you were coming, I would have baked your favorite; fresh Brioche-a-Tete." She smiled warmly until she looked over Elaine's shoulder and spotted Jack. "Stow away?" she asked.

Jack gave a curt smile and kept his head down; staring at the slate stone flooring. Only when Elaine moved, did he. They finally crossed into the living room as Elaine and Mollie finished greeting each other.

One look to Jack, and Elaine knew he had to be looked at. But only in private. "It's been a long day, Mollie. Do you mind if we catch up in the morning?"

"Of course, dear." Mollie led her guests through the living room to the first bedroom on the main floor. She flipped on the light; then went to the second bedroom next to it and did the same thing; illuminating a smaller, more manly room for Jack. The look she gave him indicated he would be using that room and not sharing Elaine's.

A nod of his head and he entered the room, quietly closing the door behind him.

Elaine gave a small smile of thanks to Mollie and John and kissed them goodnight. She retired to her bedroom and let her bag slowly sink the floor with a soft thud. She stared at the wall that separated her and Jack and listened intently for any sign of him stirring about. She heard nothing; but then again, she was learning that he was very stealth.

By the looks on things in the kitchen, she knew Mollie was through baking and the items were on the kitchen countertop to cool, and soon she and John would be heading upstairs to bed.

Elaine took out her toothbrush, toothpaste and PDA and tossed them onto the queen sized bed, then she dully sat on the edge; her head lolling back in total exhaustion; her body followed and she let the mattress absorb her weary self. She had closed her eyes for what seemed to be only a moment but was startled to find that she had slept without moving for several hours. A glance at the clock told her it was 3:45 in the wee morning. She rubbed her eyes and ignored the core of her being that was begging her to lie still and go back to sleep. But she willed herself up and shook off the urge to follow that inner voice that kept calling her to come back and collapse into the warmth of the toasty bed. She had much to do, and far little time to do it in. She grabbed her PDA and quietly headed to the kitchen for much needed coffee.

She padded through the stillness of the house and turned on the recessed lights above the bar. The coffee maker was perched in the corner of the kitchen and was on a timer set to start in a couple of hours. Too long by half for Elaine and she started to rummage through the cabinetry for the more disgusting, instant kind of coffee. For if Mollie was anything, she was a traditionalist with her coffee. Sometimes, even French pressing for good, hearty measure.

Elaine found some Folgers's singles and put some water in the kettle to boil. She leaned against the countertop and took in the cabin. The fire that destroyed the previous home nearly destroyed Mollie. All of her beloved collections from around the world were lost and replacing them wasn't part of the rebuild. But with help from Kash, Leslie and John, Elaine managed to craft a home that was similar to the old and could create new memories. And since the original reconstruction, Elaine had been back and updated many features of the home; most notably the kitchen and bathrooms.

The original structure had been a square cabin with the center piece being a huge fireplace that spanned two stories in the middle of one wall. Elaine left the fireplace and built the house with two additional wings on either side; slightly angling them in. On either side of the fireplace, she put two sliding glass doors with built in shelving on either side of them for the art work that Kash and Leslie found to replace those lost in the fire. Some were Lladro, but mostly brilliant, exotic works of blown glass, by a little know glass artist at the time by the name of Dale Chihuly. Leslie had discovered his works in the late seventies and collected several pieces, some of which she later gave to Mollie to use in complimenting the Lladro that Mollie was so fond of and had hooked Leslie onto.

The kitchen in which Elaine was patiently waiting was affectionately known as the "West Wing", for it captured the amazing Canadian sunsets. It was Old World in style; where elegance and antique European charm met and never clashed. The warmth and smooth lines of the hickory cabinets complimented the roughness and the depth of the slate flooring, and the touches of copper and the soapstone countertops seamlessly blended and tied everything together; reflecting the grace of Mollie and the ruggedness of John. It was Elaine's favorite room.

The whistling of the kettle brought her back to reality and she quickly pulled the noisy intrusion from its burner and poured herself a cup of cheap coffee. She grinned at the thought of Mollie's reaction. A quick stir and a sip for taste and she was on her way to the living room for some early morning reading.

The journals were taking on a life of their own and they were starting to intrigue her more than she thought or wanted. To realize your parents are something different than you thought was overwhelming disconcerting at this time in her life, but she also knew that they could possibly hold a very important key into finding them.

She looked to Jack's door and decided to check on him. Gently she opened his door to find him snoring; all indications he was still alive. Closing the door, she made her way to the sectional and arranged the pillows for maximum comfort. She took off her shoes and rejoined Kash and Mrs. Scott in China. She was going to have to get past the fact that her mother had been married. Shoving that thought to the back of her mind, she picked up the PDA and continued to learn more about her parents.

CHAPTER TWENTY FIVE

Gerald and Leslie stepped into the massive courtyard leading to the Hall of Prayer for Harvest. Following behind were Kash and Alicia, her arm casually linked to his and her elegant step falling into perfect rhythm with his masculine stride. A smug smile tugged at his mouth, happy he had conquered at least one beast.

The Hall of Prayer was an incredible, breathtaking structure of Ming architecture. It was set upon a three-tiered, circular marble constitution. The Hall itself was round, with three roofs that were clad in dark blue tiles; the last pitch, topped with a gold plug. Carved dragons lined the marble ramp that led to the stairs. Leslie's fingers trailed lightly over the first guardian dragon; careful not to disturb any real or imagined spirits.

"It won't bite, but I can't guarantee that for the rest of the dragons you will come across with while in Peiping," Gerald said, encouraging her onto the final level of the Hall.

As they entered, Leslie's step and breath caught at the magnificent beauty that surrounded her. Gerald stepped closer and whispered, "Did you say something?" His smile was wide and teasing. "Don't worry; you're not the first to be awed. Come, let's look around."

Alicia took Gerald's lead and steered Kash in the opposite direction; her arm still comfortably tucked within his. He surveyed the majestic dome that extended at least fifty feet high. Its colors and designs were an intricate blend of gold, blues, greens, and dark reds, all harmonizing together. Now more than ever before he understood the significance of handing down through the generations the teachings of culture and the pride of a craft, artistic or otherwise. The Hall was a symbol of both, and he had a newfound respect for generations.

He let his attention fall to the beauty surrounding him, and she was there enjoying a lively chat with Gerald. Little doubt he was droning on about something and making it palatable with his English charm.

A gentle but insistent squeeze of his forearm brought his concentration to the petite blonde by his side. He couldn't help but compare the amenable Alicia to the sultry Leslie. One was easily handled and almost adoring, while the other, was intimidating beyond reason, hardnosed and too stubborn for her own good. And like any claim jumper worth their salt, she was laying claim to a remote piece of property—his heart and soul. To say he was a little unnerved was a bit of an understatement, but he kind of liked it.

"So, how long have you been in Peiping?" he asked Alicia, drawing his attention away from those "home in the country" thoughts.

"Long enough," was her short reply.

"Miss home?"

"Home is where you make it. Besides, this place is good for the soul."

"Well," he leaned into her, "you know what they say about too much of a good thing," he winked.

With a delicate and understanding pat on his arm, she steered him over to Gerald and Leslie, where Bryant was explaining the history of the Hall. "The Hall was built in the fifteenth century and then rebuilt after a fire in eighteen-eighty-nine. It was here, during each spring that prayers were offered for a bountiful harvest. All the dates were established by the Imperial Astronomers."

"It's impressive," Leslie said while looking at the domed roof, then to Kash. "Definitely impressive."

"A tribute to the true essence of Ming architecture," Gerald added, guiding Leslie to the exit. "Come, we have a distance to go until we see another impressive structure The Altar of Heaven."

Kash was abreast of Leslie and whispered into her ear, "That's where they sacrificed virgins."

Gerald caught wind of his comment and laughed, setting the record straight. "Close. Bull calves."

"In that case, you'd better stay behind," Leslie dryly suggested to Kash.

Kash had heard that tone before and decided to leave well enough alone and directed his regards to a more receptive Alicia. "Between peaceful moments in the Hall and sacrificing bull calves, what do people do for fun in Peiping?"

"Here," she waved a magical hand, "in the Outer City, pleasure is plentiful. There are theatres, restaurants and," she paused, "brothels."

"Two out of three isn't bad. Will you join me?" he proposed. Alicia looked shocked and surprised at his invitation. "For dinner and the theatre?" he clarified.

Relief stole across her proper British features and she nodded yes to his offer.

Gerald could feel a sudden rigidity in Leslie's proud carriage as she heard Bennett's question to Alicia and he immediately made up for it by whispering in her ear, "Dinner and the opera?" She nodded. "I'll pick you up at seven." Unexpected as it was, the soft kiss he planted on her cheek was nice.

It had been a long day and Leslie was relaxing on the sofa in the living room of the suite. She was right upon first seeing the sofa; it was more for decoration than comfort, but at that moment she didn't much care. She sat with her legs extended, shoes off and feet propped up on the end pillow. Lazily she swirled her drink as she watched Kash pat down the lapels of his charcoal grey suit. His tanned skin showed off nicely against his pressed and starched white shirt. The red and yellow paisley tie provided just enough color.

She stopped the glass short of her parted lips when he added the final touch to his suit—her trademark—black fedora. He turned around for her approval.

"Well?" he paused. "How do I look?"

"Like Errol Flynn," she stated honestly.

He smiled broadly and gathered his overcoat. "Listen, don't wait up for me."

"Oh, don't worry about that," she assured, rubbing her feet for good measure. "Have a nice time."

With a quick wink he dashed out the door.

Long stemmed wine glasses clinked and effervescent bubbles raced to the surface and popped, emitting a delicate fragrance.

"Cheers," Gerald toasted.

"Cheers," Leslie echoed.

They accepted the bubbly and then simultaneously put down their *glasses. Each gazing across the table at the other, neither wanting to break the enchanting silence. Finally, Gerald leaned forward and took a hold of Leslie's slender hand.*

"We've come a long way from that rowdy little pub on Cravens Street, haven't we?"

His remark brought a smile to her lips and a shimmering to her eyes. With one cleansing breath, the shine disappeared and she once again focused on her dinner companion.

"I'm sorry," he apologized. "It's soon approaching two years, isn't it?"

Her answer was an exaggerated blink of the eyes.

"Your friend, Bennett—he reminds me of Mark. He's the strong, silent type who's not afraid to go after what he wants."

"You mean Alicia, don't you?"

"Alicia?" he asked in a surprised tone, but understanding fully her remark. "Goodness, no. Alicia's just my assistant, nothing more."

"Um. Kash is just my photographer. Nothing more."

Like Kash Bennett, Gerald Bryant knew that tone all too well and looked down at his watch. "We'd better be going. The opera starts in forty minutes, and unlike home, we don't make a fashionable late entrance. That sort of behavior is frowned upon here."

Their walk to the theatre was about three blocks, and on the way Gerald explained the plot of the opera they were to see. "Do you know anything about the Chinese opera?" he asked.

"Only that they frown upon you being fashionably late," she replied with dimpled charm.

He matched her dimpled smile and pulled her closer to him as they walked. "Well, the opera we're going to see is about an orphan. Of all of the Chinese operas, this is my favorite.

"There's an old man named Chao. Chancellor Chao. He tries to talk the emperor out of doing something horrible, but instead the emperor turns to Tu An Ku and orders him to have Chao assassinated. Their first attempt failed, and in the courtyard, Chao denounces Tu An Ku in front of everyone. The emperor orders a dog to sniff out the wrongdoer and without knowing it Chao had been set up and must be executed along with his family members, including his unborn son. Because the mother of the child is the emperor's sister, she is spared. After smuggling the baby out of the palace, the doctor declares to Tu An Ku that the baby was stillborn and threw it out." They

reached a corner and disappeared around it with Leslie totally engrossed in Gerald's interpretation of the opera.

Kash and Alicia made their way out of the theatre and into the autumn night. Kash, ever the gentleman with Alicia, helped her with her wrap as she proceeded to finish her translation of the opera they had just seen. "Years go by," she continued, "and the orphan is adopted by Tu An Ku. One day the orphan meets the emperor's sister, and they carry on a conversation until he tells her he's the son of Tu An Ku. And you saw her devastating reaction to that. Well, the orphan goes home and tells a family friend of his experience. The friend presents him with a scroll, depicting the orphan's life and the murder of his father by Tu An Ku, his adopted father. The final scene was the son taking his revenge." She waited patiently for Kash to say something, but he didn't. "Did you enjoy the opera?" she prompted.

Bennett waited a moment before answering. "The actual opera or your version?"

Playfully she smacked his arm and they turned the corner, where they literally ran into Gerald and Leslie. "Oh, good evening," cried a startled Alicia. "On your way to the opera?"

"Yes," Gerald managed. "On your way from the opera?" Alicia nodded and Gerald locked eyes with Kash. "Did you enjoy?"

"Yes, very much." Kash's response was more automatic than genuine as he eyed Gerald's stunning companion. Leslie's smile was cool and her dimples not quite so deep as her eyes met his. He couldn't see her evening attire, because of her black cape, but it was definitely a switch from her usual.

She looked magnificent with her dark hair down and swept over to one side, revealing her smooth, creamy neck. His jaw flexed when he saw Gerald lead her past him, and for good measure, he turned and watched her walk away. Her nicely shaped legs accentuated by her black pumps and her graceful cat-like walk. He watched until they disappeared around the corner, then he turned to his attention back to the equally stunning blonde on his arm. "I'm starved," he declared. "Are there any chocolate covered almonds here in China?"

The elevator rang up, the doors parted, and Kash Bennett stepped out into the hallway, searching his pockets for his key. As he finally found it, he *rounded the corner and narrowly missed a man in the hallway. Giving a curt nod of apology, they both continued on their way.*

With irritation, Kash flopped onto his back and turned on the bedside lamp. He grabbed his watch, stared it down, and then slammed it back down onto the nightstand. Where is she? Why was it taking Leslie so long to come back? He had been back for at least two hours. He expelled a pent up, angry breath, reminiscent of those bull calves.

Leslie shut her clutch purse and handed Gerald the key. Being the gentleman he was, he opened the door and turned on the light. Like a carrot on a stick, he dangled the key in front of her, and as she reached for it, he pulled it back. His eyes twinkling, he leaned forward and took his reward. Graciously, Leslie obliged and kissed him.

"Thank you for a lovely evening," she told Gerald. "It was most enlightening."

"The pleasure was all mine," he assured her.

Leslie motioned inside. "Would you care for a night cap?"

"I'd love to," he shook his head. "But, it's late. Thank you for the offer. Perhaps another time?"

"Perhaps. Goodnight, Gerald."

"Goodnight, Leslie."

Under his breath, and his best falsetto voice, Kash echoed, "Goodnight."

Leslie locked the door and walked to her room, and before she retired for the evening, she spotted Kash's overcoat on the back of the sofa. A satisfied smile stole across her face and she closed the door to her bedroom, knowing sleep would be sweet.

Bang! A loud pop caused Kash to bolt upright in bed—his mind foggy from sleep. He turned and faced a fresh Leslie.

"Good morning," she greeted in a disgustingly happy voice. "Remember our meeting in forty-five minutes?"

Satisfied, she left him to fend for himself. Unsatisfied, he threw back the covers and made his way to the bathroom.

"Good day." Gerald extended his hands to Leslie and greeted her with a firm kiss on the cheek.

Kash did one better; not only did he kiss Alicia's hand, but her lips as well. "Hello," he cooed to a blushing Alicia.

"Did you enjoy your evening, Bennett?" Gerald asked.

Kash's eyes never left Alicia's face as he answered the question. "Oh, yes. Very much so."

"Splendid," Bryant reacted, and gave Kash a hearty slap of approval on his back.

A slightly built young man approached. He was half-walking, half-running. He removed his cap and gave Gerald an abrupt bow. Gerald responded automatically with a curt nod, acknowledging his presence.

The young man's smile was clumsy and matched his haphazard appearance. His face was smooth and clean shaven and his hair was cropped closely, standing on end. When he finally spoke, his English was broken, but he conveyed his message. "My name," he started, pointing to himself, "is Chiang. And, I, your guide."

"What happened to Kuang?" Gerald inquired, curious as to why the original guide had been replaced; especially with someone who spoke broken English.

"He," Chiang stopped, searching for the right word. "Sick. We start?" he asked enthusiastically.

Gerald shrugged his indifference, and everyone followed the young guide to their first stop, Ch'ienmen, or the traditional front gate into the Inner City.

"Here," Chiang began deliberately, "we pass through Ch'ienmen, the passageway 'tween Inner and Outer Cities. It is the tallest structure in the Outer City, with two roads going north through tunnels in wall. Off," he pointed to a scarlet walled, yellow tiled building, "That, Tien An Man, the Gate of Heavenly Peace. Come," he encouraged, and pointed to an awaiting car and smiled. "Good for feet."

On the drive over, Gerald did Chiang a favor and described Tien An Men. "The Gate of Heavenly Peace is guarded by several stone lions. Centuries ago, emperor's officials would kneel in divine proclamation. On the other side of the gate is Tien An Men Square; about one hundred squares worth. Now you know why seeing Tien An Man by car is easier on the feet.

"From here, we'll travel to Wu-Men, or the Meridian Gate. It is the *threshold of the Forbidden City. It was there, where the commoners were coerced into kneeling and groveling before the emperor. Then and only then, when the emperor was satisfied would he allow them entrance into the Forbidden City."*

"That's what kings and queens are good for," Kash remarked under his breath, ignoring Gerald's proud British glare.

They entered the vast courtyard with its Golden Water River wandering aimlessly in its marbled channel. Five arched bridges crossed the river from the courtyard to the last gate pavilion known as Taihomen.

"Come," Chiang invited. "We go up to the last gate, Taihomen, before we enter the Hall of Supreme Harmony." They fell in line behind him and crossed an elaborately carved bridge that lead to the last gate. Chiang looked to Gerald. "Perhaps you tell, my English..."

Gerald gave an understanding smile and commented on the Hall. "The Hall itself appears to float on its marble pedestals and it spans nearly two hundred feet long and one hundred feet high. The color combinations of somber red walls and bright yellow roof are in keeping with that of the Heavenly Gate and many structures in Peiping.

"You will see stretching out away from the Hall, there are smaller less significant Halls. These were used mainly for the emperors and their retainers. For five hundred years the Hall of Supreme Harmony was the center of the Chinese world. According to Chinese lore," he looked to Chiang to continue.

"This," Chiang stated, "is where earth and sky meet, four seasons unite, wind and rain join and Yin-Yang are in harmony."

At the mere mention of Yang-Yin, Kash and Leslie glanced at one another, each reading the other's thoughts and then once again, they concentrated on Gerald.

"It was here," he began, "that Son of Heaven, or the emperor, took his seat for ceremonies and to hold court. Within the red walls of the Palace City is fifteen hundred acres. Tonight we will come back here for a dinner at the pavilion overlooking Nan Hai Lake. Evening dress will be required," he informed, looking Kash in the eye, knowing full well he'd have to assist Bennett in acquiring the proper suit of clothes.

CHAPTER TWENTY SIX

"Leslie?" Kash rapped lightly on her bedroom door. There was no answer. He opened the door and stuck his head inside for a look around. No Leslie. He tiptoed in and placed a wrapped package on her bed. When he turned to leave he caught sight of her relaxing in a tub of bubbles. Curiosity got the better of him and he stepped inside the bathroom for a closer look.

Sensing something, Leslie begrudgingly opened one eye and focused in on a very dapper Kash in evening dress. Kash! Her mind screamed.

Careful not to disturb the bubbles, she lifted her head and positioned herself lower in the tub. Clutching the washcloth to her bosom addressed him in a throaty whisper. "Hello, Kash."

He took that as an invitation to sit down and chat while she relaxed in the tub, knowing full well that wasn't what she had intended. Sitting opposite of her, he flashed his best boyish grin and irritation took the place of embarrassment in her features.

She cocked an astute brow and shook her head. "What do you want?"

"I thought you might need some help. You know, scrub your back, rinse it off and pat it dry type of help."

"I can manage," she assured.

"I know," he agreed. "But I can do a better job." He reached over and tugged at the washcloth. "If only you'd let go of the washcloth, I could show you."

Leslie shrank away and threatened, "You could also get wet." She faked flicking him with water and watched him scamper for the door.

Her low husky laugh was enough to make him come back.

"What are you wearing tonight?" he asked curiously.

"Something similar to yours, but not quite as broad through the shoulders."

"You would, wouldn't you?"

Leslie just smiled.

"You are, aren't you?" He couldn't believe it. "What does Mr. Scott think of your choice of dress?"

Quiet filled the bathroom and she looked down at the bubbles. "Isn't Chiang supposed to pick you up soon? You don't want to be late," she said in a cheery British accent. She looked up, puckered her lips and rapidly fluttered her eyelashes in mock imitation of the perfect Alicia Cameron.

"You're being evasive."

"And you're being like that splinter," she whispered, "A pain in my ass."

Getting nowhere fast, he gave up and waved goodbye. "See ya."

She playfully hissed at his retreating back, knowing she hadn't heard the last reference to Mr. Scott from Mr. Bennett.

Leslie emerged from the bathroom clipping a diamond and sapphire earring into place. "Gerald, will I need a wrap tonight?" she asked.

Gerald was closing the closet door as she emerged from the bathroom. "No, darling, no reason tonight. How lovely you look," he observed with dimpled charm.

"Thank you," Leslie cooed.

As he held the door open for her, she asked, "Were you looking for anything in particular in the closet?"

"It was open, so I closed it," he lied. "Did I tell you how stunning you look?"

"No. But you did tell me how lovely I looked," she countered with a smile that rivaled his. She whisked past him and headed down the hall. "Coming?"

"Yes, dear," he answered as he shut the door and followed in her wake.

Six flutes tilted inward and resounded together. Leslie stood between the Chancellor and his Deputy Assistant. Their nods were customary and polite before they accepted the bubbling champagne.

The Chancellor took a sip and then turned his attention to Leslie. He was a small man of medium build and his face was weathered and mirrored the years of pain and suffering he and his people had endured. But in the depths of his eyes, there was a shining glimmer of hope.

While the others engaged in lively conversation, the Chancellor escorted Leslie out onto the terrace to see the lovely view of Nan Hai Lake.

"I'm looking forward to seeing your article on the tombs. I will be very much interested in the reaction of the Americans concerning our history and ancestry. Mr. Bryant has gone to great lengths in preparing and coordinating this effort and special occasion."

"Yes, he has," Leslie agreed. "As soon as the article is printed, we will be happy to send you as many copies as you wish, and whatever the response is, we will forward to you. I'm sure it will be quite favorable."

"Before you leave, I would like to read it," he gently insisted.

His request had an underlying point and Leslie gracefully accommodated him. "Of course."

He nodded his appreciation.

Leslie leaned forward on the marble ledge and gazed out at the moon's reflection on the water below. The moon was bright and reflective off the water, providing much light. She took in a deep, cleansing breath, her sharp profile outlined in the moonlight.

The Chancellor, aware of her reluctance to converse further on the article, changed the subject. "It is very beautiful here when the sky is clear and the moon is bright. More so during the Moon Harvest."

"The celebration of the moon, a Yin symbol," Leslie smiled slightly at her recall of Bennett's explanation of the Moon Harvest. She was also thankful the Chancellor had picked a more pleasant subject to discuss.

"Yes. You are familiar?" he asked, pleased that she was aware of some of their culture.

"A little." Leslie paused and sipped her champagne. "You are very proud of the beliefs and teachings that have been handed down through the generations, aren't you?"

"Yes. Those customs and way of life have sustained many generations through many trying times. We are a proud people and it will always remain a part of us."

"Will it?" she asked with a hint of skepticism. The Chancellor eyed her with distant caution, and she wasn't sure she should speak her mind in a country that truly regarded women as the inferior species, but she didn't like being considered anything less than equal. She thoughtfully regarded him and chose her words carefully.

"It will be a shame to see the ancient teachings become secondary to the up and coming communistic way."

He remained quiet, so Leslie took a more direct and heartfelt approach.

"They think nothing of playing the town bully and taking what they want, using whatever methods necessary to promote their way of life."

If he minded her outspoken criticism on communism, he didn't show it, but rather considered her opinion philosophically. "Such bitterness from such a sweet mouth. Experience teaches us much. You have such experience?"

"Of a different sort," she confessed.

Before she could continue, the Deputy Assistant appeared and whispered something into the Chancellor's ear. With a definite nod, the Assistant took his leave.

"You must excuse me," the Chancellor said politely. "Something needs my immediate attention. Please enjoy your stay, Mrs. Scott."

"I will, thank you."

Simultaneously they smiled and nodded to each other and then the Chancellor went inside to say goodbye to the others. Leslie turned her attention to the shimmering water below.

Kash stood within an arms length of her, admiring the view. He watched the moonlight dance off the midnight blue sequins of her gown, thankful she hadn't worn something similar to his. Her shoulders were slightly rounded, allowing the slit in the back of her gown to gape, exposing her smooth back.

His eyes followed the line to the flair of her hips and down to the second slit up the center seam, revealing her shapely legs. Temptation took over and he ran an erect finger down her bare back, causing a sharp intake of air.

Her gasp was audible, and the wine glass she was lightly holding, plummeted to the ground. She whirled around to face his hooded gaze and his disgustingly "happy-with-himself" smile.

Chiang walked around the pillar and announced, "Car ready."

Gerald motioned for Kash and Leslie to join Alicia and him. "Chiang will drop us at the consulate for some dancing," he said to Leslie. "You do still dance, don't you?" He asked with tongue in cheek.

Kash appeared lost in thought as Alicia took his arm and steered him away from Gerald and Leslie. "You and I, we will take a moonlit jinrikisha ride."

"Sounds charming," Kash absentmindedly commented while he watched Gerald worm his way into Leslie's favor.

The jinrikisha ride was smooth and at a fairly fast pace. Alicia positioned herself closer to Kash, prompting him to put his arm around her shoulder. She knew it was only a matter of time before he would forget the elegant beauty of Gerald's affection.

"Is it my imagination, or has the moon gotten brighter?" She wondered aloud.

Kash understood. "I'd say something romantic, but I'm not inclined that way," he revealed with an amiable smile.

"Who said you had to say anything? I prefer a man of action."

Kash obliged, his mouth descending down upon hers, leaving little doubt his intentions. It held a trace of brutality and lasted for as long as it took the jinrikisha to disappear around the corner.

The band started playing Glenn Miller's "Moonlight Serenade" and Gerald led Leslie from their table to the terrace. The music swelled in the midnight air. He took her into his arms and they began to dance.

"This is the only way to dance to this song. Under a moonlit sky with a pretty girl. Takes me back a few years."

He closed the distance between them, and like everything Gerald did, his kiss was gentlemanly and without insistence. He moved from her mouth and placed feathery kisses over her cheek and jaw.

"You women are all alike," he whispered.

"How's that?" she replied, barely recognizing her voice.

"You lure us with your feminine wiles and then stop us short with high necklines," he playfully complained.

That didn't stop him from exploring her jaw line and the soft skin behind her ear. Patiently she waited for him to discover her coolness towards his affection, and bravely he faced her and smiled his patented, understanding grin.

"Can't blame a guy for trying," he sighed, looking for a way to gracefully downplay her rejection. "It's getting late. I'd better get you back to the hotel."

Leslie could only muster a small smile in agreement.

A goodnight kiss on the cheek and Gerald poured her into the car. The *door was shut with more force than necessary and an open palm on the roof gave Chiang the signal to drive away.*

One stud, two studs, three studs popped off of Kash's evening shirt, and Alicia, with a provocative wink, slipped her hands inside the neatly tucked garment. Her touch was cool on his hot skin, causing him to shudder with anticipated delight. He returned the favor by lowering the zipper on her dress.

CHAPTER TWENTY SEVEN

"Daddy! You devil." Elaine thought to herself. She was about to advance the PDA when Jack's door opened. Speaking of the devil; he emerged looking less than himself.

His black gaze held her in check before he went to the kitchen in search of some liquid energy. Quickly Elaine shut down the PDA and put it aside. She grabbed her coffee cup and followed Jack into the kitchen. He shot the coffee maker a harsh glare and then looked to Elaine for guidance regarding the coffee.

"Give it twenty minutes and it'll make you some, or you can have the cheap stuff." She raised her cup in a mock salute.

He nodded and scoured the kitchen for the same kind of coffee as Elaine was having. He wasn't having much luck.

Sensing his frustration, she filled the kettle with more water, put it on and found the coffee singles. Tearing open the end, she placed it in a large coffee mug and presented it to him. "When it whistles, the water is ready."

He nodded.

"Are you okay?" she finally asked.

He nodded.

"Did it hit anything vital?"

He shook his head.

"Good." It was all she said, and then she went to her room and quietly closed the door to them.

Jack poured the hot water to his new found energy and stared out at the dark morning. He wondered how he was going to stall Elaine in her quest for her parents. He knew everything was being done to find them. The people in charge were professionals and good at locating. What they

160

didn't need was an amateur; and one with a damned determination to seek out the truth. Nothing good comes from the truth; at least in his line of business. He just wanted to find some time to keep her at bay and away from harm's way while his so-called friends did their jobs. He was on the verge of hatching a plan, when suddenly the kitchen was in full light. He turned to the morning glare of Mollie Shasta. He nodded his hello, picked up his coffee and headed for his room.

He nearly ran over Elaine in his haste to leave Mollie to her fancy coffee maker and a great cup of Joe. She was on her way to the bathroom for a quick shower.

"Don't touch the plane," she warned him and looked past him to see John Shasta coming down the stairs.

John gave her a quick wink and then stared at Jack. "Understand?"

Jack nodded and went into his room.

John looked to Elaine with a kindness she rarely saw. "I know there's more to your trip than fishing. Fishing of another nature. If there's anything you need; anything at all, we're here for you."

His sentiment brought tears to her eyes and she hugged his neck tightly. She nodded her thanks and headed towards the bathroom for some much needed private time.

Instead of her taking a shower, she filled up the claw tub with water; pulled the shower curtain all the way around and soaked in silence. An occasional drip from the faucet was the only noise in her little world. The more she tried to relax, the more tense she became. Every movement of the past few days kept flying in and out of her memory.

Finally, giving in, she reached through the curtain, found her towel and dried her hands. On the glass table near the tub she retrieved her PDA. Pulling it into the seclusion of her bath, she turned it on and resumed her parent's journey.

CHAPTER TWENTY EIGHT

Leslie opened the door to find the suite full of light. Hum? Kash must have come back early, she mused. Quietly she shut the door and walked to her room. She looked past the shared bathroom to the closed door of his room. The crack at the bottom revealed a light, and after an evening of gentlemanly Gerald, she was in bad need of something stimulating like Kash Bennett. She didn't know why she was compelled to see him after such an eloquent evening, but she dropped her purse, kicked off her heels and headed for his door.

A husky, tempestuous laugh escaped Alicia's parted lips as Kash dragged her down onto the bed just as Leslie opened the door to his room.

"Ka…" His name died on her lips and her heart plummeted to the floor. If she would have stepped further, she would have trampled it.

The shock on their faces mirrored her own feelings and Kash struggled to hold Alicia still, as not to disclose any of her more personal attributes. His lips were trying to form words, but nothing he said was going to ease the tension or the hurt that resided in Leslie's shocked expression.

"Excuse me," Leslie said with a crooked smile of apology.

She closed Kash's door quietly, but that mood didn't hold true through the adjoining door leading to her bedroom. With blind fury she slammed it behind her.

Kash placed Alicia to one side and handed her the chilled bottle of champagne. "Have some more champagne."

Quickly he was off the bed and through the doors, slamming each one loudly. He was upon Leslie in no time and pivoted her around into the expanse of his chest.

She didn't give him the opportunity to defend himself. "If you had wanted to screw around so badly, you could have had the decency to find somewhere else to do it other than the bedroom adjoining mine."

Enraged by her statement he tightened his grip and bore through her. "You hypocritical bitch!" he exploded. "Where have you been for the last three hours? Dancing with Mr. Manners? You're a fine one to talk about decency and morality, Mrs. Scott. Spending half the night with him while somewhere, a trusting Mr. Scott is pining away, waiting for a devoted Mrs. Scott to return."

Before she realized it, her palm came into contact with his cheek. His jaw squared at the stinging and hers clinched in an attempt to control the hot tears his words had just provoked.

Leslie swallowed hard and flexed her aching hand. She managed to keep her voice to a minimal waver when she finally spoke. "Mr. Scott's pining all right, in the pine box I buried him in nearly two years ago. Or rather, what was left after he was killed in a car explosion."

After that, any words she would have spoken would have blown him over like a feather. His regretful expression was more than she could take and she removed herself from his slackened grasp and stepped back. Hurriedly she wiped the tears away that had slipped free from her closed lashes.

The knot in his stomach matched the lump in his throat, and all the feelings he had felt over losing Mike, he felt for Leslie and her pain. There was also a selfish relief that flooded his senses, but it was short-lived and nothing gained. Tenderly he reached out to wipe away the hurt, but she pushed his hand aside.

"Please, just go."

Her request was barely above a whisper and minus that tone he had become so accustomed to. Not needing anymore encouragement, he left.

There went her Midas touch again, she feared. Unlike Greek mythology, everything she touched turned to cold, gun metal grey and not the dancing brilliance of gold. A pain-filled breath escaped her parted lips and she ran her tongue across their roughened surface, tasting the saltiness of her own tears. She hadn't realized any more had fallen. God, she hated to cry and she scolded herself for it and for what she feared the most; they weren't tears for the passing of Mark, but rather, for the threatening loss of Kash Bennett.

That very thought released the flood gates and tears spilled hopelessly down her cheeks. She cursed herself for what she considered a weakness, but on the other hand, she was thankful to know she could still feel, even if it hurt. Shaky legs took her to the bed and she gratefully collapsed on the spread, giving way to some much needed relief.

Alicia pretended to be primping in front of the mirror when Kash reentered his room. She watched him close the distance between them. His touch was as impersonal as his voice.

"It's time you left," he said flatly.

She gathered her belongings. "Yes, I suppose you're right. I'll see myself out."

It was amazing how half-way across the world, in another culture, Kash could find a bar similar to Lucy's Rathskeller—right down to the pink and blue neon lights bordering the mirror behind the bar.

Kash stirred his second double scotch. Or was it his third? Maybe even his fourth? He couldn't remember and what he kept trying to forget kept appearing every time he looked down into the caramel-colored liquid. No amount of stirring or guzzling was going to put to rest the reoccurring image of hurt welling up in Leslie Anne Scott's soft brown eyes.

Angrily he cleaned the glass and looked up into the smoke grey mirror. He squinted to make clearer the figure approaching him. As it neared, so did the familiarity and Kash anticipated the thundering slap on his back from Detective Francis X. Flanery.

It didn't happen. Instead, Flanery removed his hat and gave his balding head a pessimistic scratch. He nodded at the bartender, "Same as his," then he looked at Kash and sized up his friend's mood. "So, who licked the red off of your lollipop?"

That brought a twitch to the corner of Bennett's grimly set mouth. "Have you come all this way to arrest me or harass me?" Kash asked.

"Neither," Flanery informed him while hunting for his smokes. "However, I have come all this way to save your ass. But if this is your attitude, then to hell with you."

"Sorry."

Flanery's sharp blue eyes narrowed as he stared at Kash's grip on his drink. "Brunette's really thrown you, hasn't she?" He knew Kash as well as anybody, except maybe Mike Marrow, and he regarded him as the son he never had. And like any father, he had a protective sense about him, but he knew there wasn't a thing he could do to protect Kash from his heart—just be there if he needed someone to sound off to. More importantly, he was glad he wasn't Leslie's father, knowing Bennett's reputation for leaving a trail of broken hearts. "Good looking dame, she is."

Kash ignored his obvious comment about Leslie and shifted the conversation to something as equally depressing—Mike. "Is it really true they found Mike murdered in my car?"

"Yes," answered another man standing behind them.

Kash swiveled around to meet the somber gaze of a man that could have been Flanery's twin, except he was tall; like the elevator doors shut and he got caught in the middle, elongating his features.

"Kash, meet Mr. Briggs with the C.I.A.," Flanery introduced.

"Mr. Bennett," Briggs said as he made his way from the end of the bar and stood next to Flanery.

"Mr. Briggs believes your involvement goes deeper than Mike's murder," Flanery filled in.

Briggs narrowed his gaze and stared Flanery down for talking out of content. "Mr. Flanery, need I remind you that your jurisdiction doesn't extend to international boundaries."

"Mike wasn't a jurisdiction. He was my friend. You do know what friends are, don't you, Mr. Briggs?"

Mr. Briggs sucked in what little chin he had and blinked his droopy eyes in protest at Kash's comment. Of course he had friends. Several, but none coming to mind as he cleared his throat, hoping he could cough up the right words for the current situation. "Do you have the pendant?" he asked directly.

"No." Kash firmly responded.

"The woman?" Briggs pressed.

"Which one?"

"The brunette."

Kash looked to Flanery. "She said she sent it to the San Francisco police. You didn't receive it?"

Flanery shook his head. "Not that I know of."

"So, she did have the pendant." Briggs confirmed.

"Yeah. Some kid with a throwing star in his back begged her to take it." Kash told what he remembered happening in Chinatown that night and then he looked at Flanery. "Are you sure you didn't get it?"

"If I did, I would have known by now. This is a priority, Kash," Flanery waited a moment and then asked, "Are you sure you don't know where it is?"

165

Kash ignored the question and stared at Flanery's reflection in the mirror. "Why's he involved?" He asked, giving Briggs only a passing glance.

Used to being overlooked, Briggs patiently waited, then asked Kash, "What do you know about the pendant?"

"Nothing," Kash answered in his best monotone. "It's just a damn Yin-Yang pendant with a dragon painted on the back. What do you know about the pendant, Mr. Briggs?"

"Are you sure you can't recall seeing anything out of the ordinary regarding the look of the pendant? Unsmoothed edges?"

Before Briggs could continue, Kash grabbed the lapels of his suit and jerked him forward. "What are you insinuating? Is there something I should know about, Mr. Briggs?" Kash asked and then roughly released what he was sure to be a paper-pushing pinhead.

Unruffled by the treatment, Briggs continued. "No, it's just our officer was to pick up the pendant and transport it to D.C., but something went wrong and somehow the pendant was passed to the brunette."

"The brunette has a name. It's Leslie," Kash informed, but he was sure Briggs knew that.

"What do you know about her?" Briggs pressed.

"Nothing, really," Kash admitted. "I mean, we just met. She came from New York and World Magazine as the journalist for this assignment."

"Was she the original journalist or a replacement?"

Kash started to answer, but stopped, remembering Leslie was the last minute replacement for the original journalist.

"Hum?" Briggs wanted an answer.

"What do you know about?" Kash asked, turning the tables on the obnoxious officer.

"Very little, actually," Briggs honestly revealed. "Our problem, Mr. Bennett, is that the Russians have a contact in the U.S. and we can only speculate as to who that is. They also have a contact here in Peiping, but we do have a good idea as to the identity of that individual. We believe the American mole is going to pass the pendant to the Russian here in Peiping." He waited a moment, and then finished his worst fear. "Unless, of course, that has already taken place. Then, we're too late."

"And you believe Leslie is that mole?" Kash was reading Briggs quite well, considering he was three sheets to the wind in a sea of scotch.

"All the evidence points that way," Briggs concluded.

"What evidence?" Kash wanted to know.

"For starters, her association with Gerald Bryant, and now her being here as a replacement for the original journalist. It's just too coincidental."

Kash gave an emphatic shake of the head. "No way."

Noting Kash's defiance, Briggs took another approach. "I've read about you, Mr. Bennett. I know your type, and for lack of better wording, stop thinking with your -" he stopped short and looked at Bennett's belt buckle.

"What? You can't say it, because you don't have one. Dick!" He turned to the other man he knew wouldn't bullshit him. "What do you think, Detective Flanery?"

"I don't know, Kash," he answered honestly. "All I know is that I have several dead bodies, and apparently a pendant is missing, and Leslie was the last person to have it."

"If she kept it," Kash emphasized the word if, "it was because of the characters and the dragon painted on the back. She thinks it may be some kind of puzzle leading to who-knows-what," he defended. "Why is the Chinese underworld so interested in that pendant?"

Flanery raised his eyebrows, not at all expecting that question, and before he could answer, Briggs offered his opinion.

"Natalia, the mole, is quite clever. Probably a diversion. Like using her feminine wiles."

One look up and down at Briggs and Kash knew Natalia would have failed miserably with her usually successful tactic. "You couldn't be farther from the truth about Leslie. But, to be sure, why don't we ask her right this minute?" Kash made a move to leave but Briggs put a restraining hand on his shoulder.

"Don't be a fool. If you interfere now, we may never have a chance to recover the pendant, or capture the two of them. And, if you interfere, there will be severe consequences for you to pay," he warned.

Kash had heard enough and burned a hole through Briggs. "You certainly are special. But you're wrong on this one."

At least Kash thought he was as he walked away, feeling as awful as he did before he came to the nightspot.

"Maybe. Maybe not," Briggs offered to Bennett's retreating back.

CHAPTER TWENTY NINE

"Prick!" Elaine exclaimed, referring to Special Officer Briggs as she wiped away the tears she had spilled for her mother's anguish and the loss of her husband at such a tender age.

"I beg your pardon," Jack countered from behind the shower curtain.

His comment interrupted a daughter's interpretation of her mother's heartbreak and she was thankful for his intrusion. "Don't you ever knock?" she asked with false irritation.

"No," he bluntly replied.

The sound of running water at the sink and a toothbrush scrubbing teeth told her that he was brushing his pearly whites, and she delicately turned off the PDA and put it in a safe place on the floor behind the tub. She turned on the hot water and refreshed the heat in the tepid bath and started to lather up the washcloth when Jack poked his head between the folds of the curtain.

He wasn't smug when he climbed into the tub with her, and taking the washcloth and soap from her hands, he finished what she had started. He gently took one arm at a time and let the soapy cloth glide over her smooth skin; never taking his eyes off of hers.

She didn't mind breaking their intimacy. "Does Mollie know you're in here?"

He dropped the cloth into the water and stood up; foamy water clinging to everything, including the wound on his left side.

She frowned and stood to meet his stare. "How badly were you hurt?"

"Just a through and through. Nothing to worry about. We should get going if we're going to find your folks," he suggested as he parted the curtains and stepped out of the tub.

When she emerged from the curtained tub, he was gone. With her attitude, it might as well have been a cold shower, but she wasn't interested in romance. Not now.

She finished up and when she went to retrieve her PDA; it was gone. "Jack?" she yelled and charged out of the bathroom.

He stood in the kitchen, her angry head of steam meeting him head on. "Where is it?" she asked, spittle showering his face.

He calmly wiped his face and answered with a question. "What?"

She took a threatening step and got even closer to his face. "You know damn good and well what I'm talking about."

A surprised Mollie and John closed ranks and headed for her side. Jack sipped his coffee and watched all three closely. "You need to let the authorities take care of finding your parents. The more you read through the journals, the more they are going to cloud your judgment; and that makes it unsafe for you."

"You let me be the judge of that. I have a right to know about their lies; lives."

That slip of the tongue spoke volumes to those in the room. With that statement, the space was close and the tension was immeasurable. She stepped back, lowered her head and put her hand out for the PDA. She felt the coolness of its metal case. She closed her hand over it and Jack's. She started to back away, but his hand held her fast. Finally Elaine raised her eyes and saw the concern reflected in his brown eyes. They were soft and muted, missing that sarcastic twinkle.

She backed away and he let her go. Quietly she walked outside to the solitude of the lake and started to ready her Waco for its journey north to Alaska. But one look at the approaching weather front told her she might not be able to leave as quickly as she was hoping and needing to.

After the pre-flight check she double checked the pontoon for any damage; real or imagined, just to have something to do. She'd do anything to keep from having to go inside and face him.

A pretend cough drew her attention to the dock and John Shasta. "Came to give you some bad news; you can't fly in this weather."

"How long?"

"It's here for the better part of the day. Tomorrow morning would be best."

"Any windows today?"

"None that you should try to fly through," he warned in a fatherly tone.

She nodded in agreement. As much as she wanted to put distance between her and Jack and get on with finding her parents, she was also an extremely safe pilot; Kash had made sure to that. "I'll be a few minutes finishing up here."

John understood fully, but he didn't leave; and Elaine felt a lecture coming her way.

"I don't have to tell you he's right. You know that," he said gently. He waited a moment to see if her timber was lit, but she remained quiet; staring only at the increasingly agitated water. John took a cautious step her way. "They have means you don't and," he trailed off when she turned to face him; her tears catching him off guard.

"How long have you known?" she quietly asked.

He took great pains to be gentle in wiping away her tears and answering her question. "Before you were born." He looked around the lake; taking in its beauty. "I love to watch the change in the lake before a storm. She ready's herself; like a fortress. Protective and unwilling to give an inch to the enemy. Much like you and your parents."

His sandy white hair whipped in the wind and he pulled his collar up to ward off the chill. His dusty blue eyes narrowed as he tried to read Elaine's impassive face. "We were quite the team in the day; your mother, father and me." His voice trailed away and he hesitated to say anymore; that was for her parents to explain their choices. He held out his hand to her and she took hold. "Mollie is making some of your favorite things," he informed with a wink. "Be surprised."

"You haven't told me anything," she laughed.

"Yeah, but you know; and I don't want to get in trouble with the Mrs."

"I promise; I won't incriminate you." She linked her arm in his and they braved the trying wind as they made their way back to the cabin.

CHAPTER THIRTY

Surprisingly, when Elaine and John entered, Jack and Mollie were engaged in a lively conversation regarding recipes, of all things. Neither of them stopped to acknowledge her presence and she took that moment to slip away to her room and quietly shut the door to their bantering. The beauty of having constructed the interior of the house with all two by six walls was being able to add the extra insulation for privacy. She leaned against the six panel poplar door and strained to hear their muffled conversation. Satisfied she couldn't distinguish a word they were saying, she climbed onto the four poster bed; propped the pillows up behind her and opened the PDA for more reading. With the extra day, she was hoping to finish the journals.

She did a quick recollection of the journals and pondered who Briggs was and what his roll really was regarding the pendant and its recovery. She briefly reflected on her mother's past marriage and the anguish she had to have felt at seeing her groom murdered before her eyes. She shook that image from her mind's eye and continued reading.

It was if they were transposed to another world, somewhere far away from the agonizing events of the evening before. Kash, for the most part, had been silent and was watching Leslie with much more interest since his conversation with Briggs. He had also been suffering in silence, not only from his aching head and rumbling stomach, but from his guilty conscience gnawing at his heart.

He turned and stared at her profile, her patrician brown deep in thoughtful regard for the architectural splendor she had been taking in since they had left their hotel. He wondered where she had the pendant, since she hadn't sent it to Flanery. Or, if she had given it to Gerald. God only knew, she had plenty of opportunities. He shook that disturbing image from his mind, and joined her in observing the picturesque wonders as they made their final approach to the Valley of the Thirteen Tombs.

The Great Spirit Way was lined with huge sculptures of horses, camels, elephants, guardsmen and mythological creatures. The somber red walls and yellow tiled roofs blended perfectly with the gold's and russets the autumn season was offering.

Leslie rolled down her window and caught the clean scent of the many scotch pines that stood stoically amongst the many other trees.

Traditionally along this route, the funeral procession stopped, vehicles and horses were left behind and the march continued on foot to the tombs. But not now, there was no need and no time.

Chiang slowed the car as he neared the Dragon and Phoenix gates; the portal to perhaps the most impressive of all tombs; Yung-lo. And as with all the complexes, it too, was surrounded by a scarlet wall.

Gerald caught sight of them arriving and excused himself from Alicia and the Deputy Assistant to greet the approaching car. Chiang pulled to a stop; and Gerald opened Leslie's door. Before Chiang could assist him, Kash was out, stretching heartily, watching Gerald and his mannerly affection toward Leslie. She leaned back inside the car and pulled out her satchel, then allowed Gerald to guide her towards the entry of the tomb where two guards stood at attention. There, Leslie was greeted by the Deputy Assistant and an apathetic Alicia Cameron.

"Good day," the Assistant greeted them with his customary bow. "In the next few days you will cover a total of four tombs. Today, we start with the most impressive of all thirteen tombs, Yung-lo's. Mr. Bennett, the equipment you requested has been set up in Yung-lo's vault. It will be transported to the other tombs as you proceed."

He said nothing more, and led them into the courtyard that was full of trees, and to their right sat Yung-lo's stele. Kash meandered over and took numerous pictures at different angles, alternating cameras as necessary. Leslie didn't have a recorder, just her trusty notepad, and only occasionally she would jot down a few notations.

They passed through a pavilion that was supported by dozens of wooden columns. The ceiling was painted with lacquered dragons and the cathedral was totally empty, and handsomely decorated in gold's and blues. Kash sat down in the middle of the floor; laid on his back and took pictures of the colorful ceiling. Leslie smiled at learning he had an imagination. He caught *up with the others as they passed through the cathedral to another building where only a marble tablet stood, inscribed with the emperor's title.*

Finally they made their way to the tomb itself. Above the ground it was covered with many trees, but below, the stone chamber sunk deeply into the earth. They stepped carefully through the narrow passageway, and then down into the resting place. Several umbrella lights had been erected to aid Kash in photographing the burial vault, and the rituals inside.

The coffin itself was decorated with Buddhist sutras, and the chamber contained hundreds of treasures needed for the afterlife. Much like the Egyptians, Leslie smiled, and looked to see Kash grin, knowing his very thought. A tingle raced down her spine at the thought of them actually connecting without uttering a single word. Maybe there was hope after all, she thought, and turned back to reach out and stroked one of the many porcelain vases, tubs and earthenware in traditional blue and white.

Strategically placed bolts of colorful silks were stacked high and came to life when Kash checked his power pack for energy. He began shifting the lighting equipment for better angles. Leslie discarded her jacket; rolled up her sleeves and began translating her feelings upon entering the final resting place of Yung-lo.

She had barely heard Gerald's voice behind her. "If you need anything, Chiang will assist you. We'll see you tomorrow for the last two tombs." Gerald, Alicia and the Deputy Assistant excused themselves, and one guard and Chiang stayed behind with Kash and Leslie.

It had been a long day, and moving the equipment from Yung-lo's tomb to the second burial site had exhausted everyone. The drive back was as quiet as the drive there, and the sun was rapidly setting, and with it, the only light available for Leslie to see and write by.

Kash leaned over and took a better look at her notepad. His expression was quizzical and he made a stab at her strange form of writing. "What is that, Egyptian?"

"Close. Shorthand." A tiny smile of grateful relief spread across her weary features at his attempt in keeping his comments to her light. But that was short lived with his next question.

"How about dinner tonight?" he asked softly.

It took all she had to resist his deep, rich tone and shake her head. She turned away to avoid his steely stare. "No. I think I'll take a hot bath and fall into bed. Busy day tomorrow," she rationalized.

Kash nodded his head in agreement and looked out the window, silently kicking himself for getting into the situation.

Chiang stared in his rearview mirror at his two back seat passengers, and shook his head at their polite, but stubborn attitudes.

The torch light bounced off the narrow passageway walls. Lighting a few feet at a time, and with a supporting hand on the wall, Leslie followed the lead guard closely. Right behind was Kash, Chiang, Alicia, with Gerald bringing up the rear. This tunnel was by far the most cramped and claustrophobic of all the tombs; its ceiling and walls were jagged, and a strange, cool moisture could be felt with every breath that was taken.

Then suddenly, the guard dropped two feet down from Leslie and she stood her ground while he lit the second torch, illuminating the burial chamber. She jumped down, and the others followed. Chiang placed his torch at the far wall of the chamber, parallel to the coffins.

Leslie's breath caught as the light produced an aura around the painting on the chamber wall nearest the coffins. An octagon shaped Yin-Yang symbol with trigrams, and next to it a spectacular dragon emerging from a waterfall with Chinese characters placed at the third and seventh sides of the eight-sided form.

Leslie's wide eyed stare didn't escape Kash. It was all the communication she sent, and he understood perfectly. He was relieved to a point. At least she was right about the pendant meaning something more than just decoration.

Gerald saddled up next to her. "Beautiful, isn't it? Of all the tombs, to me, this is the most fascinating." He didn't expect her to comment as he turned to Chiang. "Come along, Chiang, we'll help Bennett with his equipment."

Whether Kash needed or wanted their help, he accepted it to speed up the process of photographing the last tomb, and putting to bed their end of the crunch. They departed, leaving only Alicia and Leslie in the chamber. Alicia watched with guarded suspicion at Leslie's curious reaction to the painted symbols on the wall.

They shared little, and had less in common, these two women, and Alicia was only too happy to keep it that way. But she held her breath as Leslie traced the dragon's claw, stopping at the seventh side. Then she studied the Yin-Yang symbol itself. Fascinated, she rubbed the eye of the Yang, and an inwardly nervous Alicia could only watch until the others returned.

Without a word, Leslie abandoned her perusal and pitched in setting up the gear. Kash repeated the same routine that he had used in previous tombs, and Leslie, too, made her notations, concentrating heavily on the chamber wall.

Leslie emerged from the tomb to catch the end of conversation that was truly one-sided; Alicia instructing Gerald; that's odd, Leslie thought. Still, she walked over towards him; like the moth to the flame.

He held out his arms and Leslie gratefully slid into their warmth and strength. "How about a celebration dinner tonight?" He whispered the question against her temple.

"Oh, I don't know," she sighed. "I still have a lot of work to do. How about if I call you when I return to the hotel?"

"I'd like that." He took a moment to wipe away a trace of perspiration from her brow. "Maybe then, we'll have a chance to catch up on old times. If Mark could only see you now, he'd be so proud."

She stole a shaky breath, and he vigorously ran his hands up and down her back to warm away the sudden chill.

"I know, I miss him, too. He was a good friend, and a lucky man. He had you. I was always jealous that you chose him, and I was going to tell him that afternoon at our meeting, but..."

"That afternoon?" she interrupted, backing out of his embrace.

"Yeah. We had some things to..."

Leslie didn't hear his explanation as she looked off into the distance and thought back to Mark and that rainy afternoon. "Do you know who it is?" she recalled asking Mark.

Mark nodded. "I'm to meet him in an hour. So, I'd better be going."

"Does he know you know?" Absentmindedly she held her arms, feeling Mark's strong hands pulling her close, and at the same time, trying to erase Gerald's deceptive affections.

"Probably." She remembered Mark answering.

"I'm sorry," Gerald murmured, interrupting her painful memory and bringing her back to the present. "Please call me tonight."

She nodded and nonchalantly kissed him goodbye.

Kash watched their affectionate display from the mouth of the tomb.

The suspicions he had been denying surfaced and his tone was severe when he called out to her. "Leslie!" His thunderous roar shot through her and she quickly removed herself from Gerald's arms. "Do you mind?" Kash growled. "I could use that film before hell freezes over." He certainly would have said more, but thought better, ad disappeared into the tomb, smarting from being proved wrong by someone as irritating as Briggs.

The Deputy Assistant shut the trunk lid of his car and turned to Kash and Leslie. "We are anxious for the article and photos to be published."

"Well, we're almost finished here, so it shouldn't be long," Kash promised.

"Not everyone is done," Leslie admitted. "I still have some things to do. Kash, why don't you ride back with the Deputy Assistant and when I'm finished, I'll have Chiang take me to the Imperial."

Kash gave a protesting glare, but she had turned her back and was heading for the tomb with Chiang close behind. She knew his answer was before it happened, but still she winced as he slammed the car door shut.

Leslie finished drawing the last character; looked to a patient Chiang and smiled. "Chiang, can you tell me what this means?" She pointed to the characters and the dragon.

"It is part of the puzzle to find the ancient scrolls that lead to the Heavenly Wisdom. With this painting was a pendant, the final piece of the puzzle. It holds two more characters. But, sadly, it is missing. It would be nice to find someday." At that thought, his face lit up.

Leslie smiled understandingly, comparing her loss with something close to an American, such as the Constitution. Maybe she could bring that loss back to the Chinese people? She wondered, and pointed to the characters on the wall. "What do they mean?"

"The one on the right means 'banks'. One on left is 'springs'. And the dragon is where the scrolls are."

"Where's the dragon located?"

"In the fall."

She furrowed her brow in confusion.

"Waterfall," he clarified.

"What is the Heavenly Wisdom?" Leslie asked, her pencil poised to make notations of Chiang's explanation.

"It is only true way into heaven. Those who hold it, master hope, wisdom and power."

"Isn't wanting power contradictory to the teachings?"

"Wisdom is power. Power of good nature. They teach the understandings, such as hope, structure of family. That is true wisdom and very powerful. It will always hold true. Shall we go?" Chiang asked, hoping he had conveyed his thoughts enough that she would be content and want to leave.

"Yeah, let's go."

The guard extinguished the torches and the dragon's secret was sacred once more. Only Leslie held the final clue, and that, she was keeping close to her heart.

Elaine touched the very thing Leslie had kept close to her heart. She now understood what Nothing was and the secret it kept. She started to continue, but was interrupted by a strong rap on the door. "Yes?" she called out.

It opened without her permission and in walked Jack with a hot steaming cup of tea. He closed the door and the distance between them before she could protest. "Mollie thought you might like some tea." He glanced at her lap and saw she had been reading the journals. "Find anything that will help?" He climbed onto the bed and sat next to her.

Too close, she thought, but she welcomed his warmth. "I've just read about the pendant and its true meaning. There are a lot of people involved, none of whom I recognize, with the exception of my father's friend, Mike Marrow. I remember him talking about Mike with fondness, and I could tell they had been good friends. Finding out that my mother had been married when she was very young comes as a shock, to say the least, but I can't help but feel her pain when she writes of losing her husband to a car bombing. This spy business is a dangerous game." Her voice trailed off as she sipped her tea. "How have you managed to stay alive, Jack?"

"Luck, really," he softly replied as he watched her take in the steamy liquid.

"No doubt luck has something to do with it, but why did you choose such a life?"

That was one question he had always dodged; even to himself. "I really don't know," he answered her honestly. Or maybe he knew, he just didn't want to say it out loud. He enjoyed what he did for a living; protecting his country in the most surreptitious way possible.

"You don't know?" she questioned, believing he knew good and well why he put, not only himself in harm's way, but her, as well.

He knew that tone and backed off the bed. He wasn't in the mood for confrontation, or explanations. "Dinner will be at six sharp. Mollie's making your favorite, so, be in a good mood when you join us," he said as he closed the door behind him, giving her no opportunity to talk back.

"Fine, Jack," she whispered. "Eventually, we will have this conversation. Especially if you want those divorce papers signed." She sipped her tea and glared at the closed door.

CHAPTER THIRTY ONE

The sun had set by the time they had emerged from the tomb, but the air was balmy, so Leslie kept her jacket draped over her arm and got into the back seat of the car; perhaps relaxing for the first time since arriving in Peiping. She couldn't wait to tell Kash about the two remaining characters and their relationship with the Heavenly Wisdom and the pendant.

Even though Leslie had only traveled to the tombs a few times, she was sure that the route they had taken wasn't the way back to the Imperial. She looked up and met the tension in Chiang's eyes as he watched her in the rearview mirror. "Chiang, where are we going?"

"Scenic way," he answered with false cheerfulness.

"At night?" she asked suspiciously.

"Just sit back and relax," he ordered politely.

Somehow, something was different about Chiang, but she couldn't put her finger on it, and she followed his suggestion and sat back, but she didn't relax. And she most certainly was on edge when they stopped and Chiang jumped out of the car. He opened the door and snatched her arm, pulling her from the safety of the vehicle.

"Please, Mrs. Scott," Chiang said quietly, influencing her with the barrel of a Colt 45 at her side. He guided her stiff carriage to an alley where a door was slightly ajar.

Still, she resisted his nudge. "What the hell is going on, Chiang?"

He didn't answer. A pair of huge hands clasped about her shoulders and mouth and yanked her through the door, easily restraining her efforts to break free. Chiang followed and closed the door behind them.

"Oh, shit," exclaimed Flanery as he tried to find a place to park.

The room was dimly lit with only one light hanging from the ceiling. A chair sat directly under it and there was a small table off to one side with various objects on top; all foreign to Leslie.

The brute holding her forced her to the chair and made her sit down. Realizing her struggling was futile, she obediently sat down and waited on pins and needles for the other shoe to drop.

Briggs pointed to himself and then took a position close to the front of the alley, obscured by a stack of skids. Flannery nodded and placed himself inside a doorway in the alley, giving a clear shot to the door where Leslie had disappeared through.

"My name is Tu An Lin." A patient, yet authoritative voice came from the shadows, and then Tu An Lin emerged, a serene smile on his face as his stare met Leslie's. A curt nod and the man that had held her earlier snatched up her left arm, pulled it up and viciously twisted it, establishing his dominance. Chiang remained just to her right, and she threw him a look that held both fear and betrayal. Relief was slight as her arm was strapped into place on the armrest. Her right arm followed the same procedure, except it was bound to the railings on the back of the chair.

Tu An Lin waited a moment, then spoke. "Mrs. Scott?"

Leslie didn't respond immediately; and she felt her head being yanked back, forcing her to pay attention to her captor.

"Don't make this difficult for yourself by being obstinate, Mrs. Scott," he warned in a patient tone.

Obviously he was a pro at this, Leslie thought to herself as she studied him. He was a round, squat figure of a man with such a pleasant face; she was having a hard time accepting his nature didn't match his looks. He looked like Buddha, but he wasn't. Too bad for him.

"We can do this the easy way or the hard way. That depends upon you," he said evenly, without rushing.

She glanced around the small table, and upon closer inspections, she found items that did look familiar to her after all: A vial, with a hypodermic needle; a pack of cigarettes, matches and a throwing star; like the one used in San Francisco. She suddenly felt a thin layer of perspiration oozing from every pore of her being. She ignored the rotund man before her and looked to Chiang. "What is it they want?"

"I thought I explained it quite clearly in the tomb earlier. We want the other piece of the puzzle. The pendant," he answered in much improved English.

Suddenly she knew what was different about Chiang. "My, hasn't our English improved?" she observed sarcastically, and then she shot a look to Tu An Lin. "I don't have the pendant," she lied.

"Come now, Mrs. Scott. We know that the pendant was passed to you in Chinatown," he persisted.

"Oh, that pendant," she recalled in an animated voice. "Well, before I left San Francisco, I sent it to the police." Knowing one lie was quickly begetting another.

"Not so according to our sources in San Francisco."

He stroked her left hand, leaving a creepy feeling running up her arm.

"You have lovely hands. Straight, slender fingers," he observed, and then touched her face, "and beautiful skin. You choose to be difficult. You choose the hard way." He moved closer to her, his brightly colored tunic collar straining against his thick neck.

"Slim, you come by your nastiness very naturally. And, where the hell is Dad in all of this?" Elaine said to no one in particular. She scrolled down, looking for her answer, and she got more than she had bargained for.

Kash fidgeted in his seat as the opera moved into the last. Alicia couldn't help but notice his restlessness, and placed a soothing hand on his forearm, encouraging him to watch the balletic fight between two of the players. The player in black lashed out at the player in red, and momentarily stunned, the character in red shook it off and retaliated.

The crack of skin meeting skin with such violent force filled the ears of Chiang, and he closed his eyes against Tu An Lin's ugly pursuit of the pendant. Leslie's head dropped to her chest and blood trickled down the front of her white shirt. The barbarian behind her grabbed another handful of her hair and jerked her head back; forcing her to look at Tu An Lin. As he stared at her bloody mouth, she concluded his smirk was permanent.

"I'm usually a very patient man, Mrs. Scott, but you seem to have pushed me to my limits," Tu An Lin reluctantly admitted. A lack of patience was usually uncalled for and counterproductive, but he tasted more than *the sweetness of wisdom, he was savoring the spoils of power, and he'd be damned if one woman was going to stand in his way of greatness. "However much you can endure, is how much I will gladly produce to locate the pendant." He wiped her bloodied mouth. "My wish for you, Mrs. Scott, is that you leave here as lovely as you did when you arrived."*

She forced herself to swallow the vile tasting blood she had been holding in her mouth, and gave a tiny laugh laced with sarcasm at his comments. "We both know you're not going to let me leave here alive, don't we?" His smirk widened to a full, nasty smile. That answered her question. "Why don't you humor me before you kill me and tell me why you want that pendant?"

What harm could that do? He figured, and if she was going to die for it, she was entitled to know the reason why. "In China, wisdom and knowledge mean everything."

"No matter how you acquire it?" she asked.

"It matters not what or how you acquire, but rather, what you do afterwards. The Heavenly Wisdom is the key to mastering wisdom; and knowledge. From mastering hope and wisdom, and understanding their features, one automatically gains the power and the respect of all."

Leslie nodded her head in understanding his twisted explanation; and still he continued. "The possibilities are endless. That pendant holds more than the key behind finding the Heavenly Wisdom; it holds something precious to your government. Something the Russians want very badly; information regarding atomic weaponry. You see," he gestured with open palms, "the possibilities are endless. We will find the pendant with or without your assistance, Mrs. Scott. But you are right on one account; I'm not going to let you live."

She closed her eyes to his madness for a moment; then she stared over at a silent Chiang. "Thanks."

"Don't worry, Mrs. Scott, it will be a totally painless death. Actually, you might enjoy it for a second or two."

She followed his gaze to the tiny table a few feet away and reckoned the contents in the vial was her passage to La La Land. "Aren't you going to give me a last request?" she asked, trying to buy time.

"Such as?" Tu An Lin recognized her attempt and humored her.

"A cigarette?"

Tu An Lin nodded and pulled out a cigarette and placed it between her dry lips and lit the end. Leslie dragged in and nearly choked, but stifled it. God, she hated cigarettes. She squinted through the smoke at the demented man in front of her and started to speak, but stopped because of the cigarette.

"Are you right handed?" he questioned.

Leslie gave an affirmative nod, yes.

"Cut her left arm free," he directed the brute.

He did so, and stepped around to take his place next to Tu An Lin, then he started to prepare the vial and needle. Leslie watched and removed the disgusting cigarette from her mouth. "I know where it is," she baited Tu An Lin.

He bit and leaned closer to her as she took another drag from her smoke. "You do?"

Leslie cocked her brow and smiled knowingly.

"Suppose you tell me?" he encouraged with twinkling eyes.

Leslie blew out the smoke she had been holding in her mouth into his face. Finally his smirk disappeared. "Go to hell," she quipped.

Fury flashed in his eyes and he violently grabbed the front of her shirt along with the pendant underneath. Leslie couldn't hide the worry in her eyes; and they stared at each other. Tu An Lin quickly replaced his furious glare with one of pleasant surprise. Anxiously he pulled down her tie and ripped open her shirt front; revealing the pendant nestled in the hollow of her throat.

She swallowed hard as his hand approached her neck. He gently cradled the object of his subsequent greatness and examined both sides. Delight showing in his features when he saw the back side and the dragon with two characters. The smirk returned and his eyes danced happily as he wrenched the pendant from around Leslie's neck.

She winced at the searing pain caused by his ripping it free, and for added measure, he dangled it in front of her face; rubbing her nose in his triumph. A new layer of sweat formed, chilling her.

Frustrated and irritated, Kash wiped a bead of sweat from his furrowed brow; then checked his watch again, hoping the opera would end soon. He speculated it was coming to a close when the player in red knelt to the ground and bowed his head in anticipation of the black player's sword. Impatiently Kash looked to his watch again, ignoring Alicia's offended glare. He wondered if Leslie had returned to the hotel, or if she was keeping company with Gerald? He sat back, sorry he had accepted Alicia's invitation in the first place. No he was wishing for the end to come soon.

Leslie looked past the pendant dangling in front of her nose to Tu An Lin's oh-too-happy-face. "Now, who's going to hell?" he proclaimed.

Her blood was racing and pounded loudly in her ears. Think! She told herself as she looked to the small table and the pack of cigarettes. Lunging forward toward Tu An Lin, she stuck the burning end of the cigarette into his eye and ground it out; then she kicked him back into the charging enforcer.

A shrill of pain came from Tu An Lin as he dropped the pendant into her lap and grabbed his face. Leslie secured the piece and got up from the chair, pulling it around to the front, her wrist still bound to the railings. Ignoring the pain, she swung the chair at the rushing brute, and repaid the many favors by breaking it over his head and shoulders; sending him crashing to the floor. She finished him off with a few swift kicks to his head.

Out of the corner of her eye, she saw Chiang make a move toward her. "You son-of-a-bitch," she growled and gladly beat him down with the remainder of the chair until he fell to the floor, unconscious. Then she frantically stripped her rope burned wrist free from the railings.

Weary and trying to catch her breath, Leslie headed for the door and freedom. She ripped it open, only to see Gerald standing there. She stopped short; staring into the depths of his betraying, azure blue eyes.

He spotted the pendant in her hand, and his tone was as indifferent as his stare. "Give me the pendant, Leslie. I won't hurt you, I promise."

"Did you promise Mark, too?" She paused, expecting an answer, but knew his action was beyond explanation. "You fucking bastard!" She lashed out and brought her foot up into his groin with all the strength she could muster.

He snapped his legs together in pain, capturing her leg. She balanced herself, and tried to pull free, but he held tight; and reaching out a shaky hand, he clutched her throat.

"This is for Mark," she hissed. Doubling her fist, she let one fly, hitting him square in the face.

He released everything and fell backwards, holding his face.

Leslie shoved the pendant into her pants pocket and headed for through the door, but she didn't reach it soon enough.

Tu An Lin hurled a throwing star at her, slicing open her right arm. Crying out, she grabbed the wound, trying to staunch the bleeding. She glanced back at his contemptible one eyed glare; then she rushed out into the alley.

She started off toward the way she had entered the alley earlier, but came to an abrupt halt when a man emerged from the shadows of a doorway. Turning tail, she ran in the opposite direction, and the out-of-shape man lumbered after her.

The man had guessed right and made every turn for turn that Leslie had. She stopped and heard him half running, half walking, and then she grabbed the nearest thing she could find; a trash can lid. She waited and timed it perfectly; nailing the man right in the face. The bang echoed off the walls and he crumpled like a mighty oak to the pavement; out cold.

"You folks have everything here at the British consulate," Kash commented, looking for a way to stimulate a conversation that was going nowhere fast.

"You mean the nightspot?" Alicia confirmed.

"Yeah, it's nice." Stimulating? Hardly. He was bored and not hiding it very well. He didn't want to be with the accommodating Alicia. Instead, he would rather have been with Leslie, enjoying an evening of her stiff-necked, highhanded, bright and charming company.

The waiter approached them; momentarily taking his mind off his the vixen that had wielded her way into his heart. "Would you like a glass of sherry? He asked Alicia.

"No, Stolichnaya on the rocks, please."

Kash stole a curious glance, then order his usual. "Scotch."

Tired of the existing tension, Alicia thoughtfully confronted Kash. "You've been pensive all night. Do you want to share it with me?" She paused, hoping he'd answer. He didn't. "Sometimes it helps to talk about it and get if off your chest," she encouraged, trying desperately to gain his trust.

"Thanks, but it's okay now." He gave her a relieved smile and relaxed back in his chair, anxious to finish his drink and get back to the Imperial and Leslie Anne Scott.

Kash stepped inside the suite and reached for the light switch and stopped when he realized the lights were already on. A grin stole across his face; Leslie must be back, he hoped.

Putting the key into his pocket, he glanced down at the floor and saw her satchel. The handle on one side was saturated with blood and droplets of red led into the living room. His smile faded as he saw the top of her head slumped to one side in the chair. He hurried towards her, calling her name. "Leslie? Leslie?"

She didn't answer.

He reached her side and found her clutching a nearly empty bottle of scotch. No wonder she didn't answer, he thought. She was apparently passed out. That was the least of his concern. He winced at the ugly mark under her lower lip and noticed the right sleeve of her jacket was soaked and red-stained. The blood had run down her arm and dribbled onto the floor next to the chair.

Training took over and he checked her vitals and found them to be normal, indicating no immediate danger. He started to take the bottle from the cradle of her bosom and met with resistance when she suddenly came to.

Her head was heavy, her mouth dry and the inside of her eyelids felt like sandpaper. Did she look as bad as she felt? She wondered. Deliberately blinking several times at him, she pulled the bottle closer into the crook of her arm, away from his insistent hand. "Mine," she declared selfishly.

He managed to wrestle it away from her death grip and placed it on the coffee table for safe keeping. Gently he cradled her face and touched the ugly mark under her lip. Her expression held little pain, dulled no doubt by the scotch. Grabbing the lapels of her jacket, he pulled her forward to his chest. She offered no help, occasionally jabbering as he struggled to remove the bulky clothing. He threw it aside and placed her back in the chair, thankful it was a wingback and would hold her steady while he ministered to her arm.

The blood had dried, causing her torn shirt to stick to the wound. He reached back and grabbed the bottle of scotch and flooded the wound with it.

That brought her around, and a tiny cry escaped her lips. She bravely tightened her jaw to the pain.

"Damn you," she said through clenched teeth, recalling his comments in San Francisco. "Scotch is for drinking, not doctoring."

As she had with him; he ignored her comment and pulled the torn shirt away from the injury. It was an angry, deep slit, shaped like a half moon. "What happened?"

"Isn't it obvious; I got the shit kicked out of me."

"I can see that. Why?"

She didn't answer and he didn't press.

"Sit still," he ordered. "I'll be right back."

She rolled her head to one side and watched until she could no longer, and even in her numb state, a sweet euphoria flooded her senses, leaving goose bumps in its wake. Oh, she liked the feeling that erupted in her when she thought of Kash Bennett. It was a sensation long dormant, but not forgotten. She was basking in the impression when he returned with a washcloth and towel.

He was happy to see she hadn't budged, though he doubted that she could have in her condition, but still, he took nothing for granted, especially with Leslie. He poured the remainder of the scotch on the slit to flush out any impurities. With his forefinger, he squeezed it shut causing the rest of the liquor and blood to ooze out.

A wave of nausea forced Leslie to sit still, or she would have gladly complained like he did in San Francisco. He wasn't delicate about dressing the wound, either. He tightened the handkerchief bandage and started to attend to her busted lip, but she turned her head away. Treating her like the spoiled child she was, he forced her head back around and gave her a settling glare.

"Just let me look at it." He pulled her lip down and found a cut similar to the one he had acquired back home.

She blinked her bloodshot eyes and attempted to speak. "'atches 'ers."

"Yeah, it does," he agreed, understanding her less than perfect enunciation. Unlike her other wound, there was a better way to treat this particular type of hurt. Tenderly he kissed it, with no complaint from her.

She was pliable under his lips, and he was careful not to be too forceful. Finally, she eased him back, her eyes holding a trace of regret in their dreamy depths. "I'm in no condition to get smacky mouthed with you. Not tonight, anyway." It was more of a request than a plea and Kash nodded his understanding.

He stymied a laugh that was building over her words, "smacky mouthed", and he held his thumb and forefinger close together, indicating a small kiss for his efforts. She smiled and allowed him that reward. He placed it on the other side of her bruised lip. He didn't stop there; he continued to her ear and whispered, "It's time to put you to bed." He could feel the heat of her flushed skin against his lips; it was delicate, like her skin.

"Alone?" she purred.

"Alone." He confirmed with regret, but not before he satisfied his curiosity and examined further the softness of her neck. He drank in the creaminess, savoring the texture beneath his lips and her sultry moan was heaven to his ears. The sweetness came to a bitter halt when he discovered the rough, red maul on her neck. He pulled down her shirt collar and followed the line all the way around to the other side of her throat.

Eyes closed and oblivious to his discovery, Leslie rolled her head to one side, inviting him to indulge them both. His brow knitted in fury and he roughly pulled her face around to his. Suddenly, she was more alert.

"You've had the pendant the whole time, haven't you?" Kash accused. "And by the looks of things, you don't have it anymore, do you? Did you hold out for more and Gerald get a little impatient? Did he decide to take it from you, Natalia?" It was out before he could stop himself, but he wasn't sorry, only saddened that deep down he still harbored suspicions about Leslie and her involvement as described by Briggs.

Her brow deepened in a confused and hurt frown and he released another wave of his pent up anger.

"Oh, you're good, Natalia. Briggs was right, I should have thought with my brain and not," he paused, searching for better phrasing than Briggs had used.

It was a tiny opening, but Leslie took advantage, and even though she may have been slightly inebriated, she wasn't brain dead, and his cruelty had just pushed her over the edge. The liquor had dulled her coordination, but she managed to shove him away and through sheer will power she stood before her accuser. "God damn you. How dare you accuse me of whatever it is you're accusing me of?" It wasn't much but it was all she could think of to say at that moment. She was hurt and confused, and didn't mind showing it. Just a second ago, he was kind, almost loving in his attention; then, bam! He changed into a regular Dr. Jekyll and Mr. Hyde, only without the makeup.

"You've sold us right down the river, lady. You've sold every free country down the goddamn river," he rambled. "Hell, even China."

"What?" she yelled in exasperation. "For some lousy volume of the Heavenly Wisdom?"

"What the hell are you talking about?"

"Right back at you," she countered.

"Trying to turn the tables isn't going to help," he warned. "The Russians found a great one in you. I'm sure Gerald loves having you as a comrade in espionage and in his bed."

"Through, Romeo?" His glare held a trace of confusion and she explained. "If you weren't so busy playing Romeo, I would have gladly explained." She waited a moment for the comment to soak into his hard head. "So, that's what you think about me?" Even in her condition, she understood where he was coming from and relieved that she would have the opportunity to reason with him. But, then again, maybe not, considering their rocky track record. Or maybe, she should just let him sit and stew for a while. It'd serve him right, she justified to herself.

"It's what I know to be true," he regretfully replied.

Judge, jury and hangman, she wanted to say. "What you think you know," she corrected. "I'm not a communist spy, but I have a pretty good idea who is, and has been for years." She took in a shaky breath and then filled him in. "Two years ago, on my wedding day, I watched my husband killed in a car explosion and burned to almost nothing. Coincidentally, Gerald was there to pick up the pieces, literally. Well, it never dawned on me that Mark's best friend was the mole he sought to bring in that very afternoon. Not until tonight, anyway."

"You saw him tonight?"

He sounded more hurt than angry. A mood she could better deal with. "Yes."

"He did this to you?" he asked looking at her bruised lip.

"No." She laughed and touched her smarting lip. "Some fat man Chiang works for hit me. That was for the other side of the pendant."

He cocked his head to one side, silently questioning her explanation. Not sure to believe her, but wanting to. "What we saw on the chamber wall?"

She nodded. "The back of the pendant is the final clue in locating the Heavenly Wisdom. Apparently when one acquires the Volume, one also gains wisdom, hope and," she paused, recalling Tu An Lin's round, full-of-himself face. "Power. That's what the fat man wants."

"I guess he got more than he bargained for."

"You mean the information concerning atomic weaponry?"

His eyes darkened, and she sensed a storm coming. "How did you know about that?"

She raised a questioning brow to him, turning the tables on him. "How did you know?" He didn't answer. He just stared in that threatening way. "There wasn't any bargains tonight, Kash." She reached into her pants pocket and pulled free the unlucky charm and gladly turned it over to Bennett's upturned palm. "Take this, please."

He closed his hand over the pendant and her weary hand, and held on tightly. She figured it was his way of offering an apology for doubting her and her loyalty. She accepted with a wan smile.

"And Gerald?"

"He got what was coming to him."

Kash raised his eyebrows urging her to explain more fully.

"I fed him his balls."

Somehow that didn't surprise him and he eased the grip on her hand, but didn't release it. There was something else nagging him and he wanted an answer. "That isn't your jacket," he observed quietly.

"No," she agreed. "I sort of borrowed it from some man that was chasing me in the alley."

"He just gave it to you?" Kash filled in the missing piece to her explanation.

"No," she simply told him.

His hooded gaze prompted her to elaborate.

"He chased me and I knocked him out cold with a trash can lid. Then, I took his jacket, got my stuff and got the hell out of there."

His laugh was loud and it assaulted her throbbing head. "You Ko'd Flannery with a trash can lid?"

"Yeah. Who's Flanery?"

As quickly as he laughed, he became serious again. "A cop from San Francisco. Because they found Mike murdered in my car, they believed I was somehow involved with the pendant. Then some pompous ass named Briggs, with the CIA came here and said you were probably the Russian plant named Natalia. Well, Flanery had stuck through uglier messes than *this one with me and he came all this way to prove Briggs wrong, and clear my name. Some friend, huh?" His eyes misted at the loyalty shown by Mike, Flanery and Leslie and realized he had never thanked any of them.*

"Yeah, like Mike." She tenderly stroked the hollow of his tightened jaw. "I'm so sorry about your friend. I'm truly to blame for that, and I…"

He put a silencing finger to her parted lips. "It's okay. As long as I don't lose you."

Relief washed over her tired features. "Did you really think that I was a Russian spy?"

"Naw," he lied and looked at his shoe tops, hiding the embarrassment he felt. He knew she knew he had entertained thought of her being Natalia, but he reasoned, "You had plenty of opportunities to give Gerald the pendant. Besides, I know who the real Natalia is. She made the mistake of ordering Stolichnaya. Only a true Russian drinks vodka on the job."

"Alicia," she said knowingly, and he nodded. "Now what are you going to do?" Tensions receding, the alcohol she had consumed was starting to take its toll. He watched her sway slightly and put a steadying hand to her shoulder. "Put you to bed," he finally answered.

"Alone?" she bravely asked.

"Alone," he sadly confirmed. Without any effort, and no complaints from Leslie, he picked her up and carried her to her room.

Elaine was exhausted. She felt as if she had just lived her parents experience in China. She flipped to the section in her PDA for notes and with her stylus she copied down more names; Flanery, Tu An Lin, Chiang and, of course, Briggs. She didn't know why she was recording the names, only that she had a feeling that somewhere, sometime, she was going to run across them again.

She looked at her watch and pulled her cell phone from the nightstand and dialed Sam Winston's number in Alaska. She waited while the phone to connect.

"Hello?" Sam Winston bellowed.

"Mr. Winston this is Elaine Bennett. I'm calling to see if you have any news regarding the search for my parents, Kash and Leslie Bennett."

There was a long pause and Winston finally spoke. "I talked with your brother not too long ago. I would have thought he would have called you with our decision."

"Your decision?"

"We've decided to go from rescue to recovery," he regretfully informed her. He waited a moment for her to say something, but she didn't. "I'm sorry, Miss Bennett, we feel that with the current weather and the amount of time they have been missing, we don't a choice but to assume they," he stopped when she cut him off.

"You have assumed wrong, Mr. Winston. My parents are still alive and we need you to keep looking for them. I'm on my way up to Juneau and when I get there, I except something better than your current efforts." She hit the end button on her phone and cut off any excuse he thought he might offer.

Then she dialed Lane's cell phone. It went immediately into his voice mail. She listened to his outgoing message as she walked to the door and opened it up to Jack talking on his phone.

He turned away from her and faced the stone fireplace, his voice dropping several decibels. She turned off her phone and made a bee line for Jack's. She plucked it out of his hand and launched into her brother.

"Lane?" She said with deadly calm.

"Elaine, put Jack back on the phone," he demanded.

"No. You tell me, little brother, why you can't call and let me know the status concerning our parents? Hum?" She prompted.

"You listen," he began in a threatening tone. "You have no idea the shit you are stirring up. The danger you have put our parents in by running around thinking you are some super sleuth."

"Don't put this on me," she said evenly, surprising even herself at how composed she was considering it was her worthless, piece of shit brother. "I know you know more than you lead on, or that you'll ever tell me, but I'm still their daughter and I have a right to know what you have found out. And if you're not willing to tell me, I'll find someone who is." Before he could rebut, she hung up the phone and threw it back at Jack. "You're either with me or him. You decide."

She walked into the silence of the kitchen and to the side of Mollie who was busy preparing the night's dinner. "Is there anything you or John can tell me regarding my parents?"

"I think you've learned enough. Perhaps after dinner, we can talk more. But until then, get some rest. You're going to need it when you travel to Alaska." Mollie continued peeling sweet potatoes as Elaine left the kitchen.

Jack made an effort to speak with her, but she warned him off with a wave of her finger. He let her go to the seclusion of her bedroom knowing full well after she got some rest; he would have some explaining to do.

CHAPTER THIRTY TWO

Elaine stirred beneath the throw and lazily straightened out the kinks from her much needed nap. At the end of her stretch she realized she wasn't alone. She stiffened and Jack knew she was aware of his presence. Taking in a deep breath, she steeled her emotions and spoke in a husky whisper. "You better have a good reason for being this close."

"None that you'll find acceptable," he replied in a lazy drawl. He placed a gentle hand on her arm and began to hypnotically rub her flesh in a slow, circular pattern. "What would you like to know?" he offered.

She sighed under his touch and took her time in answering his question. She turned over to face him; her mouth touching his. "We can discuss it after dinner with John and Mollie," she said as she kissed his slightly parted lips.

Before they could take it any further, a polite knock came on the door. "Dinner's ready," Mollie announced through the poplar.

"Hum, I hungry," Elaine declared as she extricated herself from Jack's seductive hold.

"Me, too," he agreed, as he tried to hold her in place, but without success. "For something else."

"That would be dessert," she called from the door.

"My favorite course," he said, holding the door for her to go through.

It was a short walk from Elaine's bedroom to the dining room. There she found the Duncan Phyfe replicated dining room table dressed in its finest. From the linens to the silverware to the crystal drinking and wine glasses, and of course, the English bone china; everything was perfect, reflecting the kind of hostess Mollie was; tasteful. Oh, and the smell emanating from the adjoining kitchen, was sumptuous.

Mollie was busying herself with collecting the wine glasses for the Bordeaux that would be served to complement the rack of lamb. Elaine chipped in by filling the antique water glasses with room temperature water and freshly sliced lemons.

Jack accepted a glass of wine from John, and the two of them stood back and watched the "little women" plate the food and put the finishing touches on Elaine's favorite meal.

"Come and get it," Mollie instructed as she stood by her chair and waited for her guests to seat themselves; then she sat.

Elaine looked at her plate and then to Mollie. "Mollie, why didn't you ask for some help?"

"Oh, you know, dear, too many cooks in the kitchen," she answered with a wink.

Jack cleared his throat and looked at Elaine.

"I know I can't cook, but I could have helped with the wine," Elaine defended as she cut a piece of lamb and deliberately took a bite.

Jack could have sworn her eyes rolled back into her head as she enjoyed the first nibble. He followed her lead and immediately understood why she was so enamored with the meal.

It was obvious for the whole of her marriage that Elaine was not the typical homebody and for sure she didn't know the difference between sauté and simmer, but that didn't mean she didn't know great food when it hit her palate. She savored the lamb; tasting the Dijon mustard, garlic and rosemary rub that made the tender meat so flavorful. She never got tired of eating this dish. She prepared her fork with the lamb and sweet potato rosti. The oregano in the rosti bolstered the delicious flavor of the lamb.

It was so quiet in the house; the only sounds were the utensils clinking the fine china and the occasional, "Oh, this is so good."

Mollie took the compliments in stride and enjoyed the meal; especially when Elaine went into the kitchen to refill her plate. When she returned she had another lamb chop and a healthy heaping of the white asparagus with lemon butter and truffle sauce. "Leave room for dessert, dear," Mollie reminded her.

With truffle sauce running down her chin, Elaine asked, "What's for dessert?"

"Floating Islands," Mollie replied with gleam in her twinkling brown eyes.

"Oh, that's my favorite," piped up Jack as he headed to the kitchen for another bottle of wine. He returned and refilled everyone's glass. The wine had a full bodied and rich red fruitiness that reined in the boldness of the lamb chops. It was not only soothing, but harmonizing to the meal, and it had taken the edge off of Elaine; allowing her to relax and enjoy the special meal Mollie had prepared for her.

With seconds devoured, the dinner party sat and awkwardly stared at each other. It was if they were strangers, and the only thing in common was the delicious meal they just shared. Mollie broke the silence by getting up and clearing the table. Elaine popped up and started to help; only to be shooed away like an annoying gnat.

"Out of my kitchen, girlie," Mollie ordered in a firm, no nonsense tone.

"At least let me clear the table and refill the water glasses. Maybe get the coffee?" Elaine pleaded. She hated that Mollie went to all that trouble to prepare a sumptuous meal and then had a dirty kitchen waiting on her. The least she could do was let her clean up. Better yet, let Jack tidy up while the rest of them visited with each other.

"It'll wait until we've enjoyed our dessert, and then I'll let the dishwasher take over. Now, fill up the water glasses and I'll put on the coffee for later."

Elaine had filled the glasses and like the rest, she waited patiently for Mollie to come back to the table. When she did, she placed before her guests a dish of fluffy meringue dumplings floating in a sea of delicious rum flavored crème angelise sauce.

"Bon appétit," Mollie announced, and then sat with her guests to enjoy Elaine's favorite dessert.

"Mollie, where did you find this dessert?" Jack asked in between bites.

"Oh, it must have been when the cold war was starting to take hold, that I ran across a dear friend from days of old, and we got to chatting about cooking and then Julia told me about this lovely concoction, and I tried it, and it has been a favorite ever since."

"Not *the* Julia?" Jack questioned with surprise.

"Yes, dear. The one in the same," Mollie clarified.

"Wow. Small world." He looked to Elaine as she chased a bite of her dreamy meringue through a pool of decadent sauce; her concentration solely riveted on capturing the elusive morsel.

The dishwasher had found its rhythm by the time Mollie had served the coffee and joined her guests in the living room. John had stoked the fire, sat in his favorite wing backed chair, and lazily planted his feet on the ottoman before him. The fire warmed him from the soles of his feet through the top of his head. Shortly, he would be ready for bed.

Jack broke the enchanting silence the crackling fire had cast over the full and contented dinner party. "So, Mollie, exactly how did you know Julia?"

"Hum." Mollie sipped the rich, dark roast coffee she had prepared for everyone; put her cup down on the end table next to her chair and chose her words carefully. "I was young, probably fifteen or sixteen, and my father worked at the headquarters of the OSS in Washington. Like a gym rat, I hung around the office with my father when able, and at the time, Julia was a research assistant. I remember one day I was volunteering in the file room and I had a stack of folders; I could barely see over them and when I rounded the corner to enter the room, Julia was walking out and I nearly spilled the whole lot of them as we narrowly missed running each other over. From that moment, we became friends. She was older than me by, oh, thirteen or fourteen years, but so kind and refreshingly funny. We kept in touch through the years, and when I followed my father into the service our country, our paths crossed in Paris where she was she learning what was to be her legacy. She was simply an amazing soul."

Mollie became very quiet in her reflection and recollection of days gone by. She sipped her coffee and paused; her eyes peeking over the rim of her cup to an expectant Elaine. She then let the cup rest in her lap as she explained how she came to know Leslie Anne Walker. "Your mother. Your mother was an insistent, young recruit that not only was mysteriously beautiful, but she was smart, and she had a knack for being able to see beyond the assignment. There was a group of us that were sent to London and we worked alongside the British. That is where Leslie met and fell in love with a dashing young Brit, named Mark Scott."

"Was he handsome?" Elaine asked in an off handed, solemn way.

"Oh, no," replied Mollie, almost laughing at the notion of Mark Scott being anything like Kash in looks. "No, dear. Not even close. But he was charming and brave, with a cobra like wit that struck before you knew what was happening. He made your mother laugh. And, God knows we all needed it in those days." Mollie looked for John to start filling in the blanks.

He took his cue and began telling how they came to meet Elaine's parents. "After we had finished SO training with the OSS, a handful of us were sent to London, where we were introduced to members of the OSE; their version of our OSS. Totally separate from MI6. We then were sent to Scotland to train alongside their OSE."

"How was that?" Jack asked.

"Brutal," replied John and gave a litany of what they learned. "We were taught how to parachute over rugged terrain, hand to hand combat, weapons, demolitions, communications, tailing someone, losing a tail, and the do's and don'ts of being captured. The hardest part was learning how to change your appearance."

"Seriously?" Jack commented.

"Well, that, and that damned obstacle course. It wasn't fit for a billy goat, let alone humans. I walked away from that with more injuries than anything out in the field."

"This is where you met my parents?" Elaine asked.

"I met your father. I met Leslie a little later."

Elaine cocked her head, encouraging more information. Mollie obliged.

"Your mother had done her training before John and Kash. She was trained and briefed and brought back to London to await her assignment. She was the consummate spy. Well rounded in every way. They just didn't want to send her in to be a typical saboteur. She was well versed in not only intelligence, but counterintelligence. And, she could handle herself. She was diplomatic, but she knew when to cut her losses and disappear."

"And, now?" Elaine wondered aloud.

"Now, more than ever, her skills will keep her alive. And, your father, too," Mollie reassured her.

"So, where does Mark Scott fit into this story?" Elaine queried.

"Well," Mollie began, "Mark worked for MI6; he wasn't in any way connected to the OSE. After Leslie and I arrived, she went to Scotland for training and I stayed in London as an analyst. She came back, awaiting her assignment and when she finally got the call, the OSE, OSS and MI6 were called for a joint briefing. Mark Scott was the one MI6 sent. Like all men who met your mother, he was captivated by her beauty and poise. For being so young, she was well beyond her years.

"She went off and did her assignment. Very successfully. Then, she came back to London to await a new mission. This was nearing the end of the War, so tasks were limited for women operatives and time was more abundant. Mark came in the office one day for the assistance of bringing in a mole, and that's where it started. It was a whirlwind courtship and a surprise marriage. And, then," Mollie's voice trailed off as she looked down at her lap.

John took over. "Then, on their wedding day, Mark was going to meet the mole and bring him in. He got as far as his car and it exploded."

"Leslie was inconsolable," Mollie remembered. "But she held it together for the job. The OSS and OSE needed a pretty girl that was fluent in Italian for a job in Bellagio, on Lake Como in Italy. Behind the scenes we knew it was more dangerous than her previous assignment in France. And, we knew there was a chance she wouldn't be coming back. She took it, and I, like many, thought it was a suicide mission. And when we lost contact with her, we assumed the worst. But like that Phoenix, your mother's code name, she rose out of the ashes and made it home safely.

"She tried giving up the spy business once the war was over and the debriefings were done. She settled in New York and began her journalistic career. Mostly, on works of art. But, she just couldn't stay away. So, when the OSS became the CIA, she rejoined. She wasn't happy at first, most of her assignments were state side; following up on subversives, Communistic sympathizers. She hated it. Then came China. And, as you have read, a lot more happened in China than just laying the foundation for our intelligence operations and helping MI6 with their mole. How far are you into the journals?"

"I'm in China, where she learned Gerald Bryant was the mole, and the killer of her husband." Elaine sipped her coffee and studied Mollie's taunt features. " Are you suggesting there are more?"

Mollie looked to John and he gave a curt shake of the head; warning Mollie not to go there.

"Where are the rest?" Elaine quietly asked, knowing the answer.

"When the time is right, we'll discuss it," Mollie answered firmly. "Go to Alaska and see what that yields. Then come back here and stay as long as you like. Everything you will need will be here."

Jack grimaced over Mollie's comments and flexed his jaw. He saw a hornet's nest, and usually the best defense against a hornet was to run, and he knew Elaine wasn't about to do that.

"Did my parent's go fishing for something other than the kind with gills?"

"Yes," Mollie replied honestly. "In every spy organization, someone turns. Early on we had such an individual in our ranks. He wrecked havoc, and through the years your father had started to piece together Intel that pointed to someone he thought to be dead."

"Mike Marrow." Elaine barely said his name above a whisper.

"Yes." Mollie confirmed. "Your father believed Mike to be somewhere in Alaska. The remoteness offering plenty of cover, and still close to his mother Russia.

"Mollie!" John sternly called out and rose out of his chair.

A settling look from Mollie and he dutifully sat. "She doesn't need to know that."

"She's like her mother; resourceful. She would learn about it sooner or later. And, besides, Jack's here to help not thwart. Right, Jack?" Mollie directed her steely stare toward Jack, daring him to cross her.

"Right," he regretfully lied.

"Liar." Elaine called him out.

"We've been through this," he patiently explained. "Our world can get you hurt or worse, killed. And if that happened, I couldn't face your folks. I'm responsible for keeping you out of harm's way; and that's what I'm going to do."

Mollie cleared her throat and then finished her coffee; all the while, staring down an exasperated Jack, daring him to comment further. He didn't.

"So, where did my parents go?"

"Somewhere between Craig, Angoon and Juneau," John answered, keeping it simple and to the point.

"Is that why my parents took annual fishing trips to Angoon? They suspected he was in that area? It's not exactly close to Russia, he should have been in Nome or Wales," Elaine observed.

"No, they started the fishing trips because they enjoyed them. But one trip in particular, your father heard someone make a comment about San Francisco and Lucy's Rathskellar. Of course, Kash immediately turned to see the source and when his eyes met Mike's, they both knew.

"Mike then used the fishing patrons and put distance between he and your father and Kash was unable to catch up. But he knew, and they've been searching for him ever since."

"This just keeps getting better and better," Elaine commented while rubbing her throbbing temples. What's Lane's roll in this? Is he going to be a problem?" Elaine asked pointedly.

Jack looked to John and Mollie, then firmly answered, "No."

"I would have preferred Mollie or John answering that."

"I would imagine he will try to throw a few monkey wrenches your way, but Jack will make sure you're not impeded on finding your parents," Mollie conclude. Getting up from her chair, she headed for the kitchen.

John collected Elaine and Jack's coffee cups and followed his wife into the kitchen, leaving an estranged silence in the living room.

"We better get to bed. Long day ahead tomorrow," Jack said as he got up and headed for his room.

Elaine watched his retreating back and then went into the kitchen with Mollie and John. She hugged them both and headed for her room.

CHAPTER THIRTY THREE

Sleep wasn't coming easily for Elaine, so she pulled the PDA from its charger and resumed reading about her parents' mission in China, and sub-conscientiously she was planning her trip for the morning.

Kash waited patiently for a very pale Leslie to emerge from the bathroom and crawl under the covers he had been holding up. She slipped beneath them and looked up miserably to his sympathetic face.

"Feeling better?" He asked the question gently, knowing she wasn't.

"One always feels better after getting fountain faced," she weakly informed him.

"You shouldn't have had so much to drink," he playfully lectured.

"I know that now." She gave a regretful smile and he tucked her in. He planted a kiss on her forehead, and she closed her eyes to the unpleasantness of the evening.

There was a polite knock on the door. Hearing it, Kash came out of the bathroom. A towel secured around his waist, his hair wet and combed back and the start of shaving cream on half of his face. He padded quietly to the door and whispered, "Yes?" His timber was intentionally low, so as not to wake Leslie.

"The coffee you requested, sir." The attendant said through the closed door.

Cautiously Kash opened the door to view the attendant and the silver tray he was carrying. Coffee, cream, sugar and a nice big glass of tomato juice. He took the tray and nodded his thanks, then kicked the door shut, hoping it hadn't disturbed Leslie. Being extra careful, he tiptoed past her door; thankful for the most part, that she had had a peaceful night.

He had just poured himself a steaming cup of coffee when the door announced another visitor, and this time the knock was severe and impatient. "Yes?" Kash asked, his tone matching the knock.

"It's me," growled the visitor.

Recognizing that voice, Kash opened the door to find Flanery with Special Officer Briggs. He motioned for them to come in, and as Flannery walked by, shock registered on Bennett's face when he looked beneath the brim of the detective's hat. "You look like a goddamn raccoon," he teased and followed them into the living room. Even the stone-faced Briggs had a hard time maintaining his dull composure.

Flanery found little humor in Kash's early morning banter, and tilted his head to stare up at Bennett's amused features, unmasking not one, but two black eyes and a piece of white tape across the bridge of his badly broken nose and swollen mouth. "Your Amazon friend tagged me with a trash can lid, then stole my jacket," he informed with much indignation.

"Coffee?" Kash offered, trying to smooth over Flanery's obvious irritability. They both accepted with simultaneous nods. Like twins, Kash thought. "Cups are over on the bar. Help yourself," he directed, while back peddling to his room. "Excuse me."

They helped themselves while he dressed, and as soon as they sat down, he returned in neatly pressed slacks and a crisp white shirt. Flanery had never seen him look so jake. Must be the dame, he concluded.

Kash grabbed his coffee and sat in the chair Leslie had occupied the night before. Briggs stared suspiciously at the floor beneath and the droplets of blood. Kash noticed the special officer's furrowed brow. "She was hurt last night by Chiang and his friends. Her theory was correct that some kind of puzzle was connected to the pendant. The characters and the dragon lead to an ancient volume called the Heavenly Wisdom."

The special officer's face remained unchanged throughout Kash's explanation. He could have cared less about the Heavenly Wisdom, and it showed. He vocalized his one thought and concern. "So, what you're saying is that these people took the pendant from the woman. Well, it seems they got more than they bargained for. Terrific."

I didn't say that at all." Kash pulled the pendant from his pocket and held it just out of the reach of Briggs. "She had it ripped from her neck, recovered it, and didn't surrender it to Gerald. Natalia wouldn't have returned, and if she did, she wouldn't have brought this with her." He watched Briggs for any wrinkle of change. None. But he was satisfied he *proved the special officer wrong about Leslie, and he didn't have to belabor the point. "Do you have any idea who Natalia is?" Briggs stubbornly shook his head. "Well, I do. And it's time to bait the hook." He tossed the pendant to Briggs, then sat back and enjoyed his coffee.*

Kash cheerfully sat down across the table from Alicia. It was ten o'clock and most of the breakfast club had departed. "Good morning," he greeted.

"Good morning," Alicia echoed. "A good night's rest seems to have improved your mood." She paused to look at the door. "Where's Leslie? I would thought she'd be joining us."

"I was going to say the same about Gerald."

"Apparently he didn't find his way home last night," she discreetly volunteered.

"Neither did Leslie." He reached into his pocket and pulled free the pendant and fingered it under the table, out of Alicia's sight. "I was a bit on edge last night, so I started to work on the article. You know, coordinate photos with words and I wanted to look at Leslie's notes. So, when I went through her satchel, I found this." He placed the octagon shaped object in front of her, with the dragon side up.

"Well," she said, a tiny bit exasperated. "Isn't that lovely?"

"And deadly," Kash added.

Kash flipped it over to the Yin-Yang side and carefully watched her reaction. She gave very little away, until she touched the eye of the Yang.

"It's not there, Natalia. The CIA removed it."

She smiled wittingly at him.

"You shouldn't have ordered that vodka last night. Now, where's Gerald?" Kash looked past her to see Briggs approaching in a too small waiter's jacket, carrying a silver tray.

Alicia never answered, but rather, opened her purse and started to pull her gun, but the blunt insistence of the special officer's 45 barrel beneath the tray, persuaded her to abandon the idea. He motioned for her to put her purse on the table. She did so without taking her eyes off of Kash.

"I've heard it's lovely this time of the year in Siberia." It was all Kash had to say to the Russian beauty, then he pocketed the pendant and left the breakfast room.

Alicia stared after him, knowing she would meet Kash Bennett again and the outcome would be different.

"You rock, Daddy. Wonder what became of Natalia?" Elaine looked at the clock and determined she could squeeze in some more light reading. She knew there were several pages left and she couldn't imagine what the rest could be about. The recovery of the micro film and the subsequent capture of Natalia, Elaine could only speculate it was finding the Heavenly Wisdom or Gerald, or both. She read on.

A gentle shake urged Leslie to open her heavy laden eyes. It took a moment, but she focused on someone she did and didn't know. Finally she recognized the man behind the raccoon face.

His stare was rigid, and he watched as she crawled up the headboard of the bed in fear before he presented her a glass of tomato juice. "Here, drink up," he ordered sternly. "Make you feel better."

Her eyes never left his as she took the glass and sipped the juice. "Oh!" Her pained expression told him the doctored juice had been administered. She started to put down the glass, but Flanery persuaded her to finish its contents. Reluctantly she did so.

"Family remedy. Hair from the tail of the dog that bit you. You're much more the lamb this morning, than the lion of last night. Lucky for me." He took the empty glass and placed it on the nightstand. She tried to get out of bed, but he put a restraining hand on her shoulder, and she sank back against the pillows. "Just sit still and relax. Let the tail wag you for a change," he said with a blackened wink.

"About last night," she began sheepishly. "I, uh, am very sorry. Had I known who you were…"

Flanery cut her off with a wave of his stubby hand. "It's all right. I'm quite frequently mistaken for a Chinese thug. Maybe because I cover Chinatown in my precinct?"

His melancholy gaze lightened with her apologetic smile, and their earlier tension subsided.

"Where's Kash?" she asked.

"Fishing. He'll return soon enough. In the meantime, he's ordered you to sit still." Flanery showed as much emotion as he was going to, and winked again.

He closed the door behind him, and Leslie cautiously slid out of the bed. Steadily she worked her way to the bathroom. Sure she was going to be seeing the tomato juice she had just swallowed, she held her breath until it settled into its proper place, her stomach. Quietly she closed the bathroom door.

The Chinese man gave a toothless grin as Kash placed a handful of money on the table between them. No sooner was it laid down and the old man scooped it up and shoved it into his pocket. For generosity's sake, he handed Kash an extra box of shells. A smile and nod accompanied his gesture.

Kash smiled and packed the 38 in the back of his waistband and the 45 in the front. He zipped up his leather jacket midway and placed the boxes of ammunition in his jacket pockets. A nod of thanks to the old man and he disappeared through the beaded doorway.

Leslie emerged from the bathroom rubbing her wet hair vigorously with the bath towel. She stopped short and gave a guarded smile to the equally apprehensive Flanery.

"You don't take orders very well, do you?" he observed.

Just as she started to answer, Kash walked into the living room. He placed his tote on the sofa, looked over her still pale features and noticed her pressed pants and starched shirt. "Those clothes won't do where we're going. You got anything rugged?"

A little hurt that he had ignored her basic condition, she answered anyway. "A pair of jeans I brought just in case I wanted to get ugly."

"Go get ugly," he told her with a teasing grin.

She took that as a compliment. "May I ask where we're going that requires me to get ugly?"

"Scroll hunting."

"Won't we have company?"

"Probably."

"Won't that be dangerous?"

"Definitely."

She had played this scene before and she wasn't about to have the same consequences. Two hurts in two years was too much. "Shouldn't we just let the Chinese authorities handle this?"

"Where's your sense of adventure?" Kash mocked her comments from San Francisco. He turned her around and gave her an encouraging pat on the backside towards her room.

With her safely out of sight, Kash looked to an amused Flanery and pulled free the 38 and45. "I'm anticipating company. Can you drive us to the pass?" He knew the answer and added. "Thanks."

Their drive to the pass was a bumpy and dusty one. Sitting in the back afforded Leslie on luxury; she was able to stretch out. Closing her eyes was a consideration long forgotten; the bumping and jarring only caused unnecessary nausea. She rolled the window all the way down and allowed the air to funnel in and swirl about her throbbing head. Its coolness offered temporary relief.

Kash turned around to meet her still bloodshot and swollen eyes as Flanery pulled the car off the bumpy road onto something definitely off the beaten path. It was more than Leslie could take lying down, so she sat up and steadied herself for more jostling, but suddenly Flanery brought the car to a halt in front of a dilapidated shanty.

As they got out of the car, a stooped over man led two saddled horses from the barn. Following behind was a packed mule with canteens, ropes, bed rolls and two bulging satchels. Kash walked over, lent a hand, and paid the man handsomely for his time and trouble.

As they talked, Leslie casually approached the spirited paint with familiarity and stroked his thick neck and soft nose. He stomped his hoof with delight at her attention and when she stopped he showed his discontent; shaking his mane and gently nudging her to continue. A couple of hearty pats settled him down and then she headed over to Kash.

"Where is it we're headed?" she asked, feeling she had waited long enough for an explanation.

"What was the first character on the pendant?" Kash wanted to know, looking at the mountain range, not paying any attention to her question.

"Red," she replied, irritation creeping into her features and tone.

Ah, sweet music to his ears. He was glad to hear that "tone", even if it meant she was on the verge of temper, he was happy to see her old self reappearing.

"Then, mountain," she said out of the blue, and he ignored that, too. She decided to look at the range as well. "Well, we've found the mountains; in all of their autumn splendor."

The light bulb went off above his head at her comment, then he looked back to the range. Blends of gold, yellows, russets and finally a hearty patch *of somber Chinese red. He sighted it and logged it into his memory, then called to Flanery, "You'll handle everything on this end?" Their handshake was firm and bonded from years of friendship. "See ya."*

"Yeah," Flanery agreed. "Keep an eye on him," he instructed Leslie.

She gave him an assuring wink before pulling her fedora into it usual position.

Kash guided her over to her horse and helped her mount. A quick adjustment to her stirrups, then he mounted his horse and pulled the pack mule between them.

Leslie's lively horse didn't wait for Kash to assume the lead. It bolted forward in a rambunctious and agonizing pace. Feeling as if her spine was going to go through her skull, she pulled back on the reins and slowed the beast to a tolerable gait. She settled back into the saddle and the rhythm of the horse beneath her and then took in the wondrous sight of the colorful mountains ahead.

"Scroll hunting, indeed." Elaine whispered to herself as she shut down the PDA and set her phone alarm for three hours later. She put the alarm on vibrate as to not disturb her next door neighbor. She was dressed and ready to go. Her things packed and all equipment charged.

She closed her eyes and thought of the tranquil fall mountains in China and sleep came fast; so did the alarm.

CHAPTER THIRTY FOUR

"Oh," Elaine moaned with great displeasure as she pulled free from her bosom the vibrating phone. Grabbing her gear and a note for Mollie and John she tiptoed out of her room, placed the note on John's chair and left the house as quietly as possible.

She made her way down the steps to the dock and towards her Waco Sea Plane. She mentally ran through her checklist for making a quick getaway; thankfully the nasty weather had dissipated and the air was crisp and the sky was crystal clear.

She easily untied the float plane and boarded the pontoon to store her gear in the front cockpit. "Oh, shit!" she cried out.

A sturdy hand kept her from falling into the cold Lake Shasta water.

"What the hell are you doing here?" she asked in rough whisper.

Amusement played upon Jack's face as he asked, "Now, you weren't going to leave me behind, were you, Elaine?"

"Fucking a, I was. Shit!" She threw her gear at him. "Store that," she hissed and climbed into her seat. "And don't puke on me this time."

Dutifully, Jack did as he was told and strapped in, making sure he was firmly in place just in case Elaine got another burr up her ass and decided to roll the plane several times in hopes of extricating him somewhere over the Canadian mountain range. It didn't happen.

Admiralty Island, or Kootznoowoo; the Fortress of Bears, as the Tlingits referred to it, was nestled between Stephens Passage and Chatham Straight. The Tlingits, inhabitants for over one thousand years on the island, called it such because of the brown bear population. The bears out number their human counterparts three to one. They have a great life on the island; plenty of roots and berries, not to mention the salmon. In fall they start to head to the upper slopes to sleep away the winter season.

From the time Elaine was old enough to remember, her family vacations revolved around the rugged beauty of Alaska. From polar bear watching at Point Barrow, to sending off the rowdy fisherman from Dutch Harbor in the Aleutian Islands for fall crabbing, to fly fishing with her father in the peaceful streams of Angoon, spare time was spent together as a family. Kash was home and not on some archeological dig, Leslie put aside her causes for the arts and Lane sulked for the month while they roughed in the Alaskan wilderness.

Their last family vacation consisted of only three, for Lane had more important things to do; law school and such nonsense. He never really had a sense of family. Yet, he campaigned as a judge on family values, character and morals. He wouldn't recognize any of those if they knocked him upside the head.

A thought threatened to ruin Elaine's happy trip through memory lane; were those vacations solely for the family, or even then, were they looking for the mole? She shook that consideration from her mind's eye and concentrated on something more important; her final approach to Angoon and hopefully her parents.

By the time they had arrived at the Angoon Sea Base, the wind had picked up and the landing was less than smooth, and Elaine's passenger was only too happy to let her know that. She was now sorry she let him have the headset.

As they were tethered, they climbed out and grabbed their gear. "What?" he asked defensively as they made their way to the outbuilding for a little paperwork and to meet their ride to the Tanner's Creek Lodge. "What?" he asked again.

"Really, Jack, how is it you're a spy?" she asked in a whisper.

"What is that suppose to mean?"

"You're such a pussy when it comes to flying. I mean," she started and he cut her off.

"Your kind of flying, yeah. Barrel roles, barely clearing mountain ranges, hardly flying above the ground and then climbing vertically. Yeah, damn straight I'm a pussy," he admitted as they opened the door and his voice careened off the walls, alerting everyone that was within ear shot that he was indeed a pussy.

Snorts of laughter filled the tiny building as Elaine smiled at the attendant and signed her paperwork. "Lucky me," she told the weathered face across from her at the counter.

"Good to see you again, Elaine," welcomed Bert Simmons. His weathered skin crackled under his smile and his piercing blue eyes gave Jack the once over before he gave Elaine her copy of the paperwork. "The usual, Elaine; have it filled and ready to go?"

"Yes, please. Thank you, Bert." She folded the paper and put it in her backpack and called to Jack, "Come on, Pussy, Mama Cass is waiting."

"Jezus Christ." Jack imitated in his best Scottish James Bond brogue.

Chuckles followed them out the door as Elaine spotted Cass Anderson waiting by her trusty Jeep Commander. Cass was the jack of all trades at the Tanner's Creek Lodge. A place founded by her mother, Tansy Anderson and Tansy's sister, Veronica Barrows.

As they approached, Cass opened up her arms and greeted Elaine and then popped the hatch of the Commander to store their backpacks. She gave Jack a curt nod and offered him the backseat while she opened the passenger door for Elaine.

"You made it just in time. This is the last week for tours; weather is starting to shift; I can feel it in my bones, or lack of them," Cass giggled, staring at and gesturing with her right arm, which was missing an elbow.

She had the same infectious laugh as her mother, and those who visited always commented on how Cass looked just like Tansy; Pete and Repeat. Her long blonde hair complemented her bronzed skin and large blue eyes. When she talked, it was with a smile and her white teeth glistened against her tanned features. "So, how long you stayin'? Do you want a charter anywhere? Cause you know the Mama Cass is at your disposal anytime you need her." Cass offered up her time and her charter boat, the Mama Cass.

"I'm afraid not very long. Just long enough to try and decipher if my parents are in the vicinity, or I'm chasing my tail."

"We held their room for you. I'm sure they just took a detour and didn't tell anyone. You know how those two kids are," she speculated, trying to soothe an anxious Elaine.

Before they knew it they were at the Tanner's Creek Lodge. A quaint three story structure made of native timber and glass and offering spectacular views from every angle; whether it was of the bay or the forest it backed up to, with the meandering creek, for which the lodge was named; everything was in place for the vacation of a lifetime; activities abound if that's what one desired. Or, if it was peace and quiet you were in need of, the trails and the streams nearby offered the best of nature. Whatever your poison, the Tanner's Creek was more than happy to accommodate. From packed picnic baskets with your favorite foods and drinks, to a rousing good time with nightly poker or board games; with prizes for the winners. The Tanner's Creek never disappointed. If you didn't have a good time, well, they always thought you should have.

Jack grabbed the backpacks and followed the ladies up the steps to the massive double doors that led into the lodge. The moment Elaine walked in, the earthy, calming smell of cedar overtook her and she immediately relaxed. That, and one of the sweetest smiles on the planet was coming towards her with arms open wide; Tansy Anderson pulled her into her bosom for a bone crushing hug. They released and Tansy took Elaine's face between her two hands and stated, "Talk about Pete and Repeat. You are so your mother's daughter. You may have daddy's coloring, but you look like your mother."

"Oh, that's a bad thing?" Cass questioned with a bright smile.

"Not at all," Tansy said back as Veronica entered the room with a tray of some of Elaine's favorites; champagne with Chambord liquor and raspberries at the bottom, served with homemade almond flavored ladyfingers.

"Welcome back," Veronica offered the goodies to Elaine and Jack, then put the tray down. A quick hug and she disappeared back into the kitchen with three more glasses of champagne; handing one to Tansy and Cass. "To a happy ending," she toasted to Elaine.

All raised their glasses to each other and let the chilled bubbly fill their bellies. Elaine and Jack dipped the delicate cookies and watched the champagne fizz with delight at the sugary concoction.

Tansy motioned for them to sit in the circular great room of the lodge while Cass took their backpacks to their room. They settled into the front of the fireplace, which was the center piece of the lodge. Set in the middle of the lodge, it had four openings; one on each side of the room. Its uneven stone pattern matched perfectly with the lodge pole furnishing in the great and dining rooms. The fire in the middle was massive and its warmth was enough to heat the lower and second levels of the lodge.

Elaine plopped down in the rocking chair and propped her feet on the ottoman as she sipped her champagne and enjoyed her cookie. Tansy and Veronica sat on the leather sofa and let the fire add warmth to the drinks. Jack's phone rang and excused himself to the far corner of the dining room; away from Elaine's acute hearing.

Tansy leaned forward as she spoke to Elaine, "What's the plan for him?" she asked nodding her head in Jack's direction.

"A very short leash," Elaine replied with a smile. "As much as I want to trust him, I can't. He knows something and he's not telling me. Which means, I'll have to find it out on my own." She finished her champagne and her thought. "I tried ditching him at Mollie and John's, but he was in the plane, waiting for me. So, I guess we're tied at the hip for a while. And just like our marriage, neither one of us is willing to give in to the other. Which ought to make finding my parents a snap," she concluded with a touch of sarcasm.

Jack came back and looked at the three upturned faces before him; he wasn't sure he wanted to sit down, but he did, in a rocker next to Elaine. He sipped his champagne and offered nothing of the conversation he just had.

"Don't make me ask, Jack," Elaine warned.

"You just did," he corrected her and quickly summarized his conversation. "There's rumblings," and he left it at that while looking at Tansy and Veronica.

Elaine got his drift and informed him, "You can speak freely, Jack."

He understood that tone and continued. "There's more than just a score to settle. This mole, this mole your folks have been chasing is the head of a powerful Russian family. One that has not only infiltrated their own government in Russia, but I'm pretty sure ours. They have ties to the middle east and every terrorist organization you can name, including those in Europe and Asia. They have a lot of natural resources in Russia. Untapped resources. But they're lazy, for lack of better terminology. And according to sources, they're helping Iran with resources, and in turn, Iran is returning the favor, if you will. That aside, why don't we fly on up to Juneau and see what Sam Winston has found out?"

"God, Jack, can't you just for once say what they're doing and or wanting?" Elaine popped off, ignoring his comment about Juneau, her patience waning with his lame, end run explanation for things.

"No, I can't. This isn't what you do for a living. But until we find your parents, you're involved, whether I like it not. So, like that large dog on a short leash, I'm here to keep an eye on you." He finished his champagne and started for the stairs.

"Room number eleven, Jack," Tansy called out to his retreating back.

He said nothing and disappeared up the stairway to their room.

"Sure you don't want another room," Veronica offered.

Elaine smiled and shook her head, then looked around the room. "Where's Cass?"

"Oh, she went off to get a last minute arrival. She'll be back soon. You hungry? Need anything?" Tansy asked a far away Elaine.

"Naw, I'm fine. Thank you, anyway," Elaine replied as she rose and handed her champagne glass to Tansy. "Maybe a trip to Juneau would do me good," she winked and headed towards the stairs and Jack Phillips.

CHAPTER THIRTY FIVE

When Elaine opened the door to their room, Jack was pacing, his hands thrust deep into the front pockets his jeans. He threw her a threatening glare and stabbed the air with a stern finger in her direction. "You want to find your parents?" he asked with controlled anger. "Then stop being such a control freak and let me help you. I know you think I'm buddies with Lane. But I'm not," he emphatically explained. "I keep Lane close because I have to, not because I want to."

"Why?" she calmly asked, knowing that her intuition about Lane was correct all along.

"He's into something, and I'm pretty sure,+ he doesn't realize it. His ego's so big he can't see it's been standing in front of him for a while." He crosses the room quickly. " But Lane aside, I can't leave your side. You understand why?"

"You mean it's not because you love?" she thrust his way, catching him off guard. "Let's fly to Juneau," she suggested.

She grabbed her backpack and headed for the door. He put his hand over hers on the doorknob and gave a little squeeze. "Me, too," she echoed and they left.

The weather was like good cop, bad cop. One day good, and then bam, suddenly the winds were whipping the seas up into a frenzy; making take off and landings less than comfortable. Just ask Jack. The flight to from Angoon to Juneau was nearly sixty miles, and luckily for them, they could fly into Juneau's Merchant Wharf and be a few feet from the Pacific Area Seventeenth District Coast Guard's station.

Their final approach took a while because there were numerous float planes lined up for landing. Looking down upon the wharf, Elaine saw that every slip was filled with a cruise ship; five in all. As Cass had stated, this was the last week for cruises and shore tours.

Finally, it was their turn and she, as gently as she could, eased her plane down onto the choppy sea and pulled it to the deck. Tied off, she and Jack climbed out and grabbed their respective gear. Used to, Elaine would have jumped out, given instructions to top off and then gone on her merry way. Now, she had become more aware of her surroundings.

She tossed her keys to the attendant, and as she was instructing him about topping off, Jack had walked away and was shaking hands with a man she could only assume was Sam Winston. "Thank you," she said to the attendant, tipping him a twenty, then leaving to catch up with Jack.

Sam Winston was a tall, shallow faced man, with thinning hair and a middle aged paunch. What strands of hair he did have, were being whipped about by the inclement weather. He ignored their flap and offered, with an extended hand, they go inside the Coast Guard's headquarters.

Inside, Lt. Mark Wilson greeted them and took them directly to a small ready room near the back of the facility. He shut the door behind them and asked, "Coffee?" There were no takers.

Elaine looked at the enormous map of Alaska that covered practically every inch of the wall. On the white board; a description of her father's WACO Sea Plane, its tail or registration numbers, last location of transponder and updated pictures of Leslie and Kash; smiling and enjoying themselves at the gala fundraiser hosted by Lane. He would be so pretentious, she thought, to send that kind of picture.

Markings and push pins on the map showed their search areas. Elaine could see residue of several marks where they had been and were not successful, leading to new marks and pins of hope. She pulled a chair out and sat down, encouraging the others to follow suit. It was her way of controlling how long this meeting was going to last and how much information she was going to gather.

"First off," Lt. Wilson began, "Let me say, we know how devastating it is to hear we are going from a rescue to a recovery." He stopped and clinched his square jaw.

Elaine saw how hard it was for him to speak of the missing flyers.

"Mark, I know how hard it is for you to conduct this search. You have flown with my father. And I know he thinks the world of you. And, I know he appreciates the time, energy and resources you and your fellow guards are putting out there to rescue them, and so do I."

"Yes, ma'am. That WACO plane of your dad's; it's a relic, but in top notch shape," he said, shaking his head in disbelief that it was missing and couldn't be found.

"I know, and that's what's so puzzling. He's a gadget's man. The latest GPS and transponder; new autopilot." She gave a stunted laugh and added, "Hell, if he could, he'd have a coffeemaker on board."

Everyone gave a short laugh and then they fell silent again, the gravity of the situation weighing heavily in the air and in Elaine's heart. On the plane ride over from Angoon, she was hell bent on giving everyone involved a piece of her mind, but now, her unhappy opinion didn't matter. She could tell by the look on Mark's face, he was devastated that he hadn't been successful in finding Kash and Leslie; but why stop now. She was going to will them to continue, And, if not them, she needed to know all they knew so she could carry on the search and find her parents.

Elaine took out her PDA, turned it on and started to jot down some notes regarding where they had been and where their latest efforts were being concentrated. "I take it by the big red circle around New Tokeen, that is where contact was lost?" she asked, looking expectantly for their cooperation.

It was Sam Winston that spoke. "Look, I can appreciate you're wanting to continue, but we've all discussed the possibilities of them being alive and the prospects at this time of year are nil at best."

"And I appreciate you relaying to me the bullshit of information my brother wants you to, but I know otherwise." She looked to Mark Wilson, his handsome face somewhat shocked, but silently thankful she spoke his sentiments. "So Mark, explain your board."

"We know their last stop was in Craig. As you can see, X does mark the spot where we lost connection with the transponder. We searched that area extensively, and as much as the weather these last few days has allowed, we have searched Sea Otter Sound, Davidson Inlet, and Warren Channel for rescue efforts." He then hesitated, but continued. "For recovery; Shaken Bay and Sumner Straight."

217

The room was deathly cold and too quiet; with the exception of Elaine's stylus clicking feverishly over the surface of her PDA. She got up and went to the map; her mind's finger tracing the flight pattern from Craig to El Capitan Passage. She turned back to Mark, "No debris field?"

He shook his head, "None that we could see or determine."

She absentmindedly tapped her PDA, looked at the map and said out loud her one nagging thought since the disappearance, "Even if the plane goes down, the transponder keeps emitting its signal. Who disabled the transponder and why?"

Not a soul around the table, including Jack, could answer that question.

"Do you have notes on exactly where your aircraft and boats have been searching?" she asked Mark.

He nodded, opened his file and handed it to Elaine. Sam Winston sent a disapproving glare Mark's way.

Elaine gave the notes a quick perusal and handed them back to Mark. "Could you make me a copy?"

"Yes, ma'am."

"Seriously, Lieutenant," Winston warned, but was cut off by Elaine.

"I don't believe you're the Rear Admiral in charge here, Mr. Winston. The Rear Admiral is a good friend of my father's, and you, Mr. Winston, are a friend of the other Mr. Bennett; the one who doesn't count."

With that said, Mark left the room to make Elaine her copies and Winston got up from his chair and followed the lieutenant, barking after him like petulant ass Elaine knew he was. She turned to look, at Jack, who remained silent through the whole meeting. She raised her eyebrows and dared him to comment.

He did. "Glad you chewed someone else's ass out for a change. I don't think I have enough left for that ravishing temper of yours," he mocked.

"Yes you do," she countered with a smile.

He drew a white hand towel from his backpack and waved it in surrender. "I'm on your side," he proclaimed, getting up and packing his towel. "Let's go find them."

Upon walking down the hallway to the front of the building, they ran into Lieutenant Wilson. He smiled and handed Elaine a manila envelope with copies of their search reports. "Rear Admiral sends his regards, ma'am. We'll keep searching right along with you, and what we find, you will get a copy. May I have your email?" He readied his PDA and she happily sent her contact information to him. "Thank you. Fair winds and following seas, ma'am. Sir." He acknowledged Jack with a curt nod.

CHAPTER THIRTY SIX

Sam Winston was nowhere to be found when Elaine and Jack left the Coast Guard station; and just as well. Elaine was sure he was on the phone with Lane spilling their plan, but at the moment, she didn't care about him and his wants and needs. Oddly enough, she couldn't remember when the last time was that she cared anything about Lane.

If possible, the wind had picked up and it was making walking a little more of a chore. And to complicate matters, scads of cruise ship tourists were meandering about, paying little attention to those around them; only interested in what they came to see that they don't have back home.

Elaine threw Jack a look and cocked her head toward her favorite restaurant in all of Juneau; The Open Wide. As they made their way, float planes galore were lined up in front of the most popular eatery for miles. They hurried up the steps and into the building.

Amongst the crush of tourists, Elaine caught the eye of one of the owners, Jackie Dotson. She was stationed at the hostess stand, directing the wait staff as if she were conducting a symphony. Seamlessly, people were being shown to their seats and waiting was kept to a minimum.

A buxom blonde, nearly a head shorter than Elaine bounded towards her with arms open wide. "Where have you been, girl?" Jackie lamented to Elaine. She looked Jack up and down and then stated, "I see you brought your bags with you."

Elaine smiled and then looked at a fake smiling Jack. "Can't leave it in the plane; it likes to play with things. Push too many buttons. Real and imaginable," she commented with a smile.

"Hungry?" Jackie asked, knowing full well the answer.

Elaine nodded and Jackie whisked them off to one of the private dining areas on the second floor. More lodge pole furnishing greeted them in the secluded space. The table was big enough to seat six very comfortably, eight was a squeeze, but cozy. A spinnaker and a chart showing the exact location of the restaurant was on one wall and a picture of sunset in Juneau was on the opposite wall. Steins were already filled with water and lemon, and Jackie rushed in with a basket full of homemade cheese straws.

"Samantha will be in momentarily. Can I get you anything else? Your drinks?" she asked, her velvet brown eyes shimmering with delight that they were there.

"Water with lemon is great," Elaine replied, looking at Jack to see if he wanted anything else.

"I'm good, thanks," he said, looking over the menu.

Everything on the menu was oversized; thus the name Open Wide. Burgers were stacked and three times the size of normal restaurants, and instead of French fries, one got loaded potato halves, not wedges. Every drink, no matter what, was served in a stein. Even the silverware was extra large. It would make sense, though, considering the size of the owner, Harlan Dotson, Jackie's husband.

He was a big man that filled up the opening to the private dining space. His laugh was a big as he was and his handshake firm, like a Hoosier preacher. Jack grimaced as he was greeted by Harlan and his boisterous shake. "Good to see you again, old man," he told Jack with a hearty slap on the back. He was more reserved with Elaine and his hug was firm but not overpowering. "The little lady told me you two were here. Good to see you both," he said looking back and forth from Elaine to Jack. "And together, even. Who would have thought that? Sit, sit," he insisted, motioning for them to sit back down.

They did and he looked at them expectantly. "What?" Elaine asked with a knowing smile.

"Nothing," he replied, understanding full well her smile. "So, Elaine, the usual?" he asked, nodding his assumption.

"That obvious?" she asked looking at her closed menu.

"Yep. Haystack it is. Jack?"

"Surprise me," Jack answered, knowing he was going to have to open wide for any meal that was placed before him.

"You got it," Harlan said as he whipped past the curtain that gave them privacy.

"Wonder where Samantha is? I thought she was going to wait on us." Elaine casually mentioned as she sipped her water and looked at Jack perusing the dessert menu. "You won't have room for any of that, and besides, if you eat any of that, you might put the plane overweight," she teased.

They wooed and awed over the homemade desserts ranging from apple and cherry pies, to margarita sundaes, and then the curtain was pushed back and their meals were being placed before them. Elaine's Haystack was set up an oversized chilled pewter plate. The crisp iceberg lettuce barely peeking out at the bottom of a heaping stack of thinly battered and deep fried onion straws. On top of the lettuce was seasoned ground beef with scallions and a blend of Monterey and Colby Jack cheeses. As always, she didn't know where to start, so she picked a side and dug in with the gigantic fork and pulled out as much variety as she could for her first bite. The creamy homemade chipotle ranch dressing that was under the straws, provided just enough zip and tang to complement each ingredient. The look on her face told Jack she had found Nirvana.

He looked at his burger, trying to figure out what was on it; he couldn't. So, he smashed it down and picked it up with its wrapper and readied his mouth to receive Harlan's best. He barely got his mouth around the work of art and bite down. Condiments oozed and left their residue on his mouth and chin as he chewed the delicious medium rare burger stuffed with Blue Cheese. He looked at Elaine and smiled. For once, he was speechless.

Laughing at him and his messy self; she took his face in her hands and kissed him. Then she took her napkin and wiped his lips and chin, enjoying the moment and the tasty residue.

They were half way through their meals, when Samantha Dotson bounced in. "Ta da!" she announced and hugged Elaine. "How is everything?" Her green eyes twinkling like her father's as she looked over their plates and the little damage they had done to the food.

"Too much as usual, but delicious as always. How have you been?" she asked Samantha.

"Great. Looking forward to a break when the cruises stop. Oh," she began with animation, "It was so nice seeing your mom and dad the other day."

Elaine's smile faded and her fork thudded to the table. "You saw my parents?" she asked an obviously confused Samantha.

"Ah, yeah," Samantha stuttered. "Everything okay? I mean, they seemed fine and they were with another couple. I just thought they were all fishing together. You know, like they usually do this time of year." Samantha's words were barely audible at the end of her sentence as she stared at Elaine's ashen features. "What's wrong?"

"Samantha," Jack started, "did you notice anything unusual about Mr. and Mrs. Bennett? Did they seem hurt, or anxious?"

"No, they looked healthy, and their appetites indicated they were okay. Why? Are they okay?"

"Notice anything else about them?" he pressed.

"They did seem really quiet, and Mr. Bennett tipped me with a gold nugget. Kind of like on the down low.

"You mean so the other couple didn't see him do it?" Jack asked.

"Yeah, and he squeezed my hand really hard, so that I felt the nugget." She looked to Elaine. "What's going on?"

"Their missing, Sam. I was told their plane had gone down and we've been searching for them ever since. We just came from the Coast Guard and got the latest update, but they obviously didn't tell us anything like this," Elaine replied with more hope than she felt she was allowed to have. She looked to Jack and then to Samantha. "Does your mother still have her Wrangler?"

"Yeah," Sam answered. "You need it?"

"Yes, but it has to be on the down low," Elaine instructed.

"Not a problem. We're so busy, she's not going to notice and if she does, I will tell her I let you borrow it. Do my parent's know that Mr. and Mrs. Bennett are missing, sort of?"

"No. Let's keep it that way for the moment," Jack suggested.

Samantha nodded and headed out of the suddenly close space to fetch her mother's keys, leaving an obviously shocked, but hopeful Elaine. She didn't have to say a word to Jack. She frantically pulled her backpack up to her lap and pulled free her wallet. She was searching for money to pay the bill when Samantha entered the private room. "Sam, exactly how long ago did you see my folks?"

"Two days ago."

"And the couple they were with, could you describe them?" Jack asked.

"Very average. Um, the guy was small, short. You could tell that when he was young he was handsome, like Mr. Bennett, very crisp looking. Neat. The woman; she was petite, with blondish grey hair. You never know by looking at your parents and this couple that they were elderly. They all moved really well and nobody appeared hurt," she concluded and handed her mother's keys to Elaine. "I hope I've helped."

"More than you know. How much for lunch?" Elaine asked.

Sam gave a wave of the hand. "You know Mom and Dad think your money is phony. So, put it away."

Jack handed her a fifty. "Your tip."

Sam shook her head and tried to refuse the generous offering. "I got a gold nugget." She winked and then looked to Elaine and added, "Unless you want it back?"

"You keep it," Elaine said and gave Samantha a healthy hug. "We'll be back shortly with your mother's Jeep. Thank you."

They grabbed their packs and made their way through the throngs of tourists and out the side door of the attached gift shop. They found Jackie's Jeep Wrangler at the back of the property and climbed in. Jack waited until they were headed out and away from the Open Wide restaurant before he spoke.

"Where are we going?" he asked.

"To the mine," she pointedly answered.

"Why?"

"Because of the nugget, why else?" she replied in short order. She couldn't understand his questions. "What part do I need to explain?"

"All of it."

"Are you trying to be a smartass and ruin the significance of this moment?"

"No," he answered defensively. "I'm just not following you on this."

"You don't have to. You're sitting next to me." She took a sidelong glance his direction and saw his frustration. "We're headed toward the Glory Hole, or the AJ Mine. Well, actually, a little mine not far from the

AJ Mine; an offshoot, if you will. In my early teens, my dad and I would go exploring in the mines. We found this little, hideaway-of-a-mine that only locals visited and played in. The tourists always kept to the AJ Mine. And one day, we found some nuggets and we kept them. As a matter of fact, my dad gave me the largest one, and it ended up being your wedding ring. As for the rest, Dad put them in a pouch and told me that they were his bread crumbs. So, if anything ever happened to him, follow the bread crumbs. And, that's exactly what we're doing."

She put the Jeep into low gear and they climbed Basin Road, past Perseverance Trailhead. She looked into the mirror and noticed they had company. She was just about to mention it to Jack, when they turned off on a dirt access road she had passed. They followed Basin Road until it came to an end. There she parked the Jeep, pocketed the keys and opened the back door to get her backpack. She opened the pack and double checked her flashlight. Jack did the same.

"We've got a hike. So, I hope you've got good boots on." She shone her light on his feet and was happy he did.

"Are we going in the original mine or what?" he asked as they traversed the rugged terrain.

"No. We're going about two miles or so past," she answered. Her feet light and sure as she made her way to her childhood discovery.

"I suppose there's not an easier way or access?" he asked after stumbling for the umpteenth time on roots and ground cover.

"No. Do you want me to slow down?" she solicited sweetly.

By his silence, she took it that her pace was okay and she continued; and though it was daylight, her flashlight helped illuminate their path. Their pace was slowed as they made their ascent up Mt. Roberts and past the AJ Mine that was built in 1912, and was closed in 1944, but not after producing eighty-eight million ounces of gold. Once they came upon the out buildings, and the terrain had leveled off; their push to their destination quickened.

There was a substantial amount of overgrowth on and around the buildings and mine opening. Doors and windows were missing and the timbers that held the structures together, were precariously propped up with loose pieces of wood and steel girders. When Elaine looked down, she could see the Gastineau Channel and the numerous cruise ships in the harbor. She kept moving, with Jack closely behind for about another mile and a half, then she headed around and up the steep face of the mountain.

She grabbed trees to pull herself along until she reached a clearing. "We're here," she announced to a relieved Jack.

The mine opening was barely recognizable from the lush greenery that encompassed it. When Jack pulled down some of the growth, there stood an entry that was barely passable. Into the frail gap of the rock, two by twelve's had been affixed in a crisscross fashion to keep out unwanted trespassers like Elaine and Jack. And with the over grown brush, the mine entry was well concealed, and it looked like it had been years since anyone had ventured inside.

Jack shone his flashlight into the entry and Elaine squeezed between the boards and carefully stepped down the rickety steps, and what daylight was available was absorbed into the walls of the mine. Jack threw his pack inside and it landed next to Elaine. She waited patiently while he contorted himself to fit through the narrow opening of the X; catching half of what he was wearing on the boards. When he finally did make it inside, it was with a thud at her feet. Embarrassed he got up and gave her and the opening a menacing glare.

He took the flashlight back and shined it on the walls, ceiling and floor of the mine. Testing the steps by tossing their backpacks on them, they deemed them safe enough to travel down the rest of the way into the main tunnel. The mine was cold, around forty degrees or so.

As they went deeper into the mine, the walls bore pot marks here and there. These were holes where spikes were driven in for dynamite to be set and used to blow rock out for discovery of gold and tunneling. Jack made a mental note as they moved further into the depths of the mine.

There were several off shoot tunnels and Elaine took one, and then another, and then she reversed and found yet one more passageway, and that was enough for Jack to comment. "I don't suppose you have any breadcrumbs?" he asked, tripping on the railroad track, again. "Dammit! Is it my imagination, or are we climbing?"

She ignored his comments, totally focused on the task at hand. "We're not far from where my father and I discovered our little fortune," she explained as they came upon a round clearing where numerous tunnels converged with multiple tracks running side by side. Several old mining cars were stacked one behind the other. Jack pulled on the first one in line and it moved easily considering it had been sitting for some time in the cold dampness.

"But how is that going to help us find them?"

"I don't know, Jack. I just have a feeling. Haven't you ever followed your gut?"

"Outside of down the aisle with you? No. My situations rarely call for me to use my gut. The Intel I receive is suppose to be factual, not presumptions or full of hunches."

Elaine looked above one of the tunnels and read the sign, "This is it. Number 3. Let's go."

She was off before he could protest and along the way he noticed the tracks had become almost nonexistent. So traveling for him was easier; no more stubbed toes. This tunnel was winding and it felt like they were still going uphill.

Suddenly, Elaine stopped and looked back at a niche and stood in its entry. She closed her eyes and drew in a deep breath. She hadn't imagined it, she thought. "Mom's been here," she whispered.

Jack watched with great interest and said nothing as she examined the small space.

She shone the flashlight inside and saw some graffiti on the rock wall. She let the flashlight crawl over every inch of the space. Crates had been turned over and used as seats. Cans of spray paint were discarded after they were used to make the colorful statements, and next to the crate closest to the art was a waded up Kleenex. She walked over and picked it up; gently taking in its aroma. "It's mom's own special blend; Raffinee and Opium. Spicy and freshly sensual," she mused. She held the flashlight steady on the graffiti and within its complex picture she found her mother's upside down and backward handwriting.

"What the hell is that?" Jack asked, taking the flashlight from Elaine and holding it steady while she took her cell phone and snapped a photo of it.

"My mom's way of communicating. When she was in school, she had a friend named Gwen who used to write upside and backwards out of boredom."

Before she could continue, Jack hushed her and turned off the light. They listened intently and heard voices speaking Chinese. He groped in the dark and found a good sized rock, stepped out of the niche and threw it down the tunnel, way ahead of their current position. Grabbing Elaine, he pulled her into a cut out in the wall, behind and right of the opening. The only noises were the occasional shots of wind through the mine and dusty footsteps running their way. If they stopped at the niche, hopefully they would only shine their light in the opening; revealing just the graffiti and crates, and not their tucked hideaway.

It took them what appeared to be only seconds as they rounded the bend and rushed by the tiny niche. Elaine made a move, but Jack kept her still. Suddenly the niche grew full of light as one of the intruders gave a quick look and then joined the rest of the team down the tunnel in pursuit of Jack's rock.

Jack counted to five and then eased out of the tuck with his hand firmly around Elaine's wrist. "Stay close to me," he said barely above a whisper as he hugged the tunnel wall and moved at an agonizingly slow pace so not to alert their pursuers; and when they rounded the soft bend in the passageway, Jack flipped on the flashlight and then they began to run as fast as the old mine would let them. And the mine wasn't letting them without incident; Jack caught his toe on a railroad that sent him tumbling. The tunnel behind them was illuminated and Jack looked straight at the source. A warning shot singed past his head and careened off the tunnel wall.

"Jack, old friend," came the call from Slim, and then he admonished in Mandarin the one who shot at Jack and Elaine, but it ended with the name of "Boris".

"That son-of-a-bitch is everywhere!" exclaimed Elaine, righting Jack and heading for the clearing.

They came to the circular spot where all of the tunnels met and with one single thing on his mind, Jack threw the backpacks and hoisted Elaine into the first mining car. Giving it all he had to make it move, it started down the tracks, slow at first, then picking up speed; as they now were going opposite of uphill.

Hurried Mandarin let them know their unwanted guests were closing, and that they, too, had found the mining cars. Rusting wheels began to churn and Jack knew the race was on to the mine's opening. He pulled free from his waistband his Sig Sauer, flipped the safety off and readied the chamber.

The cars had picked up quite a bit of speed and were jostling back and forth, and getting off a shot that would count was nearly impossible. Jack was biding his time, waiting for the right moment before he fired his weapon.

Elaine wasn't waiting; she perked up and fired two rounds in the vicinity of Slim and his merry men. They bounced off the walls and it took a great deal of discipline for them not to return fire.

"Where did you get that gun?" Jack demanded as he peered over the edge of the car, measuring their lead and how fast the others were gaining.

Before she answered, their car came to an abrupt halt and they were pitched headlong out onto the floor of the mine. Because of erosion, the tracks had ended, and as they were righting themselves, warning shots filled the air and bounced off the walls and ceiling, causing exploding rock to strike Elaine in the face. She turned and fired twice, giving Jack the chance to grab their gear and then she lead them out of the maze.

They knew it was going to be but seconds before Slim and his men had the same unfortunate accident they just experienced. Only theirs was going to be worse; they would find the back end of Jack and Elaine's car. That sudden stop was going to hurt.

They heard the crash and the screams, and though they had a substantial head start, Jack wasn't counting on that to deter Slim. Blindly he searched his backpack and found what he was searching for. As Elaine kept running ahead, he stopped and plugged one of the pot marks with a stick of dynamite. He lit the fuse and ran, catching Elaine by the nap of her jacket he threw her down as the stick explode, sending shock waves throughout the mine.

He picked her up and they ran as fast as they could, the mine fall in behind them, nipping at their heels. As they neared the entry, Jack rushed past and launched his body through the wooden X, giving Elaine a clear shot of getting out safely.

They stumbled; sliding down the mountain side, avoiding the trees they had used earlier to help in their climb. Narrowly missing the last tree, Elaine, rolled to her left and plunged into the creek at the bottom. Jack had grabbed a tree and slowed his descent. He sat for a moment and then gingerly made his way down to Elaine. He offered a hand and she climbed out of the creek and sat on its bank to collect her thoughts and control the fear that was threatening to erupt from her every pore.

Jack took off his jacket and placed it around her shoulders and vigorously rubbed her arms.

It took a moment, but Elaine finally spoke. "How did he find us, and how did we miss seeing him?" she asked through chattering teeth and racing heart. She willed herself to calm down. Adrenaline was a funny thing; every sense was acutely aware, but the dangers that followed after the rush could be devastating to the human body. She felt her heartbeat starting to slow and match Jack's low timber.

"Easy of both accounts. He has unlimited sources and there were numerous cruise ships with many Asians touring the last frontier," he deduced. He looked back at the mine opening and then to Elaine. "Is there a back way out of that mine?"

"Yeah, but it's about three to four miles back from the niche with the graffiti. So, if they're alive, they can get out. But it will take time. Let's not wait around to see if they do," she encouraged, getting to her feet and pounding through the stream to the other side. "Just exactly where did you get that dynamite?"

"Same place you got the gun," he shot back.

CHAPTER THIRTY SEVEN

Harlan Dotson watched as his wife's Jeep Wrangler peeled into the parking lot and skidded to a stop in her parking spot. He dragged slowly on his unfiltered Camel cigarette and watched Elaine and Jack extricate themselves and their gear from the Jeep. Elaine was a little wet and Jack was a little dusty. They approached him as if nothing had happened.

"Did you hear that racket up there by the mine?" he asked. Neither spoke. "You do that, Jack?"

Jack's wink was all he had to say as Elaine handed Harlan the keys to Jackie's Jeep. "Tell her thank you, Harlan. I'll keep in touch and let you know what more we find," Elaine said as she hugged her good friend.

He pulled free her father's nugget and tried to hand it to Elaine. "Sam wants you to have this. For luck, if you will," he said. "She's like her mother; can't keep a secret."

She shook her head and wouldn't have any of it. "There's plenty more of that from where this one came from. Tell her thank you. Her information," she stopped short, a catch sticking in her throat and heart. She sniffed loudly and said, "Her information has made a difference."

The plane ride back to Angoon was a cold one for Jack. He not only was up front, but he was the quintessential gentleman and let Elaine keep his jacket to keep her warm. The heater provided little against the cold wind whipping at his face and it was an hour flight at best. All he wanted was a hot shower, toddy and bed. And he wouldn't be against having Elaine's warmth snuggled up next to him either.

He smiled and to pass the time he went back in time to when their love and marriage was carefree and full of trust and respect.

It was an architectural fundraiser for the preservation of the

Conservatory of Flowers at the Golden Gate Park. A number of notables had attended the dinner and like so many occasions, Jack was running late and when he had arrived someone else was sitting in his seat, next to his wife, enjoying her company. Instead of finding a table, he found the bar and indulged in a few cocktails before heading to the auction.

The auction began and several items were sent home with some of San Fran's most elite citizens. Then came a pen and pencil set from Cartier. It was antique rose gold and marble from the late eighteen hundreds. The bidding began with Elaine staking first claim. Then Jack upped the ante and raised the stakes. Their war began and ended with Elaine claiming the price.

But Jack wouldn't be outdone. He intercepted her at the claim station. She looked ravishing that night; deck out in emerald green. The gown showing off her best assets; her long shapely legs. He presented her with her favorite cocktail, an Italian Margarita, with a kiss of lime.

"Thank you," she drawled, as she took the drink and her vintage set in its tortoise shelled box.

"That's quite a beautiful set," he remarked, looking at her bosom where she had precariously let the box rest as she sipped her drink.

"Thank you," she simply replied.

"I was wondering if you'd be interested in selling the set?" he gently inquired.

"Oh, I'm sorry. No. It's a gift," she informed him just as gently.

"For whom?"

"My husband."

"Oh, that's too bad. I was hoping I could entertain you and try and talk you out of it," he admitted.

"Hum," was all she said as she molded her body to his and tenderly tucked the antique box inside the pocket of his white dinner jacket. "Yeah, well, the last time you entertained me, you talked me *into* something else. That marriage thing. Remember?" She gave a throaty laugh and kissed him favorably, even though he had missed dinner.

He had missed a lot of dinners and other important things in their marriage, and as they approached Angoon, he regretted everyone of them.

CHAPTER THIRTY EIGHT

The weather the next morning wasn't fit for man or beast. The winds were howling and the bay and sea were kicking up a fuss. Elaine looked out their window knowing she couldn't fly in this weather; well, safely anyway. And if there was anything she was, she was a safe pilot.

She took her freshly made cup of java and sat on the loveseat by the window and continued to stare at the unhappy waters of the bay. The Mama Cass bobbed and weaved as relentless waves crashed into her hull and threw her against the bumpers on the dock that were used to protect her. No charters today. It was excruciating to watch the time slowly tick away, and to be so isolated and not have the ability to do anything except wait was horrible. God, she was bad at waiting, she thought. Little, if any patience for it.

Frustrated, she got up from the loveseat and sat at the tiny desk where the mini personal Keurig brewer sat; ready to percolate another cup of outstanding coffee. Earlier, she had run down to the second floor and plugged her phone into the computer and was able to print pictures of their discovery in the mine. She had also loaded the images onto her PDA. To compare, she put them side by side, lining up the scrolled graffiti, with its uneven totem poles, so she could see the entire artwork and message.

She got up and found her compact in her backpack and then returned to the desk, where she took the photo in which her mother's handwriting was in and turned it upside down. Then she placed the mirror over it, at an angle. She read out loud her mother's words, "Your aim." She thought for a moment, looked again and repeated, "Your aim. What the hell?" She wrote it down on her PDA and began examining the rest of photos for more clues.

Amazing what one can find when they set their mind to it, she thought. Within the totem poles of the graffiti, she found a bent arm with a bulging muscle. She circled it and made a notation in her book. Its paint was fresh, not damaged by years of dewy dampness. "What do you do when you bulge your muscles?" she asked out loud and Jack startled her with a response.

"You impress," he said, posing like a bodybuilder with his biceps bulging in nothing but a bath towel wrapped around his waist.

"Very funny," she said, looking over his toned and newly showered self. His only flaw, a nasty through and through on his side, complements of Slim. "Nice, but funny. Come and take a look at these photos and this symbol left by my mother?"

He padded over, holding the ends of another towel draped casually over his neck and shoulders. He looked at the photos and then to her PDA with the words in quotations, "your aim". "Couldn't she have just written it out, instead of being so cryptic."

"She was a spy, Jack, what do you think? Obviously her training is coming back full circle and she left it for the likes of you to find; another spy. Go figure."

"So from left to right, we have," he began as he was looking over the photos, "your aim and a bugling muscle. Anything else?"

"I just started going over the photos a few minutes ago. Let's see," she muttered as she carefully scanned the rest of the photos. She was about to stop, when at the last totem pole she saw a buccaneer's hat, with a skull and crossbones. "Buccaneer's hat with skull and crossbones," she said, slightly more animated than before. Now she felt like they were getting somewhere.

Jack had rejoined her, dressed in jeans and a thick, woolen sweater; it's buttons at the top left undone, showing his white undershirt. "Show me?" he asked.

She did, and then he leaned on the desk, and stared out into space.

"Tell me you're thinking spy stuff here," she encouraged with a touch of sarcasm.

"You're so much more beautiful when you're not sarcastic," he bit back with his own brand of sarcasm.

"So I've been told," she rebutted sweetly. "Repeatedly," she added.

He looked down at the desk, and under all the photos, the phone and the PDA was a map of Alaska. Her aviation map to be more precise. He gently intruded into her space and moved her gadgets away to get a better look at the map. "What's in Craig?" he asked because she had it circled in blue.

"Outside of one of the few paved roads on Prince of Wales Island? Not much, around fifteen hundred residents. We'd stop on occasions, but not like in Hydaburg, where they have the Totem Pole Park. But, John did mention between Craig, Angoon and Juneau, those were important points of interest to my folks, and Mark said this was their last *known* stop." She reached for her PDA and photos; her stylus pecking away at the "your aim" , buccaneer's hat and arm. "It's like Pictionary, and I was good at that game. So, let's approach it that way."

"I sucked at that game," he solemnly revealed.

"I know," she confirmed. "Okay, "your aim" isn't self explanatory, but they are words. The buccaneer's hat with the skull and crossbones. We know the skull and crossbones stands for poison, or poisonous substance."

"Or military," he interjected, and at the same time they said, "Captain!"

She grabbed the map and located New Tokeen where her parents' transponder went dead. " New Tokeen. New Tokeen is near El Captain Passage," she blurted out with excitement.

"What's near there?" Jack asked.

"El Captain Cave," she answered, circling approximately where the cave would be located if it were on her aviator map. "All right, one down and two to go," she stated with renewed enthusiasm. "Jack, since you're in the business, what is hot button or zone right now, and what is Slim's interest?"

"Slim's interest is mainly drugs. But it's not to say he hasn't formed new alliances," he answered, recalling the name Boris in the mine tunnel.

As if she were reading his mind she piped up with, "Who's Boris?"

"You heard that, did you?" he asked with a smile.

She nodded her head, yes, and raised her eyebrows prompting him to fill in the blanks.

He got the hint. "Boris comes from an old time Russian mafia family. The clan is called the Vory, or vor v zakone. Which means, thief in law. Back in the day, pre World War II, these thieves were the elite in organized crime. They were born out of the prison camps established by Stalin. They lived by a code to completely be subjugated to the laws of being a criminal. They stole everything. They didn't work a traditional job. Thievery was their job. That meant if Vor didn't have a blanket, the Vor stole it.   "And, they had a code of conduct that was rather severe; the Vor had to forsake their families, they could have a lover, but no family. They couldn't have a job. They only lived off of what was gleaned from thievery or gambling. After the fall of the Soviet Union, the Vory gained access to the most prominent of politicians and their ways quickly spread through post Mother Russia countries.

"Boris is a progressive Vor and so is his family. Where typically the Vory didn't associate with arms smuggling or drugs, Boris and his family have embraced them with open arms. No pun intended. This has happened in large because the competition to stay afloat in their economy. They have moved into not only the former Soviet Bloc countries, but places like Madrid and New York."

He was quiet for a moment, and then he bent down and kissed the top of her head. "Now you know why it concerns me to have you involved. They're not nice people, and their code of conduct is just not exclusively for their own. Understand?"

"Believe me, Jack, right now, I'd rather be at my drafting board peeling layers back on an old house, and not some old mystery that's made its way into the twenty-first century. Can you riddle me this; what kind of spy are you?"

"I'm like your mother; I'm a saboteur. My cover was the construction industry. Go in and build new buildings and tear down old governments," explained matter-of-factly.

"Is Jack Phillips your real name?"

He hesitated for what seemed forever before honestly answering. "No. Jack is, but Phillips is not my real last name."

Tears welled in her eyes, clouding everything she thought was true. "Are we even legally married? Or was it, or rather I, part of your cover?"

He wiped her tear-streaked face. "Yes, we are legally married. If you recall, you signed the certificate first, and then, I signed my legal name, folded it and put it in the breast pocket of my tux. I gave it to your father to put in a safe deposit box, where it has remained ever since."

"I don't suppose you're going to tell me my real married name?"

"To keep you safe, no."

"So, the divorce papers?"

"More for Lane's benefit," he admitted.

She stood and looked him square in the eye. "You put me through hell, all because my brother is into something he doesn't realize?"

"No amount of apologizing is going to help, is it?"

"I didn't say that," she muttered against his soft mouth. "I didn't say that at all," she finished by devouring the soul before her.

Recklessly they found the bed and fell into the softness of the down mattress. Their want and need for each other was consuming and nearly combustible. Every touch, every kiss, every stroke was searing, yet soothing. Each giving and taking as much as the other; neither giving in until there was nothing left but a sweet surrender. They fell asleep, clinging to each and the beautiful memory of just what happened.

Elaine tenuously opened her eyes to find Jack propped up by pillows, fully clothed, sipping coffee and trying to figure out her PDA. She gracefully stretched out the kinks of their lovemaking, and then propped up on one elbow, staring at her PDA, then to her husband. Before she could protest he was defending his intrusion.

"I'm your husband; I'm entitled," he mocked and lightly shook the silver gadget.

"You're entitled to what we just did," she said, looking at the clock, "several times and several hours ago. Nothing else."

"How does this thing work?" He shook it for good measure, trying to get a rise out of her.

"What, Mr. Spy Man can't figure it out?" she teased as she got out of bed and started for the bathroom.

"Where are you going?" he asked.

"To the bathroom and a much needed hot bath," she answered, gathering her clothing as she went.

"I could help," he cheerfully offered.

"I'm not young anymore, Jack. That's why I need a hot bath" she countered, blowing him a kiss and then shutting and locking the door, ensuring privacy.

When Elaine emerged from the bathroom, Jack was still on the bed, happily reading her PDA. "What fancy-ass contraption did you use to break my password?" she asked, full of indignation.

He picked up a small gadget with a USB cable with two male ends and waved it triumphantly in her direction; his eyes never leaving her PDA. "I don't know what it's called, I just know how to use it."

"That's debatable," she huffed after seeing the USB with two male ends. "I see I got screwed twice today," she muttered to herself.

"Oh, it was more than twice, sweetheart," he chimed in. "Have you been able to decipher these diaries and put them into some semblance of order?" he asked, somewhat frustrated that he wasn't being able to *read* between the lines.

"Yeah. I've got this little doohickey with cords and stuff," she playfully retorted, and he settled her with a stern look. "I don't know, Jack. It's like my work; I'm able to peel back layers and blend. I just look at these journals and my parent's like one big onion. I peel a few layers here and cry a little there, but I'm managing to understand what they were doing in and through the diaries." Then she made light of the situation. "It's kind of like that old commercial, 'Ancient Chinese secret, huh.'" She laughed and tugged at him to stop reading the PDA. "Come on, there's probably a poker game going on downstairs."

He still gave her a look of frustration as they headed downstairs for some rootin-tootin fun.

CHAPTER THIRTY NINE

They didn't have to go far to find Tansy or Veronica; they were in the thick of things in the great room. Laughing, refilling glasses, and taking plates after guests were through noshing on the most delightful appetizers, was a seamless task for Tansy, Veronica and Cass.

Making sure all guests had their drinks topped off, Tansy announced, "Poker, anyone?"

The room erupted in boisterous applause and wolf whistles. As the patrons were excited about the evening's festivities, Tansy and Cass prepared three tables with 5 chairs, new decks of cards and an ample supply of poker chips.

Sherry went around to each guest and had them pull a piece of paper from the top hat she was carrying. The paper was marked with either a one, two or three. There were four of each number in the hat. Whatever the number pulled, was the table at which the player sat. Tansy, Veronica and Cass, each sat at a table and was the dealer for that group.

Tansy systematically rounded up the one's and placed them at her table. Veronica, the two's, and Cass the three's. A side bar was at each station, and it was filled with peanuts, pretzels, Goldfish and popcorn. Drinks were served between hands and at breaks.

Thankfully, Jack and Elaine were seated at different tables. Jack always hated the fact that Elaine was the superior poker player between the two of them, and had the better poker face; literally and figuratively. She really missed her calling; she would have made an exceptional operative, he thought. He caught her eye and brushed a finger over his nose, like the cons in the movie, *The Sting*. She laughed.

Each dealer laid out the rules of the tournament: They would play ten hands, then on the eleventh hand, the person with the least amount of money would have to bet "all in". They'd either sink or swim. This process would repeat itself until there was one player left at each table. There would be two breaks between these initial rounds. Everyone bought two hundred dollars in chips; the ante was ten dollars, and the raises were unlimited.

Tansy rang her favorite copper dinner bell, signifying the start of the tournament. Chatter slowed, while people looked over their hands and contemplated their wagers. Elaine sat at Tansy's table along with Betty and Bob Brown, a couple from Vancouver, and a very stylish looking gentleman named, Kevin Shaunessey, originally from Wisconsin. The Browns' were in their mid-sixties and just recently retired. Bob had been a hospital administrator, while Betty was an auditor for an insurance company. They were a chatty couple, especially with Tansy. But, then Tansy had a way of getting people to open up and share.

Kevin, on the other hand, was rather close with his information and more interested in the hands that were being dealt than idle chit chat. Between he and Elaine they had the lion's share of the winning hands.

Jack on the other hand, was losing, and losing big. He had his reasons; he wanted to join Elaine's table and keep an eye on the gentleman sitting across from his wife. On the last hand of the first round, Jack bet it all as required and promptly bowed out; even though he held three aces. "Just not my night," he lied, as the rest of the players neatly stacked their chips and got up for refreshments.

Veronica leaned over and gathered Jack's cards. She took a peek, and her blue eyes shot open at his hand. He put a finger to his lips, pleading with her to remain quiet. She did. He leaned over and gave her cheek a sweet peck and whispered, "You'd be a lousy poker player." He winked and went to grab some food and beer with the others of his table.

Three players were out. Then six, and finally eight, with one table left to set the final four. It had come down to Tansy's table with Kevin and Elaine vying for the third and final seat in the tournament. Kevin had slightly less money than Elaine, so the final hand required him to go all in. Reluctantly, he did so.

The tension was palpable, Kevin didn't like losing and Elaine read that in his narrow brown eyes. She picked up on his twitches early on and recognized his good from his bad. When he had a good hand, he would lightly stroke, only once, the tee in his perfectly trimmed, salt and pepper Van Dyke. With a bad hand, he played with his crested ring. He liked his hand. With all bets placed, Tansy nodded to Kevin to show his hand.

Triumphantly he placed his cards down; four of a kind, all eights. Chatter filled the air as Kevin looked expectantly to Elaine to beat his hand.

"Kevin has a dead man's hand. Four of a kind. And in eight's, no less. The infinite number," Tansy announced. "All right, girl, show us what you've got," she said to Elaine.

Calmly Elaine revealed her hand; a Royal Flush in all spades. And she, along with everyone else in the room, watched Kevin's face go slack. His brown eyes narrowed at the loss, but to his credit, he did attempt a wan smile of congratulations to Elaine.

"Well played," he managed and rose, excusing himself to the surrounding group.

They parted and he headed upstairs. Hushed whispers followed him until he disappeared by the stairs, then the remainder of the participants grew rowdy and started taking sides; placing bets on whom they thought would win out. Amazingly, Elaine was the favorite.

With bellies full from either Veronica's awesome appetizers or the beer from the Alaskan Brewing Company, the players took their places at Tansy's table and the crowd gathered around, watching intently to see who was going to rein as the tournament champion. The rules for this match up were set forth by Tansy, "One hundred dollar ante and a two hundred dollar minimum for the raises. May the best man or woman win."

The players consisted of Murray Atkins of Shreveport, Louisiana; he cleaned up at Veronica's table. Then from Nashville, Tennessee; Boyd Chastain, who won everything in sight at Cass's table. And, last but not least, Elaine.

Though she was odds on favorite, she didn't start out that way. She was not having the best of draws, but she hung in there, and after the first ten hands, Murray was low man on the totem pole. On the eleventh hand, he went all in; and won. So, the next hand was sudden death for the first round of the final and Elaine was low. She put *all in*; and won.

They played four more sudden death hands to whittle down to the final two players. All bets were in, with Boyd, *all in*. He presented his cards and he was busted. Nothing but a pair of fives. Murray was a little better with a pair of jacks, but it was Elaine that cleaned up with two pair; kings and aces.

The finale was anticlimactic as Elaine cleaned Murray's clock. She took her winnings and quietly instructed Tansy to donate to the local school for whatever they deemed necessary.

Sometime during the last few hands of the finale, Kevin reappeared. His distant observation wasn't lost on Jack, and before Elaine could get out of her chair, Jack bear hugged her and whispered, "Kevin's been missing in action for quite some time. He enjoys Russian Standard Vodka."

She smiled and pretended he had said something totally different. "I can't help you're such a lousy player," she lied to cover up.

Jack shrugged his shoulders in mock defeat as Kevin approached with a fresh bottle of Russian Standard. He lifted the bottle to Jack in an offer to share his favorite brand. "Why not?" Jack asked.

Veronica and Cass had brought out fresh glasses and a variety of after dinner drinks, as well as more munchies for the hungry crowd.

Kevin offered anyone who was interested, to join him in a toast to the new champion. He raised his glass of neat vodka in a salute to Elaine and her triumph. "A toast, to our lovely champion. My she live long and spend our money wisely."

A variety of "here, here" and a chorus of "cheers" rang out through the great room. The vodka raced down Elaine's throat and spread a cool warmth throughout her being. She shuddered at the creepiness of it and looked to Jack, who was casually observing Kevin's interaction with Murray, as Murray recounted his last, losing hand.

It was nearly two in the morning before the group started to dwindle in numbers and Elaine and Jack threw in the towel to exhaustion. They thanked Tansy, Veronica and Cass for an exceptionally fun time and bade everyone left a goodnight, including Kevin.

"Is it me, or is Kevin creepy?" Elaine asked as Jack opened the door to their room.

"In a GQ kind of way," he replied, flipping on the lights and heading toward the bathroom.

"What do you make of him?" she asked through the bathroom door.

She waited patiently for him to emerge and answer her question. "He's not to be trusted," he stated the obvious. "But, we're leaving in the morning, and we probably won't ever see him again," he remarked with confidence as he pulled her into his arms and kissed her. "I'm ready for bed," he exclaimed. On his way to their queen bed, he shed ever stitch of clothing and climbed in, fluffy his pillows for extra measure. He flipped her side of the covers down and patted where she needed to be. "Come on. We're going to be busy later. We need our rest."

Following suit, her clothes led a trail to the bed and she climbed in next to her husband. The only thing she was wearing was a tribute to her mother and father's adventure; the Yin-Yang pendant. A sweet little peck and he turned his back to her and promptly went to sleep. She turned off the light and waited for about ten minutes for the sandman to visit. He didn't. So, she groped in the night and found her PDA on her nightstand. She turned it on and it illuminated the dark space. She found where she had left off in the journals and resumed reading. Her last account, she had left them in a mountainous range in China.

Kash swiveled in his saddle to check on a very quiet Leslie and found her shifting uncomfortably in her saddle. He glanced down at his watch and then pulled his horse to a stop.

He remembered the last time he was surrounded by so much foliage; it was his South American trip with Marrow. This trip was totally different; fresh autumn air as opposed to the stifling heat of the jungle. The incessant chatter of the tropical birds and Mike Marrow, compared to the tranquil pines, maples, and the quiet beauty of Leslie Anne Scott.

He watched her bring her horse to a stop next to him and he took pleasure in pushing her hat back. "Let's take a break," he suggested.

Ah, sweet music to her ears. She dismounted the paint and gave a hearty stretch. Kash found a lower limb and loosely tied off the horses and mule. He took a generous swig of water from his canteen, then offered some to Leslie.

Without hesitation, she took a gulp and wiped her mouth with the back of her gloved hand and passed the canteen back to Kash. She noticed the path they had taken was virtually fresh and the trees surrounding them were mostly somber red, with a few in resplendent gold and a few yellows mixed in here and there. She leaned against the sturdy trunk of one of those somber red trees and watched the horses fidget as Kash checked their cinches and bridles.

He pulled two guns from his saddle bag and placed one in the front and the other in the back of his jeans. Sauntering over to her, he ignored her curious frown and switched places with her. Leaning against the tree he managed to keep her within the circle or his arms. A little tug and he had her resting comfortably against his length.

She caught sight of a bead of sweat rolling from the hollow of his neck and down his chest. Inadvertently she licked her lips and watched the droplet disappear into the fibers of his shirt. Bracing herself against his chest, she boldly captured his lower lip and playfully nipped it. She repeated the process with his upper lip before devouring both in a host of sweetness. The sensuous rubbing of his hand at the small of her back only added to the heat radiating through her lightweight shirt.

She didn't want it to end, but she could feel his need growing and reluctantly she drew back, cocking her perfectly arched brow in a silent "thank you". Tease, reflected in the silver of his eyes. He held her closer and dared her to continued. Her cheekbones raised in a restrained smile and suddenly embarrassment flushed her face. She looked down to hide it and her smile faded as reality set in. She stared at the pistol tucked inside his waistband. She tapped the handle, pushing it further into his pants.

"Careful," he sounded off, delicately capturing her hand.

"Do we need these?"

"Well, I'm sort of attached to them."

Her dimples registered his insinuation and then suddenly she was serious once again.

"Yes. Speaking of," he stopped and took the pistol from his back, gave it a quick inspection and shoved it into the back of her well fitted jeans. She arched her back at the uncomfortable intrusion. Kash lifted her face to his. "Just in case."

"Terrific," she whispered. "That's all I need to do; shoot myself in the ass."

He planted a reassuring kiss on her pouty mouth and steered her back to her horse. He handed over the reins to the mule. "Your turn to persuade this beast."

"Um, I have a way with beasts," she said with smile and brought the mule into line.

Nighttime had fallen quickly, and so had the temperature. Kash had finished bedding the animals and returned to the campsite where fresh coffee, dried fruit and day old bread greeted him. Leslie poured them coffee and he gratefully received the steamy liquid. Kash began to eat heartily and she wondered if he was even chewing his food.

"You haven't fully explained our business here in the wilderness. I have a pretty good idea, but only an idea. Why don't you enlighten me?" She took another sip of coffee and waited patiently for him to think through his answer.

While he thought, he shoved more bread into his mouth, then he started to answer her question. She listened to his muffled reasoning and ignored his manners, or lack of them.

"Our business," he started, then washed down his bread with a gulp of coffee, "is to find the Heavenly Wisdom, and place it into the right hands." He touched her bruised lip. "Instead of the wrong hands."

"Why are we doing this?"

"Nobility. Righteousness. Or perhaps to ease my conscience and soften my end of the crunch."

She understood completely. "Do you know where the scrolls are located?"

He shook his head and popped a piece of fruit. "That's where you come in. I need that drawing of the pendant."

She patted down her shirt pockets, then the back of her jeans and pulled free a folded piece of paper. Pushing the plates aside, Kash pressed the blanket smooth and she laid out the drawing to study. He pointed to the "red" and "mountain" characters. "These two, we've figured out. We're in the mountains amongst the most vibrant patch of red. Also, this is the closet red range to the burial grounds." He tapped the two remaining characters. "These two, I don't understand."

"According to Chiang," she pointed to the third character, "this means 'banks'. It could mean lake, river or shoreline?"

"Probably lake or river. Tomorrow we'll start checking the ground and trees for any sign of moss. We find some, we'll know there's a source of water nearby."

Leslie gave him an astonished look.

"Boy Scout. What about the fourth character?"

"It means 'springs'. Can't be the season, or the freshest time; we're in autumn. Maybe water channeling from one source rising…"

"To the surface," he concluded her thought and repaid the favor with an astonished nod. "Boy Scout?" he teased.

"Dad was a Scout Master. Possibly a hot springs." She got them back on course.

"Possibly. What about the dragon?"

"It's where the scrolls can be found, and those lead to the Heavenly Wisdom."

"And where do we find the dragon?"

"In the fall. The waterfall. Find the bank and springs," she began.

"And find the waterfall, you find the dragon and the scrolls," he finished. It was nice they agreed on something. Amazing to Leslie and frightening to Kash. "I suggest you get some sleep," he said as he settled against his saddle. "The change in elevation tomorrow will be tiring."

"Yes, sir, Mr. Scout Master," she mocked with a three fingered salute.

Before she could bed down for the night, she had to clean up. Like the obedient woman Kash knew she could be, she cleaned and packed the plates, then settled beneath her blanket. Forcing herself to relax, sleep finally came, for the both of them.

Abruptly Kash opened his eyes to a dwindling fire and hurriedly doused it with the remainder of the coffee. Careless, he chastised himself and strained to hear past the smoldering as to where the animals had been bedding for the night. They were restless. He checked a sleeping Leslie and quietly moved towards the horses and mule.

On the way, he carefully moved from tree to tree, stopping only to listen for noises foreign to the surroundings. He started to slide to the next tree, but ducked down when he saw two black clad figures milling about the horses. Using the shadows of the trees, he worked around to a better vantage. A twig snapped under his weight and he winced at its deafening crack. Holding his position, and breath, he waited and listened for their reaction.

A high pitched shrill exploded behind him and he dove out of the way of a sharp edge saber. Rolling up into a crouch position, Kash eyed his hooded attacker. His adrenalin pumping and his heart pounding in his ears, he started to lunge, but two arms encircled his chest and held him in check. He didn't struggle, but every muscle was tense, prepared to defend.

The attacker raised the blade to his shoulders, parallel to the ground and prepared to strike. Kash didn't wait; using the man behind him for support, he kicked past the saber with both legs and wrapped around the attacker's neck. A quick twist and crack, and Kash let his enemy fall to the ground. Driving the second man backwards into a tree offered freedom, but only for a moment. Fending off two jabs, Kash delivered a kick to the abdomen and backhand to the face, throwing his assailant off balance. Grabbing the back of his tunic and the waistband of his pants, Kash rammed him head first into a nearby tree trunk.

The sound of his head splitting and neck breaking echoed throughout the silent trees. Leslie closed her eyes and turned her head away from the sight, sound and smell of death. She had reached the horses, who were well aware of the destruction around them, and offered a soothing, reassuring pat to their necks. "Sssh. It's all right," she cooed to them. It was really more for her benefit that theirs. "Calm down, now. It's all right."

They stopped their thrashing and ceased their whinnies, but still nervously stomped their hooves. Kash gave the rope a hard yank and forced them to be still.

He showed no sign of weariness from the encounter as he carried the saddles from the campsite and prepared the horses. He felt her stare and turned to her. His voice was steady and commanding, reflecting no remorse for his actions, but no arrogance, either. "Go back to the camp, pack the gear, the bedrolls and bring them to me."

Without a word, she headed back to the camp, and on her way, she listened intently for any noises that weren't created by her. As a precaution, she pulled the revolver from the back of her jeans and held it uncomfortably in her hand. It didn't nestle affectionately in her palm like a small kitten or puppy. The contrary, it was cold and hard, unyielding, expecting her to fit to its inflexible shape.

She reached the camp, released and checked the chamber. It was full. A flick of the wrist and the chamber snapped back into place. She shoved the revolver into the back of her Levi's, then gathered the gear for Kash.

They had been traveling for hours, and the past hour the journey had been slow because the terrain had roughened and the elevation has increased. The horses and mule continued up the steep climb, despite their loads and the length of time they had been ascending without a break. Kash realized it and looked around for a relatively flat plain to rest the animals.

Dismounting was a chore for Leslie, every muscle screamed in protest when she swung her leg out of the saddle and it hit the hard ground. The jarring sent a shock up her length, letting her know she was slightly out of shape where riding was concerned. She pulled the collar up on her jeans jacket to ward off the morning chill.

Kash scooped up the reins and affixed them to an upstart bush. The animals delighted in barley having to extend their necks for a refreshing nibble. That triggered Leslie's stomach, as she just knew it was hard pressed against her backbone from lack of food, and from the looks of things, relief was far from sight. Kash seemed able, but not willing to unpack for an early lunch. Instead he stuffed the canteen into her sunken belly, offering her liquid nourishment to tide her over until dinner.

The tepid liquid did nothing but stream its way down to her stomach and become absorbed. Having had enough, she offered it back to him; and a definite shake of his head was his reply. Putting the lid in place, she secured the canteen to his saddle horn and stared blankly at the sword Kash had taken from one of his attackers.

Curiously she ran a finger down its ornate sheath, and shivers raced down her spine. The creepy kind. Those most associated with fingernails scraping down a chalkboard. She couldn't understand why he had taken it, and at the moment, she didn't care to know.

Leaving well enough alone, she journeyed over to Kash, finding him in an all too familiar pose; leaning up against the trunk of a mighty oak. Hesitating not, she molded her body to his; and then her lips to his. A deep throated groan filled her ears as he deepened their intimacy, surprising her with a delightful exploration of her mouth with his tongue. Stroking and probing lightly, he invited her to do the same.

The soft rustling of leaves broke through the enchanting spell she had cast, and Kash, careful not to interrupt their embrace, protectively pulled her closer. Cautiously he opened one eye to spot the source of the unsettling.

A black clad figure, similar to those earlier that morning, took his aim with a throwing star. In one motion, Kash seized the gun from the back of Leslie's jeans; ceased their embrace and shoved her to the ground for safe keeping. Before he could align and fire, the throwing star was hurled and neatly cut through the material of his shirt, penetrating the taunt muscle of his shoulder. Ignoring the pain, he fired three consecutive shots, falling his enemy.

After the shots, it didn't take Leslie long to collect herself. She grabbed the Colt 45 from the front of his jeans, and out of the corner of her eye, she caught sight of the second intruder lurking nearby. She turned and their eyes met. Chiang! her mind registered.

Mrs. Scott! he immediately regretted. She pulled the slide back, engaging the first bullet, then she took off after the retreating Chiang.

Kash extended a forbidding hand in her direction and watched her race after Chiang. "Leslie!" He cried out in pain; looked at his wound and scowled at the neatly sliced half moon. "Shit!"

Leslie pulled up and strained her ears for any sound of Chiang. Hearing his sudden movement, she jerked her head around and spotted him running through a small clearing. She raised the 45, sighted and squeezed the trigger. A loud crack filled the air, followed by an agonizing cry. She continued after him, hell bent on evening a score. Her eyes narrowed in their search, finding trickles of bright red on the ground; clashing with the scarlet of the autumn leaves.

She slowed in her pursuit, and Chiang, weakened by loss of blood pressed himself against a tree, listening for any sign of his pursuer. She pulled even with him and then started to go the opposite direction. He relaxed for only a moment, then he grimaced as the sweat from his brow rolled down and cooled the heated end of the barrel that rested against his temple.

A hand to his shoulder, she encouraged him to slide down the tree trunk and sit on the ground. He obeyed the silent order, gnarling his lip at the pain in his leg. The barrel left his temple and was positioned directly in front of his face; aimed at an angle that ensure instantaneous death if fired.

The cylinder moved to just under his chin; raising his head. He complied, but his eyes remained lowered. He didn't want to look into the betrayed depths of her expression, knowing she was thinking about that night with Tu An Lin. That night he offered no help.

An eternity seemed to have passed before he finally looked up to her face. She was a very unpredictable woman; instead of the clinched jaw and eyes black with revenge, her expression held a combination of pity and sorrow.

"You've hunted before," he noted.

"Yes," she replied solemnly.

"And now you must be humane and put the wounded prey out of its misery," he finished her thought for her.

"Yes."

"So be it," he accepted.

Chiang looked up at her with steady, knowing eyes, just like that wounded buck on her first hunting trip with her father when she was eleven. Now he was the one with the sorrowful expression. She hesitated only a moment, then slowly she raised the 45 and placed it between his eyes.

Her conscience fought with her dark side, and the need for revenge and preservation. She had made the decision, when Kash jammed his thumb between the trigger and firing pin. A quick jerk and he wrenched the Colt from her hand. Her black glare tried to penetrate the steel gray wall of his stare.

"You were going to kill him, weren't you?" Kash asked in an unbelieving tone.

"Do we have a choice?" she coolly rebutted.

"When it comes to one of our own, yes." Kash extended a hand to Chiang and helped him up.

"What the hell does that mean; 'one of our own'?" she questioned sarcastically. "Oh, I see."

"No, you don't see."

"Apparently you're the one who can't see," Leslie threw back. "I suppose the other three men with Chiang were also our own? You know?" she drilled. "The one's you managed to kill in a six hour period."

"No."

"No, what?" she interrupted. "You don't remember?"

"They weren't our own," he ground out.

She nodded toward a silent Chiang. "Neither is he."

"You're sort of right." Kash gave in and Chiang gave him a worried

look. "He's an operative for the Chinese government. Something like our CIA," he informed her with great pleasure, hoping it would clear the air and bring her down off her high, spirited horse. It only added more fuel to the fire.

She bore a hole through a relieved Chiang, but her words were for Kash. "That's real easy for you to say. You weren't the one tied to a chair, taking punches and slaps from a fat, bald man, and watching out of the corner of your eye, 'one of your own' shrinking back into the shadows, lifting not one finger to help." She touched her bruised lip and looked to Kash. "Thanks for keeping me so well informed."

She stalked away, leaving Kash to tend to Chiang and vice versa. If he could have, he would have dragged her back by that thick mane of hers and set her straight, but he had neither the strength nor the time. Instead he sent a stinging not to her retreating back. "Just like that pendant, huh?" He hoped his words soaked in and stung, but he doubted it. From the look of things, they just reverberated off the trees.

Little did he know his words hit home, and they did sting, but she wasn't going to show it. Least of all, to him. Holding her carriage straight, her head high, and keeping an even stride, she made her way back to the horses.

Kash helped Chiang mount his horse, careful not to disturb the make shift bandage on his leg. For the most part the bleeding had stopped and the searing pain had subsided to a dull ache.

"Flanery was right. You are interested," Chiang teased with a broad grin.

Kash gave him a settling glare, but it didn't detour Chiang.

"She has a point, you know? You've known about my infiltration into Tu An Lin's operation for some time, yet you never said anything to her. Especially since she was in the middle of it all."

"I had my reasons," Kash defended. "Besides, she put herself in the middle of it all."

"That's not the reason. You actually thought she was the Russian, didn't you?"

Kash didn't respond.

"Not that lady. She should have been Chinese."

"Have you forgotten she was going to kill you?" Kash reminded him.

"And with good reason. If I were her, I would have, too. She showed loyalty; to you." Chiang pointed out.

"You'd better get going," Kash changed the subject quickly. "I can handle it from here."

"Yes, I can see how you were handling things," Chiang chided. "One thing," he cautioned, "There's one more family member lurking behind. Possibly the most dangerous of the four. Be careful."

Kash nodded his appreciation and spurred Chiang's horse on.

Elaine stopped for a moment to recount Chiang's actions until this point. What exactly was his role in the Chinese government? Hopefully, it would be pointed out later. But she noticed by the amount of pages left; she was coming to an end with these particular journals. Looking at the clock it had taken but a half an hour, so she continued, bound and determined to finish, and see where this all led.

She took a peek and listened to Jack's breathing. He was sound asleep. Before she resumed reading, she took her stylus and made a note about Chiang.

The sight was deserted when Kash returned. As if he expected to find her there waiting. Only his horse remained, still tied to the bush. An irritated yank pulled the reins free and he hauled himself into the saddle. A slight protest from his stiffening shoulder was ignored, and he reined the beast in the direction Leslie had taken.

Loyal! my ass, Kash thought as he remembered Chiang's description of Leslie, but he forgot to add stubborn and too headstrong for her own good to his list of compliments of Leslie Anne Scott's sterling personality.

Atop the view was breathtaking. For as far as the eye could see, autumn colored clouds shared intimate space. Wavering slightly from side to side, they beckoned one to delve into the kaleidoscope of russets, ambers, sanguine and speckles of green. The sky above, a robin's egg blue, devoid of any clouds, allowed the sun to pour freely its nourishing light onto the land below.

The tiny brook that Leslie had first seen about a mile or so back had grown into a moderate stream, and its water tripped over protruding rocks, then resumed the chase downstream, eventually finding its way to the small spot. The banks were smooth, undisturbed and crystalline in appearance.

She leaned on her saddle horn and studied the unusual brightness of the banks below. The pattern continued along both sides until the stream disappeared around the bend to her left. Looking at the banks, there wasn't an easy way down, so she spurred the horse on and followed the stream from above.

Leslie's detour from the stream side to the springs side had taken a little more than an hour to complete, and not far behind a fatigued Kash followed. The autumn sun was going down quickly, and typical of Indian Summer, so was the temperature.

Leslie had felt like she had crossed over into another dimension; the line between night and day. The stream side was bright, cheery and crisp. The springs side was dark, moist and threatening. Maybe with morning light it would become less suspicious, she hoped.

She gave a wary look to the hot springs below, emitting its eerie mist, daring anyone, including her to enter its bowels. She took the dare and led her horse and the pack mule down a jagged path to the mouth of the springs.

The fire was burning, the coffee perked and the dried fruit was ready for consumption. So where was Kash? Leslie wondered and checked her watch for the umpteenth time. Was he so seriously injured that he was unable to track her? Or was he just hell bent on teaching her a lesson? Hopefully, it was the latter.

Another hour, and a half a pot of coffee later, she checked the jagged path she had taken and still no sign of Kash. Waiting had become tedious, and muscles had tensed from worry and long hours of riding. She looked to the hazy springs and reevaluated it state. From a distance, it was threatening, but up close, it was soft, dreamy and inviting.

It didn't take her long to undress and dive into the opaque warmth of the springs. She surfaced and took in a deep, cleansing breath; allowing the stream to warm and refresh her senses and clear her foggy head. The heat felt wondrous around her sore muscles, providing a soft, constant massage. Swimming farther out, she didn't see the intrusion at the camp.

Like a mermaid, she dove down to the bottom of the springs, and swam back to the bank. The camp fire provided enough light for Kash to recognize the form swimming toward him, and he stepped closer for a better look.

The fog, light near the bank, swirled around his pant leg. He watched her surface, the mist parting to allow her access to the cool autumn air.

Glorifying in the contrast, Leslie closed her eyes and ran warm water over her cool face and she smoothed her dark mane back away from her face. Looking down at the misty water, she started her ascent, unaware of Kash. Waist deep in water, she finally looked up to see the silhouette of a man. A man she was quite familiar with.

Kash extended a beckoning hand to the emerging figure; and willingly she placed her hand in his and allowed him to lead her out of the vaporous springs. The mixture of heat from her body and the coolness of the autumn air, left an aura of mist that clung to every soft, feminine curve of her being.

The heat she felt rising wasn't from the springs or embarrassment, but rather, a natural warmth generated from a deep need that had been lying dormant for nearly two years. Two years seemed forever away as she stepped with surety toward Kash.

His gaze lingered up her long, shapely legs, past her slim hips and smooth breasts before stopping at her face. He lifted a hand to trace the subtle line of her jaw, pausing just under the small dimple of her chin. Tugging lightly, he encouraged her to part her lips and swiftly he claimed them in a drugging kiss, wanting, needing to taste their intoxicating sweetness.

The roughness of his stubble left a scratchy trail of sensuality as he sought out the thundering pulse in her neck. She tipped her head to the side, giving him full approach to the richness of her neck. A domino of shivers raced down her, leaving her weakened, yet exhilarated with want.

The steel bands encircling loosened slightly, permitting her to unbutton his shirt. Deftly she discarded the unwanted piece of material, and she basked in the warmth of his body next to hers. Filling her palms with the sinewy mass of his arms, she created a score of feathery kisses from his roughened jaw down the smoothness of his chest. She stopped at the tear in his shoulder and administered her own brand of medicine.

One agreeable to him. He snaked a hand behind her and grabbed a handful of her wet trusses, adoring its thick splendor. He pulled back her head and watched the reflection of the fire dancing wildly in the depths of her golden brown eyes. His molten silver gaze drifted from her face to her breasts. His touch was firm and masterful, manipulating the nipple to a taunt, rosy peak. A peak he had to climb and explore more fully. Starting at the swell of her breast, he made his ascent slowly, savoring its softness and capturing the sensitive bud, he swirled his tongue lazily around it, bringing it to a new height of arousal. He didn't stop there, giving equal time to its mate. Sliding down to his knees, he explored the flat plane of her stomach, teasing the dimple of her belly button. He stopped just above the dark triangle that led to the heart of her womanhood and he playfully nipped the tender spot.

Weakened by his persistence, she slumped to the ground next to him, her stomach tightening in a knot of desire, anticipating the pleasures to follow. He dragged her down the rest of the way to the bedroll beneath and resumed the whirlwind of sensations he had been creating within her. Next to them the fire burned brightly, adding a warmth that wasn't necessary.

A night of peaceful slumber in one position made its presence known and Leslie stretched lazily trying to work out the kinks and sleepiness. Drowsy eyelids opened to a new dawn, and oddly enough, she was right about the hot springs. The morning light made it look less suspicious; almost friendly, and certainly romantic.

Sensing the cold morning air on her backside, she was aware that Kash was no longer sharing her bedroll. She sat up and pulled the blanket about her, then she looked for the missing Kash. There was no need, familiar arms enveloped her, pulling her up and holding her close. A playful yank and the blanket fell to a heap around her ankles, revealing the same feminine curves he had mastered the night before. Turning her around to the expanse of his chest, he welcomed her to the new day with a kiss that was as urgent as their passion the previous evening.

As much as she hated to, she ended the kiss. Aware of her present state, she looked away from his penetrating silver stare.

"What's wrong?" he asked, confused.

"You've been able to freshen up this morning," she pointed out. Running her tongue over her teeth. "Such as brushing your teeth," she made clearer her point.

"Oooh," he cooed with a playful pout. "Poor baby. Your mouth a little seedy this morning?"

"You know it is."

He laughed and lifted her face to his for a quick kiss. "You're such a snob," he teased, and placed a silencing finger to her lips. "Go get ready before I change my mind and have my way with you."

He let her go and she grabbed the blanket and walked away. "I'm not a snob," she called over her shoulder in defense. "I'm conscientious."

"Exactly. You're high-minded."

She gave a throaty laugh and made her way to her saddle bag.

Leaving the pack mule behind at the campsite made their ride less of a strain and permitted them to scale the range more quickly. For as long as they had been traveling the stream side, the bank had remained in their crystalline state. The farther they went, the more tumultuous the water became. Going from the quiet stream to nearly a full fledge raging river.

Reining his horse to a stop, Kash raised a quieting hand to Leslie. "Listen?"

She steered her horse over next to his and listened carefully. A loud, continuous roar could be heard just off in the distance and around the bend to the left of the racing river. "The waterfall?" she speculated.

"Let's find out."

They spurred on and disappeared around the bend toward the sound.

The closer they got, the more intense the roar became; almost deafening. As they rounded the bend, they looked up to find a waterfall rumbling down. At the top, water ran over the edge with nowhere to go but down. White foamed formed and bubbled at the base; jostling for position to race down the continuing river.

They pulled their horses just behind the fall and looked skyward at the structure that dominated the wall of the waterfall. Leslie's gasp was drowned out by the rushing water as she stared at the constitution before them. A magnificently sculptured dragon was emerging from the wall.

It stood erect, with its tortoise shell body facing the waterfall, and its hawk claws ready to strike. The mouth open, exposed sharp, uneven teeth, daring entry into its chamber. Leslie looked past the mouth to the flared nostrils and eyes: The demon's eyes. Cold and unfriendly, somehow sensing intruders.

She turned back to Kash, who seemed to be less impressed than herself and found him dismounting and pulling free from his saddle horn a coiled rope with a grappling hook at the end.

Sharp, curved fingers struggled to attach themselves to worn, crusty stone. *After groping wildly, they found a weakness and broke through, ensuring Kash a secure hold. Pulling hard, he set the hook and tugged on the rope to make certain he had support.*

Leslie watched impassively as he stuffed his pockets and belt with tools he anticipated he needed for the job ahead. Oddly enough, the saber that was strapped to the saddle earlier, now dangled from Bennett's belt.

He gave the rope a second pull, and scrutinized the climb to the dragon's mouth. It was a straight pull climb; nothing to brace against or walk up; since the head of the dragon extended well beyond its chest. He turned back to a seemingly patient Leslie. "This won't take long. So, sit still," he instructed.

He started his climb to the uninviting mouth. Leslie let him get two thirds of the way up before she started her climb.

A tug from below alerted him to the activity beneath his feet and he held his position and looked down at the figure climbing towards him; irritation masked his face. His yell was as loud and thunderous as the waterfall next to him. "I thought I told you to stay put!"

"What?" she yelled back, pretending she couldn't hear him. "Loud down here. And wet, too. Hurry up, the rope's getting slippery from the spray."

Accepting the obvious, Kash continued and reached the mouth of the demon speller. Holding tight to the rope with one hand, and like the grapple earlier, he blindly searched for a safe point to pull in. Locking onto a spiked edge, he hauled himself up and over the jagged teeth.

Silently he waited for his partner to reach the opening. He watched her grope around for a few seconds before he reached over and hoisted her past the threatening teeth, landing her across his lap, bottom up. He smiled at the successful maneuver. Finally, I have you where I want you. Or rather, where you deserve to be," he reprimanded.

"You wouldn't dare?"

"I never dare, just deliver."

She bit her lip in anticipation of his delivery, but instead he turned her over and smiled his patented boyish grin. "Something wrong?" he asked innocently, pushing her hat back.

He gave her a teasing wink, and allowed her to unfold her length from his lap and get up. She extended a helping hand to him. On his feet, he flicked his lighter and illuminated the inside of the dragon's mouth, divulging the secret the demon speller was erected to protect. On the far wall was a larger version of the pendant; an octagon shaped Yin-Yang symbol with trigrams.

He found two torches on either side of the symbol and lit them. The mouth that was a moment ago dingy and grey was transformed into a haunting orange. Kash stepped past his partner to examine more closely the symbol on the wall for any sign of the scrolls. Nothing. He studied, too, the adjoining walls, floor and ceiling, but saw no indication there were any scrolls to be found, or where they could possibly be located.

Turning back to the symbol, he noticed the eye of the Yang was slightly depressed. Stepping closer, with Leslie nearly in his hip pocket, he investigated the indentation further.

Sticking two fingers inside the cavity, he sensed its willingness to want to move. He encouraged the pattern to the left and watched as the Yang separated from the Yin; creating a broken line between the two.

At the same time, Leslie drew his attention to certain trigrams: Heaven and Earth, Water and Fire moved away from the wall and stopped. Looking inside each extended trigram they found neatly rolled and banded scrolls.

Carefully removing the precious parchment, they didn't notice the threatening intrusion of Gerald Bryant. Not until he drew a saber that matched the one Kash had linked through his belt. Obviously the most deadly of assailants that were following Kash and Leslie met his untimely demise through Gerald.

Simultaneously they snapped their heads around to see him standing in front of them in his khaki garb and bushman's hat. Pleased with the surprise his arrival had stirred, a maniacal smile spread across his face. He rhythmically tapped the floor with the end of the saber as he approached them.

Kash stretched a shielding arm in front of Leslie, silently coaxing her to move behind him and take the scrolls he was holding. She did, and he pushed her deeper into the adjoining wall for safe keeping. He took a step toward Gerald, but was stopped short by the saber swishing back and forth in front of him.

They said nothing, knowing what the other expected. While keeping an eye on Gerald, Kash gradually drew his saber, much to the delight of Gerald and chagrin to Leslie.

Quietly she slinked along the side wall and tried to improve her vantage. Methodically, each man stalked the other, neither willing to take the offensive and dreading to take the defensive. Recognizing that, Gerald took the initiative and whipped his saber masterfully; moving closer to Kash with each swipe, begging him to partake in a duel to the death.

Suddenly, he lunged toward Kash, striking and slicing open, again, the already tender wound on his shoulder. Kash remained steady, not giving an inch to his new found enemy.

"A new game, Mr. Bennett," Gerald promised. "This time it isn't chess."

As quickly as Gerald had struck, Kash repaid the compliment, cutting into Gerald's fair, English skin.

Gerald didn't look to his wounded shoulder, only acknowledging with a touched cackle.

"Chess of a different nature," Kash enlightened.

"Have it your way, old man."

Preliminaries aside, they started dueling, each proficient and agile in the art of fencing. Lunging, staving off calculated jabs that met in the middle of the saber and ended up at the handle, bringing enemy face to face, eye to eye. Survival for one, insanity for the other.

Kash started to take command of the duel, pushing Gerald's saber closer and closer to his face, backing him up in the process. A sidelong glance, and

Gerald had discovered the torch burning within his grasp. Kash saw it too, but too late.

The flame licked across Bennett's shirt front, causing no real damage, but it was enough to distract Kash; throwing him off guard. Gerald threw the torch aside and delivered a boot kick to Kash's chest; knocking the wind out of him and the saber out of his hand. Gerald followed with a vicious backhand to his face; putting Kash to the ground. A swift kick of Bennett's saber and Gerald removed any doubt that the duel would continue.

Frantically Leslie dropped the scrolls and looked for something, anything to throw Kash for defense. Nothing.

While she searched, Gerald stalked his prey and moved in for the kill. "Have the board set up in your head, old man? Russia's black rook to king one. Checkmate." The black rook revealed and recited his chess move to Kash.

Not quite if Leslie had her way. A frustrated cry erupted from her throat as she rushed a surprised Gerald. He didn't panic; his reflexes were far too quick and superior to her efforts and he shooed her away like an annoying fly. But it was enough for Kash to gather himself and his saber.

Leslie righted herself and charged again. Even with her stature, she was no match for Gerald's strength and agility. He ceased her aggression with a rising backhanded blow to her chest and face, hurling her backwards toward the opening and a watery grave below.

Kash reached an instinctive hand of help to her, but couldn't. Gerald was between them and a powerless scream flooded his ears as Leslie dropped over the edge and out of sight; her dark blue fedora tumbling after her.

Bennett's nostrils flared as he gulped in air and a murderous rage grew in his eyes as he focused on the black rook before him. He raised his saber, beckoned his enemy to continue their efforts of combat. This time, it was a duel to the death. Gerald Bryant's death.

A wedged hand between jagged teeth. That's all that stood in the way of Leslie and her Maker. Her breath was coming in waves as she struggled to swing her lower and upper bodies together to build momentum to bring her other hand in contact with the crusty teeth. Rapid breathing was replaced by exasperated cries of failure and pain. Like the grappling hook of earlier, her fingers desperately searched for a strong hold, anything to grab onto. Finally she successfully dug in and held on.

Kash and Gerald met once again at the handles of their sabers. "Black king at king bishop two. Black rook at queen one and the white knight at queen bishop one. Got the board set in your head, old man?" Kash asked as he drew up the final scenario for a straining Gerald.

Kash pushed him away, hoping he'd charge; and he did. A flick of the wrist and Kash sent Gerald's saber in the opposite direction and plunged his own deep into the belly of the black rook and out the other side.

With agonizing slowness, Kash pulled the blade out and Gerald proudly stifled his awareness of the inevitable. That the saber was cutting into the palms of his hands was irrelevant, as he watched the blood pour his mortal wound. Dazed, that he had lost, he staggered back towards the jagged teeth and the tumultuous water below.

As he tumbled backwards, Leslie had finally gathered enough momentum and adrenaline to grab a hold with free hand and started to pull herself up to safety. Just in the nick of time, she ducked her head as Russia's Black Rook fell from grace to his watery grave.

"Checkmate," Kash snarled through clenched teeth.

Struggling was no longer necessary when Leslie felt her weary arms being seized and the pressure of holding on was relieved.

Bracing himself, Kash pulled his stubborn partner to safety, hoping she had leaned the meaning of "sit still".

She sank into the protection of his arms and after a moment she turned to her face up to his and a mixture of emotions clouded her usually cool façade. "America's White Knight," she whispered.

"Saving the damsel in distress. And waiting his reward," he hinted.

She didn't need any more coaxing to give her thanks. His lips accepted her and he enjoyed her method of gratitude. She pulled back to measure her success, and she didn't need to look to find it; she could feel it. A knowing smile illuminated her face, and Kash held her still to savor the moment.

"So, how long have you been a spy?" she asked, deadly serious.

Kash pretended to be shocked, and uncertain where question was concerned. He raised his eyebrows and mouthed, "Me?"

She wasn't fooled. "You forget, I was married to one. Certain things you," she tapped a finger lightly on his chest, "can't hide."

He ignored her comment and turned her loose with a quick slap on her fanny. "You get the scrolls and I'll clean up," he directed. "Then we'll take the safe way down; the rope."

He started to extinguish the remaining torch, but thought better after eyeing his comrade in that light. Quietly he moved to her bent over figure; soaking in her feminine curves. He pulled free her shirt from the restraining band of her jeans. She turned and looked into the burnt silver of his eyes and knew what was coming.

"Here?" she mouthed.

"You're such a snob," he said, sending his hands up her shirt; filling his palms with her warm, tender flesh.

Clothes discarded, and beneath them, he lowered her to the makeshift bed and started a ritual she was sure she'd never tire of. He surprised her by starting at her toes. Tenderly he massaged each foot, his gaze never leaving the softness and dreamy warmth of her eyes. Snaking his tongue out, he ran it from her arch, up her taunt calf, to the soft flesh behind her knee.

Across the bridge, he went, and daringly he traveled up the length of her silky thigh, stopping ever so often to languish on the inside. He lingered at the crease of her hip and ran an erect line from the top to the bottom. His mustache hairs leaving a sticky trail of blissful rapture. Unhurriedly he gave the same attention to the other leg, draping both about his shoulder and back.

Never before in her life had a man ever made love to her the way Kash did. So complete; so unselfishly and so uninhibited. Taking her to heights and pleasures never traveled. As he neared his destination, the tiny ache that had started in her stomach, was now a tightening knot in her loins. She arched her hips instinctively and stiffened her legs to her growing need. His lips approached her moistness, but she placed a restraining hand on his cheek.

"What?" he whispered, his breath fanning her fire. She answered with an embarrassed shake of the head, and tried to encourage him to make his way up to her lips. "I'll be there soon enough," he assured her, capturing both of her hands and holding them slightly away from his face. "But there's something I want us both to discover." His breath felt like fire on her most delicate of flesh and soon it was an all consuming blaze that was totally out of control. The thunderous roar she heard wasn't just from the waterfall.

Kash stood nervously outside the door. He ran a hand over his neatly combed hair and brushed off his evening jacket before applying a sturdy rap on the door. There wasn't an answer; he knocked again. "Leslie? Come on, *honey, we're going to be late for the state dinner." Still there was no response. "Les?"*

He leaned against the door frame and tried again; pulling something from his jacket pocket. Finally, she opened the door, and with a broad grin, he dangled the Yin-Yang pendant in front of her.

She looked past the swirling necklace to Kash, who was admiring her choice of attire; the purple kimono he had bought her when they had first arrived.

He stepped inside the doorway and closed the distance between them. "Happy birthday."

"How did you know?" she gushed with surprise.

He shrugged and moved even closer and gave the birthday girl her birthday kiss. It was all she expected it to be; deliciously intimate. He didn't stop there, he made his way to the tender nape of her neck and nibbled lightly, drinking in her sweetness. Delicately he secured the pendant around her neck and sealed it with a spine tingling kiss. "You should be getting ready. We don't want to be late."

"We can celebrate here," she offered the alternative to the state dinner. "Your birthday?"

She shook her head. "The Moon Festival."

He liked the idea, and pulled her into the circle of his arms. "It's a very private celebration," he reminded, and playfully looked down her kimono.

"And very romantic," she added, removing his tie and placing soft kisses on his face and neck.

"Yes, I can tell." Kash more than happily agreed as she molded her body to his.

"So can I."

She gave a throaty laugh as he scooped her up and kicked the door shut to their private celebration.

Elaine clutched the PDA to her heart and silently let the tears slid down her cheeks. She was and wasn't surprised by her parent's love for one another. They had always been affectionate, but conservative in their emotions. But how lovely to know they had the same kind of deep, raw passion for each other as she and Jack.

She turned off her PDA, placed it on the nightstand and snuggled down into the bed against the length of her husband. His heat comforting and safe. Her tears streamed down his back as she kissed it lightly.

"I love you, Elaine. Like you father loves your mother," he whispered in a husky voice. He turned over to face her and his mouth found hers. He tasted the salty tears; dried them, and pulled her into his arms. Together they finally found peaceful sleep.

CHAPTER FORTY

Surprisingly when Elaine awoke she wasn't the least bit tired. Her energy had somehow been renewed. The last few days had been a drain. But this morning, this morning she felt hopeful. Something she hadn't felt, even long before her parents went missing.

Climbing out of bed, she got a chill and rushed to the bathroom where Jack was in the shower. She stepped in after taking care of morning business to find him lathered from head to toe. He threw the sponge her way and she got soapy right alongside of him. She placed a quick kiss on his slightly parted lips.

"Hey, you brushed your teeth already. How'd you do that so quickly?" He wanted to know.

"What? You pee and brush your teeth. Aren't those the first two things you do in the morning?" she asked him while she rinsed off and found the shampoo bottle.

"One of the two, yeah," he answered. "I'm going to shave," he said as he stepped out of the shower, leaving her to wash her hair.

Then for fun, she poked her head out from the shower curtain and teased, "Oh, that's the second thing you do; shave."

"That is correct," he lied as she disappeared behind the curtain, laughing at what men do.

Before Jack and Elaine even reached the stairway, they smelled the delicious concoction Veronica had been making that morning. When they made their way to the dining room, there was only a handful of people from the night before. As a courtesy to those that wanted to go on a charter with Cass, she pushed back the time, allowing the guests to get in a few more hours of sleep before heading out all day.

Tansy bounced in with two cups of freshly made coffee, one for

Jack and one for Elaine. They graciously accepted. Before they were even seated, Veronica had two piping hot plates in her hands, ready to serve them.

"Wow," Elaine exclaimed, watching Veronica put the plates on the table along with ice water with lemon and freshly squeezed orange juice. "I'll have to take a nap after this," she admitted.

The breakfast included one savory crepe and one sweet. The savory was filled with scrambled eggs, spinach and mushrooms, and the crepe was lined with goat cheese and sun dried tomatoes and complemented with a mornay sauce. The sweet one was filled with chocolate and bananas and topped with a hazelnut whipped cream. Fresh seasonal fruit rounded out the delicious spread.

There wasn't much talking, if any, as the two consumed their breakfast, and when they were done they went back their room and packed their gear and headed downstairs to have Cass take them to the sea base.

Richly deserved hugs were given and taken as they said their goodbyes and thank you's to Tansy and Veronica. "I hope when you return, it will be under better circumstances. Keep the faith, Elaine. You'll find them," Tansy encouraged with tears in her eyes. "You'll find them," she repeated, as if trying to will it to happen.

"I know I will," Elaine agreed with certainty.

"Is it always like this?" Jack yelled into the mouthpiece of his headset.

Elaine winced at the volume in her ears. "Jack," she said softly and evenly, "you don't have to yell, I can hear you just fine. And, yes, it is, because we're in an open aired cockpit. I'm sorry if you're uncomfortable, but be a manly spy and suck it up."

"How much further?" he asked in a normal volume.

She smiled, thankful he had toned it down. She checked her GPS and the map strapped to her thigh and answered, "Not much. New Tokeen is just ahead. Right now we're in El Captain Passage. I'm going to take us down for a closer look," she informed him, giving him a heads up. "Jack, take the binoculars and sweep the area and see if you can spot anything; debris field, anything that looks like a plane has crash landed."

She flew down the passage, past Devilish Bay, around Tenass Passage into Tokeen Bay. "See anything, Jack?" He shook his head no. Elaine banked to the left and retraced their last flight pattern.

"I still don't see anything," he told her as she was starting to bank slightly left. "Wait! Down there by the dock, there's a plane," he informed with some moderate enthusiasm.

Elaine straightened out the plane and peered over the right side of her plane and saw a float plane tied off at El Capitan Cave. "Let's be nosy, shall we?" she said to no one in particular, though Jack answered.

"Yes."

She taxied up to the El Capitan Cave dock and cut her engine. The plane tethered at the end of the dock sat six easily, and was not occupied. Nor did it have any official decals from the state of Alaska. Elaine took out her cell phone and took a picture of the plane and numbers. It was strange that someone would be docked this time of year. Tours usually ended somewhere near August, and all tours were reserved.

Jack had hopped out of the plane and secured it while Elaine finished shutting down and securing the cockpit. She gathered her backpack and joined Jack on the dock. "Thank you for tying us off," she said as she accepted his hand in helping her leap from the pontoon to the dock. She pulled free her flashlight and checked to make sure it was in operating order. She also pulled free her Glock and shoved it into the waistband of her cargo pants.

"My kind of woman," Jack praised and he showed her his Sig Sauer tucked in his waistband.

They started off and before they made it to the first step there was a placard telling those with boats or float planes that they were not to be left unattended. "First rule broken," Elaine admitted. "I suppose the next thing is no guns?" she quipped with typical sarcasm.

The temperature was in the mid thirties, but the wind was making it feel like at least twenty. They took to the steps and started their ascent to the mouth of El Capitan; the largest cave in Alaska, with over two miles of mapped passageways.

It took them nearly fifteen minutes to climb the steep staircase of three hundred and sixty-seven steps and reach the platform outside the mouth of the cave. The opening was an odd shape; almost resembling a bear's head; the crown and ears narrowing to a point at the bottom.

Elaine took a moment to survey the opening and surroundings; trees and more trees. From Sitka spruce to the Alaska yellow cedar; the rainforest that came up to the opening of the cave was formidable; as it guarded one of nature's most impressive wonders; El Capitan Cave.

Elaine remembered her first visit to El Cap, as it was so often referred to; it was just she and her father. Often their visits were to seek adventure, but mostly she learned to respect nature in all her glory from the excursions she took with Kash.

It had been several decades since her last visit to El Cap. She was sure some things had changed. She looked over at a tuckered Jack and asked, "Have you ever been here?"

He shook his head, gulping copious amounts of air; trying to slow down his heart rate from the tortuous climb. He couldn't believe Elaine's calm and hardly winded demeanor. "How," he gasped, "how is you're so not winded?"

"I live in San Francisco, Jack," she replied, and then asked, "How is it you're not in shape, doing what you do?"

He didn't answer, and by then his heart and breathing were somewhat back to normal. "Should we just wait here and see who comes out?" he offered, knowing she wasn't going to wait. And he was right, she had started for the mouth of the cave; her flashlight leading the way.

As they entered, the wind gave an upsweep and particularly shoved them through the opening. Elaine held her ground and got a feel for the sounds of their space. Wind and water were the primary noises, and as they carefully stepped; crushed stone took over and echoed off the close walls and the low ceiling. There was mud drawn in from the outside, and it made their journey slippery and somewhat treacherous. Oddly enough, the temperature in the cave was a balmy forty degrees; much warmer than outside. Still, there breath showed as they started making their way through the passageway and over several boulders.

"Ah, shit!" Jack exclaimed as he hit his head and scuffed his backpack on the small space between the boulder and ceiling.

Once past the rocks, the cave gently lit up on its own from small holes that led to the surface. These tiny holes let natural light filter through. Elaine stopped, and for just a moment, lowered her flashlight and enjoyed the beauty of twilight, as it was known.

As they moved forward it suddenly felt like it was sprinkling in the cave; but it was only the condensation from the temperature changes. Jack looked up and was hit in the eye with a drop from the very low ceiling. This area was the most congested spot in the beginning of the cave, and Elaine sensed Jack pulling off his backpack. She stopped and saw that he had stowed it behind small boulder. He tugged at hers and she let him pull it free and stash it with his.

The only thing he had to aid in their spelunking, was a coiled rope draped over his shoulder and a special piece of hardware. "I think we have all we need," he said, as he tugged on the rope and waved his Sig. "Come on," he urged.

It wasn't but about two hundred feet in from the opening, that they came upon a slatted, metal gate that was placed to keep people like her and Jack, and whoever was ahead of them, at bay. It was ajar; its two pad locks, opened. The only critters it allowed to pass, were two species of bats. Of which, Jack and Elaine were neither.

Jack easily moved ahead of Elaine and turned on a mini flashlight with a very bright LED light. He had it positioned above the barrel of his Sig.

She turned hers off and stashed it in the side pocket of her cargo pants. Even with his light shining brightly and lighting their passage with exceptional clarity; she was particularly in his hip pocket. He briefly glanced at her, and she recognized his annoyance and backed off; only slightly.

They came upon what was known as the *First Room*; it was a step beyond the gate. They squeezed through and were in one of the largest areas in the cave. Jack abruptly stopped, and rather quickly Elaine found her nose in the middle of his back.

"Listen," he instructed, dowsing his light to help his hearing. He felt Elaine clutch his arm for support in the blackened space.

They stood hopelessly still, and outside of the constant dripping of water and the occasional burst of wind, they both heard hushed voices. Elaine recognized one to be Slim; the others, she wasn't sure, but she guessed they were speaking Russian. "Boris?" she whispered in Jack's ear. She felt his head turn toward her.

"Not sure. Let's find out, shall we?" When he turned his light back on and had put it on a lower setting.

They began crunching their way through the First Room on the rock and cobble filled pathway; stopping at the first opening to their right to listen for the voices of earlier. It was quiet, so they deliberately moved on. The second opening on the right was a little niche that dropped down five or six feet; nothing. Their first opening to the left was a small tunnel that led to the *Twin Pits*.

Jack looked to Elaine, who took the hint. She pulled her flashlight out and illuminated the small space and started her crawl through. He stored his gun and light and followed. They traversed through several tunnels and pits and reached the bottom level. El Capitan resembled a three story home; basement, first level and a second story above the main tunnel. Right now, Elaine and Jack stood in the basement. And like all old basements, it was damp and smelled of the earth.

Where they stood, they weren't far from the *Hibernaculum*, the bone filled passage where bones from black bears were said to have ranged from approximately eleven thousand to one hundred and fifteen years old. There were also bones from brown bears, otters as well as red foxes and other various rodents. The presence of these bones meant that the El Capitan was ice free at least twelve thousand years ago.

Elaine took the lead and headed east in a maze of passageways that would narrow down and flair out again. On this lower level, few had hardly traveled, the stalactites and stalagmites were plentiful and left to create natural columns and pillars. On more than one occasion, they both had to duck out of the way of some of the soda straws, or thin hallow stalactites. The flowstone formed wavy, earth-toned patterns in the cave walls. Some of them looked like pleated curtains on opening night.

One passageway they went by, ascended to the main level; Jack made a mental note of its location and configurations. He particularly made note of the numerous soda straws above that were poised and positioned like pipes on an organ; smallest to largest.

As they made their way along an underlying passage, they once again, heard voices; much more clearly this time. From what Jack could tell, there were three. And, there was splashing of water.

"That sounds like they're near the Rockwell River. Come on," she instructed.

He followed her past a few more pits and through some tiny funnels and then they came upon a boulder fill. Nimbly, they both negotiated the haphazard pieces of rock and turned back south toward the sound of the water.

While following the sound of the voices, they sloshed through mud and silt. Jack pulled hard on Elaine and forced her light off. They hugged the cave wall as they made their way and then eased down to a ledge that overlooked the water below. There stood Slim and Kevin. They both stared impassively, at the water, their backs to Elaine and Jack. The lights on their mining helmets reflected into the water.

Even spelunking, Kevin looked like he had just stepped out of a bandbox. Slim, on the other hand, looked like he was used to crawling around in this kind of shit. He even had a rope with a grappling attached. Unlike the one Jack had borrowed from the dock.

"Are we surprised?" Elaine whispered with mocking surprise.

"So, these units, once produced, will bring a healthy profit?" Slim asked.

"For both of us, yes. Extremist don't care about profits. They care about crippling the Infidel. Literally and figuratively. You will now have the prototype, and since we've been sending most of the important raw material in the form of decorative glass, you can proceed with assembling and selling them at whatever price you have agreed upon. The assembled capacitor is the last piece for their dirty little bombs. Properly placed, the explosions should rain down and disperse enough flux to incapacitate and disrupt any and all electrical based equipment and communications. It will give them the time they need to complete their mission," Kevin concluded with same dour manner he had at the poker table.

A diver emerged from the water carrying a white box, no more the size of a handheld cooler. He yanked free his *Spare Air* oxygen unit and handed Kevin the box. Kevin immediately handed it to Slim and looked closely into the opaque mask of the diver. "Is that everything?" he asked, buying time as he pulled free his FNP-45 Tactical Handgun and spun around, firing several rounds at Jack and Elaine.

Jack pushed Elaine out of the way, and when he came up and fired, it wasn't at Kevin, rather the diver, hitting him square in the mini oxygen tank. It blasted him backwards into the water, causing enough disturbance to the sight to buy Jack some time and securing Elaine away from the fray.

By the time Jack was repositioned, Slim and Kevin were making their way along the inner passageway. Jack leaned over the ledge and fired at their retreating figures, striking boulders and sending pieces of limestone in their wake.

Kevin turned and fired a few more shots, just to make Jack take cover and give them more time to make it to the main tunnel. "Go," Kevin barked at Slim. "Get the plane ready," he ordered as he took up position behind a large boulder, waiting for Jack to show himself.

Elaine had had enough, she bolted and headed for the main tunnel. Jack stretched a hand out in vain to keep her from running after Slim, but he knew better and turned his attention to Kevin. Moving to the end of the ledge closest to Kevin's position, Jack slid down the rock face and peered around its edge.

A shot rang out and rock flew past Jack's face and he quickly returned fire, narrowly missing the fleeing Kevin. It was about a ten foot drop to the river bed and Jack made it with no problem and started after Kevin. He was sure Elaine was in the hunt for Slim.

And she was. She had slowed her progress, going past three pits and finding no sign of Slim or his white box. She stopped and listened intently for any other sounds outside of the wind and the dripping water running through the belly of the cave. Nothing. She was almost at the *Twin Pits* when she heard the sounds of a man struggling.

She doubled back and headed east toward the sound. Rounding the inner passage wall, she scrambled up the steep pathway. Her progress was slowed by uneven, jagged rocks covered in a thin layer of silt. To make matters worse, she kept dropping her damned flashlight. "Shit!" she exclaimed, picking it up for the umpteenth time and moving ahead.

She knew if she was having this much trouble; Slim wasn't fairing any better; and he had a box to carry. She came upon a short shelf; tossed her flashlight onto it and heaved herself up. Just as she righted herself, she saw light coming from behind her. She shot off to the right and barely fit into a tiny inlet to hide. She pulled her gun and flipped off the safety and her flashlight and waited.

Jack pulled himself up onto the ledge and stopped to gather his bearings. He shined the light toward the inlet and walked cautiously. Something moved in it. He raised his light and found Elaine squeezing out from the tiny opening.

"Where's Kevin?" she asked in a whisper.

"He was ahead of me," Jack answered. A little perplexed as to which way Kevin had taken. "What about Slim?"

"He was ahead of me," she repeated Jack's answer. "He came up this slope and by the time I was up on the ledge, your light was behind me and I hid."

"Does this lead to the main tunnel?" Jack asked, pulling the mangy rope he found on the dock off from around his shoulders and neck.

"Yes," she answered succinctly and turned on her flashlight. "This way," she led and he followed.

"Wait a minute," Jack grabbed her arm as he heard Kevin and Slim ahead.

"We'll lock them in to slow them down. Now, go," Kevin ordered.

"There just ahead. You stay behind me," he directed her, as he took the lead.

She didn't argue as they slogged their way through more silt and obstructing rocks. They came upon a dangling rope, courtesy of Kevin and Slim. Waiting not, Jack free climbed the rope and groped for a hold on the rocks above and pulled himself onto the floor of the main level. Not far behind was Elaine and when she reached the apex, Jack pulled her up the rest of the way.

"The opening's not far," Elaine informed him as he once again took the lead.

Unlike their first trip through the main tunnel, this one was quicker. They remembered the pit falls and areas of low ceilings and narrow passageways. They heard the clanking of the gate and the clicking of the two padlocks being shut. But they also knew that Kevin and Slim still had to negotiate three hundred and sixty seven steps down a steep staircase to make it to the dock and the plane.

Elaine and Jack still had time to catch up. Jack readied his Sig and fired two shots at the padlocks; destroying them and allowing them to push the gate open and resume their pursuit.

Kevin had heard the shots and expected that much from Jack. He urged Slim to continue. "Untie the plane. I'll be there momentarily," he ordered. He placed his mining hat in the middle of a step and then moved down thirty steps. He took up a low shooting stance and waited for Jack and Elaine. "Like fish in a barrel," he commented.

As Jack and Elaine squeezed through the last section of tight boulders, they found the opening and started down the steps. They came upon the first landing and at the bottom on the third step down, there was a mining helmet.

"Trap!" Jack yelled, and threw Elaine over the side, into the fray of the a huge Sitka Spruce.

She clung onto it for dear life as Jack jumped and emptied his clip at Kevin below. Several of Kevin's bullets hit the tree limbs were Elaine and Jack were hanging from. Groping and trying to find a foothold, Jack shoved his gun into his waistband and had both hands free to pull himself safely onto a large limb and secure Elaine.

Putting in a fresh clip, he carefully walked the large limb until he was able to jump onto the platform. He motioned for Elaine to follow and she mimicked his movements and found the platform, and then they resumed their chase.

As they were running down the stairs, Elaine heard more gun shots and the sound of puncturing metal. "Fuck! They've shot the plane!" she screamed. But gunshot wasn't the only sound. There was another plane, and it was close; like on final approach close. She heard the splash down and the unmistakable sound of the engine slowing as it was approached the dock.

The last flight of stairs went quickly and they jumped to the dock, Jack fired shots at Slim as he was boarding the plane at the end. Jack continued his pursuit, firing until his magazine was empty. He didn't have any more magazines.

He had taken cover by Elaine's plane when she had caught up. She had taken a quick look and saw the damage. She drew her gun and continued after Kevin and Slim, Jack yelling for her to stop. She didn't slow down until she saw the other plane come along side her, and its passengers; Kash and Leslie. She instinctively reached for her mother and cried, "No!" as the plane started to pull away.

A shot rang out, and another cry of *No!* came from the passing plane, as Leslie watched her daughter fallen by a bullet and tumble into the frigid waters of El Capitan Passage. The red silk scarf she had been wearing, slipped out of the plane's window and fluttered down to the waters below as the plane gathered speed and pulled up from the cove and headed off into the distance. It was followed by Kevin and Slim's plane.

Jack ran and dove into the freezing water, searching for Elaine. He found her and dragged her to the surface. Side stroking his way to the ladder on the dock, he hoisted her over his shoulder, climbed the ladder and laid her down.

He quickly assessed her condition and began to staunch the bleeding in her shoulder. "Elaine? Elaine Rene, wake up!" he yelled, and to his relief she opened her eyes.

"I saw them," she breathlessly uttered. "Tell me, I saw them?" she cried.

"We did," he replied softly, pulling her into his arms. "We saw them," he repeated, for more his benefit than hers.

She opened her eyes to him and chattered, "Satellite phone and blankets under the pilot's seat." It was all she could manage and Jack gently laid her down on the wet dock.

Before he stepped on the pontoon, he saw Leslie's scarf wafting in the water. He plucked it up, squeezed out the excess water and stuffed it into his jacket. Rummaging under the pilot's seat he located the blankets and phone. It didn't take him long to strip her of her wet clothing and wrap her in the blankets, and call for help.

Elaine didn't know and didn't care who he called, but he reassured her help was on its way. She nodded and closed her eyes to quite possibly the best and worst day of her life.

EPILOGUE

It had been a week since Elaine had caught the tiniest glimpse of her parents, and still they were no closer to finding them. If anything, it seemed like they were miles behind. In the week since, she had questioned many things: Why didn't she look at the tail numbers? Why couldn't she remember the primary colors of the plane? Why did she allow herself to become so deeply involved?

The answer to the last question gently knocked on her door and then peeked in. "Hi," Jack announced softly, carrying a tray full of goodies from Mollie's kitchen. "Mollie thought a midday snack might be kind of nice." He kindly placed the tray on the desk and helped her get comfortable before putting it on the bed. With great attention, he made sure everything was the way it should be before he excused himself and left her to her thoughts and the fresh fruit, cheese and tea.

She watched him close the door and remembered his heroic actions on the dock, and how since, he hadn't left her side. She had wanted, pleaded for him to follow up on any leads, but he insisted his place was with her. And when she was able, they would together, resume their search for Kash and Leslie. He had told her that others were tracking down leads, and that Slippery Slim had moved his base of operations from the underground tunnels in San Francisco to god-knows-where. There had been an alert posted regarding the capacitor for the dirty bombs containing the flux, and an alert to Customs for the glassware containing the uranium.

Lane was a little more than worried these days; it seemed his aide, Kevin Seaver, was missing. He hadn't returned from vacation. And when shown a picture taken of Kevin Shaunessey at the Tanner's Creek Lodge, Lane nearly had a stroke and had to admit they were one in the same. What time held for Lane and his many indiscretions, Elaine didn't know, nor did she care. But she did know that his days of thwarting her at every turn were over. And when the time came, she would worry about him and his family. But right now, she had to get well so she could resume her search.

Instinctively she reached for her tea with her left hand and winced at the pain her shoulder was still producing. The bullet had nicked her collarbone and tore through the top of her trapezius muscle, leaving a splintered mess behind. The doctors told her it would be a month before she would be able to resume normal activities, but not flying. She wouldn't be able to dead-stick for a while. Besides, she wasn't sure when her plane was going to be ready. John had been a life saver with her WACO. He had a friend from Juneau, a retired airplane mechanic, go to El Capitan Cave's dock with a barge and small crane and take her plane Point Baker for repairs.

She had thanked God on more than one occasion for Mollie and John Shasta. From the moment Jack had called them and told them what had happened, they wouldn't take no for an answer in having her stay and recuperate at their home. They had kept her warm, fed and loved beyond measure. They had treated her as if she were their daughter. She simply didn't know how she was going to repay them.

She looked at the foot of her bed and saw numerous boxes. They were Kash and Leslie's journals. The very ones they entrusted their friends, Mollie and John, to keep safe and sound. But in the event of their deaths, or in this case, disappearance, Elaine was to be given access to them.

The boxes were in chronological order; starting in 1945. John said they were from when they each joined the OSS to their last days with the CIA. It was a lot of reading, but what else did Elaine have to do? She had time; and hopefully so did her parents.

She reached behind her and pulled off the bedpost her mother's scarf. Jack had grabbed it from the icy waters of El Capitan Passage. She put it to her nose and smelled her mother's undeniable scent. She buried her face in it and let it absorb her tears. Finally, she managed to put the tray aside and smooth out with her right hand her mother's scarf. It was a deep, blood red in the middle and then it faded to gold at the ends. The pattern filled the whole scarf, and was of the San Francisco Bay. It showed the landmarks that made San Francisco, well, San Francisco. It started with the Ferry Building, Coit Tower, Pier 39, The Presido, the Japanese Tea Garden, and of course, the Golden Gate Bridge stretching over to Sausalito.

Elaine traced a finger across the bridge and stopped. She backed up and went back to the Presido, just before the bridge. There was a building that didn't belong there. She felt the ink of the San Francisco pattern; it was raised black ink. The drawing that didn't belong there was not raised. She looked over the scarf, checking for anything familiar. At the Golden Gate bridge, she saw an "s" was added to the end of the word *Gate*. "Golden Gates?" she said aloud. "What does that mean?" She looked more closely and found another drawing near Coit Tower. It looked like a cathedral with three arched towers, a stack in the middle with a dome and cross.

She stroked the scarf with renewed energy as she draped it around her neck, she looked down at the bottom edge where the signature of the original artist was and found her mother's crazy handwriting. She stumbled to the mirror and held the scarf to it and read, "Vladimir."

Her excitement took over and she rushed to the door. A wave of painful nausea washed over her. She steadied herself and gently opened the door to hear John, Mollie and Jack in the kitchen. As she made her way, she heard Jack say, "Mom, when I think," he stopped when Mollie placed a hand of warning on his arm and he turned to face Elaine.

"Wow, there's all kinds of good news to be shared," Elaine managed through shocked tears.

Jack rushed over to her and eased her down onto John's favorite chair. "What are you doing out of bed?" he asked, concern etched in his tired features.

"Learning that Mollie and John are your parents," she guessed.

Mollie and John rushed over and tried to soothe what they perceived to be hurt feelings. To the contrary, Elaine gathered Mollie with her good arm and held her as tightly as she could. "I always knew you were more than just my godmother," she barely managed as she pulled away and stared at John. "And you," she couldn't speak anymore, the tears wouldn't let her. Instead she let him hug her as gently as he knew how.

Jack stared at his feet, uncertain whether he should look her way. He knew what kind of terror she could unleash with just a look. But when his eyes met hers, he saw the softness of love from their wedding day. He returned the favor, and smiled at her recognition.

Gently he took her face and kissed her. "No more secrets," he promised.

With that she asked, "Where are the Golden Gates?" Ready to get down to business.

"In San Francisco," Jack automatically replied.

"I don't think so," she countered, pulling the scarf off and smoothing it out and then showing them the drawing in the Presido and the "s" added onto the word Gate and the building near Coit Tower. And finally she pointed out near the signature in the corner; the upside down and backwards writing of her mother. "It says, 'Vladimir'," she informed them.

"The Golden Gates are in Vladimir, Russia," Jack confirmed.

"Who's up for a road trip?" Elaine asked with a wink.

THE END